To Helen, my dear,
dearest Helen — and to
Richard, Richard II,
Lynne, Bill, and Martha

Arthur Cavanaugh

BY ARTHUR CAVANAUGH

Leaving Home
The Children Are Gone
My Own Back Yard

Leaving Home

a novel by

ARTHUR CAVANAUGH

Simon and Schuster · New York

First printing

SBN 671–20700–8
Library of Congress Catalog Card Number: 74–130468
Designed by Edith Fowler
Manufactured in the United States of America
by H. Wolff Book Mfg. Co., Inc.

Most of this material has appeared in a different form in
McCall's, Redbook and Ladies' Home Journal.

*To my Father
and to the memory of
my Mother,
who was Catherine*

The author is indebted to John Mack Carter and to his associate, Phyllis Levy, for the encouragement and support that led to the writing of this novel; and to Joan Hutzler my appreciation for her preparation of the manuscript.

A. C.

Prologue: October 1956
_____

"It's a beautiful day, we have to admit," said Father Wyzcinski, seated up front next to the chauffeur. It wasn't a remark that particularly required an answer.

We were riding directly behind the hearse and the floral car. The hearse was sleek gunmetal gray, rather than the black one of my dreams, but still I tried not to look at it. Instead, I counted the sprays and wreaths that were piled in the floral car, just as at church I had fixed my attention on the ritual of the priests on the altar.

Traffic on Queens Boulevard was scant at that hour of the weekday morning; except for traffic lights and a brief tie-up at the Long Island railway underpass, the cortege rolled along almost without interruption. It wasn't an imposing cortege, this ragtail collection of friends' and relatives' cars. Only two rented limousines, but Catherine wouldn't have wanted a grand display.

Chrysanthemums, snapdragons, two sprays of gladiola—Dad, seated behind me, asked the chauffeur how many miles did a Chrysler Imperial eat up, on the average? About twelve per gallon, give or take a little, the chauffeur replied. And then he turned the big car onto the cemetery road.

Beyond the iron fence of Calvary the tombstones and mausoleums stretched endlessly like a silent Lilliputian village. The limousine slid to a halt at the tall entrance gates, and behind us were the sounds of the other cars halting too. To the right, across the road from the cemetery, the New York City skyline rose up sheer, like mountain cliffs, from the other side of the East River. The cemetery gates were open, and after the hearse and the floral car rolled through, the driver of the hearse got out and crossed to the squat brick building at the side of the entrance. A man in

9

droopy trousers came out and frowned at the papers that the driver presented to him, then pointed down the road and gestured toward the left. The driver crossed back to the hearse, and none of us spoke in the limousine—not Dad, or my brothers, Vinny and Daniel. Marijane, Daniel's wife, who was crowded next to Lissy and me on the jump seat, turned to smile encouragement at him, but no one spoke—there was utter silence from the other cars as well, mixed with the drone of traffic on the expressway, a quarter mile or so away.

The driver climbed behind the wheel of the hearse, and my father broke the silence. "Look at those gates, nice piece of iron-work," he said cheerfully. "What was it Tilly always said about 'em? Some damned thing."

"Something fancy, that's for sure," Vinny said. "Hey, Rob, you remember?" he called to me.

I studied the wrought-iron gates for a moment.

Aunt Tilly was my mother's sister, a spinster schoolteacher with an "artistic nature." "Oh, she used to compare them to the gates of a French chateau. An *exquisite* French chateau," I specified, imitating Aunt Tilly's breathless inflection.

"That's it to a T," Daniel laughed behind me. "Everything was always 'exquisite' or 'sublime' with Aunt Tilly."

"It's funny how opposite they were for sisters," Dad added thoughtfully. "Tilly with her airs, and Cath, my old Cath, always as plain as bread." Something went wrong with his voice as he pronounced the familiar name. My old Cath . . .

The hearse and floral car moved slowly down the main ceme-tery road. The limousine passed through the gates, following at a distance, and I seemed to hear Catherine say, "Why, Calvary's a lovely place. It's so peaceful and you can find practically every-body in Brooklyn there."

She had regarded it as she would a favorite park, an ideal spot to take her children on outings. She had always enjoyed wander-ing among the headstones and statuary and searching out the graves of family and friends. At Easter she brought flowers to the Quinlan graves; returned with fresh blooms on Memorial Day, and evergreen wreaths at Christmas. She raked the autumn foliage from her family's plot and cleared away the snow from it in winter. We'd once spent a Fourth of July at Calvary—partly because it was the Depression and the excursion cost nothing beyond the trolley fare—rolling down the hill slopes in the deep summer green. Visits to Calvary served also as lessons in Brooklyn history and genealogy for us children. In pleasant weather Catherine brought a box lunch and spread out a cloth among the graves. As we munched on sandwiches she would discourse on the neighboring headstones. "Over there, down to the left, are the O'Sullivans from Herkimer Street," she would say. "Eugene O'Sullivan had the nickname of Nifty, due to his sporty manner of dressing. Looked like he'd stepped from a bandbox, with his starched shirts and creases in his trousers sharp as knives. It was Nifty who married Mary Lynch, one of the five Lynch girls from Monroe Street, each prettier than the next, except for Louise, who had a cast in her right eye. Beatrice Lynch—or was it Mary Ellen? —married Ned Gorman, the famous criminal lawyer. Where's the Gorman plot? Anyway, it's interesting, because the Gormans came from the same village in Wexford where your Grandma Quinlan was born. So, you see, it's a small world."

"What became of the Lynch with the cast in her right eye?"

"She taught school. What a queer question to ask, Robbie. You have the funniest mind."

Robbie . . . The cortege trundled along the winding, dipping road, past the mausoleums that crowned the hillocks, elaborate stone and marble dwellings festooned with carved cherubs, wreaths, and sorrowing madonnas. *Robbie* . . . I heard her call.

"If I may remark, Mister Connerty, you couldn't ask for a finer day for burying," spoke up Father Wyzcinski, intent on his role as cheerful commentator.

"Yes, and the ground not hard yet," Dad agreed solemnly. "We're almost at the plot, I think, Father. Another turn in the road . . ."

Robbie, I heard her call. The limousine followed the hearse around the turn in the road, and I glanced ahead at the slender rise of hill on the right. The Quinlan plot was situated halfway up that hill. "Come," she'd say, whenever the impulse flew at her

11

to "take the trolley and visit Grandma and Grandpa Quinlan and your Uncle Johnny that you never knew." Uncle Johnny was her brother who had died in infancy and whose name was carved in tiny letters on the square granite tombstone, JOHN JOSEPH QUINLAN, JAN. 5, 1880, NINE DAYS ON EARTH. "Isn't it strange," Catherine would muse, "Johnny's my own brother, but I won't actually meet him till I get to heaven myself." It was as if her brother resided out on Long Island, with heaven no farther away than the next train stop after Bay Shore. . . .

"Rob." Lissy, my wife, pressed my arm. "We're here," she said gently. "The car's stopped."

I looked up and saw that the hearse had halted at the side of the hill slope, but still I didn't move. "Robbie, you'll have to get out first," my father said from the rear, but I sat frozen on the jump seat, blocking his exit, and I stared ahead at the undertaker's men, who were assembling at the side of the hearse. I looked toward the hillside, where a fresh grave had been dug, the oblong of scooped-out earth covered by a length of green matting. A short distance away workmen lounged on picks and shovels, waiting to fill in the earth.

It was as if I hadn't really known until this moment why we were here, what we had come to do. *Connerty, Catherine, née Quinlan,* the obituary notice had read, *Dear wife of James V., devoted mother of*— A sharp, echoing *twiing* reverberated in my ears, the sound of the heavy metal hearse door being opened.

"Rob," Lissy said again, and I followed her and Marijane from the limousine, then turned and watched my father and brothers alight. Dad required no assistance. He removed his hat and stood facing the hearse, alone and erect. The wind ruffled his white, thinning hair as we grouped ourselves behind him.

Other car doors were opening. Figures gathered on the road edge. Charlie Cronin, my sister Margaret and her husband, Uncle Al and Aunt Gen, my red-haired cousins and their wives. The Raylmans and Luros and Mrs. Fritzle, old neighbors from Warbisher Street; Reverend and Mrs. Calkins, who'd moved into the Fritzles' house next door.

Father Wyzcinski stood at the head of the small group of

mourners; a purple stole encircled his shoulders, and he opened his breviary, ready to begin the prayers. Lissy took my arm.

First the undertaker's men removed the wreaths and sprays from the floral car and carried them up the slight hill rise. They arranged the flowers at the head of the green matting, then they came back down the hill for my mother.

The men lifted the coffin from the hearse and onto their shoulders, and bore it up the sloping hill. How lightly they carried her, I thought, moving in the procession behind my father and brothers. As lightly as the men had carried the flowers, with no more difficulty, as if the only weight to be borne was that of the coffin itself. They carried her up the hill, past the graves she had told us of so often. *Those are the McEvoys from Putnam Avenue, the nicest family. Mister McEvoy ran a grocery store on the corner of Ralph Avenue and Madison Street.* In slow cadence up the hill, and I, who had fled from this hill a thousand times in dreams, followed behind with the others.

Lightly the men lowered the coffin onto the pulleys which were visible beneath the green matting, and we formed into rows in front of the square granite headstone. JOHN JOSEPH QUINLAN, I read in the diminutive carving, then my grandparents' names, Aunt Tilly's, and under hers the space where Catherine's name would soon be carved.

Father Wyzcinski stepped forward, sprinkled the coffin with holy water, and began reciting the prayers of burial. "Deliver, O Lord, we beseech Thee, the soul of Thy handmaiden, Catherine . . ."

I closed my eyes and thought of the other missing member of the family. My sister Roseanne, buried thousands of miles away in a foreign grave. Roseanne, who had been my enemy and then my staunchest friend.

"May the martyrs receive thee, and bring thee into the holy city," Father Wyzcinski intoned. "May the choir of angels welcome thee and mayest thou, like the once poor Lazarus, be received into paradise."

He sprinkled the coffin again, and the droplets of water, glistening on the polished wood, were the tears I could not cry.

In the limousine, on the ride back to Warbisher Street, Dad announced his plans.

"Vinny invited me and I'm taking him up on it," he told us firmly, gripping the hand strap. "I'm flying out with him on Friday." Vinny was the oldest of the family and had moved to California with Peggy, his wife, several years ago. They had four children now and a house in San Fernando Valley. Peggy was expecting her fifth child at any moment and had not been able to fly east for the funeral.

"It'll do you good, the change of scene and everything," Vinny said to Dad. "The weather's been gorgeous—Peg's taken the kids to the beach every afternoon. You can have Mike's room—we'll move him in with Terry and Jamie."

"And when you get back," Marijane said, swinging around in the jump seat, "you have to promise to come to Chevy Chase. We can't guarantee perfect weather, but we'll make up for it."

"Yeah, Dad, I'll get you out on the old golf course," Dan said, jabbing him on the arm. Graying at the temples, Daniel looked even handsomer than usual in his black Homburg and Chesterfield. He was a surgeon and lived in a big glass-and-brick house outside Washington. "Soon as you come back from the coast," Dan said.

My father nodded, and there was an interval of silence. Then he turned and looked out the rear window. "I don't see the other cars behind us. There'll be thirty for breakfast at the house." Back at the cemetery, as was the custom, he had invited all the mourners to breakfast at the house. "I can spot only Al's car and the other limousine," he said.

"Everybody here knows the way to Warbisher Street," Daniel said.

The limousine scudded past the gaudy high-rise apartments, mammoth supermarkets, and discount stores that thronged Queens Boulevard, then swung into Woodhaven Boulevard, headed toward Grand Central Parkway and Brooklyn.

"The thing is to give yourself time," Vinny went on. "Put off decisions for a while. Come and stay with Peg and me, buzz down to Dan's—and when you're back here, Rob's half an hour away in the city."

"I'll sleep with the baby and you can bunk with Robert," Lissy said.

My father gripped the suede hand strap. "You're good boys," he said, keeping his voice steady. "You—you're terrific, that's all."

Vinny patted his arm. "Well, Pops, we don't think you're all bad yourself."

"Yes, you're a splendid man, Mr. Connerty," contributed Father Wyzcinski from the front seat. "Just as Mrs. Connerty was a splendid woman." Apparently unable to think of anything more on the subject, he lapsed into silence.

The limousine turned onto the parkway. We rode along the smooth asphalt and Dad looked out at the whirring trees and shrubbery. "I don't kid myself," he said. "I know what I have to do." He paused a moment and then told us of another decision he had made. "I'm putting the house up for sale," he said. "By the time I get back from Vinny's there ought to be a buyer . . . and I'm selling it."

"That's not giving yourself time to think," Vinny said.

"I've already thought about it."

Dan said, "Suppose you feel differently in six months. You can't buy the house back."

"I won't want to," Dad said. "It's what I have to do, don't you see?"

I sat silently on the jump seat, staring ahead. It was ending. The family, the house, the days of the past on Warbisher Street. This morning's breakfast would represent the last gathering in the house, the last bustle and stir of a big meal cooking in the kitchen, the platters of food carried into the crowded dining room . . .

"Don't you see," Dad said, "if I stayed on there, I'd be an old fellow chasing ghosts through the rooms. You children are welcome to any furniture or belongings you want . . . then afterward I'll be finding new quarters."

"But where?" Vinny asked.

"Maybe I'll take a room in Charlie Cronin's boardinghouse.

15

The place is like an old men's club, and I'd have company and nothing to worry about when I wanted to visit one of you boys or Margaret. I could go to Florida in the winter."

"You'll come to us if you want to get away from the cold weather," Vinny said firmly.

The car went past Snake Hill and the reservoir at Highland Park, and suddenly the Bushwick Avenue exit was in sight. We came off the parkway and went past the sprawling power plant that had formerly been the site of Troemmer's Beer Garden—twinkling lights strung over the outdoor tables and chairs, and on weekend evenings you could hear a German band playing as you strolled past. Next, the iron framework of the Broadway El jutted into view above the tree-dotted streets and cracked sidewalks, the blocks of tenements and rows of small houses that comprised the neighborhood in which we had grown up. In recent years it had become predominantly a Negro neighborhood, but black families had always lived there, and their increased numbers had not much altered the look of the neighborhood. The same children skipped rope and played catch on the streets, the same housewives trooped along with grocery bundles and shopping carts, their black faces signifying the only major change.

We dropped off Father Wyzcinski at St. Aloysius Rectory on Bushwick Avenue. Dad climbed out onto the sidewalk and attempted to give him an envelope. "No, sir, Mr. Connerty," Father Wyzcinski protested. "It was entirely my pleasure." The use of the phrase evidently struck him as inappropriate. "Entirely my privilege, that is," he corrected. "Look after yourself and enjoy California." The purple stole over his arm fluttering in the wind, he scooted up the rectory steps.

"A sap, but well-meaning," Dad said, getting back into the limousine again. "Driver, it's the next left after the second traffic light. Warbisher." He settled back as the car rolled along Bushwick Avenue. "He read the service nice, I thought."

"There was an appealing simplicity about him," Marijane offered.

"I'll say," Dan cracked.

The car went past the second traffic light, turned left, and like a book opening its pages, Warbisher Street spread itself out—the sidewalks and alleys, the back fences and scarred trees bearers of a thousand lost footprints from my childhood. It was a street of small identical houses standing cheek to jowl, each with a postage-stamp porch, side alley, and gabled roof. So closely packed together were the houses that, from a certain angle, they appeared to be one house continuously repeating itself, like the folds of an accordion. As diminutive as the houses that occupied it, Warbisher Street began and ended in the space of a single block that extended from Broadway to Bushwick Avenue—"like it lacked the sense to keep on going," my father used to remark.

Our house was in the middle of the block, on the right as the car approached it from Bushwick Avenue. "Number twenty-four," Dad said, and the chauffeur nosed slowly down the street, scanning the house numbers.

Catherine . . .

The car stopped in front of Number 24 and I stared out at the small, neat brown-shingled house. Behind me Dad suddenly said, "She'll never see it again, will she?" and I shut my eyes against a vision of newly filled-in earth and remembered a Saturday years ago, when I'd broken my arm while attempting to climb our neighbor's back fence. I'd known right off that the arm was broken, had heard the bone crack, in fact. But I'd thought that if I kept silent the pain would go away—and that by some magic the arm wouldn't be broken anymore.

The chauffeur opened the door and I stepped onto the sidewalk and helped Marijane and Lissy from the limousine. If I kept silent and ignored the pain . . .

"Know what?" Dad said, getting out with Vinny and Dan. "I'm hungry as a bear—how about you fellows?" and the three of them paced up and down in front of the house, stretching their legs.

The other limousine drew up, disgorging my sister Margaret and her husband, and Charlie Cronin. Then came Uncle Al's Buick. It was the first new car he'd ever owned and he tooted the horn proudly.

"Some buggy, isn't it, Jimbo," he called to Dad. "Took me a long time, but I made it."

"She's a honey, Al."

My big blustering uncle climbed out, followed by his equally large wife and three of their red-haired sons with their wives. Aunt Gen was carrying a foil-wrapped platter—ham or roast beef, probably—and she started up the walk.

"Why don't the girls and I go in and get the coffee started?" she said, pausing to kiss Dad, then clattering up the porch steps with her daughters-in-law.

I stood under the elm tree that fronted the walk, and my wife came up to me. Her face looked pale, the blond hair pulled back tautly from the white brow. Our first baby had been born ten days ago, a long and difficult delivery, and Lissy was still not recovered from it. "Robert, are you all right?" she said.

"Listen," I said, "I don't want you helping too much with breakfast."

"I'm okay. It's you I worry about."

More cars were parking along the curb. Slamming car doors, calling to one another, their voices carrying on the autumn air, the mourners converged on the brown-shingled house, and my father went to greet them, a host welcoming his guests.

"Really, I'm fine," I said. And I smiled at her in proof of it.

To the Irish in Brooklyn among whom I grew up, funeral breakfasts were seldom somber repasts, at least not for long. Indeed, a visitor happening upon one of these affairs would have been startled to learn that the merry rejoicing guests had recently been attendant at a burial. There is much laughter and talk and sometimes boisterous behavior, but beneath the surface gaiety the mourners are, in fact, a conspiracy. They are trying, with their jokes and laughter, to stave off the coming of tomorrow. Tomorrow—the empty bed, the vacant chair—must be held at bay at any cost; and if merriment can accomplish it, surely it is preferable to grief.

Entering the house, I hung up my coat, straightened my tie and went to help with the guests. I disposed of coats and hats, found chairs, mixed drinks, I listened and nodded at old stories, laughed at old jokes. I opened whiskey bottles, passed around cigars, fetched ashtrays, and ushered elderly parties to the dining table.

Three sittings were necessary to accommodate everyone at breakfast, and the kitchen was a babble of female voices and comings and goings through the swinging door. Aunt Gen's baked ham, sausage, bacon and eggs, hot biscuits, buttered toast, coffee by the potful—the food was carried to the table in an unceasing flow. One sitting was no sooner finished than the table was swiftly cleared and reset for another. And the past was brought forth, like bright souvenirs to be handed around.

Brooklyn in the old days—parish dances and boat rides, trolley-car outings to Coney Island; tales of ward heelers and bishops and crooked doings at Tammany Hall, of romances and marriages, overnight riches and ruin, of christenings and funerals, beginnings and endings—and woven through the reverie was a single name, taken up and chorused by all. *Catherine,* the missing guest of honor, nowhere to be seen or heard from, inexplicably missing. I listened to her name being honored, and smiled at stories about her, and I kept the smile intact on my face until it began to crack.

By three o'clock the breakfast sittings were over, but only a small portion of the mourners showed any indication of leaving. I was standing with Dad and Charlie Cronin, who was his boyhood buddy and had known Catherine as a young girl. Charlie launched into another tale about her, and it was then that I felt the smile cracking apart.

And there was one other difficulty. I could not bring myself to enter the kitchen.

Lissy made her way to me through the smoke-wreathed room. Her face was whiter and more drawn, and she said, "I'd better be going, I think."

"You helped in the kitchen too much. You were out there the whole time."

"It's not that—the baby-sitter has to leave by four, and I promised I'd be back by then."

"I'll get your coat," I said.

She embraced my father and went to bid goodbye to the ladies who sat around the dining table like members of a quilting bee. I went to the closet in the front hall for her coat and took out my own as well. She came into the hall and I helped her into her coat.

"I'll go with you," I said. "We'll get a cab."

Lissy looked at me. "Hadn't you better stay with your father?"

I pulled on my own coat. "No, it's okay. Dan and Vinny are with him."

"Dan's leaving any minute. Marijane's upstairs packing for the drive back to Washington." For the last three days Dan and Marijane and Vinny had stayed at the house so that Dad wouldn't be alone. Lissy put her hand on my arm. "Your father's doing so well, don't leave him yet."

I licked my lips. "Well, see, the difficulty's with me," I said. "I'm not doing too well. The kitchen, for instance. I can't go in there. When someone wants ice, I find someone else to get it."

"Robert—"

"I've tried very, very hard, but—"

There was a clatter of high heels on the stairs and Marijane came down. She was carrying a suitcase, and her long hair swung out from her shoulders. "Are you two leaving?" she asked. "If you'll wait a sec, Dan and I can drive you to the city."

I went over to take the suitcase from her. "No, just Lissy is leaving. It'd be neat if you could give her a lift."

My wife frowned. "Rob, if you think you'd better leave—"

"No, no, I'm fine," I said, producing the smile again.

"Just Lissy, then? It's perfectly no bother." Marijane ankled into the living room and drew a chorus of male praise, a reaction to which her sleek good looks had accustomed her. She hugged Dad, invited him to Washington again, whisked into the dining room for a round of goodbyes to the ladies, then with Dan in tow, came back into the hall.

I kissed Lissy at the door. "See you later. So long, Dan and Marijane. We have to get together soon."

Hugs and handshakes, then they went out the door.

I took off my coat and hung it in the closet. I moved among the groups of men in the living room. Charlie Cronin had taken up occupancy of the morris chair, which he always claimed for his own on visits to the house. I thought of how ironic it would be if

Dad ended up in a rooming house with his old unmarried friend. Then I saw Charlie beckoning to me.

"Robbie, sweet fella—" He grinned, gave me a wink, and held up his glass. "Could you get a bit of ice from the kitchen, and a drop more of Jameson's for Uncle Charlie?"

The kitchen—I couldn't go in there. "Well, tell me what you've been doing, Charlie," I said, pretending not to understand.

He regarded me with a tipsy eye, the grin sliding around on his wattled face. "Say, what was it yer father used to call you? Some special name, when you was real little."

"I don't remember, we had so many nicknames—"

"You was different from the others, and runty, even for being the baby of the clan. And one day your dad—"

"If you'll excuse me, I'll be back in a moment." I started away, but Charlie hadn't finished with me.

"Whoa there, aren't you forgettin' something?" he trilled, holding out his glass. "A bit of ice and a few drops of Jameson's. She was a saint," he hiccupped.

I took the glass from him. "Who was?"

Charlie closed his hand, as if taking a pledge. "Catherine was a saint and I loved her, second only to the lady I called Mom. It was why I never entered the marital state, y'know. Couldn't settle for second best."

I did my best to smile. "Mom was fond of you too, Charlie."

"Some ice, lad," he cried. "Poor Charlie needs some ice."

"Yes, sure." I turned and started through the dining room toward the kitchen. What a childish thing, not to be able to enter a room simply because it held a few memories. I skirted past the circle of quilting-bee ladies at the dining table who were still busy stitching together the patches of the past.

"She was the best neighbor God ever put next door to anybody," Mrs. Fritzle was eulogizing, while Aunt Gen, Lillian Brennan, Mrs. Raylman, and two of my cousins' wives nodded in agreement. Mrs. Fritzle scraped some errant crumbs into her cupped palm. "I tell you, there was times if I didn't have Catherine Connerty across the alley from—Robbie?"

I stopped halfway to the kitchen door, and Mrs. Fritzle twisted her bulk around to me. "I ain't had a talk with you yet." She grinned from her chair. "Lookit how tall he is, ladies. Rob was always the shorty of the family." Her hand tugged at my jacket. "Remember when you fell from my fence and broke your arm?"

If I keep silent the pain will go away, and then by some magic . . . no pain . . . "Yes, I remember," I said. "I was seven or eight, I think."

She laughed at the long-ago incident. "A little half-pint and thought he could climb that big fence. Tell me, Robbie, how many is it now? Kids, I mean."

Leaning across the table, my Aunt Gen supplied the information. "Oh, Rob's started to turn 'em out finally. Last week, a darling little seven-pounder."

There were murmurs of approval and Mrs. Fritzle said, "Well, congratulations on a swell start." Then she shook her head in regret. "I guess your mother never got to see the new baby."

Aunt Gen clucked eloquently. "No, Cath was planning a visit in a day or so when . . ." She let the sentence trail off.

Mrs. Fritzle gripped my sleeve. "I—I understand you was the last of the children to see your mom before . . ."

I shifted Charlie's glass in my hand. "Yes, I was."

"You come out to Warbisher Street on a surprise visit, like a sudden impulse. And a few days later, bingo. It was all over."

"Yes, that's right." I went past the table, and the ring of faces followed me as I approached the kitchen door. *If I keep silent and the pain goes away . . .* I stood at the swinging door, unable to push it open. Of all the rooms in the house the kitchen had been Catherine's special domain. And now . . .

I stood there foolishly, conscious of the ladies' scrutiny, and I could not reach out my hand to touch the door. Then it swung open from the other side, and my sister Margaret, her eyes puffy and red, was standing in front of me. How stout and matronly Margaret had become. And what of Roseanne, my other sister . . . ?

"Yes, Rob?" Margaret asked.

"Charlie Cronin—more ice—" I stammered, thrusting the glass at her, then next I was beating a retreat through the haze of talk and cigar smoke in the living room and out to the hall closet to reach for my coat, as though it were a reprieve.

It was then that my father came through the arch and changed the dark shape of the day for me.

I heard steps behind me and turned around, one arm already in the coat.

Dad was standing in the arch. "All finished?" he asked.

I lowered the coat's other sleeve, pulled on the coat. "Well, it's getting late, and . . ." The hall stairs rose into the dimness and I remembered my mother, hurrying up and down those stairs, skimming over the steps as though some marvelous surprise awaited her at top or bottom. "It—it's been a hard day, I guess," I said to my father.

He ran a hand through his white hair, a gesture so familiar that I was hardly aware of it. "It's Roseanne who could have helped us the most with it," he said. "But she's not here anymore."

My sister's far-distant grave, marked by a plain white cross as shown in the snapshots. "Dad, I—I'm really okay," I said. "A good night's sleep and I'll be fine."

His faded blue eyes rested on me. "I watched you on the ride to the cemetery. You kept staring at the flower car, never at the hearse. When it was time to get out at the cemetery, you couldn't move from the car. And just now, when Charlie asked you to get some ice from the kitchen—"

I attempted to make a joke of it. "Yeah, couldn't go in there. Can you tie that?"

Dad's eyes flared with grief. "Is it so easy to do? That kitchen's got your mother written all over it. Why else do you think I'm selling this house?"

"I know," I said slowly.

He looked at me, his gaze keen and intent. "But we still have to face up to it, Robbie—that's what's hard for you, isn't it? To accept that she's gone."

Carrying my coat, I went to the door. "I really think I'd better go, Dad. Lissy's home alone with the baby—" I reached for the knob.

"By hurrying away," Dad said, "it won't make your mother any more alive."

I leaned against the door and closed my eyes, as I had done at the cemetery. "Please," I said.

"You can't run away, Rob." He came over behind me and was silent for a moment. "We used to call you our violin, remember?" he asked. "The others were a brass band, but you were our violin." He was silent again, then he said, "She's dead. We have to accept it."

"Only . . . I can't seem to yet," I said in despair. "I can't . . ."

I felt his hand gentle on my shoulder. "These past few years we used to talk about it—and Cath wasn't afraid of dying," he said. "The way I see it, she's gone to heaven, just like—"

"Stop. Please." I turned to him from the door, my eyes glistening. "Listen, Dad, help me," I asked. "I'm doing badly at it."

"She left something for you," he said. "I found it last night."

I looked at him. "What?"

"On the closet shelf in her room. That's what I came to tell you about."

"What did she leave?"

"A box, with a letter taped to it. Your name is written on the envelope."

He watched me, estimating the stir of interest in my eyes.

"Dad," I said, "I can't go upstairs. What did she write? Did you read it?"

My father took my coat and permitted himself a smile. "Your name's on the envelope. You'll have to find out for yourself."

"I can't. I can't go up there. If I can't even make it into the kitchen—"

The smile broadened, and his hands pressed into my shoulders. "I remember another time years ago when you stayed out of that kitchen. Go upstairs, Rob. Make yourself do it. Look at the box. Maybe it will help."

"What box—?" Suddenly I knew which box he was talking about.

"Go upstairs and see," he urged. "It'll help you."

In the end, I suppose, it was curiosity more than any other

prompting that led me up the stairs. That, and because I knew of nothing else that would help me. Dad stood below in the hall and watched me climb the steps. At the top, where the stairs turned and gave onto the second-floor landing, I paused and glanced over the banister at him.

My father smiled up at me. "Almost there," he said.

"Sir Edmund Hillary approaching the summit of Everest," I joked.

"To the summit, Sir Edmund," he joked back.

I climbed the remaining stairs and turned at the landing. The upstairs hall stretched ahead of me, the bedroom doors closed and silent. There to my right was the room I had shared with Vinny and Dan for so many years. There the bathroom and linen closet, and the rear bedroom that Margaret and Roseanne had shared. All so familiar, and yet it was a region lost in time, with faded boundaries. At the front of the hall, the door open a crack, was the bedroom in which we children had been born. My parents' room, scented with the lilac water that Catherine had used, its scent still drifting into the hall.

I closed the door behind me and entered the small shade-drawn room. The double mahogany bed was chastely clothed in a white coverlet, threadbare from many washings. A rocking chair and a sewing table were grouped at the front window, and across from it was the bureau, and the side window that gave on the alley. I opened the closet and saw, on the shelf, the box my father had referred to. A candy box—that is, it had once contained candy. A ten-pound Valentine box, which a young husband had once brought recklessly home to his bride. I lifted the box from the shelf and carried it to the sewing table. The pink worn cardboard was shaped in the form of a heart, a gold-threaded ribbon ran diagonally across the lid, and tucked under the ribbon was an envelope addressed in Catherine's graceful scrawl.

For Robbie, it read, but when I raised the shade for light and opened the envelope, no letter was inside. Long ago this Valentine box had been my special possession, and perhaps the envelope with my name on it was to make note of this fact.

I lifted off the pink cardboard lid. All of the past was contained in that Valentine box; it lay preserved in the yellowed dog-eared photos that filled it to the rim. And something more was contained in the box—a terrible question that had haunted my childhood. A question I had never dared to ask, until it got lost and buried inside me, far beyond my reach. I had run from that question for years—it had remained lost and unanswered until only last week, when, in this very room . . .

I sifted through the stacks of yellowed photos. There they were —Vinny and Dan, Margaret, Roseanne with her pigtails, face screwed up at the camera—preserved intact. They told a hundred stories, these photos, and spoke of countless days and nights, of summer afternoons and twilight evenings abuzz with fireflies. They told, these photos, of hardships endured, of tears mingled with laughter, of a family growing up in a brown-shingled house in Brooklyn. An ordinary, even nondescript family, yet of inestimable worth, for it had been the only family I had known. Here in this photo, the woman in the apron laughing on the back steps —she was the mother of the family. The handsome black-haired man posed self-consciously in the alleyway, the blurred auto in the background signaling a memory of an auto once briefly owned —this was Jim Connerty, the father of the family.

Here are snapshots of the five Connerty children in endless poses and stages. The tall, solemn eldest son is Vincent, and Margaret comes next, prim and solemn in her First Communion dress. That scowling pig-tailed face belongs to Roseanne of course. Notice her stance, fists held belligerently, ready for instant combat . . . but as it turned out, she had no wish to fight the world.

The dainty, wispy lady in the fur piece, caught by the camera on the front porch, her hand raised in delicate protest, is named Aunt Tillybird. Surely she was always an aunt, was born and died as one. . . . Uncle Al and Aunt Gen, the red-haired cousins, Charlie Cronin, friends and neighbors—all are here in the photos, captured by the Brownie lens. But what of Robbie, the youngest Connerty, where is he? Ah, how often that cry went forth. *Where is Robbie, where can he be?* From the porch, the front door, the top of the stairs, from the kitchen, the cellar, the back steps— *Roobbbbie. Rooobbbbiiiiee, where are you?*

Look, there he is. Standing in front of the brown-shingled house, wearing his Sunday pair of knickers. He is seven years old and his left arm is encased in a plaster cast. There Robbie is, complete with knickers and arm in a sling. There I am, the boy I used to be, skinny and undersized, the different one, square peg in a round hole, drawing pictures and falling off fences, the baby of the family. That was the trouble in a nutshell, the reason I tried to climb Mrs. Fritzle's fence, and the reason I didn't cry when I fell off. And the broken arm was the beginning of the Valentine box as well.

It happened a week or so before this photo was taken. I remembered all of it. . . .

Part One
_____

1

The Valentine Box

"Rooobbbiie," called a voice from upstairs in the house somewhere.

I was out in the backyard and I didn't answer—not yet. It was a Saturday morning in October 1933. The sky was clear blue, the air smoky with burning leaves, and I was going to climb the Fritzles' fence. But I didn't want anyone knowing about it. Not yet.

I stood under the poplar tree in a corner of the yard and surveyed the row of nailed-together boards that marked off the other backyards of Warbisher Street. Trees poked above the fences here and there, and clotheslines bent with drying wash crisscrossed the air. Making a crooked line down the middle and bisecting the others was the fence that separated us from the tenement backyards of Fauber Street. Those other yards were piled with junk and tin cans and a tangle of wash lines that rose one floor above the other to the top-floor flats. There would be plenty of faces to watch my efforts from the back windows and fire escapes of Fauber Street, but I cared only that Catherine and the others in the family weren't watching.

The Fritzles' fence was the tallest of any—over six feet it measured, which was a lot of fence to climb. The family that had previously lived next door had needed an extra-high fence to keep their German shepherd penned in, and the Fritzles hadn't bothered to take it down, even though they had no dog to worry about.

If somebody could manage to climb the Fritzles' fence, he wouldn't have anything to worry about after that—not courage or strength or all-around smartness. It was a test of all three.

My older brothers, Dan and Vinny, had each been ten years old before they'd managed it. Margaret, who came next after Vinny, wasn't the type of girl to be interested in fences, and of course you couldn't believe Roseanne's boast that she'd climbed it when she was six. Roseanne could climb the fence by now, as she was constantly demonstrating for my benefit, but she hadn't been any six when she'd first made it up there. She'd been at least ten, I was willing to bet.

I wanted to be the youngest and smallest of the Connertys ever to go whizzing over the top of that fence. Imagine, only eight years old and he made it, the family'd all marvel at the supper table tonight. Robbie, that little runt, imagine it. I was shorter than my brothers had ever been at eight, and even Roseanne could long claim superiority in height over me. As Dad was always saying when I trooped up the porch steps last from church on Sunday, "Here comes the tag end of the parade. Pick up your feet, Rob."

But I wasn't too little to start school at St. Aloysius's before I was even six. My birthday was in April and I'd entered the first grade in January—and didn't I get promoted to second grade okay?

"The nuns will never keep him," Roseanne had predicted, swishing her evil pigtails. "They'll get one look at his ridiculous behavior and send him home."

"Pay attention to your own problems, miss," Catherine had shushed my sister. "Robbie will do fine at school."

That first day of class—the rows of varnished desks, the religious statues staring from pedestals, Sister Clothilde in her black nun's habit tapping her pointer for attention—I hadn't moved in my seat the entire morning long. Hadn't shifted my feet once or fiddled with my pencil box or made a sound. Hadn't raised my hand to be excused for the bathroom, even when it got urgent. ("What, must he be excused so soon?" I imagined Sister Clothilde snorting, like the Red Queen in *Alice in Wonderland*. "Home with him this instant, the wretched infant.")

I wasn't sent home, however, and by the second week of school Sister Clothilde had appointed me coat monitor.

"You hear that? Coat monitor!" I had informed Roseanne at supper. "Picked me out of the whole class."

"She'll be sorry," said Roseanne, emitting a terrible bray of laughter.

Squeezed in between Vinny and Dan at the table, their long arms reaching for bowls that I couldn't reach by half, I stabbed at my mashed potatoes in despair. No matter if I was coat monitor the whole eight grades, I'd never match Vinny's record at St. A's —the Medal of Excellence at graduation. Last year Margaret had won the fire-prevention essay contest for the entire borough of Brooklyn, and Dan was the top altar boy at St. A's. My brothers and sisters, all of them bigger and taller and smarter, even Roseanne.

But not after today. I stared over at the Fritzles' fence, studying it carefully. After today I'd march at the head of the parade. *I'll never forget the time Robbie climbed the Fritzles' fence,* my father would reminisce in years to come. *Only eight he was, and no taller than my elbow, but that didn't stop him.*

I stiffened warily and shot a look at the alleyway that ran between our house and the Fritzles'. No sign of anybody, but were those footsteps I'd heard? Dad wouldn't be home till afternoon— he worked a half day on Saturdays at the main office of the Childs Restaurant Company in New York, where he was employed in the accounting department. Dan and Vinny were off at the Bushwick High football game, and Margaret was at church, taking in the Saturday morning weddings. There was nothing in life my oldest sister liked better than brides and church weddings. Which left only one sneaky person . . .

I left the tree and went over to check the alley, just in case. Roseanne had the softest, creepingest footsteps of any living creature on earth. She was capable of surprising the Pope in his private chambers at the Vatican, Dad claimed. You looked around and she was nowhere in sight. Then, whammo, there she was, catching you red-handed at something. I peered up and down the alley for a glimpse of pigtails, but there was nothing. I'd better get busy with the fence while I was still unobserved.

I crossed back into the yard and took up my position at the tree. I'd seen the way Dan, Vinny and Roseanne had done it a hundred times. You took a deep breath, caromed over the dirt, careful to duck under the wash line, and leaped up as you neared the fence. High, high up, so you could grab hold of the top and haul yourself up. The trick was to pack enough speed into your run in order to make the leap high enough—up, *up,* like you were aiming for the sky.

I crouched down and got into my racer's stance. I took a deep breath, then another. I counted to ten, sprinted away from the tree—and as I started my wild, headlong plunge across the yard, Mom's voice floated out from upstairs.

"Roobbbie . . . are you down there?"

I tore across the yard, and her voice calling my name seemed to lift me up like a cloud and carry me in the air. *Rooo-oo-bbb-bbi-i-eee.* . . . It was terrific, my feet were hardly on the ground. Faster, faster I ran, the fence getting closer, taller, higher. I leaped up with all the strength that was in me, up, up, reached out my hands blindly—and caught hold of the wooden boards. My fingers clutched at the top, refusing to let go; I dug in my sneakers and hoisted myself slowly up. I'd done it, I'd climbed the Fritzles' fence, the youngest and smallest of the . . .

Then I made a slight mistake.

The mistake came from not having figured out what to do *after* I'd climbed the fence. I'd concentrated all my attention on getting up there, with not a thought for what to do next. I straddled the fence, and the sky seemed near enough to touch, and I could see all the backyards stretching to the last house. Maybe I was too busy enjoying the view, because the next moment I had lost my balance and was slipping off, tumbling downward. I tried to grab hold again, but it was too late, the ground was rushing up, and I put out my hands to break the fall.

I slammed into the dirt, and there was a funny cracking sound in my left arm, like a twig snapping. Bright pinwheels of color began to whirl in my head and my stomach felt sick, like I was going to vomit.

I lay on the ground and didn't move. Mom had stopped calling and it was a cinch she'd come looking for me in a minute or two. She mustn't find me like this, no one must, but what could I do to prevent it? Mustn't cry. If I could keep from crying, maybe the pain would go away.

Mom would be coming. Better hide somewhere. Cautiously I moved my legs, and an awful pain shot up my left arm. I couldn't seem to pick myself up from the ground. Had to hurry and find a place to hide. Hugging the broken arm against my stomach, I reached out with the other arm and dragged myself in relays across the yard. The pain was worse, the dizziness and sickness, but I didn't make a sound.

"Roobbbie," came a last summons from the house.

I dragged myself over the dirt until I reached the poplar tree and hid myself behind it. Then I waited for the pain to go away.

Count or something. Think of pretty pictures—the seashore and blue waves. An apple orchard on a farm. The pictures in the book of *King Arthur* at the library. It was stupid, falling from the fence like that. Wasn't it the stupidest thing you ever heard of? Wait till the family found out. *Poor Robbie, fell off the Fritzles' fence and broke his arm.* Please, they mustn't find out. If I could make the pain go away, maybe . . . maybe the arm wouldn't be injured anymore. Think of more pictures. . . .

Crouched there behind the tree, I heard the back door open. I waited, my heart hammering, not daring to breathe, the pain splintering up my arm. I counted to fifty by twos, then I peeped from behind the tree.

My mother was standing on the back steps, shielding her eyes as she searched around the yard. The wind was ruffling her apron and she clamped it down with her hand. All she was doing was just standing there, but the instant I spied her something came over me that I never could understand.

What was so special or different about my mother? I couldn't understand it. She looked mostly the same as the other mothers in the neighborhood, the same kind of clothes—housedresses and aprons, cloth coats and funny-shaped hats when she went to the store. Her face wasn't much different from theirs, really. It was a perfectly ordinary face, the brown hair salted with gray, like most of the other mothers. And yet she wasn't like them at all. Why was it?

My mother's face, for example—I could pick it at once from the crowd of housewives shopping at Bohack's or coming out of church. A perfectly ordinary face, but I could pick it out, just as, from blocks away, I could instantly recognize her coming along the sidewalk, and soon as I did, my feet would go racing toward her. She always could single me out too, her arms open and ready as I sailed toward her on the sidewalk. Seen from a distance, the other mothers on Warbisher Street looked the same, yet I never went running up to them. But not Catherine—and I didn't understand why it was so.

Take right now, for example: just seeing her there on the back steps made the pain in my arm more bearable, and some of the sick churning in my stomach went away. I watched her scout the yard with her eyes, and next she was looking straight at the tree. I crouched down, pulled in my head and legs, squeezed myself into a ball. I heard her approaching steps, then her shoes were standing in front of the tree.

"Well, look at this," she said. "What are you doing there?"

I blinked at her. "I'm sitting here," I said.

She inspected me for a moment. "Are you sure you're all right? Your face looks pale—"

A wave of pain shot up my arm, but I jutted out my jaw. "I'm fine."

"And the way your arm is twisted up like that—" She started toward me.

I pushed away from her, using my good arm to hump myself over the ground, and shouted, "Keep away from me," tears stinging my eyes. "When Vinny or Dan wants to be left alone, you don't bother them."

"Well," exclaimed Catherine, "will you listen to Mr. Temperament in person." And acting as if that were the end of it, she turned away and casually surveyed the yard.

She hugged her arms in the chill air and took in the bare, unlovely patch of earth marked off by the fence. "When I think of the plans we had for this yard," she sighed. "A bench for under the tree, lovely green grass . . . and over here at the Fritzles' side, a flower border." She was over at the fence, and it was amazing—she was standing at the exact spot where I'd fallen. "My goodness, look at the way the dirt's scuffed up here," she remarked. "What could've caused it?"

The tears smarted my eyes. "So what?" I retorted.

She frowned and studied the tall fence. "My goodness, if I had a nickel for every time your brothers fell off from this contraption . . ." She paused and threw me a sneaky look. "What I mean to say is, it's no disgrace." She edged toward me, all the while pretending to be unconcerned.

"Keep away from me." The tears flopped down my cheeks, but I bit at my mouth and paid them no mind. "Keep away," I said.

"You'll allow me to gather up these leaves, I hope," Catherine said, and scooped up a pile of dead leaves, which she carried to a basket in the alleyway. She deposited the leaves in the basket and commenced humming to herself.

Catherine always hummed while performing her chores. *Catherine* . . . that was the name Dad called her by. Somehow it described the kind of person she was, quick and laughing. The kind of person you could play jokes on, and she wouldn't get sore. Like the time Dad came home and told her that Childs Restaurants was transferring him to a new branch they were opening in the South Seas and she'd better get busy and pack.

"They don't have restaurants in the South Seas," Mom had said, ". . . *do* they?"

They had coconut restaurants, Dad explained.

"*Coconut* restaurants?"

"Certainly, Cath. It's their principal diet. They use coconuts for everything, even their currency. We'll have to learn a new monetary system. They cut up the coconuts into the equivalent of quarters and dimes and half dollars—"

Catherine wasn't stupid; it was just that any really farfetched idea was appealing to her. "Cut them up? Won't that be awful messy? The juice running over your hands, and—" Then, catching on, she waved her hand and scoffed at Dad. "If you think I fell for that malarkey, Jim Connerty—"

"You did, and don't deny it," he'd laughed. "You're so gullible, Cath, I think I could sell you the Brooklyn, Manhattan and Williamsburg bridges combined."

And she had tilted back her head and laughed along with the rest of us. Not that she couldn't get angry, like the time Daniel talked fresh to her and she chased him out the back door with a baseball bat, taking swipes at his legs. But the truth was, Catherine was unable to stay angry for long.

Rainy Saturdays were a perfect example. Rain beating on the roof and the whole gang of us—"her Indians"—penned up in the house. Noise and bedlam. Vinny and Dan roughhousing around, Roseanne stealing my crayons, Margaret complaining in a whine about something or other. The racket would get fierce—Vinny and Danny wrestling on the floor, me screaming about the crayons, Roseanne screaming that she didn't swipe them.

At a certain point, down went the mop or broom or whatever happened to be in Mom's hand. Without a word she would march through the ruckus and uproar, straight to the coat closet in the front hall.

"Hey, Mom. Where are you going?"

Without answering, her mouth set, she would stick on her hat and continue her march to the door.

"Mom, what's wrong? Where are you going?" Our concern was growing genuine as we piled after her into the hall. "Mom, hey—"

"I'm going out." A flat statement, no possible arguing about it, accompanied by a withering look. "I'm not spending a minute's more time hanging around with savages." And she would yank open the door.

"No, Mom, please don't leave."

"Come back, Mom. Where would you go?"

Hesitation. "Anyplace but here. Blow your nose, Vincent. Pull up your socks, Daniel. A pack of savages."

"But where would you go? Besides, it's raining and you don't have your coat on. Only your hat."

Frowning at us as we crowded around her, the mouth not quite as grim, "Well, I know where I'd like to go," she would allow.

So, too, did we know, and a deafening chorus would go up from us. "To Schlack's, to Schlack's!"

Closing the door, leaning against it, "Oh, wouldn't it be grand?" she'd speculate. "I can almost taste those chunks of strawberry. You know?"

Schlack's was an old ice-cream parlor down on Broadway—the best soda store in Brooklyn, Dad called it. If Mom had a weakness, it was for ice cream, and accordingly Schlack's was her favorite place in the neighborhood. However, sodas there cost twenty-five cents, as compared to fifteen or ten cents anyplace else, and so a family outing to Schlack's didn't occur very often. It was the Depression, and so far this year we hadn't been to Schlack's once.

But Catherine didn't actually need to *go* to Schlack's in order for her spirits to be lifted—the mere contemplation of it was sufficient. Leaning against the front door, the rain beating down, she would forget her anger at us. "Those chunks of strawberry," she'd say, and the fighting and noise would be gone.

One night I'd dreamed that Mom really did run away to Schlack's. In the dream I had found her perched on a stool at the marble soda counter, but when I'd asked her to come home, she'd kept right on spooning her soda, as though she couldn't hear. I'd called and called in the dream, and had awakened, still calling, and she had hurried to me in her bathrobe.

"Schlack's . . . you were at Schlack's . . . ," I'd mumbled.

"Hush, Robbie."

"You were gone . . . gone . . ."

She'd sat next to me on the cot, stroking my head until I fell asleep again. "Hush, Robbie, it was only a bad dream. Hush, now . . ."

"Well," Mom said, finishing with the leaves and brushing at her apron. "I gather you plan to spend the whole morning sprawled over there." She was certainly ignoring me a lot.

"I guess so," I replied. Another stab of pain—I kept quiet and the pain went away . . .

She crossed to the back steps, started up them. "No, I guess he wouldn't want to," I could hear her debate with herself. "I probably ought to forget the whole idea."

Boy, she was acting dumb. Hadn't she noticed *anything* was wrong with me? I could practically be bleeding to death, and she'd go right on with her thoughts. "Forget what?" I flung at her.

She turned around on the steps, still with that maddening indecision. "Well, it's this," she allowed. "There I was upstairs, pushing that fool carpet sweeper around, while the rest of the family were out enjoying themselves."

"Dad's working at the office, that's not enjoying himself," I said.

"Well, at least he's not chained to a dopey carpet sweeper," replied Catherine, which sounded reasonable enough. She came down a step. "Anyway, why shouldn't Robbie and me go someplace too, I thought to myself," she continued.

My mouth fell open, and I forget the pain that stabbed at my arm. "Where could we go?"

Catherine smiled at me. "I've got a couple quarters saved up for a treat and I thought—"

"A soda?" I asked dazedly.

"Sure, why not?" She slapped at her apron. "A soda at Schlack's."

At *Schlack's!* The prospect of it nearly propelled me to my feet. "Gee, that'd be neat." I struggled up from the ground, but then a dizziness swept over me and I fell back against the fence.

"Robbie." With a cry, Mom ran toward me across the yard. "You've hurt your arm, haven't you?" she said, kneeling down at the tree. "Let me see. Don't move it." She'd known all along what was wrong—only she hadn't wanted to add to my shame.

"It's not broken, is it?" I asked, the tears starting again.

She examined the twisted-up arm. "Don't be alarmed—it could be growing pains, you know," she comforted.

I looked at her. "You mean at eight years old?"

"Sometimes they come early. Here, let me help you up." She slipped an arm around my waist, helped me up and guided me slowly toward the back steps. "When growing pains come early, it's a sign you'll be big and tall," she went on.

"Taller than Vinny and Dan?" I asked in delight.

"I bet they'll be shrimps compared to you. We'll take these steps nice and easy. How are you feeling?"

I mounted the steps with a groan of pain. "Shrimps compared to me, imagine that."

Catherine pushed open the back door and led me into the kitchen, and it was as if the Angelus bell was ringing at St. A's. I was inside the house, safe and away from harm. That was another thing I didn't understand. Why should a falling-down old house make me feel safe and warm? It was as puzzling as trying to figure out what made Catherine different from other mothers.

It was puzzling because, as far as appearances went, our brown-shingled house wouldn't have won a prize for anything, except possibly shabbiness. It was the sort of house that children draw with crayons, wobbly and crooked, the windows and doors put in at a slant. In all honesty, it looked as if a strong wind could blow it over, shingles, roof, chimney and all. In fact, it already leaned to one side, as if the wind had started to work on it.

It was always getting into trouble, our house. The roof sprang leaks that had to be patched with tar. Down in the cellar the furnace, a great clanking contrivance, had to be poked and prodded to provide any heat, and the boiler was always on the fritz. Everywhere there were cracks in the walls, and the floors were so slanty, marbles rolled across them without any prodding from human hands. The house had six small rooms crowded with furniture so old and worn that you couldn't imagine it had ever been new. The rooms seemed constantly on the verge of bursting apart from the strain of accommodating us all and fitting us in. A junk-filled, beat-up old house like ours—how could it make any-body feel safe and protected and beyond harm? It was impossible to figure out. And yet . . .

The kitchen, into which I now came dazedly, was my favorite of any place or part of the house. I liked the dotted-swiss curtains at the windows and the sparkling glass-doored cupboard, whose shelves were stacked with plates and glasses and china cups hanging from hooks. I liked the fat black stove, and the blue-and-white tiles that covered the floor in a diamond pattern. I even liked the battered tin coffee can that Catherine kept on the sill over the sink, with flowers or a plant growing in it. I liked the smells of the kitchen, cookies or a pie baking in the oven, a stew bubbling on the oven burner, and the clean smell of tiles after they'd been freshly scrubbed. My favorite place of any to sit was the white kitchen table, covered with blue-flowered oilcloth, that stood in the middle of the floor. Sitting there meant that I usually had Mom to talk to, since much of her time was spent in the kitchen. Besides, there was always plenty of action in the kitchen, what with Vinny, Dan, Margaret and Roseanne trooping in the back door and out the swinging door that led to the dining room, or charging up and down the stairs from the cellar. It was an interesting place to be, seated at that kitchen table; anybody would have enjoyed sitting there.

At the moment it wasn't too enjoyable, however. Mom helped me to a chair and I sat down, clutching my arm as though it were about to fall off. I was getting awfully groggy, waiting for the pain to go away.

"Of course we've got to consider the possibility that it isn't growing pains," she said. "The only person to really tell us that is Dr. Drennan. I'd better phone him, don't you think?"

"What about the soda at Schlack's?" I gasped.

"Oh, no problem about that," Mom said. "We'll go to Schlack's . . . but we'll call Dr. Drennan first."

With that she disappeared through the swinging door. I could faintly hear her on the phone in the front hall, then she came back to the kitchen. "We certainly are lucky," she said. "Dr. Drennan was getting his car out. He came back to the phone and said he'd drive us to the hospital"—she paused—"then we'll go to Schlack's from there." She twisted her hands, trying hard to please me.

"It's all right. I know we can't go for a soda," I said.

She came over to the table. "Yes, we will, Robbie. I promise."

"I fell off the fence . . . and I was ashamed to have you find out," I went on.

Catherine shook her head. "Climbing a fence won't make you taller. It's hard being the smallest."

"I wish I could sit here always in this kitchen, even with my arm broke," I said, looking at her from the chair.

"Ah, Robbie, you like being home," Mom said, with a shake of her head. The next moment, she was a whirl of activity.

"Dr. Drennan told me to make you a sling. He'll be outside honking his horn any minute." She bustled back and forth through the swinging door, fashioned a sling from an old shirt for my arm, put on her hat and coat, forgot to remove her apron, and to do so, had to take off the coat. Hurriedly she combed my hair, washed my face, and clucked, "There isn't time to change your underwear."

"Why do I need clean underwear?"

An auto horn sounded out front in the street. "Good Lord, I'd better leave a note for your father. No one will know where we are!" She searched for pencil and paper, scribbled a note hastily at the dining room table.

"What are you telling him?"

"We're going to St. Mary's to get your arm fixed, then on to Schlack's for a soda," Catherine said. "He'll think I've gone dippy," she added, and the auto horn honked again.

She led me down the porch steps to the curb, where Dr. Drennan's big shiny black car was parked. A bunch of kids had collected around to admire it—a new automobile was an infrequent sight on Warbisher Street. As the kids made a path for us I realized that I'd never ridden in an auto before, only on trolley cars and the El train. This would be my first ride.

To break an arm wasn't so terrible after all.

It turned out, in fact, extremely well. The ride to the hospital in Dr. Drennan's car was downright enjoyable, even with my arm twitching with pain. We sat in the spacious back seat, rolling along, the gray upholstery deep-cushioned, and I thought of my father's ambition to own a car of his own someday. He and his brother, my Uncle Al, had owned a Model T together years ago, before either of them was married, and Dad still talked of the fun they had driving to Rockaway Beach and Bear Mountain. On Sundays, when he took us walking on Bushwick Avenue, he always stopped to watch a new Pierce Arrow or Hupmobile go gliding past. "Someday when this damned Depression is over . . . ," he'd sigh, and after that we'd walk on.

"My, but your new car is grand," Catherine complimented Dr. Drennan as we drove along. She sat on the edge of the seat, mindful of the upholstery. Dr. Drennan had delivered all five of her children, and she held him in awe. "It's very kind of you to drive us to St. Mary's like this," she said for about the tenth time.

"Don't mention it, Mrs. Connerty. I was on my way there. No bother."

At the hospital Mom was permitted to come upstairs with me, though she had to wait outside in the hall while Dr. Drennan X-rayed my arm. It was a simple fracture, and he'd get it fixed in a jiffy, he said. A nurse escorted me to a room where I was to wait to be taken up to the operating room, and Mom was allowed in there. The nurse started to undress me, but Mom said that was all right, she'd do it herself, and the nurse left us together.

"I've never been in a hospital," I said, feeling scared.

She slipped the loose white hospital gown over me and tied the strings in back. "Neither have I. Isn't bad, though." She glanced around the cold, bare room, pretending to find it attractive. "Of course, you wouldn't want to throw a New Year's Eve shindig in here, I'll grant you that."

The nurse came back and gave me an enema—for the anesthetic, she explained, closing the sheets around the bed, shutting out Catherine. It was awful, being given that enema. The warm water and the tube, and everything.

"I haven't gone away," Catherine called from the other side of the sheets. After I'd come out of the bathroom and the nurse had left, Mom helped me into the bed, perched next to me on the side, and took my hand. "Nasty things, enemas. Well, it's finished with, and you can relax."

The room was small, but it seemed very large, and so quiet and still. "About that soda at Schlack's—I don't know which flavor to pick," I said. "Tell me about the strawberry."

"Words can't describe those strawberry sodas at Schlack's!" Catherine shook her head at the wonder of it. "Those big chunks of strawberry—the first spoonful, dipping into that ice cream and syrup and fizz water—!"

"Will I have to wait long to go to the operating room?"

She stroked my hair. "Not too long. Say, I bet they're all jumping around at home, wondering how we're doing. Wait till your brothers learn you got a ride in Dr. Drennan's car."

"I bet they'll envy me," I said. But even though we kept talking, the room kept filling with silence. I stared up at the cloudy white globe on the ceiling over the bed. "When you were little, what did you want to be?" I asked, picking another subject.

My mother thought it over. "A bareback rider," she said. "When I was ten, Papa took Tilly and me to the circus, and from then on, nothing else would do."

"We don't see Aunt Tilly much."

"She's delicate and high-strung. Houses spilling over with children are hard on Tilly."

I moved my head on the pillow. "I can't think of anything to be when I grow up except a trolley-car conductor like Mr. Fritzle next door. But I might not grow tall enough. He says you have to be five feet three inches."

"You'll grow tall," Mama said.

"Will Dad take a picture of me after I get the cast on my arm?" My father was the official family photographer. He was always taking snapshots of us with his Brownie, and one of my favorite pastimes was to round up the snaps that were kept in a drawer of the dining room sideboard. There were snapshots going back to when we were babies, posed on a blanket or tucked in the wicker buggy that had been bought for Vinny and used by each of us in turn—I could spend hours poring over those snaps. "He'll want to take my picture," I said. "After all, it's the first broken arm in the family."

"He'll take a whole roll," Catherine said.

"We couldn't afford a whole roll of film." The light globe shone down from the ceiling, and I closed my eyes. "Gee, one minute I was on top of the fence, and the next minute down on the ground." I listened to my heart thump and pictured the operating room upstairs. "Are you ever scared?" I asked.

My mother looked down at me. "All the time. I was scared when I saw you hiding behind the tree and knew right away you were hurt. But you didn't want me to know, so I played along with it, but I was good and scared."

"I mean, scared bad."

She thought that over too, wrinkling her brow. Then, "The only time I'm scared is when I think about something happening where I wouldn't be able to look after my Indians."

"You mean, if you died, like?"

"I don't mind dying, I guess, provided my job's done," she answered with a firm nod. "I just wouldn't want anything to happen . . . while my family still needed me."

The ceiling light stared down at me, like a clouded eye. "Remember that night I woke up crying?" I asked, reaching for her hand. "I dreamed you'd gone away."

"That's silly. Where did you you think I'd gone?"

"To Schlack's, for a strawberry soda."

My mother laughed, and the sound of it filled the room, chasing away the silence, and suddenly I had it figured out. About why she was different and why I could pick her out in a crowd. I finally understood—it was because she was *my* mother. She was ours, she belonged to Vinny and Dan, Margaret, Roseanne and me. Belonged specially to us, and we to her.

"Oh, Mom," I said, getting scared again, and hung onto her hand. "I could have had anybody, Mrs. McGovern, or Mrs. Fritzle, or anybody. But it was you."

That wonderful laugh. "What on earth are you talking about, Robbie?"

The door opened then and a man in white came in wheeling a table in front of him. He rolled it to the side of the bed and asked, "This the little soldier? Think you can climb aboard, sonny?"

"Yes, sure he can," Catherine said.

And I did.

•   •

I figured it out about the house too—the reason why it could make you feel warm and safe, even though it was half falling down. But it wasn't until I got home that I figured it out.

It was afternoon by the time I woke up in the hospital, still sleepy from the anesthetic. I opened my eyes, and the room was blurry and out of focus. It smelled of ether, and I could feel something heavy encasing my left arm.

"Rob?" A man leaned over the pillow—it was Dad. "He's coming to," I heard him say, then Mom came around from the foot of the bed. "How are you, champ?" Dad asked.

I recognized the clouded eye of the light globe staring down from the ceiling, and lay groggy and still for a moment. "Is it . . . over yet?"

Dad grinned. "Everything but the soda at Schlack's," he said, and that woke me up more. My father's bigness loomed impressively over the bed. Six feet three inches tall—the Connerty height, it was known as—and arms strong with muscle, he reminded me of the picture of a woodcutter that was in my second-grade reader. His hair was coal black and wavy, he talked in a booming voice, and took long, vigorous strides that were hard for anyone to keep up with, including Mom. It was strange to think, considering how big and tall he was, that he worked at a desk in an office, entering figures in a ledger. A desk in an office, when he should have been a lumberjack chopping down trees in a forest. He leaned closer over the pillow. "How do you feel?"

I looked at the plaster cast on my arm. "I guess you'll want a snapshot of this with the Brownie."

He gazed quietly down at me. "Ah, Cath, don't he look small in this bed? I don't know where we got a half-pint like Rob." He reached out and cupped my chin in his strong hand. "The others are like a—a—brass band blaring away, and Rob is . . . I don't know . . . a violin."

"A violin?" I asked.

"Well, violins need careful handling—they shouldn't go trying to climb Fritzle's fence."

I sat up against the pillows. "Will I have to go to school on Monday?"

His face creased into a broad grin and he said, "Cath, I think the violin is ready to go home now."

We went home in a taxi—my second automobile ride in a single day—and when the cab pulled up to the brown-shingled house and Dad helped me up the porch steps, Vinny, Dan, Margaret and Roseanne came running out the door to crowd around me.

"Let's see the cast," Vinny said. "Gosh, feel how heavy it is."

"You could get movie stars to autograph it," Roseanne said, pushing closer for a better look. She screwed up her face and sucked on a pigtail. "Did they give you ether at the hospital? Ick —I bet it was lousy."

"I didn't throw up from it," I said proudly, and added, "I don't have to go to school Monday either," before I went into the house.

"What, just from breaking an arm?" Roseanne squawked.

I was given Vinny's bed to sleep in that night. My own cot was in a corner of the small bedroom, jammed between the bureau and the wall, whereas Vinny's bed was next to the window, from which you could look out at the alley and part of the Fritzles' backyard. The room was crowded enough with two beds, and when I'd come along, nothing but a narrow foldaway cot would fit into what space was left.

"One more kid and we'll have to start using the cellar," Dad used to remark.

I fell asleep as soon as my head touched the pillow, and in the morning Catherine brought up my breakfast on a tray—cornflakes with bananas. Usually I was last in line for the Sunday funnies, but I had first crack at them that day. And in the afternoon, while I lay half dreaming, Catherine came into the room with a surprise for me.

"This'll keep you entertained," she said. "The snapshots you're always looking at—I rummaged in the sideboard and rounded 'em all up." She sat next to the bed and handed me a stack of Brownie snapshots. Margaret in her christening robe, Vinny holding a balloon in the wicker buggy . . .

"And I dug up something for you to keep them in," Mom went on. "Look what I found in the cellar." She held out a large pink candy box for me to inspect. It was heart-shaped, with a gold-threaded ribbon pasted across the lid.

"Where'd it come from?" I asked.

"That crazy palooka I married, didn't he lug it home to me on our first Valentine's Day." Mom shook her head at the foolish extravagance of it. "Ten pounds of chocolates—well, I couldn't throw the box out after it was finished."

She handed the box to me and I held it for a moment. "It's beautiful," I said and ran my hand across the gold ribbon.

"It's to keep the snapshots in, so you'll always have 'em handy. I knew it would come in useful someday."

I smoothed my hand over the pink cardboard, then I opened the lid, gathered up the snapshots, and placed them in the box. I kept my head down so that she wouldn't see my eyes. "I'll look after them good," I said. "And you don't have to buy me a soda at Schlack's."

"Oh, yes, I promised," Mom reminded me. "Listen, it's a rare enough treat, with the Depression and all. Avail yourself of it."

My father was standing in the doorway. "How's the patient doing?" He came in and stood behind Catherine, his arm resting lightly on her shoulder. "Think you might want to hobble downstairs for the Sunday-night radio programs?"

"Maybe," I said. Under the plaster cast my arm ached, but I felt happy and safe and warm—and right then I figured out what it was about the house.

It was this: the house was my parents. *They* were the house, it was made of them.

Dad said, "Don't hide your face, Rob. What's wrong?"

"Nothing's wrong," I answered, hugging the box—and that was the whole truth of it.

2

Hanna—for Hope

"Copybooks open, class," said Sister Ethelbert to the third grade the next year. "Too often in our study of geography," she addressed us, "we neglect our home area. We can list the population of Tokyo, or the leading exports of Brazil, but what do we know of our own town or city? Pens ready, class." She rapped on her desk with a ruler. "Let me see how many facts you can write down about your native Brooklyn. Begin!"

I dipped my pen in the inkwell, chewed on the end for a moment, and proceeded to scratch in a woeful script, *There are five boroughs in New York City: Manhattan, Bronx, Staten Island, Queens, and Brooklyn. Brooklyn is the largest and has the most people. It has Coney Island and is sometimes called the borough of churches. This is because there are churches all over the place . . .*

My pen wavered to a halt and I commenced chewing again. None of what I had written was describing Brooklyn at all. I knew nothing whatever about the other boroughs—had set foot in Manhattan no more than twice—and it now looked as if I didn't know a lot more about my native borough. What was Brooklyn? How could I describe it?

It was neighborhoods, I thought: a hundred different sections, connected by trolley-car lines and El trains. It was a batch of neighborhoods with odd-sounding names that made pictures in your head: Red Hook, Flatbush, Greenpoint, Crown Heights, Fort Greene, Cobble Hill, Brownsville, Prospect Heights. Sometimes a neighborhood was named after the main street that ran through it, such as Eastern Parkway, or, in my own case, Bushwick Avenue. When somebody asked me where I lived in Brooklyn, the answer was "Bushwick."

Or, if you were a Catholic, you could answer by supplying the name of your parish. "Where you from?" "St. Aloysius's," you answered, and the other person knew that you lived in the Bushwick section. If somebody answered "St. Francis Xavier," it meant that he lived near Prospect Park. "Our Lady of Perpetual Help" meant Bay Ridge, "Nativity" meant Classon Avenue, and if you answered "The Cathedral," it meant downtown around Fulton Street and Borough Hall, where the big department stores, restaurants and movie palaces were located.

Brooklyn was neighborhoods, and the truth was that all you really knew about the borough was your own neighborhood. You knew the street names and houses and tenements and storefronts, the library and churches and schools and movie theaters. Like the back of your hand, you knew the vacant lots, alleyways, backyards, trolley tracks, front porches and stoops, the cracked sidewalks and trees and gutters. New York was a distant place where people worked, traveling back and forth on the El, but what counted in their lives was their neighborhoods. You were born in a neighborhood and sometimes spent your whole life there. Or you might marry or grow rich and move away, in which case you acquired a second neighborhood. That's what had happened to Mom and Dad. My mother was from St. Gabriel's parish, Dad grew up in nearby Holy Queen of Martyrs, and when they married they settled in St. Aloysius, two miles away. Two miles, yet it was a whole other world.

Brooklyn has many different sections where people live, I wrote in my copybook in the third grade. *However, some of these sections are the same and some have nothing in common . . .*

My pen stopped again as I thought of something that every neighborhood in Brooklyn shared, along with the rest of America. For how long it had been going on, I wasn't certain, just as nobody could predict when, if ever, it would end. But it was certainly shared by the rest of the borough.

I dipped my pen in the inkwell again and wrote, *On second thought, one thing that all the neighborhoods of Brooklyn have in common is the Depression.*

• •

In the house on Warbisher Street the Depression was like an extra member of the family, an eighth place laid at the table, and the only difference was in how my parents regarded it. Dad took the Depression very seriously, as though it were a long, sobering sermon at church. On the other hand, though Catherine acknowledged hard times as a fact, she didn't pull down her eyebrows worrying about it.

I remember that day in January when my mother more or less invited the Depression straight in the door. It's what it amounted to, though she didn't think of it in that fashion. To her it was simply that the doorbell rang one morning, and naturally she went to answer it.

It was after nine o'clock, I was home from school with a cold, and the house was quiet and dozing. Dan, Margaret and Roseanne had gone off to St. Aloysius's, and Vinny, who had to take two trolley cars to get to Brooklyn Tech, and left earlier. I lay on my cot, the blankets pulled up, and listened to the quietness. It didn't seem normal not to hear shouting or footsteps downstairs, and I decided that I liked it for a change. All yesterday I'd sweated and tossed under the blankets, swallowed aspirin and hot lemonade, and wondered if I was dying. The fever was gone today, so I wasn't going to die, at any rate.

In fact, when Catherine came upstairs to clean, she discovered me getting out of bed. "What's this?" she asked, lowering the carpet sweeper to the floor.

I mustered a weak smile as I pulled on my bathrobe. "Well, I still feel sick, but I think I can make it downstairs."

"Oh, you can?"

I hobbled to the doorway. "I'll try, at least."

She propped a hand on the carpet sweeper. "Funny how you improved the minute it was after nine o'clock and too late for school."

"Yeah, I know . . ." I wobbled down the hall to the stairs and started down, holding onto the railing. The radio was downstairs. "Just Plain Bill" "Ma Perkins" and "Our Gal Sunday" were downstairs. . . . "Would it bother you, Mom," I inquired weakly, "If I turned on the Emerson?"

She leaned over the banister. "Go right ahead. And, Robbie?"

"Yes?"

She caught my eye. "In case you think you're foxing me—back to school tomorrow."

"Yes, Mama."

In the living room I settled myself in Dad's morris chair in front of the radio, pulled over the hassock, propped up my feet, and reached out to switch on the dial. *Briiingg,* the doorbell rang. Another beggar, I thought.

Strangers were always ringing our bell—peddlers, dry-goods salesmen, men offering to wash the windows or clean out the furnace for fifty cents. It was the Depression, and even young men came to the door, a lost, watery look in their eyes, to ask for work, or for food or old clothing that we might be able to spare. There were also unsavory types who showed up on front porches, and for that reason the housewives on Warbisher Street made it a practice to check from their windows first. Often they did no more than that: part the curtains, glance out, and go back to their kitchens.

My mother would have liked to emulate the neighborhood ladies, only she couldn't get herself to do it. The glance out the window was what did her in—or perhaps it was the simple lure of the doorbell.

"I'm a sap about it," she admitted. "I go running to the door like I expect to find Queen Mary there."

Dad had a different appraisal of it. "It's half female curiosity and half you can't turn your back on anybody. Every bum in the neighborhood knows it too."

"Now, no, they don't."

"Oh, no? First they try the rectory, then they head for you."

She called downstairs to me now. "Was that the bell? Who could it be, I wonder?"

I turned in the morris chair and looked out the window. "It's— I'm not sure—some kind of woman, I think." On second glance, the figure on the porch was that of a woman, all right, but unlike any I had ever glimpsed. She was as big as a truck driver and garbed in outlandish attire. The moth-eaten black coat was several sizes too small and tied at the waist with wrapping twine; raw, hamlike hands protruded from the worn sleeves, and clutched in the hands was a bulging canvas satchel, on which was emblazoned *Weber's Baths, Coney Island's Finest*. The woman's feet were thrust into heavy ankle-high work shoes, partially unlaced, and perched airily on her head was a girlish summer straw hat, astir with ribbons and cherries. She was tall and strapping, and she stood, feet planted wide apart, staring at the door with a mixture of patience, fear and expectation. She stood there unprotestingly, as if she were long accustomed to waiting at doors.

"What do you mean, some kind of woman?"

"Sort of a lady bum," I shouted up the stairs.

There was a pause, during which, I knew, Catherine was deliberating; then, sure enough, she came bustling down.

Clucking her tongue, she glanced out the glass oval—"Look at the poor creature"—and swung open the door. I stood behind her as she asked, "Yes, can I help you?"

The woman stepped back; her hands twisted at the canvas satchel, and she gazed fearfully at my mother. "Pliss, lady—" She pointed across the street, her German accent as thick and clumsy as her shoes. "The Werners, you tell me vere dey are, pliss? No answer the bell."

My mother looked over at the green-shingled house that stood across the street from ours. "Why, they moved away last week," she explained. "Mr. Werner's plant closed down, you know, and—"

The woman's mouth formed a wide O of disbelief. "They gone, you mean?"

"Mr. Werner got a job in Philadelphia, to manage a plant there. It came up unexpectedly," my mother explained. It was a frequent happening in those years, families moving away without notice, cars loaded with belongings, steering toward jobs in other cities. Familes vanished also because they could not meet the rent or keep up mortgage payments; they hired ice trucks, piled them with furniture at night, and were gone by morning. Our neighborhood in Brooklyn had never been prosperous; to me it had seemed as if the houses on Warbisher Street had been *built* to look shabby and run-down. But there had been a settled quality about the neighborhood, a sense of permanence, as if the little houses and the people in them would always be there. That quality had disappeared.

"*Moved?*" The woman stared across at the green house, at the windows that gaped back at her emptily. "Last Thurday," she said, "I got to stay home, take my boy to clinic—" She turned frantically to my mother. "What I gonna *do?* The Werners was my Thursdays."

"Your—?"

"My Thursdays. To go by their house and clean. I got now only Mondays, the Sanders."

"They should have let you know," Catherine sympathized. She looked at the stiff, chapped hands, which were purple at the knuckles. "You have no gloves."

"Aaah," the woman cried, dismissing so minor a worry. "Lady, my boy is in hospital. If tomorrow I don't have five dollars for hospital—"

My mother shivered in the cold January air that swooped in from the open porch. The Depression was a familiar presence in our house. I remembered the Friday night last year that my father had come home from Childs with his pay envelope reduced nearly by half. After supper he had spread out the bills and coins on the dining room table.

"There, that's what we've got now, Cath," he'd said. "Thirty-five instead of sixty. We'll never survive."

He shook his head and regarded the huddle of bills as though they represented a puzzle to which there was no solution. Each Friday it was his custom to distribute his pay into envelopes marked *Food, Mtge, Church, Amus.*, and so forth. I think he must have torn up the *Amus.* envelope that evening, because after that we stopped going to the movies. We didn't take trolley-car rides to the Prospect Park Zoo on Sundays or to Rockaway Beach in the summers, and there were no visits to Schlack's even on Mom's birthday.

It took Dad a long time to figure out how many bills to put in which envelope that Friday. On Sunday we started putting pennies instead of nickels in the collection basket at St. A's; we signed up for free lunch at school, and Vinny got a job delivering groceries to earn his high-school expenses. Dad brought home a shoe-repair kit and learned how to fit new soles and heels; he taught himself barbering, and a stool in the cellar became our barber chair.

Every evening my mother was busy sewing in the living room, turning shirt collars, patching trousers, making over Margaret's dresses for Roseanne while from the Emerson, H. V. Kaltenborn told of new shutdowns and idle assembly lines. Dad listened and shook his head. "No way out of it," he would declare dolefully.

I remember the smile on his face when he came home in November and told Mom that he was being given some overtime work at the office. One of the men was on sick leave, and Mr. Carlson, the boss, was going to pay Dad extra to stay late a couple of nights a week and finish the work. At supper that night we talked excitedly about how we'd spend the extra few dollars. Roller skates, movies! A new coffee pot, new oilcloth, a hat for Mom! But each week the overtime pay, while it lasted, disappeared into Dad's envelopes without a trace. And when my father sat in his morris chair at night and thought no one was looking, a worried, almost frightened look would come on his face.

"You have to remember the hard times of his childhood," Mom told us one night after he'd shouted at Vinny for losing some money that was in his pocket. "When Dad was fourteen years old his father passed away," Mom explained. "He had to quit school and work to support his mother and Al. Sometimes they didn't have enough money for coal to heat the flat. And now bad times seem to have come back. It's natural to worry."

"But you don't worry," Vinny said.

"Yes, I do," Catherine said. "When I have time for it."

Shivering in the doorway, Mom didn't appear to have time to worry now either. All that apparently concerned her were the woman's raw, chapped hands.

"You've got to have gloves," she said firmly. "I have an old pair, the lining's half out, but if you'll wait there a—"

"*Lady, pliss*—" As Catherine moved from the door the woman stumbled into the hall after her, an arm outflung. She was breathing heavily. Wild-eyed, she put down the satchel, tugged at the straw hat. Fear, desperation, stunned surprise, blind panic—all had raced over her broad face. Now, tugging at the straw hat as though to render her appearance more fetching, she swung her arms and tossed a gay, roguish smile at us. "Hey, lady," she announced with a noticeable lack of tact, "your house look like it could maybe stand a good cleaning. Hanna clean it smick-smack for you, eh?"

Catherine blinked at her from the stairs. "I—well—"

The woman gestured at me. "This your boy? Hey, you skinny kid," she shouted playfully, "why you not in school?"

I pulled at my bathrobe. "I've been sick. It was almost bronchitis."

"*Ja,* I bet." She wagged a finger at me. "Listen, I hope you work hard by school and learn. Ask Hanna what iss not to read or write." She whacked me on the shoulder—"Ahh, you are good boy"—and smiled up at my mother, as though only terms needed to be agreed on. "Hanna clean whole house for you, lady, cost only a dollar." My mother looked at her helplessly. Slowly the woman nodded in understanding. "*Ja* . . . iss too much, a dollar. By you iss hard times too." She shook her head in self-anger. "What iss matter with me, to come in your house like crazy person?" The thick clumping shoes traced a path to the door; the rough red hands reclaimed the canvas satchel. "Forgive Hanna," she said.

"A dollar"—Catherine watched the door open—"you should charge more for a day's cleaning."

In the doorway the woman shifted the satchel and tried to smile. "You no worry. I find work, I be okay." She shook her finger gently at me. "No forgets, sonny. Study hard, learn good by school."

She was gone.

The wind whipped at my mother's skirt as she ran out onto the porch. She hugged her arms against the cold. "Dollar's not enough," she called. "I'll pay two, not a cent less."

The big, heavy, mute shape reversed direction on the sidewalk, the row of dog-eared houses outlined behind her. Her face struggled hard to comprehend. "You—?"

I saw my mother clap a hand to her mouth. "If Jim—" She bit her lip. "We won't tell him, that's all. Those poor hands," she clucked, going to the edge of the porch. "Well, come in, no sense standing in the cold."

Then she held open the door for Hanna.

Johanna was her name, pronounced "Yo," with a long, rolling "Hahhhhna": Johanna Haegle, Austrian born, but she bade us, and the rest of the world, to call her Hanna.

That first day she hung up her coat—ignoring the moth holes, she invited us to feel of its superior weave. "Some nice coat, eh? I find in ash can,"—and whipped open the canvas satchel. Dramatically she drew out the tools of her trade: dusting cloths, soap, a scrub brush, an apron, a pair of shapeless carpet slippers (also plucked from an ash can). The apron was faded and patched and fastened at the waist with a safety pin, the carpet slippers were lined with chunks of cardboard, but as Hanna herself remarked, rolling up her sleeves, "I no here for fancy ball. Okay, lady, where we begin?"

She made a swift survey of the house, then threw herself upon it, cleaning everything in sight. In and out of rooms she moved, up and down stairs. She washed the windows, attacked the furniture with cloths and whisk broom, shuttled the carpet sweeper over the rugs. She mixed pails of soapy water and scrubbed the bathroom, the kitchen tiles. Hunched over on her knees, a hand reaching to pull the pail behind her, face rosy and content, she made her way slowly across the floors, swinging the sudsy brush in wide, amiable half circles.

"Austria must be an interesting land," I remarked to her as the morning progressed. I had abandoned the radio in favor of following Hanna from room to room. It was more entertaining. "I regard all foreign lands as interesting," I informed her.

"*Ja,*" she muttered.

I stood alongside as she mixed a fresh pail for the kitchen. "I intend to travel far and wide one day. I don't as yet know what career to follow, but I hope it includes lots of travel."

"No foolin'." She knelt down with pail and brush and scrubbed her way across the blue-and-white tiles.

"Geography's my favorite subject at school. Actually, I hate to miss school like this, you know."

Hanna didn't really need a conversation partner; as she scrubbed she entertained herself with bursts of foreign song. Swoosh, swoosh, would go the scrub brush, then an outbreak of melody. *"Wien, Wien, nur du allein . . ."*

"I'm practically an honor student," I persisted. "I hope to win a scholarship to high school when I graduate—St. John's, maybe—and from there, who knows, to college."

Swoosh went the brush in vigorous arcs over the tiles. "Ah, vunderful! Hanna never go to school. Since little girl, work only."

"If you let him, Robbie will talk your ears off," Mom warned, poking her head through the swinging door. "He's the gabby member of the clan."

"He talk funny for little kid," observed Hanna. "He grow up different, I bet."

"Roseanne says I'm a freak," I confided, and paused to mull over the stream of chatter that seemed to pour incessantly from my lips.

When it was noon Hanna held up her hand, policeman style, and waved Mom away from the stove. "Who working here, lady? Sits down. *Hanna* fix lunch."

Watching Hanna prepare lunch was like observing a resourceful oversized chipmunk sniffing out edibles in a forest. She opened the icebox and studied the shelves. "Ah, you got nice chunk meat here, lady."

"It's only the leftover from a rump roast," Mom apologized.

"We make stew," declared Hanna. She foraged in the vegetable bin and came up with carrots, onions. In a twinkling the whole was stirring in a pan on the stove. She seized the blue-enamel coffee pot, filled it with water, and spooned coffee into it. To this she added an egg shell plucked from the trash—"Make coffee clear, no bitter taste"—and set the pot to boil. "What we give the skinny kid?" she asked, rummaging through the vegetable bin and unearthing a bag of potatoes. "Hey, skinny kid, you like fried potatoes? Hanna make vunderful *Kartoffeln*. Where iss pepper, salt?"

In a daze, Catherine watched the delicious lunch materialize: the stew bubbling in gravy, the potatoes asizzle in a frying pan, while over the kitchen floated the rich aroma of Hanna's coffee. For my mother there would never be anything as tasty as one of Hanna's improvised stews, no brew more fragrant than her boiled coffee. For me—and later for my brothers and sisters—Hanna's fried potatoes, hot, brown-crusted and spicy, would be a perennial wonder.

For her own lunch Hanna claimed a jar of bacon drippings from the icebox. She swabbed the lard on slices of bread—"Since little girl, iss my lunch. In Austerlitz black bread we use"—and sat down at the table, big and ample-bosomed. Steam curled from the radiator, warming us; the blue-and-white tiles sparkled from Hanna's scrubbing.

Before eating she bowed her head, blessed herself, and recited a prayer in German. "Komm, Herr Jesus . . . ," she intoned.

"I never heard that prayer," I said.

"I teach to you," she offered. "Iss nice prayer, ask Jesus to be guest at table vhen you eat." She picked up the bread and munched it happily. Wisps of hair escaped delicately from the knot skewered at the back of her neck, and her broad feet, I noticed, were tucked daintily under the chair legs. Despite her size and girth, there was a quality of littleness about Hanna.

She sipped the hot coffee, ate the lard bread, and told us about herself. The depression was an old story in Austria, she explained. As long as twelve years ago there had been no work for her husband, Josef, a baker by trade. So he had emigrated to America, found work in a bakery in Brooklyn, saved his money and sent for Hanna after their son was born to join him. "With my little boy I cross ocean alone," she described. "Twelve days and terrible storms, but ship not sink, and ach, so happy we are to be with Josef! Then at bakery one day where he work iss accident. Was—how you call?—boiler explode." Hanna's coffee cup clacked down on the saucer. "My—my Josef was took away in ambulance. Two days screaming in hospital . . . then he die."

She ran her hand over the blue oilcloth. "Terrible things can happen in life," she said, nodding her head, "terrible, but you got to haff *Glaube*—what you say in English, *faith? Ja,* you got to go on." The hand brushed at the oilcloth. "I haff child, I must go on."

By the time of Josef's death the Depression had started in America and she had not been able to find work. She had walked the streets. "I go to bakeries, but no jobs, iss everywhere the Depression." She jerked her head determinedly. "Hanna not give up. Walk, walk the streets. Then I find building in Greenpoint what needs janitor, take care of halls, furnace. They want man for job, but I beg, beg. Picks up ash cans, show how easy I carry. Get down on knees, show how good I scrub. 'Okay, job is yours,' they say, and the happiness I feel"—she smiled and clapped her hands—"I cannot tell you. In return for janitor I get free apartment. Two rooms in basement, no window in bedroom, but iss fine. Then I go out, look for work as cleaning woman. Walk, ring doorbells. I have son, I must work."

Hanna's son was named Emil; he was fourteen years old, and all of her dreams were centered on him. Her biggest dream was that Emil would not only finish high school—in itself an achievement—but would go on to college as well. But then her smile dimmed and she rubbed again at the oilcloth. "What iss word for ear sickness when it—?"

"Mastoids?" my mother supplied.

The hand stroked the oilcloth in apprehension. "*Ja,* that is why Emil in hospital. If it no clear up, doctors must operate him." She looked at my mother. "Hospital iss one place what scare Hanna. They take Josef there, he die . . ."

My mother reached out to the square, blunt hand. "You mustn't worry. Our Vinny had an ear infection like that and they didn't have to operate."

"I went to the hospital with a broken arm," I told Hanna, waving my left arm over my head. "Look, it's fine now."

"Iss true?" asked the broad, flat face. The head nodded, a hand went to her breast. "In her heart . . . Hanna keep hope," she said.

Her palm whacked the table, she pushed back her chair. "Talk, talk, iss work to be done." She stood up, threw her shoulders back, and gave my mother a smile. "What we do now, lady? I wash dishes, then we wax floors maybe?"

Dan was the first one home from school that day. Handsome Dan, he was called. He had hair like Dad's, curly black, a cleft in his chin, and a flashy smile, and at thirteen his shoulders were already filling out.

"Hey, buddy," he greeted me, slamming the front door and flinging his books on the hall table. There was no doubt that Dan would inherit his share of the Connerty height: he was at least three heads taller than me. "I got your homework assignment from Sister Edward," he told me. "She says to bring it in tomorrow, buddy."

"What if I don't have the right books?"

"That's your tough problem."

He sauntered into the kitchen, came back munching a peanut-butter sandwich. Just then Mom came down the stairs, a jacket folded over her arm. Dan asked, "Who's the Mack truck in the cellar? I noticed the light on down there and—"

"That's Hanna, and don't talk smart-alecky," Mom said, marching past him. "And not a word to your father, understand?"

"Hey, wait a minute. What are you doing with my jacket?"

Calmly, my mother continued into the dining room. Her head was upraised, as when pursuing a righteous cause. She put the jacket on the dining table, dug into her apron pocket, and out came two crumpled dollar bills, which she smoothed with her hand. "Don't think it's the house money," she said, glancing up at Daniel and me. "I happened to have a little extra tucked aside, in case of emergencies. Not a word about it, understand?" She went to the cellar stairs and called, "Haaaana," with an air of satisfaction.

The whole family was familiar with Catherine's mysterious sums of money that were "tucked aside" for what she regarded as emergencies. How the money was accumulated she never disclosed, and her notion of an emergency was highly flexible. It included practically anything—a pair of gloves for Margaret to wear to a party, flowers for Vinny to take his prom date. On such occasions she would disappear into her room, emerge with some bills, hand them over, and caution in a vaudeville whisper, "Don't let on to your father."

"I guess you could call Hanna an emergency," she reflected now, coming back to the table and smoothing out the bills again.

The cellar stairs groaned, and the big hulking figure trooped into view, lugging two large bundles of old newspapers. She had spied the stacks of paper earlier in the cellar and inquired, "I guess you sell these to junkman, eh, lady? Hanna can take? *Ja,* you sure?" It seemed that she collected old newspapers in the building where she was janitress and brought them weekly to a dealer. "Pull in wagon, sometimes I make twenty-five cent."

Straw hat bobbing, shoes clumping, Hanna made her way to the dining room table. "Vell, lady, we get plenty work finish," she commented happily.

"Roseanne, I'd like you to meet Hanna," Mom said to my sister, who'd come into the archway with her schoolbag.

"Who is she?" Roseanne asked.

My mother didn't quite supply an answer but counted out the two dollars on the table and said, "I won't hear of a cent less." She hesitated, and added a quarter from her apron pocket. "That's for carfare."

Hanna's expression as she stared at the money was as if she were beholding the United States Mint. She twisted at her hands. "Ahh, lady . . ."

"Why, the wonderful work you did for us." Mom smiled. "You're underpaid, if anything."

"Can—can pay hospital," Hanna said, gathering up the bills. She raised her eyes gropingly to my mother. "In other house I work, iss not like this. Vat—?"

Catherine folded Daniel's old jacket and handed it to her. "It might fit your son. No, go ahead, our Dan's outgrown it," she lied.

Hanna stroked the jacket wordlessly, then placed it in the canvas satchel, where it joined the scrub brush, the carpet slippers, the patched apron.

Mom went over to her, already a loyal ally. "Could you come

next week?" she asked. "We'll have to keep it quiet from my husband for a while, he worries so about things, but—" She raised her chin in the manner of Joan of Arc. "Maybe from now on we can be your Thursdays, Hanna," she said.

She waved Hanna goodbye from the porch, then gathered us in the dining room for a lecture, which she repeated as both Vinny and Margaret joined the circle. "You children know I don't usually conceal things from your father—never mind that pious look, Margaret—but sometimes women have to do things on their own initiative. They just have to forge ahead," she finished up.

"I'll say," Dan commented. "It's the Depression and suddenly we've got a maid."

"She's not a maid, she's a friend," Mom corrected him. "What's more, she's coming next Thursday—so long as my extra money holds out. Hanna needs us, and perhaps"—she tilted her head in thought, and a puzzled look came into her eyes—"perhaps we need her as well. And none of you are to spill the beans about it. Okay?"

"Sure, Mom," we agreed. "Sure, okay."

We didn't spill the beans either—and for a good reason. Hanna came back the next Thursday, and the next after that, and by then none of us would consider betraying Mom's secret. It would have meant losing Hanna.

She cleaned the house. She scrubbed the floors, washed our clothes and hung them to dry in the backyard, her sturdy figure planted like a tree against the winter gales. She cooked lunch for Catherine and afterward set up the ironing board in the kitchen, disposing of the basket of freshly dampened shirts and blouses, bursts of song accompanying the iron's hiss. She washed and cooked and ironed, and did something more for us, which wasn't as simple to identify. I knew only that on Thursdays we didn't lag on the way home from St. Aloysius's. We headed straight for the brown-shingled house, for the kitchen, the hissing iron, and Hanna's joyous greeting.

"Ahh, Robbie, your cheeks from the cold," she would exclaim, rubbing her warm hands on my face. "Here, sits down, I make soup to fatten you up. Roseanne, look, I find ribbon in trash can, iron it smooth to tie pretty in your hair. Sits with your brother. Ah, here is Daniel, so handsome. Such vunderful family."

"We're not so wonderful," Roseanne told her. "Sister Miriam Jerome said I was slothful today. How's Emil's ear?"

"Ach, is all better almost. No have to operate."

As we sat with her in the kitchen Hanna kept an anxious eye on the clock. Each minute that ticked by increased her nervousness. "Come, hurry mit soup. By four o'clock I must be gone. Shhhhh!" She stuck a finger to her lips. "We can't let Papa know yet."

"I'll pack your satchel, Hanna."

"Stay there, Hanna, I'll get your coat."

We waved her down the street from the porch. "So long, Hanna," we called, watching her set off with her satchel down Warbisher Street. "See you next Thursday."

And we would wait till the next Thursday came. Even on the other days of the week there was something of Hanna that lingered over the rooms, warm and nourishing, like her soup. At night when Dad switched on the radio and listened, with head shaking, to the news reports—the number of jobless in Cleveland, the relief lines in Detroit—it was as though we could hear Hanna singing in the background.

Of course it was bound to happen that he would find out. When he came home that first Thursday he glanced around in amazement. "Great Scott but the house is clean, Cath. How'd you accomplish it?"

My mother set the meat platter down, avoiding his gaze. "Oh, I just pitched in."

"Clean the windows too? They're positively shining." He had remarked on the gleaming waxed floors and the stack of freshly ironed shirts in his drawer. "Where'd you get the soup?" he'd asked, sniffing at the stove. "Smells good."

Four o'clock on Thursday was Hanna's deadline to scurry out of the house. Prussian troops might have been after her, such was her haste as she collected her bundles and fumbled with the wrapping twine on her coat. And one Thursday—the fourth she was at the house—my father arrived home early.

My mother had gone downtown to Fulton Street that Thursday

on the scent of a yard-goods sale. Dan was in the cellar, Margaret and Roseanne were upstairs, and I was in the kitchen with Hanna. It was nearly four, and she was finishing with the ironing.

"We don't realize how vital the decimal point is," I was instructing her. "Sister Edward told us about this man today, he made out a check for ten dollars, only he forgot the decimal point."

"*Ja?*" The iron swished hurriedly over Margaret's school jumper.

"Well, what happened"—I heard the thud of the front door closing—"the other man cashed the check for a thousand dollars. On account of the missing decimal point. It goes to show you."

Hanna looked up from the ironing board. "Ahh, iss Wincent getting home," she said, "he stay at the school for basket—what game iss?—practice." She put down the iron and sang out, "Wincent! Come in kitchen, gets warm."

There was silence, then my father's voice asked, "Who is that in there?" Another silence. "Who the hell is it?"

"It's him," I whispered. "It's my father."

Hanna stared wildly at the swinging door that led to the dining room and the front of the house. She moved, as if to make a last-ditch break for freedom, then crossed herself, and stared, hypnotized.

The door opened; my father stood there. He was holding a compress to his jaw. He looked at Hanna. "Who the dickens are you?"

She gawked at him, seized the iron, and plunged furiously into activity. "Am Brunnen vor dem Tore," she sang, "Da steht ein—" She glanced up at the door, as if noting my father's presence there for the first time. "Goood evening, sir." She smiled, waving to a chair. "Sits down. Rest you feet."

"Robert," my father said, shifting the compress with a faint moan, "who is this person? Surely you must know."

But Hanna was hurrying toward him from the ironing board, her gaze on the compress. "Vat iss matter," she murmured. "Ahh, toothache, *nein?*" She guided him to a chair, clucking in sympathy. "Sits. Iss need ice, make pain go away." She sped to the icebox, chopped some ice, rolled a wet towel around it, hurried back to his chair. "Der, press against face, feel better."

My father leaned back in the chair and regarded her weakly. "Please. Just tell me who you are. That's all."

She stood back, smiling, and put out her hands. "Who I am? I am Hanna, who else?"

By evening my father's toothache had abated, but not his displeasure with my mother.

"Deception," he cried, "pure out-and-out deception. Not only you—the whole family's been in on it, apparently."

"I admit it was sneaky," Catherine conceded. "I won't argue about that, Jim."

He paced up and down the living room carpet. "Total stranger in the kitchen. Singing away, ironing to beat the band. I gather you've been paying this person wages."

"Two dollars every Thursday, plus carfare. I make her take the carfare."

My father gestured broadly. "Think nothing of it, Catherine. What's two dollars to us? A mere nothing."

"Until today it was from my own money," my mother pointed out. "She rang the bell, Jim. Her little boy was in the hospital, and the way she stood there in that awful coat, and no gloves for her hands—"

"Two dollars," my father repeated, circling around the sofa. "We can spare it easily. Sure, when I divide up my pay on Fridays in those blasted envelopes—why sure, there's always money left over."

"The extra overtime you got at the office, Jim—I kept thinking of that."

"Only for two months."

"You'll get more, wait and see."

Dad paced up and down, gesturing at her. "What's money to you? Brought up in the lap of luxury—"

"Papa wasn't rich. He owned a small business, that's all."

"You and Tilly never knew what it was to go without. I remember when Al and me had to steal from the coal yard or freeze."

Dad stopped his pacing and confronted Mom from across the carpet. "You betrayed me, Catherine. Or haven't you heard the Depression's still on?"

"Yes, I've heard about it," she flared back at him. "How could I help it—it's become your favorite word." She went over and gestured at the radio." You and Gabriel Heatter and H. V. Kaltenborn. Oh, I know there's a depression—but I went to the door one Thursday, the door of this warm house, and I saw a woman who had no gloves and a string tied round her coat so it wouldn't fall open. I looked at her and I didn't feel like I was so bad off. And . . . and there was something in her face that made me feel ashamed."

"Cath . . ." my father said.

She turned and faced him. "Standing in the cold, hands raw from it, but there was hope in her face. No reason for it, but there was hope. I brought her inside. She scrubbed the floors and cleaned—and she brought hope into the house with her. She made me feel different, Jim, as if there was really hope for us all. I didn't know how I'd pay her, or keep on paying her, but I asked her back. She needed us, and I guess I figured we needed her. Times like these, if you can do something for someone else . . . that means there's hope, doesn't it?"

My father looked at her, started to speak, changed his mind. "I can't imagine why you're against H. V. Kaltenborn, Catherine," he said. "H.V.'s the soul of optimism."

My mother turned and beckoned to me in the hall. "Okay, Mister Big Ears, upstairs to bed. You too, Roseanne."

"Good night, Mother," I said. "Good night, Father."

The next morning at breakfast my father was silent, and my mother didn't refer to the subject either. But that night—it was Friday—when he came home with his pay envelope he spread the bills on the table and got out the envelopes marked *Food, Mtge, Church, School, Amus.*

"Carlson spoke to me about some extra work on Saturdays," he said to Catherine. "He thinks he can fix me up."

Then my father took out a fresh envelope, put two dollars in it, and wrote across the front, *Hanna—for Hope.*

3

The Easter Dress

I remember Christmas Eve the next year and my father trumpeting into the front hall, late from work. He was waving his pay envelope. "Anybody home?" he called excitedly.

Mom was in the kitchen, but the rest of us were sprawled in the living room. A program of Christmas carols was playing on the Emerson and we were discussing where to buy a tree. We'd waited until Christmas Eve because the prices for the leftover trees could be counted on to plummet dramatically by then. After supper Mom planned to go scouting along Broadway, where trees were for sale on almost every corner—green rows of pine and fir propped against the ropes that were tied to the lampposts and El pillars. We'd already checked the stands in the afternoon, and the going price for a good-sized tree was still a dollar. Earlier in the week it had been two dollars, and Mom had predicted that it would go down to fifty cents, maybe a quarter, if we waited long enough. The trick was in calculating exactly how long to wait before the last of the decent trees were snapped up by other astute bargain hunters.

We couldn't afford any new tree ornaments or lights this year. All afternoon Vinny had toiled in the cellar repairing the old strings and testing the bulbs. He'd repainted the old crèche as well, pasted cotton on the roof for snow, and glued the head back on the statue of Saint Joseph which had broken off last Christmas. We would have a tree—a nice one, if we were lucky—and the crèche to put under it, and if there weren't many gifts to open on Christmas morning, there was sure to be something for each of us.

"Where's Mom?" Dad shouted from the hallway. "Cath, Cath."

He came into the living room in his frayed herringbone coat and sailed his fedora into the air.

"Ask me the news. Go ahead," he demanded when Mom trotted in from the kitchen.

"What is it, Jim?" she asked, wiping her hands on her apron.

He grinned and waved the pay envelope at her. "I got paid today. Is this or is this not my pay envelope? Well?"

She swiped at the envelope. "Yes, of course, you big palooka."

"Count it, why don't you." He shook out the bills from the envelope and they floated onto the carpet. "There's ten extra bucks floating around on that rug, Catherine old sock."

Margaret jumped up from the sofa. "Dad, you got a raise, how perfectly splendid." Ever since she'd started Girls' Commercial High School last year Margaret had taken to using phrases like "perfectly splendid" and "absolutely enthralling." It was her announced goal to become "a genuine lady," and not a minute went by that she wasn't practicing at it.

Roseanne flew across the carpet and flung her arms around Dad. "Hey, Pop, are we rich?"

"Nobody gets rich on ten extra dollars," Daniel said.

"Count 'em, ten extra bucks," Dad said to Mom, who was on her knees gathering up the bills. "Am I right?"

My mother stood up and counted the bills. "My goodness, ten extra dollars!"

"Hey, Dad, that's great," Vinny said.

My father stood in the center of the living room and spread out his arms, including all of us in their wide circumference. "It means," he said, his voice shaky all of a sudden, "it means we're coming through. We're not going under. We're still in the ball game."

Mom tucked the bills in his pocket. "Well, I could have told you that."

"If you're not a wonder," he said, turning to her. "Went and hired Hanna last year, and look at you now, cool as a cucumber. I guess you never had nightmares of losing this house to the bank. I could see the foreclosure notice posted on the door, clear as anything."

"We'd have found another house," Mom said. "We'd have stayed together. That's what counts—all of us staying a family together." She reached up and kissed him. "Fish stew for supper, are you hungry?"

Forgetting that his overcoat was still on, Dad followed her into the dining room. "Ten bucks more a week. Do you realize it adds up to five hundred and twenty dollars a year?" he asked, and the swinging door whooshed shut behind them.

"Five hundred and twenty dollars." Dan whistled slowly. "We could buy a car for that."

"Or a fur coat for Mother," Margaret said. "Something suitable, like muskrat."

There were no cars or fur coats, but we didn't bother that Christmas Eve about waiting for fifty-cent trees. As soon as supper was over, the whole family paraded out, and Dad bought the first tree on Broadway that caught his fancy. It cost a dollar, and after that he marched into Woolworth's and bought new lights and strings and a box of gilded ornaments.

We put up the tree and strung and decorated it the minute we got home. When finally we had finished, it rose against the living room window, straight and tall, its branches spreading over the carpet, sparkling with tinsel and aglow with red, blue and orange lights. We brought up the crèche from the cellar and placed it under the tree and arranged the statues of Mary and Joseph on either side of the manger. Then Dad found a shepherd's figure in the cellar that Mom said had been lost for years, and we placed it outside the crèche, its crook pointed toward some invisible Christmas star.

Bedtime was forgotten and we just sat in the living room admiring the tree and talking about the ten-dollar raise. "If we saved it all for two years, you could buy a car," Daniel kept saying. "We could go to Niagara Falls, Florida—"

Dad sat on the sofa with Catherine, his arm around her, and smoked his pipe. "No cars for paupers like us," he sighed, pausing to draw on the pipe. "Maybe someday, though. Say, when I think of the times Al and me had busting around in that old tin lizzy— Cath, I don't believe you're listening."

My mother jerked her head up from his shoulder and blinked. "Yes, I am. So much to do tomorrow . . ."

Roseanne and I lay on the carpet near the tree. "If I had ten extra dollars I'd spend it on movie magazines," she mused, while I gazed drowsily at the empty manger in the painted-up crèche. We would not place the figure of the Infant in the manger until morning, since Jesus himself wouldn't be reborn until after midnight.

"Just tell me if I have more than one present," I asked.

"Yes, you do. Now, up to bed," Mom said. "You too, Roseanne."

I curled up on the carpet. "Dad, what did you mean before?"

"What did I say, fella?"

"That we're still in the ball game."

He sucked on his pipe. "I meant that we haven't been struck out by that tough old umpire, the Depression."

"Oh . . ." The tree lights shimmered, the tinsel sparkled. My eyes closed and I dreamed that angels with golden wings were carrying the Infant down to the manger on Warbisher Street.

We didn't buy a car and take trips to Niagara Falls or any other faraway places, but on the Fourth of July weekend that summer Dad took us on the Long Island Railroad to Rockaway Beach two days in a row. He bought us hot dogs, French fries and orangeade, and treated us to rides on the roller coaster at Playland. He brought his Brownie along and took snapshots of us belly-whopping in the waves and kneeling, pyramid style, one on top of the other, on the beach. We all posed for snapshots except Mom, who refused to be photographed in her bathing suit.

"Keep away from me with that Brownie," she kept warning Dad.

"Now, Cath. It's not as if that gay-nineties outfit you're wearing is revealing. A nun would be happy to pose in it."

"I'm not a nun. Just keep away."

So Dad waited his chance and sneaked up on her from behind an umbrella. The very instant that he was aiming the Brownie, Catherine spotted him. She gave a yelp and lunged for a towel to cover herself, but he clicked the shutter anyway.

Of all the photos in the Valentine box, the slightly out-of-focus snapshot of Mom in her bathing suit, yelping as she reached for a towel, became everybody's favorite. Everybody's, that is, when the candy box could be pried loose from me. By now I'd come to regard both the box and the snapshots as my exclusive property. Mostly I kept the box in the dining room sideboard drawer, tucked under the folded American flag that we took out each Decoration Day to drape from the porch. I kept an eye on that sideboard drawer, and when anybody headed for it, I usually was there first, grabbing hold of the snapshots. Roseanne went storming to Mom to complain about it one afternoon in March.

"Make the rat hand it over. Maybe the box is his, but not the snapshots. Right, Mom?"

"Rooobbie," came Mom's voice from the kitchen. "Hand over that box this instant or you'll get your ears clipped."

"But it's mine."

"This instant—you hear?"

Back stormed my sister, and there was no choice except to surrender the Valentine box to her grasping hands.

"Oooh, if I'm not your enemy, Robert Connerty," Roseanne snarled, carrying the box away. "Ooooh, if I won't pay you back double and triple for this."

It was no idle matter, a threat like that from Roseanne. God only knew what damaging information she might have on me, or would immediately make it her business to acquire. Only last week she'd caught Dan smoking in the cellar. Crept down the cellar stairs, not a sound, and caught him puffing away behind the coal bin. God only knew what price Dan had to pay so that she wouldn't squeal on him.

I decided that I wouldn't be cowed, and followed her to the dining table. "You get the snapshots all bent," I said. "You wrinkle up the corners."

Ignoring me, Roseanne plopped herself down at the dining table and opened the heart-shaped box. Even a best friend would have to admit that Roseanne was a sorry-looking sight. Freckles were spattered all over her face, arms, and legs. Mean, squinty eyes were pasted above a shoe-button nose, and of course there were the horrible pigtails to top off the whole picture.

Actually, the pigtails had to be blamed on Mom. Back when she was expecting Roseanne, a salesman had come to the door one morning selling shampoo. It was a brand called "Precious Darling," and Mom had bought several bottles, chiefly because of the picture on the label. It showed a little girl—Precious Darling, presumably—with long, wavy golden tresses that hung in lustrous glory to her waist.

Mom somehow had the notion that this was a sign that her baby would have beautiful golden tresses too. As Dad commented, it was a mistaken notion. Roseanne was born bald, and her hair, when it grew in, was ruler-straight and the color of straw that had been left in the rain. Nevertheless, Mom kept hoping it would *turn* golden and wavy, and for this reason she braided Roseanne's hair and kept it long.

"Tilly's hair was dark till she was seventeen, then it turned almost blond," Mom said, in proof of her conviction. "I promise you, sweetheart. If there's no change by the time you graduate from St. A's, you can have it cut."

"Okay, but when I graduate from St. A's, that's positively it."

I looked at my sister's dank braids as she pawed through the stack of photos. "Your hair hasn't turned golden or wavy yet," I pointed out.

She held up the snapshot taken of me when I'd broken my arm. "Too bad it wasn't both arms. Plus a leg," she said.

"It'll never turn wavy or golden."

She thumbed through the snaps. "Here it is," she whooped. "Here's old Mom in her bathing suit. The expression on her face slays me." And she rocked in her chair, laughing.

But there was another snapshot of Catherine, which I came to prize above any other, and it was taken a month later that year. It was a special Easter for our family because, for the first time since the Depression, each of us had something new to wear. New shoes for all of us, plus a new hat and purse for Margaret, a suit for Vinny, new sports jackets for Daniel and me, and a puffed-sleeve dress for Roseanne. Not only that, but Dad had insisted that Mom buy a whole new outfit for herself as well. He put the money in her hand—twenty-five dollars he'd earned from overtime—and refused to take any no's for an answer.

"Oh, dear," Mom said when she finally accepted the money.

Not that she wasn't pleased, but selecting a new dress or hat was an experience that filled her with doubts. "I get afraid I'll look like a walking Maypole," was her explanation. It took her several trolley trips downtown to the Fulton Street dress stores before she found what she wanted. All the hats this Easter looked like upturned flower pots, she said, and the dresses were like Mother Hubbards. When finally she selected her outfit, she wouldn't show it to anyone or even talk about it.

On Easter morning, I remember, we were ready to leave for Mass and waiting downstairs in the hall, and no sign of her. It was getting late, and Dad kept checking his watch and moving from the front door to the stair post—then all at once Mom appeared on the upper landing. She was wearing a lilac print dress with a matching jacket and a pink-flowered hat. She stood on the landing, clutched her prayer book and white gloves, tremulous as a bride, and glanced down at us, as though for courage.

She came down the stairs, steadying her hand on the banister. "Well, for pete's sake," she said. "Somebody say something."

But nobody answered. We stood in the hall, gaping up at her, and at the door Dad seemed to have turned into a statue.

Mom's hand trembled on the banister; you could tell from her face she was worried. "What's wrong, is it the wrong color, or what?" she asked frantically.

Still not speaking, my father slowly crossed to the foot of the stairs, his mouth open.

"What is it?" she asked desperately. "What's wrong?"

"It—it's that I was afraid I'd never see you in another new dress," he said. "Oh, Cath, you're the queen of them all!"

Sunlight broke across my mother's face. "You like my dress? I—I'm still not sure about the hat. It's a toque."

"It's a hat for a queen," Dad said.

Catherine lifted a hand nervously to the pink veiling. Shyness had overcome her and her gaze was fastened on Dad. "Really?"

she said, and came down the rest of the stairs and accepted the arm that he held out. Then they walked out the door together, straight past the rest of us.

We sat up front in a pew together at St. Aloysius's, a lineup of Connertys, Mom at one end of the pew and Dad at the other, and all through Mass he kept turning to look at her over our heads. We walked a rambling route home, and on Broadway Dad abruptly turned back and dashed into Sheehan's flower shop. He came out of the shop with a bunch of violets, wrapped in foil, which he presented to Mom with a courtly bow. All the way home she sniffed at the violets, and when we reached the brown-shingled house nothing would do but that my father had to run inside and get the Brownie.

He came out with the camera and posed Mom alone on the porch steps, then squinted into the viewer and called out instructions. "Raise the old chin, Cath. Hold the flowers in front. Never noticed before, but I think you've lost some weight."

Mom kept her head raised, the violets held stiffly in front of her. "You mean, it's noticeable?"

"Definitely thinner."

"Well, you're correct—I had to get this dress a whole size smaller."

Dad bent over the Brownie. "Smile now . . . hold it!"

She smiled, and the resulting snapshot was my favorite of all in the Valentine box. It showed my mother posed on the steps in the lilac dress, the sun lighting her face, the violets sweet in her hand, and it didn't appear to me that she looked thinner in the least.

Jobs were still scarce, but there were some to be had if you went out and looked hard for them. In the fall Vinny started college. His plan was to register for night courses at Brooklyn Polytech and get a day job that would pay enough to cover his tuition and allow him to contribute to the household. But Dad turned thumbs down on it.

"I had the same notion too," he said. "Night school, and I'd work full time at the office. Three years, and I just about got through my high-school courses. You're going full time to Polytech, buster. A part-time job should be enough for your expenses. We can take care of the household."

"Part time is harder to find, Dad."

"Not if you keep looking."

Vinny made the rounds of employment agencies, and the week before classes were to start at Polytech he found a job as a relief elevator operator at the Williamsburg Savings Bank building on Hanson Place. Six hours a night plus Saturdays, and he had enough left over from his salary to give Mom a few dollars every week.

Dan took over Vinny's old job at Ferretti's fruit and vegetable market on Broadway, but instead of being just a delivery boy working for tips, Mr. Ferretti handed him a green smock and made him a full-fledged clerk. Daniel was starting his sophomore year as a scholarship student at St. John's; Margaret was in her junior year at Girls' Commercial, and even she went and found a job—part-time clerk at the big Woolworth's on Broadway and Wilson Avenue. She was assigned to the ribbon counter.

There were jobs to be had, except in the case of Roseanne and me. After a while it gave us a left-out feeling, especially on Saturday nights, when Dan, Vinny and Margaret made a big show of handing over a portion of their earnings to help Mom with expenses.

After the supper dishes were washed, and still in her apron, Catherine would sit at the kitchen table and, each in turn, Margaret, Vinny and Dan would step up and plunk some bills on the blue-flowered oilcloth until a small pile had accumulated. Catherine would gaze at this, speechlessly.

Every Saturday night, standing off to the side at the cupboard, Roseanne and I were silent witnesses to the scene, until one night, refusing to watch anymore, and scowling under her blotchy freckles, my sister stamped out and banged the kitchen door behind her. I didn't follow her, because the part was coming that I'd waited for: the expression that lit Catherine's face as she regarded the handful of bills. Clearly, she thought this gesture of her Indians was the nicest thing in the whole world, and it was taking place right there in her kitchen. However, from what I could make out, no sooner had Vinny, Margaret and Dan handed over the crumpled bills than Mom was handing most of the money back to them.

"Nonsense, you need a new pair of shoes," she would declare, folding Daniel's hand over a five-dollar bill. "Margaret, what about that dress you want at Namm's? Here, start saving for it. Don't be silly, I'll have plenty left over for the house. We're having prime ribs for dinner tomorrow, thanks to this. Vinny, aren't you taking out a young lady tonight? Here, don't argue with me." And some more bills would be pressed into my brother's hand.

From beside the cupboard I watched it all and vowed that someday I'd plunk a thousand-dollar bill in front of Mom and refuse to accept one cent of it back. Buy yourself a fur coat, I'd tell her. Buy yourself a diamond necklace.

Roseanne, however, was more practical in her attitude. Hunched down on the living room sofa, she didn't confine herself to useless fancy daydreams but was obviously searching her thoughts for some kind of action to take.

It took several days of brooding, then one afternoon she caught up with me on the way home from St. A's and tipped me off about her plans. For Roseanne to permit herself to be seen walking with her dopey kid brother was a unique event, but she was so worked up that she didn't seem to care.

"Okay, so you're only ten and I'm only thirteen," she said, swinging her schoolbag. "I fully realize it disqualifies us from taking out working papers."

"We can't get jobs. It's stupid to think about."

"Oh, can't we?" She stopped on the sidewalk and punched me on the arm. "What about jobs where nobody would know our age?"

"That hurt," I said, rubbing my arm. Roseanne could punch worse than Daniel. "What jobs wouldn't they know our ages?"

She gave me another punch. "I guess you never read the ads in back of magazines. I guess you never heard of write-in jobs."

She was right, of course—the backs of magazines were filled with advertisements for work-at-home jobs. Like selling greeting cards or door-to-door magazine subscriptions.

"That's a terrific idea," I said, still rubbing my arm.

Roseanne didn't punch me anymore; she was too excited to bother. "Well, first of all, let's get some magazines," she said, and we proceeded to search through the trash cans on Warbisher Street, for we had nothing at home except her movie mgazines. It took us a while, but we found a discarded copy of *Woman's Home Companion* plus a *Liberty* that some coffee grounds had been wrapped in but which was still readable.

We hid the magazines in our schoolbags, and as soon as we got home, headed straight up to Roseanne's room to check over the job advertisements. We went upstairs so that Mom wouldn't find out about our scheme.

"What are you two children doing up there?" she called up the stairs after a time.

"I'm helping Robbie prepare for a history exam," Roseanne shouted back. She was an excellent liar, always ready with a likely story, I had to admit it.

We combed through the magazines, and an ad in the *Woman's Home Companion* leaped at my sister's eagle eye. It was a job advertising for people to address envelopes. *Earn at home at your leisure,* it read. *Applicants must apply in own handwriting.*

"Wouldn't you know I'd have lousy penmanship," Roseanne moaned. She brooded a moment. "If we could get Margaret to do the letters in that itsy Palmer Method she won the medal for . . ."

"We can't," I said. "They'd be on to us once we started work."

She reached into her schoolbag and pulled out her copybook. "Well, we'll just have to write our best."

"We can't write on school paper. It'd give us away entirely."

She cuffed me on the shoulder. "Good thinking, Rob. I'd never of given you credit for such brains." She sat on the bed, sucking on a pigtail. "Let's see . . . we'll have to sneak downstairs and get Mom's stationery from the dining room sideboard. That is, *you'll* have to."

"Me? Why me?"

"Don't argue. Come on."

She stood guard on the landing and hissed instructions as I

crept down the stairs. The front hall and living room were perfectly still, and the only sound was that of Mom singing in the kitchen. My heart hammered madly—answering ads was the best excitement I'd ever heard of. I tiptoed into the living room, through the dining room arch, and over to the sideboard. Hardly breathing, I slowly opened the drawer in which the Valentine box and flag were kept. Underneath was an accumulation of other objects—an old checker set, old Christmas cards, a box of string and ribbon, and Mom's box of blue stationery. The drawer slid open noiselessly.

The singing in the kitchen stopped. "Who's in there?" called Mom's voice.

Moving fast, I removed the box of stationery, put it on a table in the living room—for later convenience—then hurried back and pushed open the swinging door. "I came down to find out the time," I said.

Catherine was peeling potatoes at the sink. "What about the clock in my bedroom?"

"Oh, I forgot. Roseanne's helping me study my geography."

"She's being unusually helpful. I thought it was history." She put a hand to her brow, then leaned against the counter.

"*Plus* geography. Aren't you feeling good?"

"A bit tired, that's all." She straightened up and started another potato.

"Well, I see that it's four o'clock. Thanks, Mom."

I let the door swing shut, then I dashed into the living room, snatched up the box of stationery, and raced pell-mell up the stairs. Roseanne was waiting for me tensely at the landing.

"Did you get it? Neat going, Rob." She grabbed the stationery and hurried into the bedroom. "I've got a story all worked out. We'll write that we're an elderly unmarried brother and sister living on relief."

She sat on the floor and snitched some plain blue sheets of notepaper from the box. "We'll say that we were once wealthy but have fallen on evil times, and that our pet dog, Spot, is on the verge of starvation." She handed me a sheet of paper.

"Will they believe us, you think? Maybe we ought to skip the part about Spot."

Roseanne glared at me. "Haven't you any sense? They might not care a hoot that we're elderly, but nobody turns down a starving dog."

"You're absolutely right." I squatted down opposite her, propped the sheet of notepaper on my schoolbag, and unscrewed my fountain pen. "It's very fortunate—only last week we practiced business letters in class. It's more fun when the letters are real." Painstakingly, I copied out the address of the Excelsior Envelope Service, North Clark Street, Chicago, Illinois.

The letters, when we finished them, wouldn't have won medals for penmanship. Roseanne's handwriting had a tendency to travel uphill, while mine headed downward.

"It's really okay, since we're supposed to be elderly," she pointed out, addressing the envelope.

Before we were done that afternoon she'd found two other ads to answer, and for each she invented an entirely different application. To a greeting card company in Des Moines, Iowa, she wrote that she was "an attractive middle-aged widow in contact with many smart friends," whereas I became "a semi-crippled Army officer desirous of extra income." The third ad was for a door-to-door cosmetics saleswoman, and naturally only Roseanne could apply for that. It was her most imaginative reply. "As a former Miss America contestant and Hollywood starlet," she wrote. "I constitute a walking ad for glamour and beauty."

We sealed the envelopes, sneaked out and bought stamps from the machine in Montuori's drugstore. Roseanne parted with a quarter from her savings to purchase the stamps. She marked it down in her copybook as "A business investment. We'll have to keep records, you know."

Each afternoon we hurried home from school and pretended to be casual as we scanned the day's mail, which was kept on the hall table. If Mom suspected that we were up to some scheme or other, she made no comments to that effect. We checked the mail for three weeks, and when no replies were forthcoming, we finally confessed to her what we had done. She sat us in the kitchen and gave us chocolate cake.

"I had a notion it was something of the kind," she said. "So much of my stationery seemed to be going."

Roseanne speared a hunk of cake in despair. "It was our rotten penmanship that did it."

"Now, you listen here," Mom said, and her voice was severe. "I don't want either of you carrying on about earning money. Eat your cake and do your jobs at school—that's more than enough."

"No, it's not," Roseanne protested, and flung down her fork.

She refused to give up, and after school a day or so later she dragged me with her to the Bushwick Avenue branch of the Public Library. Roseanne was a frequent visitor at the branch and assured me that she was on personal terms with Miss Willis, the children's librarian. Sometimes when Miss Willis was especially busy, she allowed my sister to sort out the piles of books, put them on the carts, and get them ready for the shelves. That became the basis for Roseanne's next attempt at employment.

She hauled me down the steps to the children's basement entrance and ordered me to comb my hair. Then she peered through the window bars at Miss Willis's desk. One side of the desk was marked "Check Out" and the other "Check In," and the books on this latter side were piled as high as Miss Willis's head.

"Look at her, she's stamping books in and out like a maniac. Perfect opportunity," Roseanne said, and turned back to me. "Here's the plan. We wander in there, and I'll remark to Miss Willis how overworked she seems, then we'll pitch in without waiting to be asked. We'll sort out every book in the dump, and when she sees what a fantastic job we've done . . ."

She gave my hair a final swipe and dragged me after her through the door. The children's room was swarming with customers. You couldn't get near Miss Willis's desk, what with so many kids thrusting books at her.

"My goodness, but you're swamped," Roseanne called to her with a flattering smile. "Well, thank heavens my brother and I happened to come along. Don't give it a thought, Miss Willis."

She signaled to me, and we commenced unloading books from

the desk and stacking them alphabetically, according to author, on the carts. It took us a solid half-hour's work. Roseanne smacked the last of the books in the cart, went over to the side of the desk and stood there smiling pointedly. Miss Willis was still acting like a maniac with her pencil stamper, but finally she looked over at my sister.

"I wish you wouldn't keep grinning like that, child," she said. "It unnerves me. What is it you want?"

The smile stayed on Roseanne's face. "My assistant and me, we cleared off all the returned books for you."

Miss Willis peered over her spectacles. "Did you? How thoughtful. Pick out some nice reading for yourselves—libraries aren't meant for loitering." She pushed at her spectacles and went back to her stamping.

Roseanne remained silent until we were outside on the street again. Then she kicked at the library fence in fury and rage. "We ought to go back in and unload the damned carts," she said. "Just pile the books back on old stupid's desk." Tossing her pigtails, she lunged down the steps, as if to carry out her threat.

"No, don't, she'll have us arrested," I yelled. "Listen, we'd better give up, that's all."

My sister kicked savagely at the library entrance door. "We . . . are not . . . giving up," she growled between her teeth. "And you—what help are you?" she snarled at me. "You're nothing but a millstone around my neck. Ahhh, come on."

The whole way home she didn't speak another word, and it wasn't difficult to surmise that she was about to turn into my enemy again.

But she didn't—not yet, at least. In a last-ditch effort, Roseanne decided that what we needed to do was to prowl around the neighborhood, looking for opportunities. We employed our roller skates for this mission, since it permitted us to cover the area more swiftly. Frankly, though, it didn't strike me that we accomplished much. All we did, really, was to roller skate up and down Broadway under the El tracks and spy on Margaret and Dan at their jobs.

We showed up at Woolworth's nearly every afternoon, despite

Margaret's complaints about our presence there. "I look up from the ribbon counter and there they are, hiding behind the housewares counter, watching me," she wailed to Mom. "Can't you please keep them away?"

"Calm down, Margaret, and explain—what harm are they doing?"

"One of these days, Mr. Fergus, the floor manager, will kick them out. A lovely scene that will make."

The Woolworth's where Margaret worked was the biggest five-and-ten in the neighborhood. It was a wonderful shiny, busy place, with long aisles, dozens of counters, a soda fountain, and a basement section downstairs. Roseanne and I always removed our roller skates before venturing inside—there was no sense in *asking* for trouble. And we soon learned to keep out of Mr. Fergus's path. He was a short man—what Mom would have called a dandy. He wore a mustache and pencil-striped suits and bustled around issuing orders to the clerks, scribbling notations on bits of paper and listening to customers' complaints. If trouble broke out, Mr. Fergus was on the spot like lightning, snapping his fingers with authority. Margaret thought very highly of him, however. "He's a gentleman, with high principles," was her stated opinion.

"He's a midget," was Roseanne's.

Pretending to be customers, skates clanking at our sides, we strolled the aisles, headed by a circuitous route for the housewares counter at the rear of the store. There the aluminum pots and pans provided a handy cover from which we could observe the ribbon counter over against the wall.

Margaret was waiting on a customer in her usual ladylike manner. "Three and a half yards of cerise velvet? Certainly, madam." She smiled. She unrolled a spool of ribbon, measured the length on a yardstick, snipped it off with a flourish—"A lovely shade, may I comment"—tucked the ribbon into a bag, and rang up the sale on the cash register. "Thank you, madam. Do come again."

"What a bunch of baloney that madam-ing is," commented Roseanne from behind a stack of Wear-Ever frying pans.

"I like it when she rings the cash register," I said. "I like the *piiiing* sound it makes."

"You'll never catch me behind a ribbon counter. That's for old-maid types like Margaret and Aunt Tilly. Me, I'd take cosmetics."

I'd noticed, from our many journeys through Woolworth's, that only the prettiest girls seemed to work at the cosmetics counter. I wasn't sure that Roseanne, with her screwed-up freckled face and ropelike pigtails, qualified for the position, but I couldn't tell her that; one misspoken word and she could turn instantly into an enemy, scowling in that hideous manner and threatening God-knows-what dire punishment. "Yeah, you'd be neat at the cosmetics counter," I agreed.

"Boy, could I sell lipstick and face powder for Woolworth's," she said as we watched Margaret gush over another customer at the ribbon counter.

"Especially the face powder," I said, eying my sister's freckles. Right away I knew I'd said the wrong thing.

"Face powder, on account of my freckles, is that what you mean?" She turned and punched me on the arm. "Is it?"

"No, Roseanne. Honest to God. I swear."

"Come on, I'm tired of this joint. Let's check up on brother Daniel," she snarled, shoving down the aisle. Out on the sidewalk she clamped on her skates and streaked down Broadway under the El tracks. I didn't catch up with her until, panting, I reached Ferretti's fruit and vegetable store several blocks away.

Roseanne was at her post behind an El pillar. I skated up behind her, and we watched the doings at Ferretti's. Attired in a green smock, Handsome Dan was waiting on a giggling girl customer. Black curly hair slicked back, he selected three fat grapefruit for her, tossed the fruit up, caught them nimbly as a juggler, and dropped them into a bag. It was astounding, the increase of girl customers at Ferretti's since my brother had donned his green smock. A whole gaggle of girls were clustered around the bins of bananas, oranges, Idaho potatoes and lettuce that bordered the sidewalk. All of them were ignoring the other clerks and waiting for Handsome Dan to be free. "Ten cents' worth of grapes, please, Dan," a girl requested as he turned to her.

"Did you hear that idiot?" asked Roseanne in disgust. " 'Ten cents' worth of grapes'—any excuse to be near him. What an idiot, not to know it's what's inside a person that counts."

"Inside?" I asked.

"True beauty comes from within, you dope."

We watched the scene a minute or two longer—Dan was juggling bananas now, while a girl looked on adoringly—then Roseanne turned away and muttered, "Let's go home." She stooped down and removed her skates. I followed suit, and we headed back toward Warbisher Street on foot.

Roseanne had given up—and before we reached home she had turned into my enemy once more. She skulked along the sidewalk, the skates banging against her legs. "Just wait'll I get my hair cut, then everybody can watch out," she growled.

"Maybe we'll still get an answer to one of the letters," I said. "It's in the realm of possibility."

She kicked at a pebble, which went zigging to the curb. "I hate it, don't you?"

"Hate what?"

"Being the damned youngest in the family. Like Dad says, it's the tag end of the parade."

"He says that about me."

She hunted out another pebble to send zigging. "It applies the same to me. Sometimes I almost think . . ."

"What, Roseanne?"

"Why did they bother having us? Maybe we were afterthoughts and they really didn't want us."

I stopped dead on the sidewalk. It was a possibility that had never occurred to me before. "Why wouldn't they want us?" I asked.

She swung around angrily on the sidewalk. "Look at yourself. Are you such a bargain?" she demanded. "What do you do that's so great? Hang around, that's all, and be a pest. What good are you? Oh, forget it, I don't know what I mean," she broke off. Then, sprinting away from me, she raced over the cracked cement toward the brown-shingled house. "First one there gets dibs," she hollered over the flying pigtails.

I ran after her as fast as I could. I closed my eyes and pretended that the porch was the Fritzles' fence and that I'd leap over it this time for certain. But as I ran I kept thinking of what Roseanne had said. *Not wanted us?*

Naturally my sister reached the porch first, but as I rounded the front walk I saw in my mind the Valentine box of photos, clearly enough to touch it. I saw the stacks of snapshots that Dad had taken of his children, and it was proof that he cared equally for each one of us. He wouldn't have taken all those snapshots of Roseanne and me unless he loved and wanted us. And however much he wanted us, Mom doubled him in it. Sure as the sun and the moon, she did.

"You lost," Roseanne said when I'd reached the steps. "What's there to look so happy about?"

"I don't know," I answered, "but I am."

There was everything, it seemed to me, to be happy about. There was Dad's new raise in pay, another five dollars added to the ten, which had chased the worried, driven look from his face. There was Catherine to be happy about, looking pretty and glowing in her new Easter outfit. There were the lively goings-on in the brown-shingled house—Vinny dressing for Saturday-night dates, Margaret sighing over fashion magazines, Daniel strumming on the secondhand banjo he'd recently purchased. There were Saturday-night trips to the movies again. Only last week Dad had taken us to the Halsey Theatre to see *A Tale of Two Cities.*

"It's a love story," he'd explained beforehand to Mom, who wasn't familiar with the Dickens novel. "It's about this guy in Manhattan and this girl in Brooklyn—the two cities, see—and some gangsters kidnap her . . ."

I think that Mom only half-believed this explanation and when we reached the theater and she saw the pictures of the costumed actors on display outside, she scoffed, "What are you talking about gangsters? What sort of gangsters wear capes and wigs?"

"Old-fashioned gangsters."

"I'll bet. You can't tell me Ronald Colman's playing a gangster."

"He almost pulled your leg again," I said as we stood in line at the box office.

"Only almost, the big palooka."

Mom cried at the movie, and at the end, when Ronald Colman mounted the guillotine, I caught Dad wiping at his eyes. I spent the walk home in a trance, endlessly chanting, with gestures, "It's a far, far better thing I do . . ."

"Than I have ever done," Roseanne chimed in, marching up the porch steps as though to her death.

"Gangsters," said Mom behind her. "If you're not the limit, Jim Connerty."

There were movies to be happy about, and big roasts for Sunday dinner, and family parties again. Genuine, honest-to-goodness parties—my confirmation, Vinny's graduation, Thanksgiving Day—at our house and at Uncle Al and Aunt Gen's, with swarms of cousins tumbling and chasing through the rooms. For such a long time family gatherings had been occasions of gloom, at which the men gravely discussed the latest financial crisis and the women formed a worried circle of their own. But now the parties rocked with noise and horseplay, and the dinner table was heaped with food. Sunday roasts were plentiful enough so that Charlie Cronin could be invited to share them once more.

"Say, Jim, why don't we ask Charlie for next Sunday?" Mom suggested one evening after supper. "It's been so long since we gave him a good feed."

Charlie had been coming to Warbisher Street, but only to play pinochle with Dad and talk at length about the old days, when they were boys together in Holy Queen of Martyrs parish. Charlie had been the star boy soprano at Holy Queen, and later the lead tenor, much in demand at other parishes, which was how he'd met Mom at St. Gabriel's and introduced her to Dad.

"When I think of his lonely existence in that rooming house . . . ," Mom went on. "I'll fix roast lamb, it was always his favorite."

Dad got up from the morris chair. "So you're up to your old tricks again."

"I can't imagine what you mean," Mom said.

He grinned at her. "Who will the candidate be this time? Let's see, there was Rose Hennessy, and that other female from the

88

Ladies' Altar Aid Society, the one who had the government bonds—"

"I don't know what you're talking about; I'm only asking Charlie for a nice dinner," Mom said and flounced through the swinging door to the kitchen.

I didn't know what Dad was talking about either, but he called up Charlie at his rooming house and invited him to dinner, and promptly at one o'clock on the following Sunday the front doorbell rang. I opened the door, revealing Charlie on the doorstep, turned out in his best attire. He wore an Irish pepper-and-salt suit, a pink shirt with a contrasting white collar, a stickpin in his tie, and his hair was parted in the middle and plastered into curls at the ends, like someone in a barbershop quartet.

"Ah, the Connerty violin, as Jimbo refers to his youngest tot," he greeted me, ducking nimbly into the hall. "For your gracious mother." Handing me a bouquet of jonquils, he cupped a hand to his mouth and danced to the living room arch. "Jimbo, did I hear mention of a drink?"

You wouldn't have believed the fuss that Catherine made over the jonquils. She arranged them in a vase and carried them into the living room, where Dad had already poured the dinner guest a glass of Jameson's whiskey.

"What gorgeous blooms, Charlie," Mom said, beaming at him. "You shouldn't be so extravagant."

"Let us all kneel, a saint has entered the room," said Charlie back to her. "Cath, you've gotten thinner."

Mom put the flowers on a table. "So everybody's been telling me lately. If I keep it up, I'll be back to my girlish figure."

Charlie raised his glass to her. "The niftiest figure in St. Gabriel's parish, bar none."

Mom inclined her head with a kittenish air—"Charlie, you always did exaggerate"—and excused herself to return to her cooking. "Roast lamb, your favorite," she tossed back at him, whisking through the swinging door.

Her behavior at dinner was even worse. You'd have thought Charlie was the king of Persia from all the attention he received. She poured water for him from her Waterford pitcher, a prized possession, and seated him in the place of honor at her right—not that she stayed in her chair for more than a minute at a time. She was too busy hopping in and out of the kitchen with various platters with which to tempt Charlie's appetite. He had second helpings of everything, and she urged third helpings on him. She carried on as if he'd never tasted food before.

"More lamb, Charlie? What about more broccoli? Don't forget to save room for my peach pie."

"You're too good to me, Catherine. After this feast, I ask you, how can I return to the dismal fare at the Blue Ribbon cafeteria?"

When the meal was finally over, Charlie could barely rise from the table. He belched and staggered into the living room, singing Mom's praises with every step. "What a jewel she is, Jimbo. What a fortunate man you are to have snared her."

Mom was clearing the table with Margaret and Roseanne. "The Blue Ribbon cafeteria, indeed," she said, tssking. "If a man is deprived of decent home cooking, what sort of life is that?"

"A lonely life," answered Charlie, accepting another glass of Jameson's.

After the dishes were washed and put away, Mom appeared with her sewing basket and installed herself on the sofa. "You menfolk go on with your talk," she said, threading a darning needle. "Don't let me interrupt you."

Menfolk? As far as I could recollect, it was a term my mother had never used before. I noticed that it didn't take her long to interrupt the conversation either. About a minute, I estimated.

"Jim," she said, "did I tell you I ran into Loretta Brophy at Bohack's yesterday?"

My father favored her with a curious smile. "No, Cath, you didn't. Tell me, how is Loretta these days?"

She stitched at a sock. "The gas company's given her another promotion. After all these years Loretta must have a pretty penny tucked away, I'd imagine."

"Plus she has that spacious apartment on Menahan Street," my father added. "I imagine she's an excellent housekeeper too."

"Oh, spotless."

"And her cooking?"

"Well, if I were half as good a cook as Loretta Brophy . . . ," Mom said, her darning needle stitching away. "I'll never forget the meal she served the Ladies' Altar Aid."

During this odd exchange of information about Loretta Brophy Charlie had remained surprisingly silent, but now he spoke up. "Miss Brophy is unattached, I take it," he said.

Mom's needle paused in midair. "Why, Charlie, how did you know?"

"I guessed," Charlie said.

My mother put down her darning. "Yes, she is single, and how she stayed single is a mystery to me, Charlie. With all of Loretta's outstanding traits, and her—"

"Perhaps it's her weight problem," my father contributed blandly.

There was a slight pause. "Miss Brophy, I take it, is over-weight," said Charlie, shifting in his chair. Mom started to reply, but he held up his hand. "Understand me, Cath, I've always found fat women to have jolly personalities."

"Loretta's far from fat, Charlie." Mom shot a murderous look at the morris chair and attempted to continue her darning. "Plump, yes. What you'd describe as a womanly figure, but the loveliest rosy complexion and—"

"Rosy complexions are pleasing," Charlie said.

"And her hair, Charlie. A beautiful auburn shade that doesn't ever need a permanent, it's so naturally wavy."

Charlie held up his hand once more. "Another plus for Miss Brophy. But answer me this, Cath."

Mom gazed at him helplessly. "Yes, Charlie?"

He pulled his bulk to the edge of his chair. "Can she cure a broken heart, answer me. What can she offer a lonesome rooming-house bachelor to erase the memory that haunts him each night as he dines at the Blue Ribbon cafeteria? Can she make him forget a former love?"

Catherine appeared to be getting extremely nervous and ill at ease. "Oh, now, come on, Charlie," she faltered. "Surely you don't still think—"

"Think of what?" he demanded of her. "Of the two loves in my life? My sainted mother, and when she was laid to rest, a certain slip of a girl I glanced upon at St. Gabe's, more radiant than the sun?"

My mother was fidgeting with the sewing basket. "Honestly, Charlie."

"More radiant than the sun, I tell you. More beautiful than Lillian Russell."

Dad lowered his pipe and looked at him. "Great Scott, Charlie, who could such a paragon have been?"

"He means Mom," I gasped from the hassock in the corner of the room where I always sat.

Charlie turned a baleful gaze on me. "The violin is equipped with big ears, I see. No, I confess my secret. I'm not ashamed to admit that when Jimbo here escorted a certain angel down the aisle of—"

"Charlie, how about another helping of pie," Mom interrupted hastily. She stood up from the sofa. "With ice cream on it?"

Emotion had not sufficiently overcome Charlie for him to refuse the offer of pie. But when the front door closed on him at last, Dad leaned against the door and began to laugh. His laughter boomed into the dining room, where it seemed to irritate Mom considerably.

"Think you're so smart, don't you, Jim Connerty," she flung at him, as he came laughing to the table.

He wiped his eyes. "I can't help it, Cath. There you were, leading him on, and he—" Another fit of laughter attacked him. "He outfoxed you, as I knew he would."

"Outfoxed me—how? I only wanted to invite him to dinner."

Dad leaned toward her over the table. "Stop pretending. You were at your old matchmaking game, and he turned it right back at you." My father placed his hand over his heart and imitated Charlie's impassioned prose. "No, I confess my secret, I'm not ashamed to admit that when Jimbo here—"

Mom got up from the table. "I refuse to listen to any more ridicule."

"Surely you could have thought up someone better than Loretta Brophy. She tips the scales at a hundred and seventy, I'll wager, and 'rosy' hardly describes her complexion. 'Mottled' says it better."

"Will you kindly let me pass," Mom said huffily.

"Besides, we've got a much likelier prospect for Charlie in the bosom of the family. I'm surprised it's never occurred to you."

Mom glared at him. "If this is some sort of a joke . . ."

"Catherine, don't tell me you refer to your own sister as a joke?"

"Tilly? Don't tell me you have the gall to stand there and suggest that Tilly and Charlie—"

"It's a perfect idea," Dad said. He turned from the table and started for the front hall. "Let's get Tilly on the horn, and if she's free for dinner next Sunday—"

"Jim Connerty, don't you dare." Like a pistol shot Mom was out of the dining room, charging after him down the hall. "The very notion of a delicate creature like Tilly teamed up with—"

She grabbed for Dad's hand as he reached for the phone. He turned to her, his eyes twinkling, and said, "You're so gullible, Cath. I swear, I could sell you the Brooklyn, Manhattan, Williamsburg—what is it?"

Catherine swayed forward, reached out to him, and steadied herself. "I'm all right," she said. "All the cooking and running back and forth . . ."

Dad gripped her arm. "You're going to Drennan for a checkup," he said. "Even Charlie noticed how thin you are."

"Really, it's just fatigue." She placed a hand on his cheek and smiled at him. "Charlie coming to Sunday dinner again . . . As you've said, it means we've come through, doesn't it? I was never worried about it, Jim. Not truly worried."

"I know, but sometimes not worrying can be a fault of yours," Dad said. His hands framed her face and he kissed her and held her against him. "Bless you, Cath, but you never heed a warning, loud or soft."

"I must be hard of hearing," Mom laughed.

And who was to guess that the warning had already been sounded?

4
Laugh in the Rain

The happy times continued for another year, and then in April, a week or so after my eleventh birthday, something happened in the brown-shingled house. It began, as everything did in our family, on a minor, ordinary note—a thunderstorm. But afterward I used to dwell on the half-forgotten child's dreams I'd had of Catherine running away to Schlack's for a soda and not coming home when I asked her to. Over and over again I thought of that dream and wished desperately that it had never occurred. For what happened that April was that the dream came true . . . and with it came a secret fear that I stumbled upon by chance among the snapshots in the Valentine box.

"That Fulton Street, I don't like it," said Hanna one Thursday afternoon early in April. She sat waiting for my mother in the front hall, her satchel packed and ready. Catherine had taken the trolley to Fulton Street to have a look at the department stores, and she was late getting home.

"All doss million trolleys and cars—I bless myself double when I go by that Fulton Street," Hanna said, and, suiting action to her word, she made the sign of the cross on her forehead.

Roseanne and I had been home from St. A's for more than an hour. "Don't worry, Mom's crossed Fulton Street a million times," my sister said. "Go home, Hanna. She'd hate to delay you."

Hanna shifted the satchel to the other side of her big, cumbersome feet. "Vat time iss?"

"I'll go see," I offered, and ran into the kitchen to check the clock over the stove. Beyond the coffee tin of flowers on the window sill the backyard was dimming, but there was still plenty of light in the sky. I ran back to the hall and announced, "It's twenty of five. That's late for Mom. Maybe she *was* run over."

"Trust you to find some reassuring words," Roseanne said, throwing me a look. "Honest, Hanna, nothing's happened to her. If you'll just go home—"

With a sudden groan, Hanna bolted to the door and out onto the porch. She peered down Warbisher Street, searching among the groups of pedestrians for sight of my mother. "Ach, *mein Gott*, I remember when Josef did not come home," she murmured, coming back inside.

Roseanne put an arm around her. "If Mom had an accident, we'd be notified by now. The hospital or police would have contacted us," she said, with surprising good sense. This past year Roseanne had grown three inches taller. Her school blouse stretched across her chest and her skirt hiked up above the scrawny knees, in need of lengthening. She was graduating from St. A's in June, which meant that her braids would soon be gone. Mom had already agreed to take her down to Mr. Pierre's, a beauty parlor downtown on Bridge Street, in time to have her hair bobbed for graduation exercises.

"Do you want Emil worrying?" she went on to Hanna. "He'll think something's happened to you."

Hanna sat down at the phone table and resumed her vigil. "No, I vait."

She folded her hands resolutely, and I sat down next to her on the telephone bench. "Don't worry, nothing bad happens to Mom. She's a walking good-luck charm."

"A vat?"

"A walking good-luck charm."

Hanna's face wreathed into a smile. "You funny, Robbie. Always talk different from anybody."

I sighed and settled down on the bench for a chat. The time might as well be put to *some* use. Just as I was about to launch into the subject of Emil, Hanna's son—he worked in a garage at present—a loud clap of thunder hit the roof. There was a flash of lightning, followed by another sharp clap, then the quick, heavy spatter of rain.

Roseanne opened the door. "It's coming down in buckets. Oh, it's gorgeous," she cried, stepping onto the porch. I joined her, and she went to the rail and stuck her hands out over it. "Isn't it wonderful? Oh, it's wonderful, just feel it," she shouted.

Another loud thunderclap, and the rain pelted down even harder. The pounding sheets of rain obscured the sidewalk and the people ducking past the house. I stretched out my hands too, while from the doorway Hanna admonished, "Children, you get vet."

"Feel it on your face, Rob," my sister cried, and I lifted my face and let the cool rain splash over my nose and cheeks.

"I love rainstorms. Don't you love rainstorms?" I cried.

Roseanne pointed down the street. "Look, the gutters have turned into raging torrents. For two cents I'd get wet all over."

"Wet all over, wet all over." I spun around the porch, arms flung out in a dance.

"Look at the poor drenched people," Roseanne said. I went back to the rail and we watched the figures scurrying along, some holding up newspapers or shopping bags for cover, all of them soaking wet. Water dripped from their hats and coats and splattered from their shoes.

"Dare me to run out in the street," Roseanne said.

"Dare me back," I said.

"Okay, double-dare!"

Shrieking, we started down the porch steps and onto the front walk. "Wait, look," I yelled. "Down past the Raylemans' house— look who it is."

And I pointed several houses down the street, toward the slight, trim figure I was always able to recognize. It was Catherine, hurrying along the sidewalk.

Roseanne darted back up the steps. "She's drenched. I'll get an umbrella."

I ran out onto the sidewalk and waved my arms. "Mom, Mom."

She glimpsed me and waved back at once. The rain poured on her, but she was laughing in spite of it. The Easter dress from last spring, the lilac-print dress and jacket, hung from her like something washed in from the sea. The pink-flowered hat was a sodden ruin, she had no paper or parcel to shield herself, but she was laughing as she hurried up the street. The dress clung to her, outlining the slight figure, emphasizing its thinness. Despite Dad's cautioning, she hadn't been to Dr. Drennan's for a checkup, as he wanted.

"What a downpour," she called to me, still laughing as she neared the house. "It feels good."

At the moment that Roseanne raced down the steps with the umbrella the rain abruptly stopped. The hard, pelting noise was turned off, as if by a switch, and magically, within seconds, the sky was blue and pink again. We both ran down the sidewalk to Mom.

"There'll be a rainbow in a minute," she said, looking up at the sky. "We'll get to make wishes." She wiped the streaming rivulets from her face and chin. "Look at the two of you—drowned rats."

"You're late. Hanna was worried and wouldn't leave," Roseanne informed her as we went up the porch steps.

"Wouldn't leave? Oh, Hanna, forgive me," Catherine said to the lumbering figure who stood in the doorway with an outstretched towel.

"Never mind, lady, dry you'self, pliss."

"I got to poking around A and S and forgot the time," Mom explained, coming into the hall. She took off the pink-flowered hat and brushed the rain from it in despair. "Look at my poor hat. I never found a prettier one. Listen to my shoes squeak."

"Pliss, lady, dry you'self."

Catherine took the towel, but, as with other things, she didn't use it for herself. Instead, she rubbed briskly at my hair and shirt, then handed it to Roseanne. "Better go upstairs and take off that blouse, miss, or you'll catch a chill," she said. "Hanna, you shouldn't have stayed. What a good, dear friend you are."

Hanna's eyes were wide with concern. "That awful Fulton Street, I vorry you have accident."

Mom laughed and pressed Hanna's hands. "Don't you know nothing like that ever happens to me?"

"It's like I told you. She's a walking good-luck charm," I piped.

She walked Hanna onto the porch and urged her down the steps. "Now, hurry along, or Emil will worry. Yes, you told me. Ox-tail stew, it's on the stove, and I have only to heat it. Goodbye.

Thanks again, Hanna. See you next Thursday."

She came back to us in the hall. "Is it past five? Your father will be home and I won't have supper heated. Roseanne, I told you to go upstairs and change your blouse—"

"But Mom, we're forgetting about the rainbow," I said, and the next thing, the three of us were hurrying onto the back steps and gazing up at the sky. High above the backyards, above the Fritzles' fence and the tenement rooftops of Fauber Street, bands of pale green, pink, and blue arched through the sky.

"How beautiful," said my mother quietly. "Hurry, children, let's each make a wish before it disappears."

We linked hands, closed our eyes, and concentrated hard. I opened my eyes first and turned to Catherine.

"I wished for happiness for all," I announced. "Does it spoil it to tell?"

"No, Robbie. What a nice thing to wish."

Roseanne touched the wet lilac dress and forgot about her wish. "Mom, you're shivering. You'd better change into something dry at once."

"Just let me start supper heating," Catherine said, hurrying back into the kitchen. But very likely it wouldn't have mattered. Even if she'd changed her dress, it was too late for caution to make any difference.

Fixing breakfast in the kitchen the next morning, she sneezed and coughed, wiped at her eyes and nose, tucked the handkerchief in her apron pocket, and went on with her routine. Vinny, Dan and Margaret had already left, and as I came in the swinging door Dad was gulping the last of his coffee. He was lecturing Mom about her cold.

"Keeping that wet dress on—if I'd been home I'd have spanked you."

Mom stiffened, then bent over, handkerchief ready, as another sneeze gathered force. Her face puckered up, the eyes squinting shut—"*Aaaaaaaa-chew.*" She wiped her nose and followed Dad through the swinging door. "It's a humdinger, I guess. Have a good day at the office."

I heard him say in the hall, "Seriously, Cath, even if this clears up by tomorrow, I'm taking you to Drennan. It's long overdue."

"I'll be fine in a day or two." Back in the kitchen—"Now, Robbie, what'll it be, cornflakes or Wheaties?" Midway across the tiles she stopped and reached for the handkerchief. Roseanne pushed open the door. "Morning, Roseanne. Pour some milk for— *Aaaaaaaa-chew!*"

Roseanne and I arrived home together that afternoon. She hadn't been walking with me since last year, and right away I made the mistake of bringing up the subject of job-hunting again.

"We're both a year older," I said. "I bet we could think of schemes that would work this time."

She shrugged. "All that letter writing was childish. I'm finished with that kind of stuff."

We neared the brown-shingled house. "You've got to admit it was fun. You thought up such neat ideas—"

She tossed a pigtail over her shoulder. "You don't seem to realize I'll be getting my hair bobbed in a few months."

"What big difference will that make?" I asked, which was the mistake.

Roseanne punched me on the arm. "Plenty of difference, you little creep. Oh, why do we have to be bothered with you?" She trooped up the porch steps, slammed the front door. "Mom, we're home."

There was no answer. "Mom," Roseanne called again, flinging down her schoolbag, and still no answer.

Catherine was on the sofa in the living room. She lay there with her back toward us and made no move to get up as we hovered uncertainly in the archway.

"Is your cold worse?" my sister asked softly, but neither of us made a step toward her. We had never seen Mom lying tiredly on the sofa in the middle of the afternoon. She must have heard us, for the next moment she was on her feet and struggling to make light of it.

"Catnapping, a fine how-do-you-do," she said, smoothing her housedress. "Well, children, tell me how school went today. I hope you behaved yourselves." She plucked a crumpled hankie from her apron pocket and wiped her chapped, reddened nose. "I bet I know two hungry Indians who'd appreciate some milk and jelly sandwiches"—starting for the dining room.

"I'll fix them," Roseanne said.

"Only take a minute." Mom went past the dining table, then swayed and reached for the table to steady herself.

"I—I believe I'll let you make the sandwiches," she said to Roseanne. "Perhaps if I lie down for a bit more . . ." She started back toward the sofa and I noticed that perspiration beaded her face. It was another signal, as there had been signals stretching back for months.

There was her thinness. And the slow climbing of the stairs on occasion. The pause to catch her breath on the landing, and the evenings after supper when she sat longer than usual on the sofa, the sewing basket idle on her lap. Not very alarming signals, unless you added them up—and if we hadn't, it was chiefly because Catherine herself gave them no attention. There were other more serious warnings, but these, we learned, she had kept to herself.

When Dad got home he sent her upstairs to bed and phoned Dr. Drennan, who prescribed aspirin, a mustard pack and rest. That night I lay awake and listened to the sound of the terrible wracked coughs that seeped through the thin wall that separated my parents' bedroom from mine. I heard the pad of my father's feet as he got up to attend to her.

"I'm worried," I heard him say. "Tomorrow I'm asking Dr. Drennan to come over."

I didn't go downstairs right away the next morning. It was Saturday, and Dan and Vinny were off at work, and I had the room to myself. It was a luxury to be taken advantage of, so I lolled in bed, and after a while got up and dawdled over to the bureau. I opened the bottom drawer, which was mine. After my birthday last week I'd pushed the shirts and underclothes to a side and cleared a space for the cards and gifts I'd received. Daniel had given me a penknife and from Vinny I'd got a Mickey Mouse wallet. Already there were three dollar bills in the wallet, one each from Uncle Al, Charlie Cronin and Margaret. Three dollars was more money than I'd ever had before, and trying to decide how to spend it was as enjoyable as the spending itself would be. Perhaps more enjoyable—for how would I feel once the money was gone? I laid the wallet back in the drawer and inspected next the water-color set that had been Aunt Tillybird's gift. The tin box bore a picture of a mountain scene, with "Made in Switzerland" printed in small letters at the bottom. The wonderful part about Aunt Tilly's gift was that at last it had solved the future for me. All this time I hadn't been able to think of anything to be, when I grew up, other than a trolley conductor or possibly a Woolworth's floor manager. Now I had another idea, thanks to the watercolor set. I couldn't understand why I hadn't thought of it before.

I carried the birthday hoard to my cot and spread the objects across the blanket. Cards, dollar bills, penknife, wallet, water-color set—I knelt on the cot and touched each in turn. What I planned to get for the wallet was one of those name-and-address cards that read, *I am a Catholic. In case of accident, kindly summon a priest.* The nuns at St. A's had instructed us that we should always be fully prepared at any moment for death.

I sat back on my heels, glad that I'd wished on the rainbow after it had rained on Thursday. If Mom and Roseanne had also wished for happiness, that made three of us wishing for it. It was bound to come true. *In case of accident, kindly summon a priest* . . . I knelt on the cot, listening.

I gathered up the birthday gifts and put them on the desk. Then I stood at the window next to Vinny's bed and looked down at the alley. It was what I'd been doing since waking up, really— listening. And if I heard no cough from the next room . . . Eleven years old and still pretending, I thought to myself. No better than a five-year-old. *In case of accident, kindly sum-mon a . . .*

I went into the hall, which stretched empty and still from the front bedroom to the stair landing. I trod the brief distance over the frayed strip of carpet to the front-bedroom door, which was closed. No sound of coughing . . . I pushed open the door qui-etly. The big double mahogany bed was unmade, the sheets rum-pled . . . and the bed was empty! Mom's cold was improved, she'd gotten up and gone downstairs to fix breakfast, same as always.

I ran back to my bedroom, shucking my pajamas en route. Knickers half on, socks dangling, shirt unbuttoned, I ducked into the bathroom to wash. I brushed my teeth, combed my hair, tucked my socks under the elastic bands of my knickers, and envisioned the scene downstairs. Mom would be in the kitchen, fixing pancakes, maybe, as she sometimes did for Saturday breakfast. I could already taste the pancakes. Two big stacks, drenched in syrup, and the kettle whistling on the burner—

Halfway down the stairs I stopped. There was a procession in the hall below—a procession of sorts. Roseanne was at the head of it, but for some reason she was walking backward, staring at Mom and Dad, who came next. Dad was propping Mom up, leading her to the stairs. He hadn't gone to the office today. He always worked a half day on Saturdays.

"You're burning with fever," I heard him say. My mother's head sagged against his shoulder. "What crazy nonsense, refusing to stay in bed," he said, helping her up the stairs.

Mom couldn't seem to get her breath, except for a rattling sound in her throat. Her head lolled crazily. "Please, I'm all right, Jim—"

Dad gestured to me to stand back on the stairs. "We've got to get Cath to bed. She almost fainted in the kitchen."

I pressed back against the wall, and, as they passed me, Mom turned and tried to smile, but the smile wouldn't form. Dad led her up, then he was racing past me to the phone in the hall. I stayed on the stairs and watched him lift the receiver and dial a number. There was a wait, and he glanced frantically up the stairs. "Hello, is Dr. Drennan there? Well, where can I reach him?" His face was harried and tense. "Yes, it's an emergency," he said into the phone.

He hung up and paced up and down the narrow hall. He didn't seem to notice me on the stairs. He kept running his hand through his hair, and when the phone finally rang, he leaped for it instantly.

"Hello, Dr. Drennan?" he said. "It's Jim Connerty. You'd better come over, Cath's very sick."

I couldn't seem to move. It didn't necessarily work out, wishing on rainbows, I thought, holding onto the banister.

Dr. Drennan arrived about half an hour later. Dad whisked him up the stairs, and Roseanne asked if I wanted to play cards while we waited for them both to come down again. She brought out her special deck of cards with the pictures of famous racing horses on the backs that Uncle Al had given her last birthday, and we sat at the dining table and played five hundred rummy. Roseanne was a scary opponent in cards, yowling with pleasure each time she scored a point. I expected the usual behavior today but she was quiet and subdued and I even managed to win the second hand.

"You don't have to let me win," I said.

"Who's letting you?" She stacked the cards together and handed them to me. "Come on, winner shuffles."

She won the third game, after which I got up and went to the sideboard.

"Don't tell me you're hauling out those snapshots again," she said.

I lifted the Valentine box from under the flag and carried it back to the table, carefully put the lid to one side, extracted a batch of snapshots. Catherine in her bathing suit, Vinny in the buggy, Margaret in the knitted baby cap and sweater . . .

Across the table from me Roseanne dealt out a hand of solitaire for herself.

"You know, it was crazy what you said to me that day we were coming up Warbisher Street last year," I remarked, lifting out another batch of photos.

Roseanne laid a red ten of diamonds under a black jack of clubs. "How would I remember some conversation from last year?"

"It was about us being afterthoughts—the tag end of the parade. If we were, Dad certainly took lots of baby pictures of us. Why, just count 'em," I said, and separated the baby pictures into groups.

Roseanne went on with her game of solitaire. "The same number for each baby, huh?"

"Well, look for yourself. Here's seven of Vinny and a batch of Margaret. Look how many there are of—"

Suddenly I gathered up the snapshots and put them in the box. "You got tired of that favorite pastime in a hurry, I notice," Roseanne said as I returned the Valentine box to the sideboard drawer.

I closed the drawer, and for some reason my hand was shaking. "Play you another game of rummy," I said, going back to the table. But then we heard footsteps on the stairs.

We stood together in the archway and watched Dr. Drennan's black bag swing against his trousers. He was talking to Dad, who was behind him on the stairs, but the talk stopped when they saw us in the hall. Dr. Drennan said, "Well, young man, come show me how's that left arm doing? Hold it up, swing it back and forth."

It was exactly what he'd said to me when he'd arrived. I went to the stairs, raised my arm, and swung it back and forth. "How is my mother?" I asked.

"Yes, sir, you've got the full use of it." Dr. Drennan rested the black bag on the phone table, reached into his vest for a fat gold-edged pen, uncapped it, and wrote briskly on a pad of paper. "Have these prescriptions filled at once," he said to Dad. "Remember, plenty of liquids, and I want her temperature taken every half hour. If it goes above a hundred and two—"

"I'll call you at once," Dad said. He glanced at the slips of paper, then escorted Dr. Drennan to the door. "It's not pneumonia yet?" he said. "I'd prefer that you level with me, Doctor."

Dr. Drennan turned in the doorway. "No, but quite honestly, I don't like the lung congestion. We have to watch her very carefully."

"She only came down with the cold two days ago."

"Pneumonia can develop very swiftly. Keep me informed, Jim."

"Thanks for coming, Doctor."

Dad closed the front door. "Roseanne, I want you to make hot lemonade," he said, going to the closet for his coat. "After you've given Mom the lemonade, put on your roller skates, it'll be faster, and get Margaret home from the five-and-ten." He opened the door, the slips of paper from Dr. Drennan clutched in his hand. "I'm going to Montuori's."

"Dad," I called.

"What is it, Robbie?"

"Can I—I—nothing," I said.

The door closed, and Roseanne hurried to the kitchen and heated water for the lemonade. She scrounged in the icebox for a lemon, squeezed the juice in a glass.

"Let me take it upstairs to her," I said. "I'll pay you money. My birthday money."

She mixed the hot water and lemon. "Out of my way," she said bossily, carrying the glass toward the stairs. "If you want to be useful, get out my roller skates."

I got out her roller skates from the cellar landing, then waited until she came back downstairs. She needed a skate key, and I hunted around for one in my jacket in the hall closet. She clamped on the skates, opened the door, clacked over the wooden porch. From the doorway I watched her skate down Warbisher Street.

I stood at the stairs for a moment, went up a step, then another. I turned at the landing, went down the hall to the front bedroom. The door was open a crack, so I could peer in.

The shades were pulled down, and the dimness was filled with a labored sound of breathing. I looked at the bed, the rumpled sheets, and at Catherine's face, drenched with sweat, on the pillow. Her head tossed from side to side, then it turned and looked toward me down the bed.

"Robbie . . . is that you?"

"Yes," I answered.

She struggled to raise her head from the pillow. "Wh-why aren't you outside playing?"

"I don't know," I replied, and a large tear ran down my cheek. "Guess what?" I said.

"Yes?" The ragged, wheezing sound of her breathing was frightening to hear.

"I suddenly have it figured out what I want to be when I grow up," I said.

She struggled up from the pillow. "Do you? What did you decide?"

"An artist," I said. "It's the water-color set from Aunt Tilly that made me think of it. I wanted to tell you first."

Hair disarrayed, she propped herself up on her elbows, her arms thin and quavering. "An artist, imagine that. Weren't you nice to tell me first." She fell back on the pillow. "Listen, Robbie, listen to me. Don't worry, do you hear? Promise you won't."

"I promise." I wiped at the tears that wetted my face. "I mustn't bother you," I said, and turned away.

When Dad came back with the medicine he hurried up the stairs without taking off his coat. Then Margaret got home, and there was lots of hurrying up and down the stairs. I don't remember when Vinny and Dan arrived, but Margaret cooked supper for us, we listened to the radio afterward, and at some point Dad phoned Dr. Drennan to report on Mom's temperature. It hadn't gone over a hundred and two, but her breathing was no better, I heard him report, and after that he sent me to bed. I undressed myself, washed my face and hands, and climbed into my cot. The water-color set, the wallet and penknife and birthday cards were on the desk, where I'd left them, but I didn't go over to look at them.

I woke up once during the night. Perhaps I'd heard footsteps in the hall. I wasn't sure, but Catherine's voice echoed through the thin wall.

"Jim," she cried out faintly. "I can't die, don't you see? My job's not done yet . . . I can't leave you behind."

I didn't listen anymore but clapped my hands over my ears and kept them there, until, in the dark, dark room, I fell asleep again.

Somebody was jiggling me awake. I heard somebody call my name. I wiggled down under the blankets and tried to go back to sleep.

"Rob . . . come on, fella. Wake up."

I blinked an eye open. Vinny was leaning over the cot, nudging my shoulder. "That's the fella," he said. "Come, now, up and at 'em."

I opened the other eye. Sun streamed in through the window; Dan's bed was empty, the blankets hurled back. "What is it?" I asked.

"Time to get up for Mass," Vinny said, rumpling my hair.

"What time is it?"

"Seven thirty."

I burrowed under the covers again. "Mass isn't till nine. Let me sleep some more."

He shook me firmly, pulled off the covers. "We're going to eight o'clock Mass today. Get up, now, you hear?"

I sat up in bed, wide awake. "We never go to eight o'clock. Why today?"

Before he could answer, Dan poked his head in the doorway. "Is he up? Dad says to hurry, for Pete's sake." He darted off down the hall.

"Why eight o'clock Mass?" I demanded.

Vinny lifted me from the cot, put me on the floor, went to the chair for my clothes. "Don't ask so many questions, okay? Just button your lip and get dressed." He threw some clothes at me.

As we came down the stairs Margaret was standing at the bottom. "Oh, good, he's ready," she said.

"Aren't you going to eight o'clock too?" I asked her.

"We're all going to different masses today, Robbie. Now, please cooperate for Mother's sake," she said, and on the hall table I noticed a gold-edged pen.

Margaret combed my hair while Vinny waited at the door; Roseanne and Daniel came in from the kitchen, and they all talked and joked with me, and I stared at the pen.

"Well, let's get moving," Vinny said, grabbing my hand and steering me firmly out the door.

We walked up toward Bushwick Avenue in the morning sunshine, and my brother started talking about his elevator job, the interesting passengers he carried in his car.

"A night elevator in a bank building, you wouldn't think you'd meet exciting types of people, would you?" He led me briskly up the street and kept hold of my hand. "Well, you'd be wrong. The variety of types who work nights in a bank would amaze you. On the surface they're perfectly ordinary, but then you start learning about 'em. We have a key-punch operator, for example, who plays championship chess. Another quiet-looking guy turns out to be a top marathon runner. Did I tell you about the Hollywood actor?"

"No, you didn't."

"He only played bit parts in movies, but he was in scenes with Dick Powell and Ruby Keeler. At present he's working nights while waiting for a break on Broadway."

We turned into Bushwick Avenue and started toward St. Aloysius's, two blocks away. Not many people were out yet, a few old ladies coming from seven o'clock Mass. The avenue was quiet, and near deserted; then from somewhere in the quiet I heard a siren, and a moment later a white ambulance turned onto Bushwick from a side street. *St. Mary's Hospital* was painted in red lettering on the side. The ambulance sped past us, headed toward Warbisher Street, but Vinny didn't turn to look at it. Neither did I. I stared straight ahead at the yellow hulk of St. Aloysius's on the next block.

"What other different types of people work at the bank?" I asked him, listening to the screech of the ambulance siren.

He kept hold of my hand. "Well, let's see. I told you about the chess player. Oh, yeah—there's another guy, who climbs mountains every vacation."

The siren faded away behind us. We stepped down from the curb and crossed to the other side. "Vinny, excuse me a minute, my lace is untied," I said.

"You're a good kid." He stopped at the curb and released my hand.

I bent down over my shoes and pretended to tie the lace. Then, as I got up again, I spun around, crossed back to the other curb, and started running along Bushwick Avenue.

"Robbie," Vinny shouted, and I started to run faster, past the houses and fences and street lamps. "Robbie," Vinny shouted, and I could hear his footsteps gaining behind me. "Robbie, don't."

I turned into Warbisher Street, raced over the pavement, past Mr. Luro, who was tending his garden, past the MacAllisters' new car and the tree that had been split apart by lightning.

"Robbie," Vinny shouted.

The ambulance was parked in front of the brown-shingled house, as I knew it would be. As I ran toward it, I saw the front door open and two white-coated attendants came onto the porch carrying a stretcher. Dad and Dr. Drennan walked behind them, and huddled in the doorway were Dan, Margaret and Roseanne.

A cry ripped from my throat. "No, Mama. No, plea—" Vinny's hand clamped over my mouth, and he half lifted me from the pavement as he seized me from behind.

"Don't let her hear you," he gasped. "Mom has pneumonia. Dr. Drennan came earlier and ordered the ambulance. She didn't want you to see."

He held onto me, his hand over my mouth, and after a moment I stopped struggling. Up and down the street, neighbors were coming onto their porches to look on as the attendants carried the stretcher to the curb and hoisted it into the rear of the ambulance. Dr. Drennan and my father climbed in, the ambulance door shut with a loud, reverberating *twiiing*, and I watched helplessly as the white vehicle drove down Warbisher Street, its siren screaming, taking Catherine away.

She was on the critical list at St. Mary's for five days. If you phoned the hospital and inquired about Mrs. Connerty in Ward E, you were told, "The patient's condition is critical." Roseanne phoned, and that was the reply she was given.

Dad was at the hospital each night, and at home we behaved in an unreal manner, like characters in a play.

It was Daniel who'd taken me to my first stage play the winter before. The name of it was *Three-Cornered Moon*, and it was performed by the St. Brendan's Players in their church basement. A girl in the cast had sent Dan tickets, and he brought me along so he wouldn't have to go out with her afterward. We sat up front in the basement auditorium of St. Brendan's, and the curtains parted on the stage, which was made to look like a living room.

There were chairs and sofas, windows and doors, and during the course of the play the actors kept going in and out of these doors —that is, when they weren't busy answering the phone. I didn't understand the action too well, but I envied the actors because they had so much to keep them busy and dashing around.

Our house became like that stage house: everybody hurrying in and out of doors, the phone always ringing. The neighbors called or rang the front bell. Aunt Gen and Aunt Tilly phoned two or three times a day to ask the latest news, inquire about visiting hours at the hospital and whether Mom was up to visitors yet. Mrs. Fritzle knocked on the back door, concerned about our welfare—who was looking after us and cooking our meals?

That first night Dad didn't get home from the hospital until ten o'clock. Margaret, who had cooked supper, kept a plate warm for him, and we grouped ourselves at the dining room table while he ate and told us about Mom's condition. "It's lobar pneumonia, just as Dr. Drennan was afraid," he said. "They've put her in an oxygen tent to help her breathe. She—she's mostly unconscious. . . ."

The front doorbell rang and it was Mrs. Luro from up the street. She had seen the ambulance leave earlier and wanted news of Mom. Then it was the phone and Aunt Tilly again, wanting to talk with Dad. That night was the beginning of the stage house, of the phone ringing and neighbors coming to the door.

After Dad talked to Aunt Tilly he sat at the table, not drinking the coffee Margaret had poured him. "She was unconscious when I left her," he said. "I leaned over the oxygen tent, even if she couldn't hear me, and told her not to worry about us, we'd manage fine." He looked at each of us in turn. "So I guess we'd better make some plans, huh?"

We listened quietly while he outlined the new regime for us. Margaret was to be in charge of the house—she would stay out of school and take time off from her job at Woolworth's. Roseanne was to help out with the housework; we were all to do our share. "Any fights or griping about it, and you'll have me to reckon with," Dad said. "The point is, to keep the family going, each one carrying his share of the load. When I'm not home, Vinny will be head of the family. I promised Cath she won't need to worry about us, and she won't." His hand tightened into a fist. "The next few days will tell the story. If your mother can get through the crisis . . ."

"What's that?" I asked. "What's a crisis?"

"It's the turning point. If she gets through it, she'll be out of danger. We'll all pray that she makes it. Matter of fact, why don't we say a rosary right now?"

The others got up from the table and filed into the living room with Dad and knelt in a circle. I turned away and went into the kitchen. It was dark in there, but moonlight shone in through the window and glimmered on the plates from supper that were drying on the drainboard. The clock ticked and the tea kettle was in place on the stove. A flowered apron hung, ghostlike, from a peg on the wall.

I sat down in the darkness at the wooden table, and my mind went drifting around in the darkness. I heard my name being called. Margaret came through the swinging door.

"Robbie, we're waiting for you to join the rosary." She stood in the doorway, but I looked at her blankly. "Rob, you mustn't sit alone in the dark like this, with no one in here," she said.

I held onto the sides of the table and looked at her. "Don't say that. Don't say no one is here," I insisted. "There is."

But I went with her to the living room and all of us knelt in a circle, with Dad at the head, and recited a rosary. And after that night I didn't go into the kitchen anymore, except to get something to eat or drink. As Margaret had said, there was no one in there.

In the stage play Daniel had taken me to at St. Brendan's the characters all spoke in exaggerated voices and struck poses as they performed their various activities. Each day now it seemed that we were imitating this strange behavior.

Margaret was overly cheerful about taking charge of the house. She cooked breakfast, made beds, ran the carpet sweeper, and greeted me like a stage mother when I came in from school. Roseanne was her faithful assistant, dispatching me to the store with grocery lists, planning the menus for dinner. "Connerty residence. May I help you?" was her new style of answering the phone. As they fussed over their tasks, she and Margaret held a continuing discussion about redecorating.

"I'd want to throw out everything and start fresh," said Margaret.

"I'd do over the living room entirely," said Roseanne. "I'd do it all in white, like Joan Crawford's living room."

Like stage children, we flocked around Dad when he came home, pale and exhausted, from the hospital at night.

"Supper's in the oven," sang Margaret.

"Let me hang up your hat and coat," I offered with politeness. "Has Mom had the crisis?"

He took off his coat slowly. "No change . . . still the oxygen tent."

I carried his hat and coat to the closet. "Oh, well, it'll be all right. We'll do our share, and she'll be home before we know it."

Dad was the only one who didn't play a stage part. Taut and worried, lapsing into silence in the middle of a sentence, distracted and forgetful, he moved like a sleepwalker from one day to the next.

On Thursday night Uncle Al and Charlie Cronin came home with him from the hospital. That was the night, I think, that we gave up being stage people acting in a play. Things had started to slip out of control even before Dad arrived home. Margaret burned the veal cutlets for supper, and Roseanne refused point-blank to clear the table when dinner was over.

"Must I remind you of Father's instructions?" Margaret fumed, cranky and out of sorts.

"Oh, stop using that ritzy voice, like you're at the ribbon counter. As for clearing the table—" Roseanne leveled an accusing finger at me. "Why can't the artist get busy and do some work? All he does is fool around with his sissy water colors."

"I'm painting some pictures for Mom," I protested, which was true. After school each afternoon I'd gotten out the water-color set and practiced copying pictures that I'd clipped from magazines. I remembered how bare and white the rooms at St. Mary's were. It would be nice if Mom had some water-color drawings to brighten the walls. "Anyway, I went to the store twice today, and—"

"Twice today. Big deal."

Margaret banged the table, rattling the dishes. "I request you one more time to clear the table, Roseanne."

Daniel came into the archway. "Is she giving you trouble, Marg? I'm the head of the house in Vinny's absence." He sauntered over to Roseanne, "Clear the table," and slapped her across the face.

Roseanne didn't cry; she never would let herself cry. She bowed her head, the imprint of Daniel's hand flaming on her cheek, and began to clear the table while Dan sauntered back to his radio program in the living room.

Dad didn't get home until ten o'clock. Charlie and Uncle Al came barging in behind him, Charlie waving a bottle, which he proceeded to unwrap. Dad got some shot glasses, and the three of them sat around the dining table, talking and taking sips of the whiskey. I wanted to show Dad the water-color drawings, so I sat in a corner next to the china closet and waited for an opportunity.

"She's putting up a grand fight, Jimbo," Charlie said, smacking his lips. "She couldn't talk much in that oxygen tent, but when I said goodbye she smiled at me. Gave me a grand smile."

My father shook his head wearily. "I don't know . . ."

"She'll pull through, I haven't a doubt of it." Uncle Al reached for the bottle and poured more whiskey into his shot glass. His hair was black, like Dad's, but his face was beefy and red, he was shorter by half a foot, and his belly sagged over his trousers. Uncle Al lived in Bayside and was employed as a truck driver by a beer company. "I forgot to mention, Jimbo," he said. "If you'd like to send any of the kids out to us, Gen says she'd be tickled to have 'em. It might ease the pressure."

Dad drained his shot glass. "This family's staying together. I'm not parceling out my kids."

"Here's to Cath," Charlie toasted, as if at a wedding. "Here's to the grandest girl St. Gabe's ever turned out."

My father stared bleakly at the table. He was silent for a moment, twisting the shot glass around. "I can't help it—I blame myself for her illness," he burst out unexpectedly. "I keep thinking how I might have saved her from it."

Uncle Al leaned over and patted his shoulder. "Ah, now, Jimbo, you've been the best husband in the world to Cath."

"Have I?" Dad shot back. "She'd lost all that weight, and what did I do about it? If I'd sent her to the doctor sooner . . ." He ran his hand through his hair. "She never thinks to look after herself. After we were married and she kept having babies—I wanted her to slow down and get her strength back. That's where the trouble started—too many babies too fast."

Too many babies . . . I sat up in the chair, suddenly alert.

Charlie poured another drink for Dad. "This is what you need, Jimbo. Here you go." He pushed the shot glass toward him.

My father pushed it away. "Drennan warned us, you know. No more babies after Roseanne, he said to Cath. I tell you, we should have stopped then. If we had, she might have been in better shape now. It's myself I blame."

No more babies after Roseanne . . . I didn't know why, but I turned and looked toward the sideboard where the Valentine box lay in the drawer.

Then Charlie was shushing my father. "Little pitchers have big ears, Jimbo. Drink up, now, there's a good fella."

Dad turned and frowned at me, bleary-eyed. "Robbie, I didn't know you were there. Go up to bed."

"Yes, sir." I walked from the dining room. Charlie was urging the drink into his hand. "Another of these, Jimbo, and you'll get yourself out of the dumps," I heard him coax.

On Friday Dad came home late as usual, and not ten minutes after he'd sat down at the dining table the telephone rang. Margaret was serving him a plate of spaghetti, the phone went *brrnggg*, and I raced Roseanne to the hall to answer it. She beat me there, picked up the phone and singsonged, "Connerty residence. May I help you?"

I could tell from the way her face changed expression that the caller wasn't a neighbor or relative. She looked at me strangely and held out the phone. "It—it's the hospital. You take it."

I backed slowly away from her, shaking my head.

"Then go get Dad. Hurry, you fool. The doctor's waiting. It's the *hospital*."

"I—I can't." I shook my head frantically.

"Dad, it's the hospital," Roseanne called in a high voice into the dining room. "You'd better come."

I heard his footsteps approach and glanced around for a place to hide where I wouldn't hear what was being said on the phone. The kitchen, I thought, and started through the archway. My father collided with me, pushed me aside, hurried to the phone.

"Yes, this is Mr. Connerty. What is it, Doctor?"

It was too late to hide. Where was there to hide? I stood with Roseanne, both of us rooted there. Margaret and Dan came into the archway, and none of us spoke, even after Dad hung up the phone.

"It's the crisis, they want me at the hospital," he said quietly. He went silently to the closet and put on his coat. He didn't seem frightened or upset; almost calmly, he went to the door and opened it.

"Pray for her," he said before he vanished into the blackness of the porch, the door shutting behind him.

I don't remember that any of us spoke or moved until Dan, squaring back his shoulders, finally said, "You heard what he asked. Let's get the prayers started. Robbie, Roseanne, all of us."

We followed Daniel into the living room and knelt in a silent circle on the worn carpet. Margaret took a rosary from her apron pocket, blessed herself, and began the Apostle's Creed. "I believe in God, the Father Almighty, and in Jesus Christ, His Only Son, Our Lord . . ."

We took turns reciting the five decades. Since Vinny wasn't home from work yet, Margaret recited the last decade in his stead. Then she rose from her knees and smoothed her apron, exactly as my mother would have done.

"It's very late. Robbie and Roseanne, go to bed," she said, just as Catherine would have instructed. Margaret wasn't a high-school girl anymore, selling ribbon at Woolworth's in the afternoon. She was in charge of a house, perhaps permanently. She went into the dining room to clear the table and I thought of the Saturday weddings at church that she'd always liked to attend; weddings seemed a long mile away from her now.

"It's late. Upstairs to bed," she said again, and I almost expected to glimpse gray strands in her hair.

We had been acting a play, because plays always turned out right in the end, but now the play acting was over; it was time to take the stage house down.

I followed Roseanne up the stairs. Without speaking, she turned in at her door, and I went down the hall to mine. I undressed and got into bed. I lay on the cot, the darkness swirling around me, and my body started to shake uncontrollably. I pulled the blankets under my chin and made silent promises to God.

I don't know when I fell asleep, but sometime toward the morning the sound of the phone woke me and I opened my eyes to see Vinny leaping from bed. He hurried into the hall, Daniel close behind, and by the time I reached the landing Roseanne and Margaret were there too. A silent tableau, we watched Vinny at the phone below the stairs.

He nodded a few times, hung up, and sat weakly on the bench. "It was Dad," he called up to us. "The crisis is over. Mom's out of danger. She's going to recover."

That was before the doctors learned it wasn't pneumonia that Catherine needed to recover from.

On an afternoon two weeks later I opened the sideboard drawer in the dining room and took out the Valentine box from under the folded flag. I carried the pink heart-shaped box to the table and sat down alone with it.

After we'd come in from school Roseanne had volunteered to go roller-skating with me. "Come on, Rob. We'll skate up to Snake Hill. It's swell weather for it."

"No—you go."

"I'm doing it for your sake. To take your mind off everything. Margaret's back at Woolworth's—we could go check up on her."

"I think I'll just stay here," I said.

"Okay, if you like hanging around a morgue." And, grumbling, Roseanne had clamped on her roller skates and careened off in escape.

The house floated in silence. I lifted off the candy-box lid. No use delaying—sooner or later I'd have to find out about the snapshots.

I drew the stacks of photos from the box and sorted through them, putting the baby photos to one side. Then, like a game of solitaire, I dealt these out on the table in rows—Vinny in his christening robe, Dan in the wicker buggy, Margaret in a sun bonnet in the backyard, Roseanne cradled in Catherine's arms—the baby pictures. Another of Vinny, two more of Roseanne.

A few bars of German song drifted from the kitchen, dispersing the quiet. Hanna had shown up today, even though Dad had told her he wouldn't be able to afford her services anymore. She'd appeared at the front door as Margaret was getting us off to school. Marched into the hall and plunked down her satchel, ignoring Margaret's explanations.

"You think I not come because you cannot pay? My friend, your mama, would she not come to me?"

"But honestly, Hanna, we can't afford—"

Up went Hanna's hand. "I haff free day today. I come as friend to help." And she had opened the satchel and fished out her apron.

It was pleasant to hear Hanna's singing; the house was so silent, the afternoons so long and slow to pass. On Saturday Catherine would be leaving St. Mary's. A special ambulance, Dad would ride with her, a long journey, up to Greenvale in the Adirondacks. I'd located the town of Greenvale on the classroom map at school. It was two inches above Albany in the mountains around Saranac Lake. Greenvale was a pretty name for a town to have.

I put the snapshots on the dining table and rubbed my stomach. It felt as if it were going to be sick, like the time with the broken arm. Greenvale . . . the sanatorium . . .

"Robbie, I must go now." Hanna pushed open the swinging door, her coat and hat on, the satchel in tow. "I make stew for supper, heating on stove. Iss not good, the way you sit alone like this."

"I'm all right, Hanna. Listen, thanks for coming."

Her big shoes lumbered to the table. "You sit and think about your mama, I bet. Worry that she not get well."

"Oh, she will," I said. "Tuberculosis is a curable disease, you know. Dad explained it to us. Definitely curable—it should take about a year."

Hanna raised a hand to her breast. "Poor lady, to haff trouble with her lungs. Who would have thought?"

"Spots on the lungs. They showed up on the X-rays." I sat up straight, my hands folded, as in school. "You see, at first the doctors thought it was pneumonia, the same symptoms, but then she started having night sweats."

"Who would have thought," Hanna repeated, with a deep frown. "Always laughing, even that day she got caught in the rain."

"She was worn out." I dug my nails into my palms. "*We* wore her out. Too many of us to look after."

Hanna looked at me closely. "I don't like how you talk. Iss nothing to blame except"—her hand gestured—"life. You must think now she get well and come home."

"I do think about it," I said, and my voice wavered for a moment. "After all, God wouldn't let her die before her job's finished."

Hanna pressed my shoulder tightly. "*Ja*, Robbie, God let her finish. I must go, but I come back again. Remember, stew iss on stove."

"Yes, Hanna. Thank you."

The lumbering tread, then the front door closed behind her—and I picked up the snapshots again. *Maybe we were afterthoughts and they really didn't want us*, Roseanne had said, walking up Warbisher Street that day last year. *Too many babies too fast,* Dad had said to Charlie Cronin and Uncle Al. *We should have stopped after Roseanne. Cath might be in better shape now.*

The afternoon light filtered in dimly from the alley, and I stared at the neat rows of baby pictures. I'd first thought to count them the Saturday Dr. Drennan had come to the house. But I'd quickly put the Valentine box away after I'd begun to discover . . .

It was useless to run from the truth. What good did it do? I moved my gaze over the rows of photos and reached the last row, the tag end of the parade, which consisted of just two photos. A dozen baby snaps of Vinny, a batch of Margaret. Ten of Daniel and Roseanne . . . but only two photos of the last Connerty baby. The number of photos showed how much a person cared. . . . *We should have stopped after Roseanne.*

I raised up my fists and brought them crashing down, scattering the snapshots to the floor. I wanted never to look at them again, never to be reminded. Wanted to set a match to them and burn away the question that throbbed in my mind. I got up from the chair, scooped up the photos, dumped them into the pink box. I clamped the lid down over the photos. It wasn't true . . . *for who else in the world loved me, if Catherine did not?* I seized the Valentine box, carried it back to the sideboard and hurled it back in the drawer. Couldn't burn it, but I'd leave it there until I could think what to do to rid myself of it forever. It wasn't true, it wasn't. . . .

"Catherine," I shouted, and ran toward the swinging door. "Catherine." I stumbled across the blue-and-white tiles, collided with the white table. The clock ticked over the stove, the coffee tin of flowers was perched on the windowsill over the sink . . . but the kitchen was empty. No one was here, my mother was gone, and I had helped—

The kitchen was a place from which to flee. I pulled open the back door, went down the steps into the yard, over to the tree—

I threw myself down under the branches that were budding with new young leaves, tender and green. Collapsed there, I looked over at the Fritzles' fence, remembering the ill-fated attempt to climb it. I'd broken my arm and Catherine had come to help with the pain. Now something else was broken and maybe never again would she be able to come. *"Catherine,"* I cried to the empty, ragged yard, and wondered what I could give in exchange for her return. Children had nothing to give, no coin of any sort to barter with. I had only my heart, and who wanted that? *Who?* I gazed over the green-sprouting earth at the Fritzles' fence and knew that I would never climb it.

"Rooobbie," Roseanne's voice called from within the house. "Rooooobbbie"—but I didn't call back. I cradled myself against the tree, and the question whirled in my mind, unspoken, unanswered, where it was to lodge itself beyond reach in the years to come:

When I was born, were my parents happy?

Part Two

_____

5

Aunt Tillybird

A year—a year wasn't so long to wait. Greenvale wasn't so far away.

On the Friday in May that my mother left in the ambulance with Dad for the day-long journey to the Adirondacks I sat in the varnished classroom at St. A's and looked without end at the map of the United States that hung from the blackboard. New York State was pale green, shaped like a lopsided heart. Albany was an inch above New York City, and an inch above that was Saranac Lake—and Greenvale was a neighboring town to Saranac. Two pale-green inches . . . not so great a distance . . .

I ran home after school to Warbisher Street that Friday. This was Catherine's house! These porch steps up which I trod, that front door and the rooms beyond—*her* house, and in a year she would be coming back again. I closed the front door and heard a crash in the kitchen.

I dropped my schoolbag and headed for the swinging door in the dining room, pushed it open. Roseanne was kneeling on the tiles, the cupboard doors were open, and scattered around her on the tiles were bits and slivers of glass.

"Mom's Waterford pitcher," I cried.

"It was an accident," Roseanne moaned in dismay, wringing her hands.

I turned and looked at the open cupboard doors. Always the Waterford pitcher had stood on the top shelf, safe from prying hands. Grandpa Quinlan had bought it years ago in Ireland for Grandma Quinlan, and Catherine numbered it among the last keepsakes of her mother. The pitcher, a silver pie service, the Meissen sugar and creamer in the china closet—nothing else was left from those other times. I noticed a box of saltines on the middle shelf, and it told me how the pitcher had met its fate.

Roseanne hurried for a broom and dustpan. "I'll pay you not to tell," she said. "I'll give you fifty cents from my graduation money when I get it next month."

I stood back and watched her sweep the bits of glass onto a sheet of newspaper. "You were climbing up on the cupboard to get crackers, instead of using a chair, and you knocked the pitcher over," I said.

She swept up the glass slivers. "So you figured it out. Brilliant deduction, Mr. Holmes."

"Swell news for Dad when he gets back on Sunday."

"Forget the fifty cents. I'll pay you a dollar." She stood up, got a paper bag from the broom closet, and emptied the dustpan into it. "I bet you feel great, getting the goods on me at last. Will a buck buy your silence? Answer me."

It hadn't occurred to me, the stunning reversal of our positions. Never once in my entire existence had I power to wield over my sister. "I'll have to think it over," I said. "Where are you going?"

She was already at the back door. "To dump this in some garbage can up the street—and why should anybody have to know?"

"Someone's bound to notice the pitcher is missing. It's always been on the top shelf."

"So I'll take my chances." She started out the door, then stopped. "Don't tell on me, Robbie. Please don't," she asked. The door closed, and from the window over the sink I watched her hurry up the alley, the paper bag under her arm.

The Waterford pitcher wasn't the only keepsake missing from the house, I thought to myself. There was another missing item, only nobody had discovered it yet. I wondered how long it would be . . .

Staying alone in the kitchen wasn't something I handled very well. It was best not to try, so I ran upstairs, got Aunt Tilly's watercolor set, and brought it down to the dining table. Two inches on a map weren't such a far distance. A year wasn't a long time to wait. . . .

I installed myself at the dining table—water colors, drawing paper, a saucer of water, and brushes. I'd clipped out some more magazine pictures, which I planned to copy and send to the sanatorium. A Florida beach scene, with palm trees and blue ocean, a New England winter landscape, snowy hills, white houses . . . I propped the Florida scene against some books on the table and studied it for a moment, dipped the brush in the water. I held the brush over the paper and seemed to hear again the crash of the Waterford pitcher.

It was a crash that each day now reverberated through our lives, bringing new changes, so that nothing was the same anymore. I daubed some color on the sheet of drawing paper and totaled up the changes that had taken place.

Margaret had left high school. Without fuss or histrionics, she'd informed Dad of her action after dinner one night.

"I spoke to Miss O'Daly, my class adviser, about Mother's illness today," she said, sitting down next to him. "The spring term has only another month to go, and Miss O'Daly says I can be excused from attendance and still be allowed to take my exams, and come back for my senior year whenever I'm able to."

Dad stared at her. "Whenever you're able to? You've only got a year to go, Margaret."

"I'll go back when Mom comes home. A year isn't long to wait, I'm only seventeen." She put her hand on Dad's arm, just as Catherine would have done. "Someone's got to look after the house," she said quietly. "If it's got to be me, I don't mind—and I'll be able to work at Woolworth's too."

"Margaret—"

"Mr. Fergus is putting me on a noon-to-six basis. It'll give me the morning for housework, and I'll be home in time to cook supper. We'll have to eat a bit later, perhaps. . . ."

"Let's wait before we make any big decisions," Dad had urged. "Let's talk it out and see if we can't—"

"We'll need all the money we can lay hands on, isn't that true?" Margaret had pressed. "You haven't said what the sanatorium will cost, but I can guess what a year's expenses will amount to."

Dad hadn't admitted it, but the question of paying the costs of the sanatorium seemed beyond any solution. Part of the expenses would be covered by his medical insurance at work, but only a part and for a limited time. The ambulance trip to Greenvale would alone cost two hundred dollars, and none of it was covered by insurance. Dad had applied for an emergency loan at a bank, and he spoke of finding a night job for himself.

He was turned down for the loan because of the mortgage payments that still had to be met on the house. He then had applied for a second mortgage, and received another "no." After that, Vinny announced that he was transferring to night college and getting a full-time day job as soon as exams were over in June.

"At least jobs are available," he said, making light of his decision. "Listen, what if it was still the Depression? I'm sure I can get forty a week—that's almost twice what I'm earning now."

"You're not switching to night college. It'll take double the time to get your degree."

"Dad, I'm not going to sit back and watch you struggle to keep from drowning. We're all in this together. Getting Mom well again has to be the main consideration."

"Ah, Vinny, I'd never ask this of you."

"You don't need to—I'm offering it. Besides, it'll only be for a year. It's not so long."

A year, a year to wait . . . and two pale-green inches to measure on a map. I daubed some more color on the drawing paper, deep blue for the Florida ocean, light blue for the sky. Then I mixed some brown for the palm trees, and in my mind the crash echoed again through the silent, empty house, like the toll of a funeral bell.

Dad phoned us from Greenvale on Saturday and reported that the sanatorium was beautiful and that Catherine had withstood the strain of the long journey very well. He spoke to Roseanne and me and said that he missed us and was leaving in a minute to catch the overnight train back to New York.

It was seven o'clock and Margaret was in the kitchen finishing supper—we wouldn't begin the meal until Vinny and Dan were home from work. Roseanne and I squatted Indian-fashion on the living room carpet, playing five hundred rummy. A lamp made a pool of light, and beyond it the darkness stretched around us. The phone rang and I jumped up at the first *brrrnngg*.

"I'll get it," I said and waited for Roseanne to stop me. She flung back a pigtail and fanned out her cards. Nobody had noticed the missing pitcher yet, and I still wasn't accustomed to having power over Roseanne. The phone gave another *brrnng*.

"Well, answer it." She scowled.

"I'd watch how you address me," I advised. "I'd be slightly careful—" Sauntering into the hall, I picked up the receiver. "Connerty residence. May I help you?"

There was a pause, as though the person at the other end was undecided about communicating any further. Then a light, fizzy voice that sounded like ginger ale said, "'Lo, there . . . might this be Robbiekins?"

I didn't often hear that voice, but surely it could belong to only one person in the world. Nobody else spoke like that. "Oh, hello, Aunt Tillybird," I said.

A bubbly ginger-ale laugh almost tickled my ear. "Ha, ha, the young gentleman recognizes me. How's tricks these days?"

"Oh, fair to middling—*tolerable*," I answered. Somehow with Aunt Tilly you found yourself talking a different language.

"Poor children, to be deprived of your mother," sighed my mother's sister. "Poor Catherine, to be so equally deprived. May I ask if your father has returned from Greenvale yet?"

The way Aunt Tillybird usually got her information mixed up was a family joke. "He only left Greenvale tonight," I explained. "The train doesn't get in until tomorrow morning."

"I thought he took the train *last* night," said my aunt. "Ah, but facts elude me so! Here I've been waiting all day for James to phone and tell me about the sanatorium and what the doctors had to say. Poor, dear Catherine . . ."

"I'll tell Dad to call you when he gets in," I offered.

"Would you, Robbiekins? I—I daresay you'll all be at home tomorrow. . . ." There was a timid pause, as if Aunt Tilly wanted to ask something more.

"Yes, we'll be home," I said.

"Yes, well . . . toodle-oo, Robbie. Take care."

A soft click of the receiver and she was gone, like a sprite in a Hans Christian Andersen tale, and I hung up the phone, wondering what she might have wanted.

"Who was it?" Roseanne asked as I came back into the living room.

I sat down on the carpet and picked up my cards. "I trust you weren't looking at my hand while I was absent," I said. "I trust you have more sense than that."

"You mean, did I cheat?" she asked.

Even with my knowledge of the broken pitcher, it was better not to push my sister too far. "I only meant—"

She glared at me and threw down her cards. "Since when has anybody ever caught me cheating? Go ahead, name a time," she demanded. "That's the trouble with families. They condemn you, no matter what." She got up, pigtails tossing, and there was anger in her freckled face, and something else, which I couldn't identify. "I wish I lived anywhere but here," she said. "In the library, or under the El tracks, or in Bohack's. Cheat! I never once cheated at cards."

She rushed through the archway as though to run out the door and never come back. But the hall was dark, and outside the street was dark. The only light was from the lamp next to the morris chair, the only person to be with was me. Slowly Roseanne came back to the living room, dropped to the carpet and picked up her cards. "Okay, whose draw?" she asked.

"Yours," I said.

Sniffily, she reached for a card. "You didn't say who was on the phone."

"It was nobody, only Aunt Tillybird," I said, and drew a card for myself.

Nobody, *only Aunt Tillybird.* . . . It summed up the family's attitude toward this fizzy, scatterbrained schoolteacher old maid, who was as unlike Catherine as any sister could manage to be. It was Grandpa Quinlan who had invented the nickname of Tillybird for his oldest daughter. Mom said it was because Tilly was so fluttery as a little girl, hopping and darting about exactly as a bird does. The nickname had stuck as the years went on, and now even Aunt Tilly used it in referring to herself. " 'Lo, there, Robbie-kins, this is Tillybird," was her standard introduction on the phone.

My Aunt Tilly taught the fifth grade in an old red-brick school building on Willoughby Avenue in Brooklyn. Art and travel were her favorite interests, and every summer she crossed the ocean in order to tour the museums and cathedrals of Europe. She never failed to send us postcards from her journeys, pictures of the Louvre or of some museum in Florence or Rome. She sent us birthday and Christmas gifts, and she was faithful about remembering special events like First Communions and graduations; but if my aunt counted for little in our lives, it was because we saw her so seldom.

Aunt Tilly rarely visited Warbisher Street, never more than once or twice a year—at Thanksgiving, usually, and to be with Mom on her birthday. The two sisters kept in daily touch via the telephone, and Mom frequently visited Tilly's apartment, but it was never explained why we didn't see more of her at Warbisher Street. Occasionally, on Memorial Day, Aunt Tilly would visit Calvary Cemetery with us, bringing along a flowered plant and a little spade with which to install it in the Quinlan plot.

"Wherever you go, plant flowers, Robbie," I remember she said mysteriously to me one Memorial Day at the cemetery. Aunt Tilly appeared to love the graves as much as Mom did, and had her own stories of the bygone lives and relationships that were traced out on the headstones. But, like everything about my aunt, her stories were invariably left unfinished. Always, in the middle of the tale, she would gather up her spade and prepare to depart. Calling goodbye, she would flutter birdlike out the cemetery gates and hail a taxi, waving from the window as the vehicle sped away.

If my aunt rarely visited Warbisher Street, we had never once been to her apartment on Clark Street, in the Heights section of Brooklyn. The apartment was tiny, Mom had said—barely enough room for Tilly herself, let alone for a noisy tribe of Indians like us. And so my aunt had remained a shadowy family figure, absent from the circle except for her postcards, birthday gifts and phone calls. She was no more than a wispy, fluttery lady whose hair was of a vivid reddish hue, as highly colored as the postcards she sent.

But how wrong I was, as the months ahead would prove, to think of her as nobody.

Roseanne scooped up a batch of cards victoriously. "What did she want?"

"Who?"

"Nitwit. Who was on the phone just now—Greta Garbo?"

"You mean Aunt Tilly? Oh, she didn't want anything," I said.

She came to the house the next day, unbidden, which must have required every frayed shred of nerve that she possessed.

Dad's train was scheduled to reach Grand Central Station at ten in the morning. We went to eight o'clock Mass, and afterward Vinny took the subway over to the city to meet the train. At ten he phoned from Grand Central and said that the Saranac train was delayed and wouldn't arrive for another hour.

We had finished breakfast, and it was raining. I didn't like the rain anymore, not since the consequences of that April thundershower, and the sound of it beating on the roof finally drove me upstairs. Upstairs was no improvement, for all I did was lie on my cot and listen to the rain. Then I tried to concentrate my attention on *not* listening to it, which worked surprisingly well.

It would be terrific, I thought, if a person could banish from his mind all the things he didn't want to think about. Like the blackboard eraser at school—one good sweep of effort, and your thoughts would be magically wiped clean. Just take hold of your mental eraser and wipe hard, and everything you needed to forget would be gone. *Catherine, Catherine . . . when I was born . . .*

"Roobbie," Margaret called upstairs to me. "May I speak to you a moment?"

I went out to the landing and called to my sister at the foot of the stairs, "Yeah, Marg?"

"If you wouldn't mind coming down for a moment, I think you could help me."

I went down the stairs and Margaret beckoned me into the dining room. She indicated the opened sideboard drawer and asked, "Isn't that where we always kept it?"

I regarded the drawer blankly and thought of the Waterford pitcher, the slivers of glass scattered on the tiles. "Where we kept what?"

"That candy box with all the snapshots." She removed the flag from the drawer and rummaged around in it. "I can't imagine what happened to that box. It's vanished, with all the photos."

"It was in the drawer the last time I saw it," I said.

Her hands sorted through the clutter of old Christmas cards, stationery and card decks. "Where could it have disappeared to?"

My glance strayed to the tin box of water colors that I'd left on the sideboard, and I picked the set up and carried it to the dining table. "Gee, Margaret, don't ask me. I haven't looked at those snapshots in weeks."

"Roseanne," Margaret called into the living room. "You haven't seen that box of snapshots, have you? It's missing from the sideboard."

Roseanne was on the sofa, reading the Sunday funnies. "If Robbie doesn't know where it is, search me."

I opened the water-color set, got out the brushes, and spread newspaper on the table. "I think I'll copy another picture to send to Mom," I said. "Did you know I finished six water colors so far, Margaret?"

She put the flag back in the drawer. "Are you certain you haven't seen it? I thought it would be nice to send some snapshots to Greenvale."

"Six completed water colors. I wouldn't be surprised if my career was in that direction. I think I'll start on my seventh. Doesn't look as if the rain will let up." I left Margaret frowning at the sideboard, went into the kitchen and held a saucer under the faucet. *Catherine, Catherine,* the clock ticked in rhythm. Water splattered over the saucer, and with my mental eraser I wiped away what I preferred not to think about.

I carried the water back into the dining room, where Margaret was still meditating at the sideboard. "It'll turn up," I said. "Wait and see, we'll find it in some odd place or other."

And I sat down to work at another drawing.

It was still raining half an hour later, and in the living room

Daniel had turned on the Emerson and was switching the dial from station to station. Daniel never liked anything except detective and sports programs. A burst of band music was replaced by a religious sermon and followed by a roll of organ playing.

"Quit that switching around," Roseanne complained from the sofa, where she was still absorbed in the funnies.

"It's after eleven, maybe we ought to phone Grand Central and check if the train's in," Dan said restlessly, and went back to fiddling with the dial again.

I mixed up some pale blue for sky, dabbed the brush in it, and as I started to paint, the doorbell rang.

It was a faint, hesitant ring, and at first no one got up to answer it. When the bell gave another hesitant ring, Roseanne went and looked out the front window.

"Eek—if there's one thing we don't need today it's silly talk," she said.

"Who is it?" I called to her.

"Answer the door and find out for yourself."

I put down the paintbrush and went into the hall. I opened the door, and poised there on the doorstep were a pair of small, dainty feet encased in rain boots. The shiny pink raincoat and matching pink umbrella made me think of water colors, and suddenly I remembered who had sent me the set—the very person who was smiling in the doorway. "Aunt Tillybird," I sang out in surprise.

"Greetings, *mon petit*." A feathery hat, drooping and rainsodden, sat on her red curls. She struggled to hold a purse and a wet cake box in one arm and to shake out the umbrella with the other. "Ha, ha, miserable day, I fear."

"I don't like the rain either," I said, with an unexpected sense of kinship. "Aunt Tilly, you didn't say you were coming!"

"Ha, ha . . ." She came into the hall—no, edged her way in—accompanied by a holiday air. "Started to phone you, then decided to hop the trolleykins instead." She deposited the pink umbrella in the rack. "Poor Cath—is your Da home yet?"

"His train's been delayed an hour."

Margaret came into the hall, tidying her hair and brushing at her dress. "Aunt Tilly, what a surprise."

"'Lo there, sweet Marguerite," said Aunt Tilly, making the words rhyme. She indicated the dripping cake box. "Some goodies from that French pastry shop on Henry Street. *Vous connaissez?*"

"Thank you, I'm sure," Margaret said, somewhat rattled.

"*Pâtisserie. Une bonne pâtisserie.* Let us hear you pronounce it." It was Aunt Tilly's practice on her infrequent visits to the house to conduct among us a running course in French. "Come, *ma chère.*"

My sister struggled to oblige her. "*Ooone bun pah-tee-suree.*"

"*Excellent, très bon.*" Aunt Tilly bestowed the cake box on Margaret as though awarding her a prize for scholarship. Margaret hurried off with it, while I took care of Aunt Tilly's raincoat and boots and the pink chiffon scarf that she unwound from her neck.

"Such nice manners. I believe you're getting tall, Robert. The famous Connerty growth."

"No, it seems to be passing me by, Aunt Tilly," I said. "I'm no bigger than you are."

"Which isn't, alas, very big at all." She turned away, the purse looped over her arm, and glanced around the hall. It was as if she'd arrived for a party but found no party under way. "His train's been delayed?" she asked.

"Just an hour. It ought to be pulling in now."

It relieved her, I sensed, to have time to prepare for my father's not always gentle teasing. I doubted that Dad intended it, but he treated Aunt Tilly as a joke, a family joke—for wasn't this what she was?

"Well," she said, advancing timorously to the archway, where she surveyed the lumpy sofa, the scarred tables and tilting lamps that bloomed in the living room. Aunt Tilly seemed to draw back for a moment. "Greetings, Roseanne," she said. "Still the long, beautiful tresses, I see."

Roseanne looked up from the funnies. "Hello, Aunt Tillybird. Didn't you hear? After I graduate from St. Aloysius's in June I'm getting my beautiful tresses chopped off."

The remark caused a moment's impasse. "I see," said Aunt Tilly, and stepped through the archway and across the carpet until her path was blocked by Daniel, who lay sprawled out full length, absorbed in a sports broadcast. Aunt Tilly halted, as before a rock or boulder.

"What ho, there, Daniel," she addressed him in a jocular tone, which Daniel appeared not to hear. Emitting a little laugh, she stepped over him, and, safe on the other side, lowered herself gingerly to the sofa. She listened attentively to the sports broadcast for a few moments. "Ah, baseball, the sports of kings," she sighed.

There was a grunt from Daniel. "I thought horse racing was the sport of kings."

Another little laugh, a gesture of the hand to acknowledge error. "Of course, horse racing, to be sure." She shook her red curls. "Ah, nothing can equal the splendors of Longchamps. That's the celebrated racing course outside Paris, you know. *Champs* means fields—"

Daniel sprang at the radio and turned up the volume. "Excuse me, Aunt Tilly, but you keep talking and I want to hear this."

She made no reply. She glanced down at her purse and clicked the round gold clasp open and shut, and it was apparent to me why she did not visit our house more often.

I stepped clumsily toward the sofa, wanting to make up for it somehow. "Aunt Tilly, you know what? The water-color set you sent me for my birthday . . ."

She looked up at me. "Yes, Robbie?"

In my anxiety the words got jumbled and twisted up, and I started the speech over again. "The water colors you sent me for my birthday—it's the favorite gift I ever received. Wo-would you care to see my efforts?"

"You've been painting?" she asked with widened eyes.

"Would you like to see?" I ran to the dining table for the drawing I'd been working on, gathered the other drawings from the sideboard, and went back to the living room. "See how many, Aunt Tilly? I was starting on another drawing when you rang the bell," I said. "I plan to send them to my mother to decorate her room."

"Really? Why, look at the landscape you copied."

"I did that one over three times."

Just then the front door slammed, and Roseanne jumped up from the sofa. "Pops, is that you?"

"Home in one piece. Train got stuck on a trestle." My father came into the hall, stamping his shoes on the linoleum. He stood in the archway and threw a big smile at us and boomed, "How'd you manage the store in my absence?"

Dan and Roseanne ran toward him, and his arms reached for them, like a blind man's. "Golly, it's good to lay eyes on you. How you been, Rosie? C'mere, Rob, I missed you too." I went over and an arm pulled me close. "I've lots to tell you about Mom."

Vinny came into the hall and set down the ancient suitcase Dad had packed for the trip. Margaret, who had been setting the table, switched off the blaring radio and helped Dad out of his coat. "I'll have dinner ready in an hour," she said efficiently.

"Tell us about Mom," Roseanne clamored. "What is Greenvale like?"

My father strode into the living room, his arms still around us. "It's one helluva gorgeous place, let me tell you. Trees and lawns, a sparkling lake, mountains in the distance. There's a main building, and then there's these cottages, six patients in each—" He stopped in the center of the room. "Why, Tilly, I didn't notice you," he said.

Aunt Tilly clicked and unclicked the gold clasp on her purse. "What ho, James." She smiled nervously. "So anxious about Catherine . . . If I'm intruding on family privacy . . ."

"Nonsense, it's a pleasure to have you," Dad said and went over to shake hands. "You'll stay for dinner, I hope. We can't promise you a fancy meal . . ."

Her hand trembled in his clasp. "How is Cath? What do the doctors say?"

"Had a long conference with 'em yesterday." Dad rubbed his hands together and turned away. "After the rain, not to mention sitting up all night on a train, I could use a drink. How about you, Til—a glass of sherry, if we have any?"

"Ha, ha—*merci, monsieur.*"

He led her into the dining room, trailed by the rest of us. Vinny ducked into the kitchen and returned with a whiskey bottle and a bottle of cooking sherry, which Margaret poured into a glass for Aunt Tilly.

"Ah, *les vins du pays*—ha, ha, thank you." She beamed.

"Sit down, Til," Dad said, slapping the chair next to him. He poured a shot of whiskey, tilted his head back, and downed it. "I don't mind if I have another," he said, reaching for the bottle. "Yes, it's a beautiful place, but we have to face that Cath is in for a long, tough battle."

Aunt Tilly was not in her chair, however. She was over at the china closet, exclaiming "Just look what I spy! The Meissen sugar bowl and cream pitcher that Papa bought Mom from *Wien*. It belonged to a full tea service, you know. *Wien,* that's German for Vienna."

My father put down his shot glass. "I confess I'm very tired, Til. If we're going to discuss—"

My aunt gazed at the china closet and crooked a finger under her chin. "I believe Cath also has the Waterford pitcher that Papa purchased on that same trip," she mused. "Imagine—it's all that's left of Mama's treasures."

"Tilly, I appreciate your interest in keepsakes and old treasures," Dad said sharply, "but if you don't mind . . ."

There was a silence. Tilly came back to the table and sat down and I wondered why she had prattled on about the sugar and creamer. Was it because it was painful to talk about Mom's illness? If so, I understood.

She regarded my father docilely and asked, "Well, James, what did the doctors tell you?"

Dad patted her hand. "Sorry if I was abrupt just now. Most of the last two days I've been riding in ambulances and trains. It rubs the nerves raw."

"Of course, James."

Dad rubbed his jaw. "Let's see, now. The doctors estimate a

year's minimum. Total bed rest for at least six months. Can you picture old Cath, who never could sit still for two minutes—"

I didn't want to picture it or to hear what else the doctors had said. A year wasn't a short time, after all, and two pale-green inches of map were beyond any distance I could travel. Doctors and pronouncements had taken my mother away, and I didn't want to hear about them.

"It'll be a rough regime," Dad went on. "According to one doctor up there, the worst part of the treatment is the psychological effect on the patient."

"Dad, excuse me," I interrupted, and went over to his chair with the water-color drawings. "I was telling Aunt Tilly about my drawings. Look, I've completed six so far, and started on a seventh."

He looked at me. "*What?*"

I laid the drawings in front of him. "I copied them from magazines. Pictures help to cheer up a room, so I figured—"

"Fella, what sort of mind do you have?" he asked in amazement. "I come back from seeing your mother, and you chatter about drawings?" He pushed back his chair and stared at me with genuine mystification. "I don't understand what makes you tick. Perhaps you can explain it."

I looked back at him, and the dining room seemed to balloon in size while I grew smaller and smaller. "I guess it—it comes from being a violin," I said, because I could think of no other reply.

The others broke out in laughter. I noticed Aunt Tilly looking at me, then Dad resumed talking and I left the dining room. I stood in the front hall, not knowing where to go. It was like the night the hospital had called and Roseanne had held out the phone for me to take—no place to run and hide. I could hear Dad's worried tones drift from the dining room. I heard Aunt Tilly say, "About the money, James. You musn't worry about the money."

No place to run or hide. I listened to the rain on the roof. It wasn't coming down as hard, and so I wandered out the door and onto the rickety porch. The rain was splashing lightly on the rail, tracing wet fingers down the pillars.

I stood at the rail and looked out at Warbisher Street's dilapidated houses. I needed to use my mental eraser, wipe all the burdensome thoughts away. I lifted my face and let the drops of rain splatter over it as if to wash away the hard thoughts. The Valentine box was missing. Vanished, Margaret had said this morning. Where was it, where had it vanished? The rain washed the hard thoughts away. . . .

There was a sound behind me, a discreet clearing of throat. I turned and saw Aunt Tillybird in the doorway. She looked tired, as if the visit had already been too much for her.

"A violin . . . is that what you are?" she asked. "The most melodious of instruments."

I shook my head and didn't answer.

Hesitantly, she came over to the rail. The drawings were in her hand. "I gave water-color sets to each of the others on birthdays gone by," she said. "But I think you're the first to care about it, Robert."

I turned from her and looked out at the street again. For an instant, in the slanting rain, I seemed to glimpse a slight figure hurrying along with some grocery bundles. Then the image was gone and there was only the street and the rain and some tears on my face.

Standing behind me, Aunt Tilly said, "We'll make Cath well, I promise . . . Robbie, what do you do with your Saturdays?" she asked, after a pause.

"I—I—" The words wouldn't form.

"These drawings are quite good," she went on. "They show a feeling for color and line. Of course you're probably not interested enough, but—"

"But what?" I asked, turning back to her.

"Well, the first necessity for an aspiring artist—"

"Oh, I'm aspiring," I assured her. "I plan to *be* an artist, it so happens."

"Then surely you frequent the museums to view the great masters?" my aunt inquired.

I wiped my face with my sleeve. "I've never seen a great master."

138

The red curls bent over the drawings. "Yes, talented. How would you like to meet me next Saturday? We could do the Metropolitan. Oh, the Rembrandts there, the El Grecos!"

"The Metropolitan Museum in New York?" I said. "Over in the city?"

"Yes," she said. "Shall we ask your father about it?"

And that was how my life with Aunt Tilly began.

6

The Saturdays

The next week passed in a cloud because there was something happy to wait for at the end of it. Aunt Tilly had asked Dad about it, and he'd said, sure, a Saturday in the city would be good for me. He said he was definitely in favor of culture, and it was unfortunate that we had so little time for it in the family. Aunt Tilly was welcome to take me, he said, and so it was arranged.

New York lay across the river, no more than half an hour away on the subway, yet I had been there exactly twice: to the circus at Madison Square Garden one spring and another time to view Macy's windows at Christmas. My recollection of those outings was blurred—the tall lighted buildings, the crowded, jostling streets, the noise and motion, the whiff of hot chestnuts from a vendor's cart. I remembered going down the subway stairs after the Macy's expedition—the underground darkness and the subway train, clacking over the bridge to Brooklyn, taking with it the last vestiges of the twinkling lights. For me New York was merely the vast, scrambling metropolis to which my father went every morning to work and from which he rode home fatigued at night. But to listen to Aunt Tilly, the city offered glorious pursuits—museums and great paintings and culture, and I was to have a taste of it at last.

As the week went by, fear began to alternate with anticipation, and I grew worried that my aunt would either forget about her invitation or else phone and cancel it. Of the two possibilities, I decided I preferred the former, for then I could still show up at her apartment on Clark Street. I was to be allowed to take the trolley to Brooklyn Heights by myself, and if I arrived at her door, how could she send me back to Warbisher Street? Aunt Tilly couldn't do a cruel thing like that, not to a violin. But if she were to phone and cancel the invitation . . . No, no, she mustn't do that.

It was definitely arranged: come Saturday, she would take me to the city. All week long I talked about it to everybody within earshot. What was surprising was that no one regarded it as a great event excepting myself.

"Some thrill, old silly Tillybird hauling you around a museum," Roseanne said, without a trace of envy. I'd wanted her to be envious more than anybody, and she wasn't at all. "Now, if you were going over there to collect movie stars' autographs, or something exciting like that . . . ," she mused.

"What are movie stars' autographs compared to great paintings?"

"More fun," said Roseanne.

I pestered Margaret every day about ironing me a fresh white shirt to wear on the journey. "I can't visit the Metropolitan Musseum looking like a bum," I said, following Margaret from room to room while she cleaned the house. "They might throw me out if I look bummy."

"Don't worry, Robbie." She ran the carpet sweeper over the living room carpet. "You'll have a clean white shirt, I promise."

I watched the carpet sweeper trundle back and forth. "You ever been to the Metropolitan Museum?"

"Just to the Brooklyn Museum, with my class in sophomore year."

"What did you make of it?"

"A lot of naked Greek statues. Please, can't you stop talking for a minute?"

Every night after dinner I consulted Dad about the outing and rehearsed the trolley-car directions with him.

"First, I go with Dan and he puts me on the Broadway trolley," I recited, getting up from the table as Dad rose. "Then I change to the DeKalb Avenue trolley and ask the conductor to let me off at Borough Hall. Then I ask a policeman to direct me to Clark Street—"

Dad was headed for the morris chair. "I think you have it down pat, Rob."

I stood in front of the morris chair as he sat down in it. "When I come to Clark Street, Aunt Tilly's apartment is a block away from the St. George Hotel."

He picked up the *World-Telegram.* "That's the ticket."

"Maybe I ought to repeat it once more, to make sure," I said. "First, I go with Dan and he puts me on the Broadway trolley—"

My father winced. "I really think you know it by heart, fella."

There was nobody I didn't talk to about it—Sister Francis Liguori at school, Hymie at the candy store, Mr. Fritzle next door. Mr. Fritzle was a trolley conductor on the DeKalb Avenue run, and I told him, "I'll be riding the DeKalb Avenue trolley on Saturday. What if I happened to get on your car?"

"I got Saturday off this week," he told me, putting an end to that particular fancy.

By Thursday, with only two more nights to go, Aunt Tilly still hadn't phoned to cancel the outing, and I waited in apprehension for the phone to ring all evening. It was preferable if it didn't ring, I reminded myself, because maybe Aunt Tilly had only forgotten about the date. Or maybe I ought to phone *her,* all friendly and polite and eager—which was the best policy? I went looking for my father for advice. Margaret was at the sideboard in the dining room, putting away the tablecloth.

"Where's Dad?" I asked her.

"It certainly is strange," she sighed. "That box of photos still hasn't turned up. I can't think where else to look. . . . He's down in the cellar."

I went to the cellar stairs, but stopped halfway down and peered over toward the coal bin, where my father was busy repairing one of the kitchen chairs. A leg had come loose and he was gluing it back on, but I wasn't looking at that. My eyes traveled past him to the pyramid of old discarded objects that filled the storage bin at the back. An old sled, a broken lamp and cracked mirror, rusty ice skates—and in the center, covered by a sheet, the wicker baby buggy that had been purchased when Vinny was born and used by each of us in infancy. Its outline bulged under the sheet, the wheels peeped out from the bottom like round black eyes. It was Roseanne who'd once remarked that the buggy would make a neat hiding place.

The stairs creaked, and Dad turned around, a bottle of glue in his hand. "Yes, fella, what is it?"

I didn't go down the rest of the stairs. "Aunt Tilly hasn't phoned or anything about Saturday—do you think I should phone her?" I asked.

He turned his attention to the chair. "I doubt if you need to, Robbie. If you're worried that she's forgotten—"

"Okay, if you think I don't need to." I glanced once more at the outline under the white sheet, then I hurried back up the stairs.

On Friday school lasted a hundred years, and the three-o'clock bell clanged as if it were heralding Christmas. I roller-skated up and down Warbisher Street all afternoon, then skated over to the library to look at the picture books. If Aunt Tilly called to cancel the trip, I didn't want to be home to answer the phone.

I sat on the porch steps and didn't go inside the house until Margaret came home from Woolworth's at six. I'd saved a task to keep me occupied—wrapping the water-color drawings for mailing to Greenvale and writing a letter to tuck inside the package.

My mother wasn't permitted as yet to write any letters home. Dad had explained that bed rest meant exactly that: lying in bed and doing nothing at all. But he had said that each of us was to write Catherine at least one letter a week—and he didn't want to hear of anybody falling down on the job. After the drawings were wrapped I sat down at the dining table and began my third letter of the week.

I carefully tore out a sheet of ruled paper from my copybook to use as stationery. *How are you?* I began. *How is the bed rest coming along? It must be boring. Can you see the trees and lake from your cottage? I hope you can.*

Guess what's in this package, I went on. *Seven water-color drawings done by my own hand. You can put them on your wall. If you can't see the trees and lake from your bed, it will be nice to look at the drawings instead.*

It was best to write the words down fast and not think about

Catherine lying sick, so far away. It was best just to keep scribbling until the page was filled. *Aunt Tilly is taking me to the Metropolitan Museum in New York tomorrow*, I continued. *So far she hasn't called it off, and Dad says he doubts if she's forgotten about it. I don't know why I'm looking forward to it so much.*

When are you coming home, Catherine? I wanted to ask. Oh, Mama, until you come home the house stays dark and feels so empty. *I'll tell you about the museum and everything in my next letter*, I finished up, racing my pen over the lines. *Trust you will enjoy the drawings. Please forgive mistakes in spelling, etc. Your son, Robbie the Artist.*

The phone rang as I was addressing the brown-paper package. "It's Aunt Tilly," Margaret called in from the hall. "She wants to speak to you, Rob."

I wrote out the post-box number of the sanatorium, the pen wavering.

"Rooobbie, it's Aunt Tilly."

Very carefully I got up from the table and went into the hall. I took the phone from my sister without comment and waited until she had gone through the archway. "Yes, Aunt Tilly?" I said into the mouthpiece.

A pause, then the ginger-ale voice bubbled and fizzed in my ear. " 'Lo, there, Robbie, how's tricks?"

"F-fine," I stammered. "Tricks are fine."

There was another agonizing pause. "About tomorrow, *mon cher* . . . Is our engagement still on? That's to say, if you'd prefer to call it off . . ."

I hung onto the phone in a flood of relief. "Call it off?" I said. "Oh, no, Aunt Tillybird, I'm counting on it."

The ginger ale bubbled over. "I, too, Robbie. Yes, counting on it!"

The fresh white shirt draped over the back of my chair was the first thing I glimpsed as I blinked awake on Saturday morning. Lemon sunlight poured through the window—I'd prayed that it wouldn't rain. Dan's and Vinny's beds were already empty . . . and on my chair I saw the white shirt.

I hastened to the bathroom to wash, although I'd given myself a thorough soaking the night before. I plastered down my hair with Vinny's bottle of Stacomb, so that the cowlick wouldn't stick up in back. Back in the bedroom, I pulled on my blue serge Sunday knickers, which Margaret had also pressed for me; my hands shook so that I could hardly button the shirt or get into the serge jacket.

Dan had put out one of his sporty ties for me to wear. He'd said last night that I couldn't go into the city wearing my rotten ink-stained St. A's tie, and he'd picked me out a sharp blue number with zigzags of purple in it. The tie was much too long, but I solved it by stuffing the ends in my knickers. I didn't look at all bad in the mirror. Aunt Tilly wouldn't have cause to be ashamed.

Dad, Vinny and Daniel were finishing up breakfast when I entered the kitchen. Dad reached in his jacket and gave me twenty-five cents to spend in the city. "Treat old Tilly to a beer, why don't you," he joked.

He left for work with Vinny, and Daniel allowed me to have a sip of his coffee, despite Margaret's loud objections.

"If he's big enough for his first solo trolley ride, he's big enough for coffee," Dan said firmly.

The coffee tasted delicious, I thought.

When it was time to leave, my brother walked down Warbisher Street with me, and we waited at the corner trolley stop under the Broadway El. Bohack's, Schmierman's Bakery, Al's Hardware, Hymie's, Jay's Outlet and most of the other shops were open, and the neighborhood ladies were already out in force, intent on their weekend bargains. I looked at the string of shops and at the flats above the store windows—the cracked shades, the flower pots perched on ledges, the sagging fire escapes and grimy brick facades. This neighborhood, these streets, were the only part of the world I had known. But today I was venturing forth on a journey to other places. My heart turned over at the enormity of it.

"Why, hello there, boys." Mrs. Raylman from Warbisher Street came waddling across the sidewalk, a mesh shopping bag over her arm. "My goodness, Robbie, you're all dressed up. You must be going somewheres," she observed.

An El train rattled over the tracks above. "I'm going to New York, to the Metropolitan Museum," I shouted over the clatter.

Mrs. Raylman frowned in disapproval. "A museum, on a lovely, sunny day like this? You ought to be out in the fresh air. It's not healthy."

The train rattled away. "I—I guess so," I said.

"Well, enjoy yourself. Morning, Daniel."

There was a clang, a hiss of sparks, a grinding of wheels, and the red-and-yellow Broadway trolley came sailing into view at the turn of the tracks. Dan signaled with his hand and the trolley began slowing down.

"Now, you got the instructions straight?" he demanded, in a last-minute quiz.

"The Broadway trolley to DeKalb—ask for a transfer—then I take the DeKalb to Borough Hall, and—"

Brakes shrieking, the trolley jerked to a halt in front of us. A bell clanged, the front doors sprang open, and a wooden footstep unfolded itself magically. "Hop on," Daniel said, boosting me onto the footstep. He shoved some coins in my hand and stepped back. "Here, buy something on me—and have a good time!" he yelled.

"I will," I shouted back, and the doors snapped shut. The bell clanged, and the trolley lurched away in a Fourth of July shower of sparks. I held onto the rail over the coin box and waved until, with another wild lurch, we rounded another turn, and Daniel was lost from view.

I deposited a nickel in the coin box, asked the motorman for a transfer, then groped my way up the swaying aisle to a seat. Nothing could beat riding on a trolley for excitement! The noisy clang of it, the wheels grinding over the tracks, sparks shooting off at each stop and start—nothing could top it! The wooden seat bucketed and shook with each turn and lurch—and I was alone, riding off to adventure all by myself.

The DeKalb Avenue trolley was even bigger and noisier than the Broadway one, and it carried a conductor as well as a motorman. The conductor went up and down the aisle collecting fares and tearing off transfers from a thick pad attached to his belt. He held a coin machine, which made a click as each oncoming passenger inserted a nickel into it. The conductor pulled a rope as we approached each trolley stop, and the rope caused the bell to clang. Before the trolley could start off again the rope had to be yanked in signal, thus providing another splendid clang.

The blocks sped past, and the look of the neighborhood began to change. The tenements gave way to rows of brownstones, then blocks of commercial buildings—auto showrooms, warehouses, offices, and the busy intersections of Flatbush and Atlantic Avenues—neon signs, crisscrossing of El tracks, the RKO Albee and Paramount, subway entrances on every corner. The trolley swung into Fulton Street and thundered past the shops and department stores of downtown Brooklyn. Taxis flashed by, bright yellow in the sun; herds of other trolleys whizzed along the tracks, in a Fourth of July of sparks.

"Borough Hall, last stop," the conductor bawled out, pulling at the rope. I was the first passenger to step onto the sidewalk, but then some of the excitement began to lessen. I stood on the foreign street corner and almost wished I were back in my own neighborhood—at least it was a familiar one.

But these strange new surroundings . . . I backed into a doorway to get my bearings. A policeman stood on the corner, chatting with an old woman who was selling papers at a stand, a scarf tied under her chin. I approached the newsstand and stood waiting until the policeman took notice of me.

"Help you, sonny?"

"Excuse me, officer," I said, twice more polite than Oliver Twist, "but I have to get to my aunt's on Clark Street."

"Clark Street, is it?" He slapped a thick arm on my shoulder, escorted me to the curb, and pointed across the wide plaza of Borough Hall with his nightstick. "Over you go that way, sonny. Straight ahead for three blocks. Left you turn, and two blocks more will bring you to Clark Street and your aunt's."

"Thank you, officer."

"Straight ahead for three blocks, then turn left for two blocks—"

"Yes, sir."

The directions were simple to follow. I crossed over the plaza, went along for a block, and realized that I was in Brooklyn Heights. The houses that lined the quiet street were old, but it wasn't like the oldness of Warbisher Street. Old in my neighborhood meant dingy and falling apart. In Brooklyn Heights it meant beautiful. The prim, gracious brownstones had lace curtains at the windows, polished brass doorknobs, and window boxes abloom with geraniums. There were dress shops, restaurants and hotels interspersed among the houses, and even the grocery stores that I passed were different. One grocery store had nothing but boxes of English biscuits tiered in the window, with a little sign that read, *Huntley and Palmer, Special Today.*

Aunt Tilly's apartment on Clark Street was a block down from the St. George Hotel. I knew it was the correct building because the address was painted on the dark-green canopy that shaded the brass-doored entrance. A Negro doorman in a green uniform was standing under the canopy, and he watched me slow to a halt and stare up at the address.

"You the nephew, I bet," he said, taking me by surprise.

"Pardon?"

"I said, is you the nephew." He grinned. "Miss Quinlan told me to keep an eye out for you."

"Yes, she's my aunt." I nodded.

"Right on the button, aren't you?" He flashed some white teeth and whisked open the brass doors. "She's waitin' for you in the lobby."

Nobody had ever held a door open for me, unless you were to count the doorman at Loew's Gates.

"Thank you," I said, and went inside.

The lobby was small and dim and quiet, and Aunt Tilly was perched on a chintz-covered chair in the corner. She was wearing a pale-colored dress and a straw hat with dotted veiling on the red curls, and the gauzy scarf at her throat fluttered as she rose to greet me. But what I noticed as I went toward my aunt across the lobby was the look in her blue eyes. It was an anxious look, as though she wasn't entirely sure I would be glad to see her. Perhaps people didn't often act glad when they saw Aunt Tilly.

"Greetings, Robbie." She stood up, her hand delicately extended, and said in surprise, "You found your way here!" as though no one had ever bothered to find her before.

The IRT subway train rocketed through the tunnel under the river, setting up a roar that made Aunt Tilly tremble. Gamely she gripped the seat next to me, and kept her skirts fastened down.

"Been to the city twice in your life?" she repeated in astonishment. "But Warbisher Street is only half an hour away. And never once set foot in the Metropolitan?"

The motion of the train rocked her back and forth, like a rag doll in a buggy. "We must plan our day for the best effect," she said. "I know! We'll start by getting out at Twenty-third Street."

"What's at Twenty-third Street?" I asked.

"You'll see," answered my aunt cryptically.

We got off the train at the Twenty-third Street station, and Aunt Tilly resolutely picked her way past the litter on the stairs. "Come, *mon cher*," she bade me as we emerged into the street.

Twenty-third Street was lined on both sides with warehouses and grim office structures, and I didn't see how it could hold any interest for Aunt Tilly. "Follow along," she said, her scarf billowing out. We walked along until we reached Fifth Avenue, and there, trundling up and down the wide thoroughfare, looking like amiable elephants rearing up in the midst of traffic, were yellow and green double-decker buses.

"The only proper way to approach uptown," declared Aunt Tilly.

"Are we taking a double-decker bus?" I asked excitedly.

"All the way up to the Metropolitan," Aunt Tilly said, but it was several moments before she determined in which direction uptown lay. She turned this way and that and made clicking sounds with her tongue.

"Uptown is to our left," she finally concluded. "To the right, you see, is Greenwich Village—one can glimpse the tip of the Washington Square arch. So picturesque, the Village—I'll take you there another time. Come, *mon petit*."

I followed her across Fifth Avenue to the uptown stop, and she waved imperiously for a double-decker bus to take us aboard. The shiny, ridiculous vehicle halted, we scrambled onto the rear platform and up the narrow curve of stairs to the top deck.

"A front seat—oh, the view is incomparable from there," exclaimed Aunt Tilly, guiding me up the swaying aisle to the front of the bus. A window glass shielded the front seat from the wind, but nevertheless Aunt Tilly's scarf blew madly, and she had to employ a hand to anchor the straw hat. "What a feast is in store for you," she cried as the glorious oversized contraption trundled uptown.

The wonders of the trolley-car ride quickly faded away. Fifth Avenue in the dappled May sunshine was a sight whose magnificence I could not have imagined. It was a canyon, formed by cliffs of towering buildings, that extended uptown as far as the eye could follow. Flags waved from every building, it seemed, bright-hued banners that heralded some special holiday declared just for us. I twisted round in my seat, craned my neck, gawked, gaped and ogled, while Aunt Tilly, shouting above the traffic din, provided a running commentary on the sights that rolled past.

"There's the Empire State Building," she said, pointing. "How it gleams in the sun—can't even see the top. Alfred E. Smith, our former governor, is chairman of the board, you know—a fitting position for a great American. And here are the shops—there's McCreery's, to your left, and just look at the gorgeous Altman windows. There's Best's ahead, and Lord and Taylor, Franklin Simon, Arnold Constable—have you ever seen such a wealth of stores?"

The bus rolled past the Public Library at Forty-second Street, and she pointed out the stone lions that guarded the entrance. Up the Avenue we went, and, as though they were personal possessions, Aunt Tilly gestured at Rockefeller Center and Cartier's and the gothic spires of St. Patrick's Cathedral. The elegant maroon mansion on the corner belonged, she said, to Mrs. Vanderbilt. "Personally, I find her a bit stuffy," she added, with a tug at her hat.

The bus went on, and still the marvels continued, a kaleidoscope of color, motion, clamor—the department-store windows, the taxis and autos, the traffic lights winking red and green, the crowds of people that surged along the wide pavements and poured in and out of the shops. Green trees poked into sight, a splashing fountain in a square—"The Plaza Hotel, Central Park," Aunt Tilly trumpeted. "Notice, if you will, the horse-drawn carriages for hire, *so* charming. And over to your right is the distinguished University Club . . . or is it the Metropolitan?" She put a finger to her lips. "Which is it? Well, an imposing edifice, at any rate." Her scarf flew; the wind rippled the straw hat. "These are the Fifth Avenue apartments and homes of the wealthy—millionaires' row. There's the Central Park Zoo—do you see it behind the trees? We'll go to the zoo one Saturday and feed those whimsical creatures, the seals."

At Eighty-second Street we left the front-row seat, descended the curving stairs, and stepped from the bus. Aunt Tilly dashed into the street, so eager to cross to the other side that a car almost knocked her down.

"Are you all right?" I asked, helping her back to the curb.

"Not even scratched," she assured me, brushing at her skirt. Grandly she gestured at the building opposite that rose in royal splendor above the trees, as magnificent as any palace.

"It's the Metropolitan Museum," my aunt said softly, as though referring to a holy cathedral.

"Hey, lady, you crossin' or what?" barked a rude voice from behind us. It belonged to a huge, beet-faced man who was evidently impatient to cross the street. "Well, yuh planning to spend the day there?" he demanded.

Aunt Tilly gave a bubbly laugh and bowed to him. "A thousand pardons, sir. Proceed ahead, by all means." He stumped past us, and she whispered, "Such colorful individualists in the city. *Les types,* as the French would say." Then once more she gazed at the museum.

"Do you know what the Metropolitan is, Robert? A world treasure house of culture and art," she said solemnly.

"It sure is big," I said. "Imagine, I never even saw it before."

"Yes . . . and today marks a first time for me as well." She turned and looked at me, her eyes blue and misty. "It's the very first time I've had a companion to bring along. I've always had to come here alone."

Then, taking my hand, she led me across Fifth Avenue to the world treasure house of culture and art.

That excursion with Aunt Tilly to the city was repeated the following Saturday, and the one after that. Half an hour from Warbisher Street was another world, whose existence I had not known about, and I required no coaxing to hasten toward it at every opportunity. It puzzled the rest of the family, for no one could figure out what attraction either the city or Aunt Tilly held for me.

"She's so damned loony," Daniel said when I returned wonder-struck from the first Saturday excursion. "Aside from Yankee Stadium, you can have New York."

"We rode up Fifth Avenue in a double-decker bus," I told him, and then went running to Margaret to relay the same news. "A double-*decker* bus, Margaret. It's better than trolley cars, no fooling."

Trolley cars, Margaret said, made her queasy. "I understand they're replacing 'em with buses soon. Personally, I can't wait. That awful clang."

After supper that first Saturday I sat drugged in the living room, visualizing the paintings that had glowed like jewels from the walls of the Metropolitan. "They have so many paintings there," I informed my father, "you could go there every day for two months and still not see them all."

"Where's this?" he asked.

"The Metropolitan Museum."

"So you had a good time, huh?" He held a match to his pipe. "Did you buy Tilly a beer, like I said?"

"I honestly can't picture her drinking beer," I said. "She bought me a lemonade at Schrafft's. She says I can go with her next Saturday, if I want."

Roseanne looked up from her book, unable to believe her ears.

"You don't intend to pal around museums with old Tilly? You can't be serious."

I got up loftily from the sofa. "I already said I'd come. Next Saturday at her apartment at ten. It has a doorman."

"Wow—Mrs. Astorbilt in person."

The next Saturday I started out from Warbisher Street half an hour early and had to dawdle around Borough Hall to use up the spare time. When I arrived at the green canopy on Clark Street the doorman recognized me right away. Horace, he told me his name was.

"She's waitin' for you, skipper," he said, and held open the brass doors.

It was on the second visit, I remember, that I wondered why Aunt Tilly waited in the lobby for me, rather than upstairs in her apartment. She was perched on the same chintz-covered chair, and it occurred to me that the more natural thing would be for her to wait upstairs. She was dressed this time in blue, and she rose to greet me with the same questioning look in her eyes.

"*Comment allez-vous?*" she said, extending her hand.

It was her announced plan to give me a French lesson each Saturday, and we had already embarked on the program. "*Très bien, merci. Et vous, madame?*" I recited for her.

She beamed approval, a feather bobbed on her hat, a strong scent of perfume wafted toward me, and she appeared to be even more animated than usual. Gaily she took my arm and tossed a jaunty "*Au revoir*" at Horace as we sailed out the door.

But when we passed a school building on the way to the subway the gaiety left her face. She paused at the curb and stared across at the ancient red-brick building that squatted behind an ugly iron fence.

"Not what we'd call distinguished architecture, is it?" she said, her eyes fixed on the building.

"Do you teach in a school like that, Aunt Tilly?" I asked.

"I teach . . . in a prison like that," she said faintly, then drew herself up, as if she hadn't intended the remark. "In life, we must make do with what is given us, Robbie." The moment was gone, and we continued along the street, but perhaps it was why we didn't go to the museum that Saturday. Outside the Clark Street subway entrance Aunt Tilly bought a *Times* at the newsstand and hurriedly turned the pages.

"Here we are, ship news," she said, "—arrivals and departures," and folded back the page. "Have you ever been to a sailing, Robbie? What am I asking—of course you haven't. Look, the *Normandie* departs at two!"

"Can you go to a sailing?" I asked.

"Just wait till you see!"

We got off at the Times Square station that day and came up into a dazzle of electric signs, giant billboards, and blazing movie marquees. Tommy Dorsey and his orchestra were appearing in person at Warner's Strand, and Benny Goodman's name shone in lights from the marquee of the Paramount. There were hot-dog and coconut-drink stands, penny arcades, souvenir stores, and about a million people teeming along the sidewalks.

Aunt Tilly led me to a bus stop. The crosstown bus would take us directly to the French Line piers, she explained, getting out some coins from her purse for the fare. "It's the most thrilling thing in the world, a transatlantic sailing," she said.

We rode the bus west along Forty-ninth Street, past tenements, rooming houses, and shabby hotels with *Transient* signs hung over the doorways. The bus turned, and suddenly, looming up directly in front of us, were three mammoth red smokestacks and a towering ship's mast that seemed to pierce the sky. The giant ocean liner *Normandie* was moored at her pier.

"Oh," I said, gaping open-mouthed, as we stood across from the pier.

"I told you," beamed Aunt Tilly. She took my hand and we threaded through the jam-up of traffic. "I've crossed the Atlantic eighteen times. What a tonic a sea voyage can be to aching nerves. Come, we'll go up onto the pier."

A line of autos and taxis stretched out from the pier entrance, and baggage was piled everywhere. Porters in blue smocks hurried to unload still more baggage from the taxis and autos, while delivery boys, carrying flowers and baskets of fruit, hastened through the entrance. Passengers alighted from the cars, the ladies with corsages pinned to their coats, the men laden with cameras and binoculars. As we approached the entrance a tangy smell of the sea blended with the porters' shouts, taxi horns, and babble of voices.

Aunt Tilly and I joined the throng that pressed onto the escalator leading to the upper pier level. There more pandemonium reigned as passengers, visitors, and Western Union messengers surged down the long shed and converged on the gangplanks that jutted from the side of the *Normandie*. The huge shape of the liner towered above the shed's roof and stretched beyond the end of the pier, several city blocks in length.

"We must seek the visitor's gangway," Aunt Tilly said with the air of a seasoned traveler. "It's generally located aft, I believe."

Visitors' tickets cost twenty-five cents and were being sold at the foot of one of the gangplanks. She purchased two tickets, and I followed her up the awninged gangway and onto the deck of the *Normandie*.

"*Alors*, we are in France," proclaimed my aunt, indicating the broad sweep of glass-enclosed deck. She went over and engaged a white-jacketed steward in conversation. "Ah, *monsieur. Permittez-moi, s'il vous plaît—*" she began.

Unfortunately the steward didn't understand Aunt Tilly's French too well. "*Pardon, madame? Pardon?*" he kept repeating, until finally she gave up and escorted me along the deck.

"The fellow is doubtless a *Breton*," she confided. "Undoubtedly he speaks a rough patois and is unaccustomed to authentic Parisian. Shall we begin our tour?"

We stepped through a doorway and found ourselves in a glittering high-ceilinged room. "*Voila, le salon de thé,*" she said. "One comes here for afternoon refreshments and to gaze out at the panorama of the sea."

She led me through lounges and smoking rooms, libraries and dining rooms. We trotted up and down a dozen stairways and along a maze of corridors and companionways, from which we could see into the luxurious cabins, where *bon voyage* parties were being celebrated with champagne glasses and laughter. We climbed to the top deck and stared up at the *Normandie*'s three tremendous red and black funnels. We explored the sun decks, descended more gangways, until at last we stood at the stern, resting our arms on the railing.

The wind snapped at the feathers on Aunt Tilly's hat, and she gazed in silence at the tugboats in the river below. "I remember my first sailing," she said. "It was on the *Rochambeau,* a dear little vessel, and I was a young schoolteacher, excited beyond telling. . . ."

She leaned against the rail, and her eyes grew soft and distant. "I shared a cabin with two charming sisters from Buffalo, who also were teachers," she went on. "What a gay crossing we had! Wine every night at dinner and dancing afterward. I met a young Italian professor, who was en route to Firenze. . . . What became of him, I wonder?"

My aunt stared out at the harbor. "Summer after summer, all the voyages since . . ." Her shoulders trembled, as if from a gust of wind. "The *Paris,* the *Berengaria,* the *Majestic* . . . all the voyages, all gone . . . ," she said, and her voice trailed off, and she followed the arc of a sea gull across the sky.

I said, "You'll be sailing back to Europe again soon. This summer probably. School ends in another month and—"

"No, not this summer, Robbie," she said.

"But why not, Aunt Tilly?"

The ship's whistle gave an ear-splitting blast, which was followed by a voice blaring over the loudspeaker. "All visitors ashore, please. All visitors ashore."

The sudden noise startled Aunt Tilly. She turned from the rail and looked around the deck. "Is it time to leave? Oh, Robbie, it's always—" Another blast of whistle drowned her out, then we made our way back to the gangplank on the promenade deck. We stepped onto the pier, and my aunt turned and cast a lingering glance backward toward the deck.

We were among the last visitors to leave the pier that sailing. We went out to the pier's end and stood at the rail in order to watch the *Normandie* depart. Other visitors gradually joined us until there was a full crowd shouting and waving at the passengers who stood lining the ship's rails.

"Wave to someone," Aunt Tilly said, lifting her arm. "There might be a passenger alone, with no one to wish her a *bon voyage*," and we both proceeded to wave vigorously at the decks. A band struck up a tune, confetti and paper streamers curled down from the rails, the whistle gave a series of mighty blasts, and slowly the gigantic liner slid from the pier. Tugboats guided her out into midstream, they pushed at the bow until it was pointed toward the sea. *"Bon voyage,"* cried Aunt Tilly, to no one at all.

She grasped the rail and watched the *Normandie*'s slowly receding silhouette glide down the river. Most of the visitors were leaving, but not Aunt Tilly.

"I thought you went to Europe every summer," I said.

She looked blankly at me for a moment. "Not this summer. I must save my pennies," she said.

It didn't make sense, and I stared up at her. "Save your pennies for what?"

"A chance I have," she answered, "perhaps a last chance"—which puzzled me even more.

By the time we emerged from the pier the sun had disappeared behind the clouds, turning the afternoon chilly and gray. I snuggled against my aunt while we waited for the bus. Another Saturday was almost over, and I understood why I had come to cherish them so.

The Saturdays with Aunt Tilly were all I had.

7
The Empty Dragon

In between the Saturdays were the other days of the week, needing to be lived through. School, and walking back to the empty house in the afternoon. Roller skating or thumbing through books at the library; sitting on the porch steps to wait for Margaret or Dan to get home. Supper, homework, going upstairs to bed. Yet in the dreary routine of those days, unexpectedly, I found something.

Tillybird had always been my aunt, but I had never really known her. Now it was to happen a second time, this same out-of-the-blue discovery of another person. It was Hanna who was responsible for it. At least she set in motion the events that led to the discovery.

Hanna, of course, didn't come on Thursdays anymore. It was June, and we hadn't seen her since April. Then one afternoon, as I entered the front hall with my schoolbag, a spicy aroma came drifting from the kitchen, accompanied by a lilting snatch of German song.

"Hanna!" I raced through the dining room, dropping my schoolbag en route. At the swinging door I hesitated only a moment, then I went hurrying over the blue-and-white tiles. "Hanna, you came to see us!"

The strapping figure turned from the stove, the strong arms lifted me up in a bear hug. "How iss my Robbie? I vurk today by Mrs. McGinty on Putnam Avenue, finish ups early, so I come here." She still smelled of soap and starch and fresh-washed clothes. "Ach, so skinny yet," she clucked, releasing me. "How iss rest of family?"

"We're okay. It's good to see you, Hanna."

She nodded and went back to the iron pot on the stove. "I make noodles and chicken for supper, fill you up good. Sits down, I fix you sandwich." She opened the refrigerator and began her delvings. "Pliss, tell me. How is my lady?"

I sat at the white table and told her about Catherine while she fixed me a sandwich of cold leftover lamb. "She's gained weight, but she still can't do anything except lie in bed. Can't even write letters—the nurse has to do it—but we write plenty to her."

"All day lie in bed? Poor lady."

"I made her some water-color drawings and she put them up on her wall. The nurse said it cheered her up."

Hanna spread mayonnaise lavishly on the bread. "Soon you go see her, maybe."

"Well . . ." I traced my finger over the blue flowers on the oilcloth. "You have to be eighteen to visit Greenvale, so that lets out everybody except Vinny. Anyway, Dad couldn't afford the train fare for all of us."

Hanna carried the sandwich to the table. "Never mind, it not be so long."

"Dad's going up there next week. He might take Vinny with him."

It was almost the same again, sitting in the kitchen and talking cozily to someone. I took a bite of the sandwich.

"And just as you say, Hanna, it won't be long. Mom's already been away for two months almost. In July it'll be three months— and by Christmas we'll only have three more months to wait."

Hanna poured me a glass of milk. "It goes fast, the time."

"Christmas is what we're aiming for," I went on. "Dad says our real present will be Mom, except the department store will have to hold her till April for delivery." *Christmas . . . six more months.* I lowered the sandwich on the plate, not hungry anymore. It was better not to think about it. "Did you know that Margaret's been made assistant head of the housewares department at Woolworth's?"

Hanna stirred the big pot on the stove. "Und take care of house too. She iss vunderful girl."

"So we're all getting along." I rubbed my hand over the oilcloth. "Hey, I forgot to tell you about my Saturdays, Hanna. Every Saturday I meet my Aunt Tilly, Mom's sister, and—"

The door slammed in the hall and there was no need to guess who it was.

"Hanna!" a voice squawked, and the next moment Roseanne came barreling through the swinging door. She looked her usual messy self. Her school blouse was wrinkled, the hem of her skirt dipped over her scratched-up knees, and her arms poked skinnily from her blouse. She dropped her books smack on the tiles and threw herself at Hanna. "The instant I caught a delicious whiff in the hall I knew it was you, Hanna."

"Roseanne! So tall you are."

"Second tallest in my class—I'm graduating this month, you know. We're making long white organdy dresses to wear." My sister stood back and struck a pose. "Notice anything different?"

Hanna studied her for a moment. "Ach, the pigtails!" she gasped.

"Discarded!" Roseanne swung the long ratty hair that now hung below her shoulders, straight as straw. "Mom always promised I could have it cut at Mr. Pierre's for graduation. Just two more weeks to wait."

"But iss sin to cut such hair," Hanna said disapprovingly. "You must not, Roseanne."

"You mean, keep it the same?" Roseanne gave a hard, jerky laugh and twisted a strand of the awful hair. "Yeah, I look adorable this way. Exactly like the picture of Precious Darling on Mom's bottle of shampoo."

She tossed her head and went to the stove, where she dipped a finger into the pot of chicken and noodles. "*Deee*licious. How've you been, Hanna? Tell us how Emil's getting on."

"That dish is for supper," I said.

Hanna retrieved the schoolbooks from the floor. "Still at the garage, that Emil. He learning to be fine mechanic. Has girl friend, name of Gwendolyn."

Trying to act cute and smart-alecky, Roseanne helped herself to another finger of stew. "Girl friend? Let me at her. Emil's my idea of a Nordic god." She wandered to the icebox, poured herself a glass of milk.

"*Ja*, thank Gott we not in Germany," Hanna said. "With them Nazis, Emil get caught in middle."

Roseanne downed the milk and didn't even bother to wipe off the ring of white on her mouth. "I'd love to be caught in a war. It'd be thrilling." She went to the cupboard and hoisted herself onto the counter.

"Hey, what are you doing?" I asked.

"What do you mean, what am I doing? You have eyes, don'tcha?" Hair streaming behind her, she balanced her knees precariously on the counter and reached up toward the shelf.

It was precisely how the Waterford pitcher had been broken. I hadn't snitched, and since nobody had discovered it was missing yet, Roseanne obviously was getting careless again. "Some people never learn," I said, "no matter how many valuables they break."

Her hand drew back. "Oh, yeah, that little episode . . ." She laughed.

"I guess some people need to be snitched on to teach them a lesson. Which reminds me, I still haven't named my price."

"Beeswax." Roseanne reached for the crackers anyway, helped herself to a handful, and shoved the box back on the shelf. "People," she said, hopping down and scooping up her books, "shouldn't threaten other people who are smarter than them. Excuse me, but it's time for my bath."

"Bath?" I called after her. "You took a bath yesterday"—and in answer the door swung shut in my face. "Oh, how I hate that Roseanne," I muttered.

Hanna was at the stove, adding some more seasoning to the chicken and noodles. "When Margaret come home, tell her cook slow for couple of hours," she said. "I must go."

I kicked savagely at the door. "Did you hear me? I hate, loathe and despise Roseanne Connerty. I hope her pigtails strangle her."

"*Ja*." Hanna nodded, unperturbed, and that might have been the end of it. I might never have made my discovery if Hanna hadn't decided that day to scrub the kitchen tiles before she left.

"At least I can do that much for my lady," she clucked, viewing the lusterless state of the floor. Off came her hat, down went her satchel. Rolling up her sleeves, she brewed a pail of steaming water and soap and attacked the tiles vigorously. Upstairs water was running in the bathtub, and Roseanne could be heard singing over the flow of the water.

Lunge-and-back, lunge-and-back, went Hanna's mop. "Poor Margaret, with no one to help make house spic-spic," she fussed. "Don't worry, soon I come again and clean whole place."

It wasn't her scrubbing of the tiles that resulted in my discovery. It was to lead to it, though, when, true to her word, Hanna came back for the promised cleaning session. But that was still two weeks away; in the meanwhile Dad went to Greenvale.

He took the overnight train the following weekend, and Vinny went with him. It meant the loss of a day's work for both of them, and to save money they went up on the Friday-night train and came straight back the following evening. It saved them the cost of staying overnight in Greenvale, though it left them only a handful of hours to spend with Mom. Dad said that even a single hour would be worth the trip, for Catherine had not seen any of us since he'd brought her to the sanatorium.

So Dad and Vinny left on the Friday-night train, and the next day I went with Aunt Tilly to New York. She took me to the Frick Museum that Saturday, we attended a chamber music concert in the museum solarium, and the paintings were sumptuous and beautiful. But all I could think of was Greenvale and my father and brother at the hospital, actually visiting with Mom. Talking to her, seeing her face, being able to touch her even. Lately there'd been moments when I couldn't summon up anymore a picture of her.

When I got back to Warbisher Street from the city that Saturday Margaret was smiling and excited. Dad had phoned before getting on the New York train and had reported that Mom's condition was greatly improved.

"He said she looks like a different person," Margaret told me.

"Different from what?" I said, crestfallen. "I never want her to look any different."

She went around the living room, straightening the antimacassars. "He said the color's back in her face and she's gained weight. The doctors think it might not take a whole year before she's cured."

I stared at Margaret from the archway. *"Honest?"*

"That's what Dad said."

"She might be home in time for Christmas?"

"It's a possibility." Margaret fussed with a new lamp, which had a crack in the frilly shade. She turned it so that the cracked part faced the wall. The lamp was another of her acquisitions from the damaged stock at Woolworth's, which Mr. Fergus allowed the employees to purchase at a nominal cost. Hardly a week passed that Margaret didn't bring home some battered item or other—a chipped tea tray, a discolored satin cushion, a broken pipe rack. The house was steadily taking on the appearance of a basement rummage sale.

She stepped back and admired the new lamp. "The shade originally had a stunning velvet bow right here"—she indicated a tear in the material—"but it fell off unfortunately."

The sound of singing floated down from upstairs. "If you stand away far enough, you can't notice the tear," I said. "I guess we shouldn't count on Mom being home by Chritsmas."

"Not count on it, but it could happen."

I turned and looked toward the stairs. "Is that Roseanne, I bet?"

"Who else? She's taking a bath."

"Another one?"

It was sort of astounding, when you considered Roseanne's past history of bath-taking. She'd always had to be dragged hollering to the tub on Saturday nights. "What's a little dirt?" she'd shrilled as Mom pushed her toward the tub and forced her to climb in. For the past week, however, my sister had been taking a bath every day. Not any quick hop into the tub either. She spent hours soaping herself and washing her dank hair, singing all the while at the top of her lungs. It was pathetic.

"Just listen to her," Margaret said, wincing at the off-key singing. "She must've spent the entire day lolling in her room—the beds were unmade when I got home, and the breakfast dishes were in the sink."

"Maybe she thinks enough baths will wash away her freckles," I commented after another burst of song.

Margaret stacked Dad's pipes neatly in the pipe rack on the table near the morris chair. A corner of the pipe rack was broken off, but otherwise it was in good condition. "It's all got to do with graduation and getting her hair cut," she said. "There's not another thing on Roseanne's mind."

Upstairs the singing broke off and was followed by a gurgle of water draining from the tub. "She didn't care anything about Dad going to Greenvale," I said. "I bet she couldn't care less whether Mom's improved or not."

Margaret started toward the kitchen. "I wouldn't go that far, Robbie. Of course she cares."

I glared at the ceiling as the hideous singing recommenced. "Boy, if I wanted to tell something, would Roseanne be in trouble. I hate to think of it."

Margaret turned back to me. "What are you talking about?"

"Oh, nothing," I said, and switched on the Emerson.

Actually, making trouble for my sister turned out to be unnecessary—trouble was headed straight in Roseanne's direction and needed no push from me.

It started as soon as Dad arrived home from Greenvale on Sunday.

He came up the front walk with Vinny, and his steps were eager and jaunty despite the two nights of sitting up in a coach train. We ran onto the porch to greet him. Eyes glowing, he put down his suitcase and reached out his arms in a bear hug.

"She's going to be okay," he kept saying as we followed him into the house. "Cath's going to win the battle." And, seated first in the morris chair, then at the dining table, handing round plates of roast pork, he described the visit to Greenvale.

"I don't mind telling you, she was mighty dragged out when I left her there in April," he confided. "Too weak to lift her head, and that terrible cough wracking her body. Well, yesterday it wasn't the same person. Am I right, Vin?"

Vinny grinned. "She was sitting up in bed, plenty of pep, and the cough's not nearly as bad. She's made friends with another woman from Brooklyn, a Mrs. Moser."

"Lives in Flatbush," Dad went on. "Really, you should have seen your mother's face when we walked in the room." His voice shook slightly. "If it weren't for the nurse, I think old Cath would have leaped out of bed. She couldn't stop looking at us."

"Did she have my drawings on the wall?" I asked.

"Yes, and shows 'em off to everyone who comes in."

"She does?" I said, and glanced down at my plate, overcome.

Daniel shook his head. "That old Cath—I bet she *will* get home for Christmas."

"She just might confound those medics and manage it." Dad picked up the carving knife and sliced off some more pork. "More meat, anybody? Margaret, this roast is delectable."

"I put apples in the pan, the way Mother does," Margaret said.

"I'll have some more." Dan held out his plate, but Roseanne was thrusting her plate greedily in front of his. "More for me, more for me," she cried. "Make it a big chunk too, Pops. Don't be stingy."

Without replying, Dad served Daniel first, then carved off another slice for Roseanne.

"Aw, it's thin as tissue," she complained. "Did you tell Mom I'm getting my hair cut next week? It's practically all I can think about."

"Evidently," my father said, and gave her a brief glance. He carved some more slices. "What Cath especially talked about were the letters you've all been sending. She keeps them in the drawer next to her bed and reads them over and over. More pork, Rob?"

I held out my plate. "I wrote her two letters last week, and I'm making more water colors for her room."

He plunked a slice of meat on my plate and handed it back to me. "Daniel, she thinks your letters are extremely interesting. She said to be sure and tell you."

My brother shrugged modestly. "I try to discuss current events with her, that type of stuff. After all, Mom probably doesn't get to follow the newspapers."

Dad served himself some more meat and sat eating for a moment. Then he asked, "What about you, Roseanne? What sort of letters have you been writing?"

My sister put down her fork. "Oh, the usual junk."

"What sort of junk?"

She swung her hair back. "Oh, about school and local happenings. You know."

"I see." Dad nodded. "How often have you been writing."

A pause. "About once a week, like you told us."

"Once a week, eh? Do you put stamps on the envelopes?"

Roseanne appeared to be considering the question. "Why, hasn't Mom been getting my letters?" she asked.

There was another pause, a longer one. "No, she hasn't," Dad said, staring at her. "Perhaps you can explain why she hasn't. I'm waiting, Roseanne, and I want the truth."

My sister flushed, but she didn't flinch under his stare. "I guess because I didn't write any," she said. "I'm sorry, Pops."

Dad's voice stayed quiet and even. "What's your excuse?"

"None," she replied, still looking at him. "No excuse."

"Don't you care enough about your mother to write her?"

Roseanne lowered her eyes. She shook her head. "It isn't because of that."

"Let's find out if it is, shall we?" Dad's voice was dangerously quiet. "Leave this table, go up at once to your room, and write your mother a letter," he ordered. "Bring it down to me, or else plan to stay in your room until your hair turns gray. Do you understand me, young lady?"

Roseanne nodded, got up from her chair. The straw hair hung limply in her face; she pushed it back and almost tripped over the chair legs as she moved from the table. Without looking at anyone, she crossed to the living room arch and stood there stiffly, a tall, gangly figure with freckles and that awful waterfall of hair. What she did next was beyond comprehension.

"Up to your room," Dad ordered.

And she said, her back toward him, "I can still have my hair cut, can't I?"

Then she fled up the stairs.

I guess we shouldn't have expected that the incident would

affect Roseanne's behavior, or inspire contrition of her soul. Apparently it didn't bother her that she hadn't written Catherine. An hour or so later that Sunday she skipped lightly down the stairs, waving a sheet of loose-leaf paper, which she handed casually to Dad in the morris chair.

"I haven't checked it for errors yet," she said.

He read the letter in silence. "It's not even a full page. Take it back and write more."

"Okey-doke," she replied blithely, and skipped back up the stairs.

"You're to write another letter tomorrow," Dad called after her.

"Right-o, *mon capitain*." Halfway up the stairs she leaned over the banister and called to Margaret, "Say, Marg, aside from broken-down lamps, would Mr. Fergus have any bargains in the beauty line?"

"Such as?" Margaret called back.

"Oh . . . bath oil, maybe. It's supposed to open the pores. Cleansing cream—all that marvelous gukky stuff." She leaned over the banister, trailed her fingers up and down the rail. "Pops, after I finish the letter, would you mind if I worked on my graduation dress? It has to be finished for rehearsal on Wednesday."

My father turned his newspaper. "It's easy to see which person you care about most in this family," he said.

Still Roseanne dawdled on the stairs, and addressed herself to Margaret again. "You'd better make my haircut appointment with Mr. Pierre tomorrow. We've only got until Saturday, you know."

Margaret groaned. "With you to remind me every ten minutes, it's not likely I'd forget."

Roseanne blew a movie-star kiss over the banister. "As Aunt Tilly would say—toodle-oo, folks," and she galloped up the stairs.

Whether or not she enlarged the letter to Mom, or wrote another letter on Monday, was never clearly established. For one thing, Dad worked late all the next week, and we ate supper without him and were in bed by the time he got home. For another, Roseanne's crazy, lunatic preparations for the coming graduation ceremonies drove everybody to helpless distraction.

Beginning at breakfast on Monday, she pestered Margaret

about making the hair appointment with Mr. Pierre. "Beauty parlors are packed solid on Saturdays," she said, ignoring her bowl of cornflakes. "I'd phone the first minute after nine, Marg."

"I'll take care of it," Margaret said.

"You won't go rushing off to Woolworth's and forget?"

"Shut up, Roseanne," Daniel warned from the other side of the table.

"While on the subject of Woolworth's, if you could persuade darling Mr. Fergus to slip you a few cosmetic preparations—"

That did it. Dan threw the box of cornflakes at her, and when it missed aim, he made her pick up every flake from the tiles.

But nothing seemed to squelch her. That afternoon, when I came in the door from school, I found her on the phone, posturing and talking in a fake Joan Crawford accent. "Is this Mr. Pierre's hairdressing establishment?" she said into the phone. "This is Miss Connerty speaking. I believe my social secretary phoned this morning for a Saturday appointment for me. I should like to verify it, if you please. My secretary is sometimes lax in her duties and—"

I slammed the door and said, "What a load of baloney."

Roseanne gripped the receiver ecstatically. "What time did you say? Nine-thirty on Saturday? Oh, thank you." She hung up the receiver and danced around the hall, her hair swinging wildly, while over and over she murmured, "Nine-thirty Saturday," like a prayer.

Then she dashed up the stairs, and in a few moments I heard the water running in the tub.

On Tuesday night after dinner Roseanne went up to her room, and she came down the stairs with the white organdy graduation dress folded over her arm. She held it out reverently, as though it were woven of gold.

"I got the hem finished," she announced, "and sewed on the sash and puffed sleeves. It's just about ready for the big event."

I went to the bottom of the stairs to have a closer look at the dress. "It's all wrinkled," I said.

"Well, of course, stupid, I've been sewing on it," she sneered. "But after it's been beautifully ironed—"

"Wrinkled, just like your school blouse," I said.

"Robert Connerty, just for that, you can't come to graduation. I'll have you barred at the door." She huffed up the stairs in outrage, but not five minutes later there was a gurgle of the tub again and, over it, my sister's voice raised in song.

By dint of sheer persistence she persuaded Margaret to bring home whatever cast-off cosmetics could be found lying around Woolworth's stockroom. It was a miserable assortment: a bent tin of mascara, a vial of horrible-smelling perfume, and a chipped, unlabeled jar of face cream.

"Naturally, you can't use the mascara," Margaret instructed. "I only brought it home to shut you up. As for that odious perfume . . ."

A smile of angels' on her face, Roseanne lifted the jar of face cream from the paper bag. "Look, it doesn't have a label. It's some miracle preparation, I bet." She unscrewed the jar, sniffed at the oily cream. "Oh, it smells heavenly. I know what it might be!"

"Poison-ivy ointment," I said.

"It's freckle cream, I'll bet anything," she rhapsodized. "Oh, Marg, what terrific luck. You're the best sister. Oh, thank you."

She flung herself at Margaret, bestowed a rain of kisses on her, then dashed up the stairs. She came downstairs to dinner with cream smeared all over her face and refused to remove any of it. She was planning a second application at bedtime, she reported.

If it was freckle cream in the jar, it was less than a miracle preparation. The next morning not a single blotchy speck had disappeared from Roseanne's face, but she wasn't discouraged. "Naturally, it requires several applications," she said. "Let's see—I've still got Thursday, Friday, plus all of Saturday, except for when I'm having my hair done at Mr. Pierre's—after all, graduation's not till Sunday."

Thursday, Friday, Saturday. Three days left to vanquish the freckles and transform Roseanne into a queen of beauty. Thursday went, leaving only two days, and Friday Hanna showed up at the door, faithful to her promise to make the house spotless for "her lady."

Hanna swept the carpets, dusted the furniture, cleaned the

floors, and still she wasn't satisfied. Descending on the kitchen, she scoured the tiles again, cleaned the stove, oven and sink. Casting about for new challenges, she removed every item from the cupboard shelves. She washed each dish, each cup and saucer and bowl, until it shone, and placed the shining lot of them on the cupboard counter to dry.

Glasses, dishes, cups and saucers—the parade of shining objects marched across the counter to greet Margaret's eye when she got home from work.

"Hanna was here," I explained. "She practically cleaned the whole house."

"That Hanna!" Margaret sighed, inspecting the immaculate line-up of glasses and crockery. "She must have emptied the entire cupboard and washed every last item." Then, after a pause, Margaret said, "Mother's pitcher . . . the Waterford pitcher . . . where could it be?"

We sat in the living room, Daniel, Margaret and I. There was silence upstairs, then a cry and the sound of Dad's belt lashing at bare flesh. There were no further cries, only the slap of the belt.

"It serves her right," Margaret said, concentrating on her basket of mending. "The deceitfulness is the worst part," she went on. "Breaking that pitcher weeks ago and hiding the pieces in a garbage can down the street."

Dan squatted down in front of the radio and fiddled with the dials. Upstairs the slap of the belt continued. "Frankly, I wouldn't be surprised if Roseanne has a potentially criminal mind," he said. "I half expect her to wind up in prison."

I sat in the corner, waiting for the lashings to be over. For years I'd daydreamed of inflicting various tortures on Roseanne. I'd pictured her chained to some horrible rack, or strapped on a treadmill, headed toward a murderous buzz saw that would decapitate her in one hideous turn of the blade. They had been richly satisfying daydreams, but I'd always pictured her screaming and shrieking at each new stab of pain. I hadn't envisioned that she wouldn't cry at all.

Something else was worrying me. The Waterford pitcher had been missing . . . and now that its whereabouts was explained . . . would it prompt a search for the missing Valentine box? Dad had cross-examined each of us about the pitcher, fixing his eyes on us, detectivelike.

"All right," he'd said after supper when Margaret had told him about the pitcher. "Can anyone tell me what might have happened to it?"

Nobody had answered, and he'd started to quiz Daniel. Next he'd turned his scrutiny on me. "Well, Robbie, what have you to say on the subject? Speak up. Speak up."

Here was my opportunity, my long-denied chance at justice. "I don't know anything about it," I said.

"Well, somebody does"—his fist had pounded the table. "Your mother treasured that pitcher. Someone knows what happened to it, and I intend to find out." His eyes had riveted on me, and I'd cursed myself for remaining silent. Why didn't I speak up? What had Roseanne done to earn my silence?

It hadn't been necessary to blurt out the guilty party's name— Roseanne had done it herself.

"I broke it," she'd said as Dad resumed his questioning of me. "It was in April. I took the pieces and hid them down the block in a garbage can. I'm sorry."

Without another word, and unbuckling his belt, Dad had marched her up the stairs. "There'll be no graduation ceremonies for you," he'd said, and a moment later the single cry rang out from the bedroom.

"Robbie, I don't want to remind you again about your studies," Margaret said from the sofa.

Daniel turned up the volume on "Mr. District Attorney" and sprawled out on the carpet. Another lash, and then there was silence from the bedroom. A moment later my father came down the stairs, looping the belt back through his trousers. He stood in the archway, and I was surprised to see the stern anger gone from his face. He shook his head.

"Didn't let out a peep. I licked her good, and not a murmur out of her," he said, almost pleased. "When I finished, do you know what she had the nerve to ask me? Dan, lower the radio, if you don't mind."

Reaching out with his foot, my brother nudged at the volume knob. "What did she ask?"

"If she could still get her hair cut tomorrow." He strode up and down the carpet. "I nearly gave her a second licking on the spot."

I sat on the hassock in the corner and reflected that nothing was turning out as I would have imagined. A golden chance to snitch on Roseanne, and I hadn't availed myself of it. A belt-lashing, and I hadn't enjoyed it—me, the victim of her rotten tricks for years. Now Dad was talking about the thing she wanted most, a haircut, and I wasn't urging him to deny it to her. All my daydreams of revenge and bloody triumph, all going to waste.

"Well, I told her to forget about the haircut," he went on. "She doesn't deserve the pleasure of graduating. Let them mail her the diploma."

What Margaret did next was equally unexpected. She stood up from the sofa, holding Mom's sewing basket, and it almost seemed as if Catherine herself were standing there, prepared to speak her mind.

"No, Dad," Margaret said. "We can't let her miss out on graduation—and I've already made the appointment at Mr. Pierre's. She's counting on it so—I'd hate to think what it would do to her."

Without commenting, my father went over to the morris chair and took a pipe from the rack. "She has guts, I'll give her that," he said. "She owned up to breaking the pitcher without batting an eye."

He spoke as if he practically admired Roseanne, but it was Daniel who delivered the final, surprising salvo. My brother rolled over on the carpet, stretched out his big arms and legs.

"Aww, let the poor runt have her lousy haircut," he said. "Don't you see? It's all she's got going for her."

The next morning Roseanne was dressed and out of the house by the time I came downstairs at eight o'clock. I was to spend the

Saturday with Aunt Tilly, and I'd gotten up early to shine my shoes and get my knickers pressed. What with last night's trouble, I'd forgotten to remind Margaret about it.

I took down the shoe-shine kit from the shelf on the cellar stair landing and asked, "Where's Roseanne?"

Margaret was washing the breakfast dishes at the sink. "She went to seven o'clock Mass."

"*Mass?*" I said. "Why does she have to go to Mass before getting her hair cut? It's not a religious activity."

Margaret wiped her hands on a dish towel. "If you've brought those knickers down to be pressed, forget it—and you'll have to fix yourself breakfast."

"What's the big hurry?"

She pushed open the swinging door. "We're leaving for Mr. Pierre's in half an hour, and I'm not even bathed or dressed."

I carried the shoe-shine kit to my room and polished my shoes. Aunt Tilly was taking me on a ferryboat ride to Staten Island today. It wasn't quite a transatlantic ocean voyage, she'd said on the phone, but it would have to do. Shoes shined, I put on my knickers, buttoned my shirt. The front door slammed below, and I heard Margaret call from the landing.

"Roseanne, is that you?"

There was no response. Margaret poked her head in the doorway. She was in her bathrobe, a towel wrapped round her head. "The reek of perfume in that bathroom is enough to knock you out," she said. "Robbie, go downstairs and see what Roseanne's doing."

"I heard her come in."

"I know, and we have exactly ten minutes to leave. Go down and remind her, will you?"

I went downstairs and checked through the living and dining rooms. The kitchen was also empty, and I called down the cellar stairs. Then I looked out at the backyard.

Roseanne was sitting under the tree as if she had the whole day to idle through.

"Well, didn't you hear us calling?" I asked, going out on the back steps. I shaded my eyes against the glare of the brilliant June sunlight. "Hey, what's wrong with you?" I demanded when she didn't reply.

She was seated on an upturned orange crate, the tree branches arching over her like a green curtain. Her back was toward me, and she had her eyes lifted above the Fritzles' fence, looking toward the sky. Her freckled arms and legs stuck out of her last year's Easter dress, which she had long since outgrown. Her hair, straight as a ruler, the color and texture of wet straw, hung to her waist, and grasped in her hands were the only two pocketbooks she owned, a red one and a blue one.

"Roseanne," I called, and still she didn't answer.

I went down the steps and across the scrubby yard. Something about the way she sat told me not to step closer or to make any jokes. I said, "You know you have to leave for Mr. Pierre's in ten minutes."

Her shoulders twitched, but she didn't turn and look at me. She kept her eyes focused on the sky, and asked tensely, "*Robbie?*"

"Yeah?"

"Do you"—she moved her legs slightly and shifted the two purses—"do you ever wonder what kind of person you'll grow up to be?"

I took a moment to reflect. "I know already—an artist. I have it planned."

She twisted the chain purse handles. "I don't mean what you'll *do*. The kind of *person* you'll be."

"I never thought about it," I confessed. "Probably I'll be the same kind I am now."

She swung around on the orange crate, her eyes wide and frantic. "Oh, I couldn't bear it," she said. "I couldn't stand it if I'm the same person."

I blinked at my sister in surprise. "You mean you don't *like* who you are?"

She laughed hollowly. "Oh, sure, I'm nuts about myself. I think I'm the cat's miaow."

It had never occurred to me that Roseanne wasn't perfectly content to remain her own horrible self. "You mean you want to change?" I said.

Her eyes swept despairingly around the yard. "I've *got* to change. It has to happen, that's all."

I moved a step closer. "Change how?"

She stabbed at the clump of grass with her patent-leather shoe. Her voice was faint and fuzzy, so that I could hardly hear her. "You know those dragons the Chinese have on New Year's?" she asked. "You know the kind? They're made of paper and they go rattling through the streets, making lots of racket and noise. But inside . . ."

"Yeah?" I said.

"Inside the dragons are empty. Inside there's nothing," she said.

"You mean you're like that?" The notion of my sister as a paper dragon dazzled me for some reason. "No fooling, you really think—"

"Don't joke about it or I'll slug you," she warned, which sounded more like the old Roseanne. "Can't you tell I'm trying to talk serious?" she asked.

"Let's say this about it," I compromised. "For an empty dragon, you sure make a big noise."

She turned to me, and the leafy branches, shading her from the sun, made her face pale and luminous, hiding the freckles. "I might as well be empty inside," she said. "Whatever's there, I can't ever express or talk about it. I can't write to Mom about it, or anything. That's the same as being empty." She stared up at me from the orange crate and on her face was a look of utter hopelessness. "Do you think I can, Robbie?"

"Think you can what?"

"Change," she said. "Don't you see, the haircut could be a beginning." Slowly she raised a hand to her hair. "If I never cut it in my whole life, I'd still never look like the picture on the shampoo bottle. But maybe if it's cut . . . it'll show something else about me that's beautiful." She dropped her hand. "Mom thought it would be my hair, but it could turn out the hair was only hiding it."

I moved closer to the orange crate. "Anyway, I'm glad I didn't tell on you about the Waterford pitcher. You didn't even have to pay me."

"It's not impossible for a person to change," Roseanne went on defiantly. "Well, is it? Answer me the truth."

"I—I—"

"You certainly seem to need time to think it over," she observed. "Well, answer me."

The back door opened and Margaret stuck out her head. "So this is where you are," she said. "I trust you're ready to leave, miss. If we're not promptly on time, Mr. Pierre won't wait."

Roseanne shrieked and jumped up from the orange crate. "Is it time to leave? Oh, I can't stand it. I can't even decide which purse to carry."

"Hurry up."

"Which one, which one?" She held out the purses, one in each hand. "Help me decide, Marg."

"Either is perfectly suitable, and if that's your awful perfume I smell—"

"The blue one," I shouted at Roseanne. "The blue is the beautiful one."

She turned to me, and if she'd had a hundred thousand dollars, all of it would have been mine. "I choose the blue one," she cried, tossing the red purse at me. "Put that in my room, will you, Rob? I'm so nervous I'll faint dead away. I'll conk out, no fooling. Wish me luck!" She sprinted up the steps and followed Margaret into the kitchen.

"I do, I wish you luck," I shouted after her as the back door closed. I stood in the yard for a moment, then I ran into the house and through the rooms to the front window, in time to glimpse Roseanne disappearing down Warbisher Street with Margaret.

"I wish you luck, I do," I called softly from the window.

Then, before leaving to meet Aunt Tillybird, I took the red pocketbook up to Roseanne's room. Margaret's room was primly in order, while Roseanne's was strewn with a wild assortment of clothes, undergarments, books, papers and shoes. Hanging from the closet door was the white graduation dress. It was wrinkled still from all the sewing and work, but once it was ironed and the wrinkles taken out . . . maybe it would be beautiful, I thought. It was possible, at least.

The dresser top was littered with hairpins, tissue, the emptied perfume bottle, and some crumpled-up sheets of loose-leaf paper. Each sheet had a line or two of untidy scrawl, but on one the script covered half the page, then, in the middle of a sentence, it abruptly ended. The handwriting was familiar, yet it belonged to a person I hadn't known existed before. I smoothed it out—Roseanne's unfinished letter to Greenvale—and read what there was of it.

Dear Mom, she had written. *It's very early and I'm getting my hair cut at Mr. Pierre's today. Let's face it, the curls aren't ever coming in, and maybe I'll look better with it cut. I'm going to Mass after I finish this letter and pray about it, so keep your fingers crossed.*

Mom, I don't write letters good. I don't know how to do it or put in words what I feel. I wish I had gotten sick instead of you, because no one would miss me. Mom, I broke something, but I'm saving up my money and when I have enough—

The sentence was left unfinished and there wasn't any more to read. I crumbled the letter back up in a ball and put it on the dresser.

What person was Daniel? Margaret, Vinny and Dad? What person, really, was anybody?

8

The Missing Saturday

"Feast your gaze," proclaimed Aunt Tilly, drawing to a halt in the gallery doorway. She tucked a sheaf of museum brochures under her arm, clasped her summer parasol intently, and studied the painting that glowed from the wall opposite. Knowledge, the air of an expert, was in her stance.

"Velázquez," she announced, "but what *is* the title of it? Oh, it's famous. Run have a look, *Robair.*" She had taken to calling me "Robair."

I crossed the parquet floor to the gold-framed painting. "Let's see, Aunt Tilly . . ."

It was the end of August, a week before Labor Day, and I'd spent the summer going on excursions with my aunt. We'd sailed up the Hudson on a Day Line boat to Indian Point, which she had compared to "a voyage on the Rhine." We'd visited the Cloisters—"pure medieval France"—and taken bus rides all over the city. A one-day boat trip to the Atlantic Highlands had brought Scotland to Aunt Tilly's mind—"I all but smell the heather"—and a day spent at Rockaway Beach she had compared to a jaunt to Brighton.

As many as three times a week I'd met her in the lobby of the Clark Street apartment and we'd sallied forth into the summer haze, Aunt Tilly armed with a parasol to ward off the blazing sun. It was, she said, as rewarding as any summer she might have spent in the capitals of Europe. "You are a natural traveler, Robair. You have curiosity, *esprit*, and excellent feet."

The summer had effected a change in Aunt Tilly. Maybe, since Roseanne's amazing revelation, I was on the lookout for unexpected changes in people, but all the same my aunt's behavior was different. Although I had yet to go upstairs to her apartment, she no longer seemed as anxious or uncertain as she waited for me on the chintz-covered chair in the lobby. The moment I appeared in the doorway she sprang eagerly to her feet. Perhaps it was simply because school was out. A prison, she had called it, and now the gates had opened for the summer and Aunt Tillybird had flown away in freedom.

"Well?" she called to me from the museum doorway. "What is the title of that stunning Velázquez?"

Four months until Christmas. Four months until Catherine came home. It still could happen. The doctors had said she was making progress. Only four months, maybe . . .

I examined the title plate at the base of the gold-framed painting. Depicted lushly on the canvas was a little boy dressed in a red silk suit. "It's called 'Don Manuel Osario de—' something or other," I called to Aunt Tilly. "And it's by Goya."

"Not Velázquez?" Her mouth opened, she pressed down on her lip and said, "Well, they're both Spanish." Thus the slight error was adjusted.

We moved through the second-floor galleries of the Metropolitan, pausing every few steps to view the paintings. The high glass-domed ceiling threw a clear light over the floors, walls and clusters of visitors, enveloping the scene in a soft translucence. The Metropolitan was a familiar labyrinth to me by now. I knew where the drinking fountains, corridor benches and lavatories were located—essential information for a museum-goer. I knew which route led to the Medieval Room, and which combination of passageways led to the basement auditorium, where art films were regularly shown. Aunt Tilly liked attending the museum's film showings. Liked them, if the truth were known, because the darkened auditorium gave her a chance to doze off and nap.

Seated next to me, her head would begin to nod as the film unrolled, and soon it would be resting on her chest. But I pretended not to notice, just as I never acknowledged the numerous mistakes she made in regard to the paintings. Let her mistake Goya for Velázquez, or Giotto for Fra Angelico. A bird, after all,

179

was created to hop and twitter and fly about, not to get facts straight. Facts were earthbound things.

"*Regardez*," said Aunt Tilly, gesturing with her parasol at another shimmering Goya. "Is it not exquisite?"

Four more months. Four more months.

"It's a knockout. Listen, I wouldn't mind painting half as good as Goya," I said.

"Notice the fantastic texture of the silk, the incredible flesh tones, the tension and stress of the composition." The words were a more or less garbled version of a museum guide's lecture that we'd heard the previous week, but I nodded attentively and let Aunt Tilly go on.

The important thing was that she cared about art. The important fact was what she had aspired to be, and what had come of it.

Aunt Tilly had told me about her life one day. We'd spent an afternoon touring the Fifth Avenue stores—Black, Starr & Frost–Gorham, Saks Fifth Avenue, Tiffany's—and, to rest her feet, we'd gone into the Plaza Hotel and settled in some high-backed chairs in the lobby. It was an elegant lobby, with marble pillars, gilt furnishings, and wonderful gilded elevators that whisked guests upstairs in crimson-carpeted cars with little cushioned benches at the back.

"The Plaza is the dowager queen of New York hotels," said Aunt Tilly, resting her head against the brocade chair. She was wearing a floppy hat that day, a faded chiffon dress, and canvas sneakers, the latter for comfort's sake. "Tell me, *Robair*," she said, "are you still as determined to be a painter?"

"Oh, it's all planned," I said. "A painter, and I'm going to live in New York and ride the double-deckers every day."

She sighed and closed her eyes. "Perhaps, if you're a successful artist, you'll reside here at the Plaza."

I took in the rich appointments, the flowers massed in ornate vases, the glittering chandeliers that hung from the carved ceiling. "No kidding, do artists get *rich*, Aunt Tilly?"

"Some have commanded princely sums."

"Honestly?" I clambered around to her in my chair. "Well, if it happens to me, I'll not only live at the Plaza, I'll invite you to lunch every day."

The thought of lunch abruptly caused my stomach to grumble. Sometimes Aunt Tilly was apt to forget about eating, and I had to drop hints on the subject. Inspecting her change purse carefully, she seldom ordered more than tea and toast for herself at the various lunch counters we patronized, though she urged a feast on me. She was cautious about spending her money, I'd noticed.

"I'll invite you to lunch every day," I went on, "and what's more, I'll paint your portrait, Aunt Tilly. It'll hang in the Metropolitan!"

"It will? My word!" Her face, tilted back against the chair, smiled softly. "I believe you're sincere, Robair."

Some ladies passed by our chairs, stopped and turned to stare for a moment. They weren't the first stares we had attracted since we'd settled in the Plaza lobby. We were an odd-looking twosome, I supposed. A boy with a cowlick and scuffed-up clothes, and Aunt Tilly in her faded dress and sneakers.

I looked at her sitting there, fingers curled around the parasol, and it put me in mind of a painting. "Tillybird, Seated," it might have been called. Her eyes rested on me, and I asked, "Aunt Tilly, did you ever want to be an artist?"

"An artist? Me?"

"Yes, did you?"

She lifted her head from the chair and considered the question. "I—well, I— Yes, I suppose it was once my ambition." She laughed, as though imparting ridiculous information. "I had an artistic nature from the very start, even as a baby. Color would delight my eye. Flowers, ribbons, the snippets of silk in Mama's sewing basket—it was a family joke how my eyes lit up when a bit of color dangled in front of me."

A family joke . . . the same phrase was still used in reference to her. Seated, head tilted to the side, a fragile hand clutching her parasol, she told me about her life. "I was so utterly different from Cath," she said. "One couldn't have guessed we were sisters. Cath was so gay and larking, so free of shadows. She was the youngest, but only by the calendar, for she always looked after me—a kind of second mother, so quick to protect and defend me. I was such a timid, retreating child, you see . . . no wonder Papa called me Tillybird. But color caught my eye! I could gaze at a single flower, hypnotized by its beauty. Then Papa gave me a water-color set for my birthday and the world changed. To be able to create with brush and paint, to express beauty—I must say, I went on to excel in art at school. My drawings won gold stars, and nothing thrilled me more than a visit to the Brooklyn Museum. Yes, I wanted to be an artist."

She sat up straight in the chair and gripped the parasol for a moment. "Papa was in the lace-importing business, you know," she continued. "Handmade lace from Ireland and France. He prospered quite nicely and might have earned his fortune. But machine-made lace, so much cheaper and more available, was a ruthless competitor, and Papa's fortunes declined. He became ill and died, and there arose the question of his daughters supporting themselves."

"Grandpa Quinlan almost made a fortune?" I asked. "Mom never told me that."

"Money never concerned Cath," laughed Aunt Tilly. "That reckless ardor for life—she embraced it, lost fortunes or not. She met a handsome young man from St. Gabriel's parish, a dashing, *penniless* young man—"

"My father," I said.

"Yes, your handsome father, and Cath didn't care a fig that he was penniless. Before that she'd gone to work at the telephone company and made a lark of it. Myself, luckily, I'd been graduated from teachers' training school, and so I was licensed to teach in the Brooklyn public schools."

"But couldn't you have been a teacher and artist *both?*" I asked my aunt.

The floppy hat, the red curls, nodded in assent. "Precisely my plan, Robair—how perceptive of you! I set my heart on exactly that course. Teach school to earn a living, and in the summer, travel to Paris to study art and paint! I saved my salary for two years in anticipation of it. I made plans, signed up for a course at the École des Beaux-Arts and sailed at last for France on the *Ro-*

chambeau. . . ." Aunt Tilly's words trailed off and she stared across the lobby at a tall china vase of flowers.

"And then what?" I asked.

"And then . . . *nothing,*" she answered slowly. "I—I couldn't get myself to actually attend class. Wasn't that foolish and absurd? I was too timid. Five weeks in Paris that first summer. Every morning I set out from my *pension* on the *rive gauche* . . . and I worried every step of the way. What if I couldn't really paint and the teachers laughed at me? To suffer such humiliation was more than I could bear—"

She turned her glance away from the flowers, tightened her fingers on the parasol. "The summer passed in defeat—and when I went again to Europe I chose a tour of the Mediterranean instead of Paris. The Greek Isles, Messina, Haifa—an enchanting tour, as was my journey the following summer to Italy." She shook her head in protest. "Each fall returning to the classroom, each summer escaping. But school grew harder, not easier to face, the years flew by . . . and oh, Robbie, my dear, if there's a lesson to be learned—"

Her voice had risen shrilly, so that it could be heard quite audibly throughout the lobby. I looked up and saw that a man in striped trousers with a carnation in his lapel was approaching our chairs.

He halted suavely in front of us and smiled at Aunt Tilly. "Excuse me, madam, but may I inquire if you are waiting for someone?"

"Waiting?" Aunt Tilly moved her sneakers and turned a dazed expression on him. "Waiting for what?"

The smile remained on the man's face. "Indeed, that is the question, madam. I am Mr. Albert, the assistant manager, and if you are not waiting for a guest, or have no other purpose at the Plaza . . ."

Aunt Tilly's face flushed, and then, putting an arm around me, she laughed and said, "Actually, my nephew and I—we're considering transferring to your hostelry. Yes, we've been staying at the Ritz and are displeased with our accommodations. Quite displeased."

The assistant manager was obviously startled, but the smile stayed intact. "Ah, yes?" He folded his hands. "If madam would care to come with me to inspect our rooms . . ."

But Aunt Tilly had another surprise for him. She drew herself up from the chair, as erectly as she could manage, and regarded him with icy disdain. "Madam would not care to," she declared. "For a traveler of my distinction—in Paris the Crillon, in London Claridge's—to be accosted in a lobby like this is a unique experience. Good day to you, sir. *Venez, Robair.*"

Chin upraised, hat bobbing, she swept across the lobby and out through the revolving door, with me in tow. It was only when she was outside that she clung trembling to the stair rail, her eyes wide and stricken.

"Are you all right, Aunt Tilly?" I asked.

There was a frightened, trapped look in her eyes, something of the look I had noticed on my first visit to Clark Street. She straightened up and pinned her gaze on the park across Fifty-ninth Street. "What an arrogant man. Well, perhaps we didn't handle him too badly, did we, Robair?"

"I think we handled him great."

"Shall we sit by the lake yonder and admire the swans?" She gripped her parasol and prepared to descend the steps. "You see, Robair, it is not necessary to lose *all* one's battles in life."

We crossed the street to the park, and at the sight of a hot-dog wagon on the corner my stomach growled again, and hunger had chased the scene in the lobby from my mind.

"Oh, dear, perhaps you'd prefer a bite to eat, Robair?"

"No, I'm not hungry, Aunt Tilly. Let's go sit by the lake."

And now the summer was almost over. In another week, Labor Day, and on the following Monday school would open again . . . and in four more months, *Christmas!*

"Beautiful. *Magnifique,*" said Aunt Tilly as we continued along the second-floor galleries. She stood back to regard another painting in rapt appreciation. "Tintoretto?"

"Canaletto," I said, reading the title plate.

"One might have guessed."

Aunt Tilly had left the city but once during the summer. The first week in August she'd taken the bus to Greenvale and visited my mother. She had come back filled with enthusiastic descriptions of the sanatorium and of Catherine's rapidly improving health. "The doctors are permitting her out of bed for part of each day," she'd told me. "She's allowed a short walk in the afternoon. I met her friend, Mrs. Moser, and we sat together in a little pavilion at the edge of the lake and chatted for hours."

I'd listened to this account of the visit in mounting despair. I had cursed my age, cursed Brooklyn and the miles that were such an unbridgeable chasm. If I were eighteen I might have gone to Greenvale myself. If only, for a few days, I could be eighteen.

"There's no question of it," my aunt had comforted me. "It won't be much longer now. Perhaps Christmas, as you say . . ."

Four more months. Four more months.

Aunt Tilly fanned herself with the brochures. "Quite humid in here, isn't it? What century are we in, Robair?"

My stomach growled—we hadn't eaten yet today—and I went over to inspect the plaque at the gallery entrance. "We're in the sixteenth," I called back. It was our custom to cover the paintings at the Metropolitan by century, allotting just so many to each visit.

"The sixteenth so soon?" Aunt Tilly turned this way and that, contemplating the galleries that stretched away on either side. "Poor Robair, you must be weary. What is that low, rumbling sound I hear?"

My stomach gave another growl. "I don't hear anything."

"Almost three o'clock and I haven't fed you yet," she gasped in sudden comprehension. "Poor Robbie, can you ever forgive me?"

I looked at her and thought of the summer that was almost over. The days with Aunt Tilly had been like a flower blooming out over the other days, lending them fragrance, sweetening the emptiness with hope and expectation, helping the summer to pass more quickly and thus hastening my mother's return. I looked at my Aunt Tilly and said, "I—I—there'll never be anything to forgive you for."

She clasped my hand. "Oh, Robair, it's been a good summer,

hasn't it? I can hardly believe it's almost over. Come, we must feed you." We retraced our path through the galleries and descended the great main stairway together, and she exclaimed, "I know! We must celebrate the summer's end. *Venez, mon cher.*"

Aunt Tilly dashed out the doors of the Metropolitan, down the steps toward Fifth Avenue. "We shall take a taxi."

"I've only been in a taxi once in my life, Aunt Tilly."

"Taxi," she cried, dashing into the street, and a sports convertible, speeding down the avenue, bore straight down on her.

I shouted out her name. I ran from the curb and pulled her back as the convertible shot past, but Tilly didn't seem the least disturbed by the near-disaster. On the contrary, it exhilarated her the more.

"Thank you, Robair. Goodness, the traffic's as reckless as in Paris today. Taxi!" She waved her hand, and after we'd climbed into a taxi, she commanded the driver, "Rumpelmayer's, if you please."

"Where's that, Aunt Tilly?" I asked.

"It's in Paris," she replied. "Paris in New York, that is. We shan't count pennies today. Not for our celebration."

Rumpelmayer's, as I learned in a few minutes, was a restaurant on Central Park South. *Confiserie* it said on the fancy awning that curved over the entrance. A gleaming brass plaque alongside the doors read *Paris, London, Genève.* French dolls and ribboned candy boxes were displayed in a window, and as we went inside, a heavy scent of pastry, ice cream and chocolate caused my stomach to rumble again.

"*Une table à deux,*" Aunt Tilly addressed the hostess grandly, ignoring the rude noise.

"What's that, miss?"

"A table for two, my good woman."

We were led to a small round table on a balcony against the wall. The snowy linen cloth was bordered in red, white and blue —the French tricolor, Aunt Tilly explained—and in the center was a silver vase of flowers. The dining room was crowded with well-dressed customers, all of them talking away while they sipped at sodas, drank tea, and nibbled at dainty sandwiches. I thought of Schlack's in Brooklyn and the soda Catherine had treated me to in honor of breaking my arm, and it seemed for a moment that I was lost and far from home. But then Aunt Tilly passed me a menu and said, "Order whatever you fancy, Robair, and simply ignore the prices. I recommend the club sandwich."

I let my eye feast on the list of delicacies. "I'm sorry, but I'm not sure what a club sandwich is."

She lowered her menu and laughed. "Of course, how would you know, confined since birth to Warbisher Street! A club sandwich, Robair, is made of chicken, bacon, lettuce and tomato—*délicieuse*, especially when accompanied by a chocolate soda."

"That'd be fine, Aunt Tilly. What are you going to order?"

She pursed her lips and studied the menu, though I had never known her to order anything other than tea and toast. When the waitress came to take the orders Aunt Tilly explained to her, "Today is a private celebration. A chocolate soda and a club sandwich for the young gentleman, *s'il vous plaît*. For myself the assorted tea sandwiches . . . and a delicious Manhattan cocktail."

"A cocktail, Aunt Tilly?"

"In celebration—why not?" She dismissed the waitress airily and smiled at me across the linen cloth. "This summer's been good for both of us, I believe," she said. "Soon I'll be reporting back to my brick schoolhouse—next Wednesday's the first faculty meeting of the new term. Usually I start dreading it by the middle of August—that dismal teachers' room in the basement, the same faces assembling, the same petty quarrels and talk—but this summer I haven't given it a thought. Do you know why?" she asked.

I shook my head, no.

"Because of you," Aunt Tilly said, reaching her hand over the linen cloth. "Because of our good times together. The numeral one may be the first in the arithmetic tables, but I confess that I prefer the numeral two.

"Yes." I glanced around the restaurant at the mirrored walls, the flowers, the trays of pastries and cakes that were arranged on a table in the center. "If I'm a famous painter, we'll come here to lunch instead of the Plaza," I said.

Aunt Tilly gazed across the table. "I've given you good times,

I've accomplished something with my summer," she said. "I went to visit Cath and saw the wonders I was helping to accomplish."

What was meant by her last statement I wasn't sure, but she went on talking and I let it slip by.

"So, you see, it hasn't been a wasted summer. Waste, Robair, can shrivel the soul." She fell silent, her glance suddenly clouded, her fingers toyed nervously with a fork. Lifting her red curls (was her hair dyed?), she smiled brightly again. "We shall not permit the summer to end," she said. "Straight through autumn and winter our Saturdays together will be our summer."

"And by Christmas Mom might be home," I said. "It's possible if she keeps improving. Dad says it's possible."

"Yes, oh, yes," Aunt Tilly exclaimed. "A parade of victories—wait and see."

The waitress arrived then. She set the club sandwich and a mammoth chocolate soda in front of me. A plate of thin little sandwiches was set in front of Aunt Tilly, then a cocktail glass was lifted from the tray.

"A Manhattan for madam."

Aunt Tilly suddenly put up her hand and quickly said, "No, I think not, after all. May I change my order, please? Tea. Just tea with lemon, if you don't mind." The waitress nodded and went off with the cocktail, and, smiling, Aunt Tilly turned to me.

"Well, Robair, there is your club sandwich and soda, looking perfectly delectable. Hurl yourself upon it. We've won the right to celebrate!"

On the day that St. Aloysius's opened for the fall term a letter was waiting for me on the hall table when I got home in the afternoon. It was addressed to "Master Robert F. Connerty" and the postmark read "Greenvale, N.Y."

Since July my mother had been permitted to write one letter home each week. The letters were addressed to Dad and usually weren't more than a page in length, but Catherine always included a message for each of us. *Roseanne, does your hair look pretty, now that it's cut?* . . . *Margaret, I don't want you tied to the house too much. Get out on some dates.* At the bottom of each letter she invariably added a postscript requesting her "Indians" to keep sending her mail. Then, *Just wait, soon I'll be able to answer each and every letter.*

We had read a dozen such postscripts and argued over how long it would be before the letters became a reality. How suddenly the waiting was over for me.

I felt too happy to remain inside the silent, gloomy house, and so I carried the letter onto the porch and sat down on the steps. For a moment I just stared at the envelope, then, with the penknife Vinny had given me for my last birthday, I carefully slit open the envelope and unfolded the closely written page.

Catherine herself might have been speaking to me.

Dear Robbie, the letter read. *The doctors say I can write a letter every day, and so I'll start with you. School begins on Monday, and I can picture you coming home with all those new books that will need covering. I picture you climbing the porch steps, hungry for a sandwich and milk. I can't be there, but I hope this letter will be waiting in my stead. . . .*

I lowered the page, because if I read too fast, the letter would be over, and I didn't want it to be over. I went back and reread the first paragraph. Wasn't Catherine terrific? Hoped the letter would be waiting for me—and it *was!*

I love all your drawings, she went on. *Every one of them is up on my wall. All the months I wasn't allowed out of bed I looked for hours at your drawings and at the photos of my Indians that I keep on the dresser. Speaking of snapshots, what a pity the Valentine box got misplaced. Never mind, you'll find it again one of these days.*

I hurried over the last two sentences. What Valentine box was she talking of, what snapshots? I didn't remember anything about a Valentine box anymore. Dad was taking new snapshots with his Brownie, and I'd started a collection of those to send to Catherine.

When Tilly was here in August, the letter continued, *she told me about the wonderful times you two have been enjoying in the city. It was so good to know that Tilly is looking after you. Each day I seem to feel better and stronger. I go to O.T., that's occupational therapy, twice a week now. Mrs. Moser and I are each hooking a rug. While we work we make bets about who will leave Greenvale first, as she's making fine progress too.*

Mrs. Moser was the lady from Flatbush who was Mom's best friend at the sanatorium. Mrs. Moser had four children, and the youngest was a boy of my age. Mom had a lot of admiration for her friend and said she was a jolly sort of person who could always make the other patients laugh.

I came to the last paragraph of the letter and sat for a while before starting it. *It's not good to hope too much,* the last paragraph read, *but I can't help thinking it won't be much longer now. I keep dreaming about Christmas and what might be. Be good, Robbie, study hard, and write soon. P.S. I miss my kitchen.*

I read the letter over, and again for a third time. I sat on the porch steps, looked out at the street, and tried to picture Catherine coming along the sidewalk, as she had pictured me arriving home from school. This very exact moment in Greenvale, perhaps, my mother was hooking a rug and thinking about her Indians. Slowly and surely she was on her way back to us. The homeward journey was already begun.

A girl was coming up Warbisher Street, dodging among the gangs of kids who were chasing around on the sidewalk. She was tall and erect, dressed in a plaid skirt and blue school jacket, a pile of books filling her arms. Her hair was bobbed short and it fluffed out in the breeze as she walked up the street. I didn't recognize her at first, accustomed as I still was to the old pig-tailed version.

"Roseanne!" I shouted, and took the front steps in a bounding leap, and ran down the front path. My sister, too, was on a homeward journey, returning from her first day in high school. Life was made up of journeys, great and small, and the starting and ending of them was the story of life.

Waving Mom's letter, I raced along the sidewalk toward my sister. Roseanne smiled and waved as she caught sight of me over the pile of books. Was she prettier since she'd made her journey to Mr. Pierre's? Was she changing into the person she wanted to be? I couldn't make up my mind.

I only knew—and perhaps it answered my question—that I was glad to be running toward her.

. .

The weeks passed, September changed into October, and every week a letter arrived for each of us from Catherine. Sometimes three or four letters would be delivered the same day, and we'd pass them around in an orgy of exchange, getting the pages mixed up, sorting them out again impatiently. Although, as Catherine had cautioned herself, it wasn't good to hope too much, each week her letters grew brighter with hope. She talked of spending Christmas with us as though no doubt of it existed any longer. She wrote that we'd find the biggest tree ever for the living room and that she planned to bake dozens of gingerbread cookies. She reminded Vinny that the crèche was stored in the cellar and that *maybe we can buy some more shepherd figures to add to the grouping. We also could use a new St. Joseph, but I'd hate to part with the old one, so forget about that.*

Toward the end of October a letter arrived for Dad. It was from Mom, and he opened it as soon as he got home that night. It was Friday, I remember, because I'd talked to Aunt Tilly about meeting her the next morning. Dad read the letter, but he didn't show it to us, as he usually did. He went upstairs alone, then came back down and said that it was better that we know about the letter. He read it aloud—and the reserves of hope, accumulated as carefully as pennies in a savings bank, dwindled away.

The next morning I took the trolley to Clark Street, and when I reached the apartment something was wrong there too.

Aunt Tilly wasn't waiting for me on the chintz-covered chair. I entered the lobby, and the chair in the corner was vacant.

"Hasn't Miss Quinlan come down yet?" Horace inquired, poking his head through the brass doors. "She's *always* sittin' there for you."

"I guess she must be delayed slightly."

Horace flashed me a reassuring grin. "Don't you bother. Miss Quinlan never missed a time with you yet. Have a seat, she'll be poppin' out of the elevator before you count to ten."

I sat down on the chintz-covered sofa and waited. It was dim and shadowy in the lobby, but outside the street was splashed with sunlight. I watched the people going past—delivery boys, old ladies with dogs, a man in a beret who I decided was an artist.

After a while I started to watch the dial over the brass elevator door. Like a clock, its hand moved from number to number, representing the floors in the building. Aunt Tilly's apartment was on the eleventh floor, but the dial hand didn't stop there once. Every so often the elevator door would open and some passengers would step into the lobby. Then the doors would close and the dial begin its circumference again. Even elevator dials made journeys.

I sat thinking about the letter Dad had read to us the night before, and finally Horace came into the lobby again.

"Miss Quinlan still not down?" This time he didn't grin but went over and frowned up at the dial hand, which was poised at fourteen. It stopped at twelve, skimmed past the other numerals, stopped again at eight. Horace took off his visored cap and scratched his head.

"I know she's upstairs. There's no way for her not to be. Tell you what, young fella." He stepped back as the elevator door opened and a lady passenger alighted. She was pulling on white gloves, and Horace bowed politely.

"Mornin', Mrs. Schuster. Lovely mornin' today."

"Yes, lovely, Horace. I'm expecting a delivery from Lord and Taylor. Will you accept it for me?"

"Certainly, Mrs. Schuster." The lady went out into the sunshine, and he turned to me. "Sonny boy, why don't you ride up to eleven and give your aunt's bell a ring. Maybe it's nothing except her clock is slow, or she didn't hear the alarm."

"I've never gone up to her apartment," I said. "Are you sure it's all right?"

Horace held the door back so that the elevator wouldn't go up. "Why, sure it is. Here—I'll press eleven for you. Step inside and up you go."

I got into the elevator, but he still held back the door. "If by some chance . . . Miss Quinlan don't answer the bell," he said, "come right down and get me. Understand?"

"Yes, Horace."

"Apartment Eleven-H. Turn right, it's at the end of the hall."

The brass door slid shut and I stood alone in the shuddering elevator. The floor numbers blinked on and off above the door. Then eleven flashed on and the elevator stopped.

I stepped into the carpeted hall and turned right, as Horace had directed. The hall was narrow and dark, save for a light at the elevator and another that glimmered dimly outside the door of the last apartment at the end.

Aunt Tilly's door was painted a shiny black, but the letter H, in gold, was faded and flecked. I stood at the door and hesitated about pressing the buzzer. It didn't seem as if my aunt wanted people coming up to her apartment. I listened for sounds in the apartment, and when I heard none I pressed the buzzer.

I could hear the ring of the bell echo inside, but there was no response—no footsteps or Aunt Tilly's voice calling in answer. Maybe I'd better go downstairs and get Horace.

I pressed the buzzer a second time, held my ear against the door. No response came, no sound other than silence. After reading the letter last night I had thought to phone Aunt Tilly and ask if it would be okay if I didn't meet her on Saturday. I was sorry now that I hadn't, because nothing was working out anymore.

What if she was ill or had had an accident? Slipped and fallen in the apartment and wasn't able to call for help or to reach the phone? I pressed my finger on the buzzer hard. There was still no response. I turned and hurried down the shadowy hall to the elevator.

Behind me in the hall a door clicked open. "Robbie . . . ?"

I turned slowly around. Aunt Tilly stood in her doorway in a rumpled dressing gown. Her red hair hung down in disarray and a thin white hand clutched at the neck of the dressing gown. She peered toward me through the shadows.

"I—I overslept," she stammered. "Oh, poor Robair."

I could not believe it was my aunt in the shadows. The rumpled gown, the hair disarrayed, like a witch's, the thin vein-ribbed white arm. "Hello, Aunt Tilly," I said.

She jerked up her head and returned my stare, and I remembered the incident with the assistant manager at the Plaza Hotel. "Come in," she said. "Come into my parlor, said the spider to the fly. Nursery rhymes are fraught with menace, don't you agree?"

She held the door open, and I came down the hall and went past her into the apartment. The door closed and she looked at me. "Poor Robair, there was so much I'd hoped you'd never see."

Hope . . . I thought of Catherine's hopes, and the letter the night before.

"It—it's a small place, I'm afraid, and much too littered," Aunt Tilly said with an attempt at a smile. "If you'll remove some of those magazines from that chair, it's quite comfortable."

There was a tiny entrance hall, and across from it a door opened on a bathroom. The apartment itself consisted of one small room with a screened-off kitchenette in the corner—and every inch of that one small room was cluttered. Magazines, art brochures, Sunday rotogravure sections, museum catalogues were piled everywhere—on the floor, the tables, the windowsill, even stacked at the foot of the daybed. The bed was as rumpled as Aunt Tilly's dressing gown; the sheets were thrown back and a wrinkled paisley spread was caught between them. Art reproductions and travel posters covered the walls. In the corner opposite the kitchenette was a large steamer trunk, pasted with travel stickers—Rome, Vienna, Istanbul. Its drawers were open, spilling over with scarves, jewelry, satin slips, tangled silk stockings . . .

Aunt Tilly gestured in despair. "Sit down, Robair."

I stared over at the steamer trunk . . . at the empty bottle that was perched on the top, half sliding off. Then I saw my aunt make her way through the litter toward the trunk. A white arm, extricating itself from the folds of the dressing gown, seized hold of the bottle.

"Remember . . . ?" she asked, gazing in horror at the empty bottle. "At the museum that day you said there'd never be anything to forgive me for."

"Maybe I just ought to go home," I said after a moment.

She held the bottle up to the light. "Imagine, not a drop left," she said, and her arm began to shake. She turned away from me, averting her face.

"Aunt Tilly, please," I said. "It's all right."

She sagged against the trunk, keeping her back toward me.

"We had such a good summer. We planned to make it last all through winter, didn't we," she said.

I didn't really understand about the bottle, or the littered room, or my aunt's behavior. But I knew that summer, at any rate, was ended for both of us. I stood among the litter of dusty magazines and said, "A letter came from Mom yesterday. It was addressed to Dad. At first he wouldn't let us read it. Then he said it was better for us to know."

Aunt Tilly turned to me, pushed back her hair. "What letter?"

"A letter from Mom. Something sad happened at Greenvale, Aunt Tilly."

She stepped toward me, half tripping over a stack of art annuals. "What's happened to Cath? Tell me!"

I twisted my hands together. "Not to Mom. To her friend at Greenvale, Mrs. Moser."

Aunt Tilly nodded. "Yes, I met her when I was up there in August. A pleasant, happy little woman."

I said, "Mrs. Moser died this week. She was getting along fine, and then she just sort of died. It's been a bad shock for Mom."

Aunt Tilly turned away and crossed slowly to the window. The light fell on her face, revealing the harsh lines and pouches.

"A shock to all of us," I went on. "Mom and Mrs. Moser were betting each other— It's not good to hope too much, I guess, is it?"

My aunt shivered and pulled at her dressing gown. "This summer was hope," she said faintly. "But it's worse without hope. Much, much worse." She went over to the bottle on the trunk and seized it again, then disappeared behind the kitchenette screen. "We surrender too easily, yes, we do," I heard her say, and next came the sound of the bottle being dropped into a waste basket. Then Aunt Tilly stepped from behind the screen.

Her face was set and determined. "I'm not going to send you home. Please . . . would you wait downstairs while I dress?"

"I—I keep thinking about Mrs. Moser, and it scares me, Aunt Tilly."

"Wait downstairs," she said. "It's not too late. Saturday's not over yet. We can still go to the city."

I went downstairs to the lobby as she had asked. Horace came over and chatted with me, and I watched the elevator dial move from floor to floor.

"Miss Quinlan all right upstairs?" Horace asked.

"It was like you said, Horace. Her alarm clock didn't go off."

He nodded reassuringly. "What'd I tell you? Wasn't nothing at all."

The elevator hand stopped at eleven, circled downward, and Aunt Tilly stepped out. She was pale, but her hair was neatly combed and she was wearing the feathery hat with the dotted veil. She came toward me, clasping a beaded purse.

"Perhaps birds aren't such fragile creatures, after all, Robair," she said with the ruin of a smile on her face.

We went, that Saturday, to St. Patrick's Cathedral on Fifth Avenue. We got off the subway at Fiftieth Street and walked toward the gray Gothic spires that rose toward the cloudless blue sky.

"Imagine," Aunt Tilly said as we mounted the broad steps of St. Patrick's. "This edifice was built largely from the contributions of the poor—the nickels and dimes of the Irish maids and coachmen who toiled in the service of the rich. It . . . speaks well of the human spirit."

We entered the cathedral doors and stepped into the vast echoing stone-enclosed space. An organ was playing in the choir loft, and its deep, sonorous tones floated out and hung in the soaring arches. Candles flickered like small brush fires on the side altars, casting shadows on the statues of the saints. The sun flooding through the great stained-glass windows turned the panes into fiery mosaics of color, and rays of light slanted across the gray stone pillars.

Aunt Tilly and I stood together in the great hushed stillness at the rear of St. Patrick's. "Sometimes . . . ," she said, staring up at the vaulted ceiling, "nothing left to us except God. . . . Shall we go pray?"

The marble-floored aisles whispered with the tread of other visitors, to which we joined our steps. I walked alongside my aunt, past the flickering candles, the white altars, and gesturing saints.

"Come," she bade me, and led the way to a small altar off the main center altar.

A statue of a young gentle-faced nun stood guard over the small altar. "She is La Bienheureuse—Saint Thérèse," Aunt Tilly said, kneeling at the altar rail. "One summer in France I visited her shrine at Lisieux. I was lonely and troubled . . . and Thérèse seemed to help me find the strength to struggle on. Ever since, I've come to her with my needs. Do you see the inscription on the altar, Robair? Let me translate it for you."

Carved in graceful letters on the altar was an inscription in French, *Je veux passer mon ciel à faire du bien sur la terre*—"I wish to spend my heaven in doing good upon earth," Aunt Tilly translated for me. "Thérèse promised on her deathbed that she would fulfill her wish . . ."

I looked at the carved lettering and thought about Mrs. Moser's children in Flatbush.

Aunt Tilly got up from the rail and took some coins from her purse. "*Bien*, we will hold Thérèse to her promise. Here, Robair, light some candles."

She gave me the coins and I dropped them into the box at the candle stand. I held a taper to the flame of a candle that was already burning.

"The first candle is for Mrs. Moser," Aunt Tilly said, and I lit a new candle with the taper. "Pray that she is at peace and that her family may be strengthened and comforted. Now light a candle for your mother, Robair."

I gazed at the banks of flickering candles and my hand shook so badly that I almost dropped the taper. "It's the smoke," I apologized, wiping at my eyes.

"Light it," Aunt Tilly said.

I lifted the taper to the top row of the stand and held it to a candle. A tiny flame flickered and then flared up brightly. A flame for Catherine . . .

I turned away from the candles and knelt with Aunt Tilly at the altar on the cold marble step. She knelt erectly and lifted her worn face to the statue of Saint Thérèse.

"Send her home to us," she prayed.

9

The Nights Before Christmas

Two weeks after Mrs. Moser's death Catherine wrote to us; *Death happens at Greenvale, and you can't hide from it behind the trees. All you can do is accept it. Florence is in heaven now, away from pain and trouble. It is her family we must grieve for. As for me, I'm grateful just to be alive. I think if I could see my Indians again, even for a minute or two, I'd be happy and not ask for more.*

Her letters were quick to recover their cheerfulness. She wrote that she was going ahead with the hooked rug she'd been making with Mrs. Moser, and that when the rug was finished, she planned to give it to Mr. Moser. She asked Dad to visit the family on Farragut Road and find out if there was anything he could do for them. Dad carried out her request, and as it happened, there was something he could do to help them. The eldest Moser son had quit high school and was looking for work, and Dad was able to get him a job in the mail room at Childs Company.

What grand news, wrote Catherine to Dad from Greenvale. *Florence always worried about that oldest boy. Keep an eye on him and try to get him to finish school at night. It's what she'd want.*

The letters regained their cheerfulness with one exception: they no longer included any expectations for Christmas, nor did Catherine speculate on how much longer she would have to stay at the sanatorium. *I'll leave when I'm ready to, I guess, and not a day before,* she wrote philosophically. Dad laughed when he read that last statement. "Evidently she was figuring on sneaking home before the end of term."

But the news about my mother's health continued to be encouraging. The doctors sent regular reports to Dad that indicated steady progress. Her weekly checkups were excellent, the hours of bed confinement had been steadily reduced; she went on walks, attended the Sunday-night movies at Greenvale, and was permitted a weekly afternoon trip to the nearby village.

Honest, I'm getting positively countrified, she wrote. *A Brooklyn girl, and here I am, hooking rugs and shopping in the village general store like I'd never set foot on a city sidewalk. Most of the hospital staff live in the village, so we get to know everything that goes on "down the hill," as they call it. Next week is the annual firehouse social, which is the biggest winter event next to Christmas for the villagers. All the local women contribute their favorite dishes to the affair, and some of the patients take part in it too. I've volunteered to bake a cake, and might even get to deliver it to the firehouse in person. Which shall I make, devil's food or Lady Baltimore?*

That was from a November letter, and her question about the cake turned out to be rhetorical. Two days after the letter was written Catherine was resting after lunch on the porch of her cottage. Resting, her face held to the winter sun, a blanket wrapped warmly around her. Resting, when suddenly blood coughed from her mouth, bright flecks of crimson, and before the doctors were able to stem it, she nearly died of hemorrhaging.

That same day my mother was taken out of the cottage and transferred to the main building of the sanatorium, where the relapsed patients were cared for.

There was always a question I asked myself about Christmas. Year after year, as the season approached, the question would take shape. November began as a most ordinary month. In Brooklyn the weather varied slightly from that of October—a touch colder, no leaves on the trees, the sky gray as slate and overcast. If there were snow flurries, usually they managed to turn into rain. But as the November nights passed and the wind whistled through the window cracks of my room and grew louder and rattled the brown shingles outside, I would think about Christmas and ask myself, *What if it didn't come this year?*

It seemed to me a reasonable question to ponder. It was like worrying about the final day of school in June. School was scheduled to end by a certain date—but what if something happened to prevent it? Everybody remembered the year the circus had been scheduled to come to Brooklyn, with big, gaudy posters announcing the opening date in every store window you passed. But then a fire had broken out in the main tent, and the circus hadn't come to Brooklyn at all that year. It had stayed away.

It seemed to me that something like that could happen with school too. Everybody knew the date on which it was supposed to close, but I attended parochial school, and what if the bishop changed his mind about it? As the nuns liked to point out, Bishop Molloy was second to the Pope in authority over us. He was boss of the parochial schools, and he could keep them open all summer if he wanted to. It was possible—that was the thing to remember. So who could guarantee that Christmas had to come?

Not the date itself, December 25. I realized that nothing short of the world's end would prevent the actual day from rolling around. Besides, Christmas wasn't confined to a single day. What I worried about as I lay in bed and listened to the November wind rattle the shingles was the *feeling* of Christmas. Something special had to start happening inside you long before the twenty-fifth or you didn't truly experience Christmas. For weeks before, wherever you went, you carried this feeling around and stored it up, and by the time the day itself came, you were so bursting with it you couldn't see straight anymore.

Always, each year, I had waited for this feeling to begin inside me. Thanksgiving Day was usually the beginning of it. The big turkey dinner, with all our Connerty relatives crowded around the table, served as a foretaste of holiday joys to come. There was always a particular moment I waited for, when the feeling truly would catch hold of me. It might happen with a Salvation Army street band blaring out "Silent Night" on a street corner, perhaps, or I'd be going along the corridor at St. Aloysius's and hear the first carol float from a classroom. Or the first December snowfall might do it—I could be looking up at the winter sky, watching the flakes drift down, white and fleecy . . . the first Christmas snow.

You couldn't force the moment to happen; the feeling had to happen by itself.

Maybe it would happen a week or so after Thanksgiving. Supper ready and no milk in the refrigerator. Catherine would fetch my jacket and cap—"Here's thirty-five cents, Rob—better get two quarts. Hurry before Bohack's closes." I'd streak down to Broadway and reach Bohack's just as Mr. Jergens, the manager, was putting out the lights before closing up. But on the way home I was in less of a rush and would dillydally along Broadway gazing at the different shop windows. My favorite shop was Rausch's Jewelry, which featured a line of Waterman pen-and-pencil sets in the window. Each set reposed in its own satin-lined case, available in a choice of styles and colors that sent daydreams spinning in my head. It was a mark of highest distinction at St. Aloysius's to own a Waterman pen-and-pencil set. You kissed the ordinary dip pens goodbye and kept the snap-open case in prominent display on your desk, casually flicking out pen or pencil as need required. Nothing carried more prestige than the gift of a pen-and-pencil set from Rausch's!

But look! Tonight the satin-lined cases had been given an extra touch of beauty. A sprig of holly and a red satin bow decorated each and every case, and the window itself was festooned with silver tinsel, glittery icicles, and silver cardboard letters strung across the back wall . . . *Season's Greetings.*

It was happening, it was beginning. The feeling was taking hold of me. One last mesmerized look at Rausch's window and I'd race home over the night pavement. I'd leapfrog over the frozen ash cans on Warbisher Street, endangering the bottles of milk. Racing along, a great shout would start swelling in my chest. Down the side alley, into the backyard, up the steps, fling open the door, into the steamy kitchen. "Mama, Mama, it's coming."

The words would spill out in a babble as Catherine rescued the milk from my unthinking arms. "Rausch's window is all decorated. All hung with tinsel and red satin bows. Christmas is coming, it's really coming!" I'd announce.

Not this year would it come, not this year. Red wasn't for

Christmas—it was the color of blood. I hadn't been entirely wrong to worry as I'd listened in past years to the November wind at night.

This year we weren't to have Thanksgiving dinner at home.

Aunt Gen had phoned Dad the week before and said, "Now, listen, Jim, I know you've always had us to Warbisher Street, and you probably want to keep things the same an' all. But name me one good reason why all of you wouldn't be better off coming to us in Bayside?"

Dad said, "It's generous of you to offer, Gen, but I think Cath'd like it if we went ahead here as usual. So far nothing's been able to break up this household—"

"Horsefeathers," said Aunt Gen. "I guess coming to Bayside isn't going to bust up your family."

"No, hardly that, Gen, but if we can manage it here—"

"Oh, sure. We'll come to Warbisher Street and pretend that Cath's not absent from the table. We won't look at her empty place and think about how she nearly died a week ago. Sure, it'll be a barrel of laughs."

"I'm only trying to say—"

"Mother of God, you're stubborn, Jim. I'll get my Irish up if you don't stop it. Al's gonna think you don't want to show up at Bayside."

"You know that's not true, Gen."

"Okay, then, why don't you come? Name me a reason."

Dad had given up arguing and said, "None, I guess. What time would you like us?"

Aunt Gen gave a shout of victory. "Make it around one, we can enjoy the whole afternoon together. It's the best solution, Jimbo. Nothing to remind the kids of any sadness, just plenty of Thanksgiving cheer."

"Sure, Gen. We'll plan to get to Bayside at one."

"Hey, don't hang up yet. Al says you talked to the doctors on Friday. What's the latest?"

"They're still keeping Cath in the main building, but she's rallying okay."

"I tell you, I could weep. All her hopes for Christmas smashed to bits. Well, you can forget your troubles with us, at least. We won't even bring up the subject."

"Yes, Gen. See you Thursday. Thanks."

My father had hung up the phone and come into the living room. Supper was over and we were listening to the Edgar Bergen hour on the radio. Deanna Durbin, the special guest star, was in the midst of singing "I Love to Whistle."

"I guess you know that was Aunt Gen on the phone," Dad had said, speaking above the singing. "The Fritzles could probably hear her next door."

Daniel rolled over toward him on the carpet and asked, "Are we going to Bayside for Thanksgiving?"

"We don't have to," Dad had said. "We can celebrate it right here, if you prefer. Just say the word, if you have any objections."

But no one had objected. The only voice was that of Deanna Durbin warbling on the radio, "Early to bed, early to rise, makes you healthy, wealthy and wise."

"What do you think?" Dad had pressed us. "If we're staying here, I'll have to call Gen right back."

"We might as well go to Bayside," Roseanne said.

"Might as well," Vinny agreed.

Dad had gone to the dining room arch and stood looking at the circle of chairs that ringed the table. "Perhaps it's best, after all." He'd walked past Catherine's empty chair, and the kitchen door swung shut behind him, while from the Emerson, Deanna Durbin continued to support her preference for whistling.

It didn't seem as if there was any reason to stay home for Thanksgiving.

To get to Uncle Al's house from Warbisher Street without a car involved a complicated, lengthy route, which was one reason that we didn't visit Bayside more often. There was the long subway ride on the Broadway El all the way to the end of the line in Jamaica, then two different buses, and after that came a walk of several blocks before Uncle Al's dilapidated, paint-peeling frame house finally hove into view.

After every trip to Bayside Dad always remarked that the combined fares were almost as expensive as an outing to Asbury Park. And the comparison was a peculiarly apt one, for Uncle Al's house resembled nothing so much as an amusement park gone slightly to seed. The frame structure, with its tilting porches, broken windows and patched-up roof, could have served as a Coney Island Fun House. The front yard was an unkempt playground strewn with broken toys, roller skates, rusted bicycle parts, old baseball mitts and other maimed objects, while from an oak tree at the side of the yard a truck tire hung from a rope, available for rides. And spilling from every corner and crevice of the house were a Coney Island gaggle of kids, our seven cousins—Al Jr., Terry, Michael, Sean, the twins, Brendan and Billy, and baby Kevin. Seven boys, all red-haired like Aunt Gen and hollering at the top of their lungs, they were ever ready for games, fights, challenges and athletic contests of every variety. Over this noisy, boisterous fun house presided my Aunt Gen, who conducted herself rather like a lady in a Coney Island ticket booth. Large and gusty, given to bursts of temper and teary expressions of sentiment, she was engaged in a perpetual round of cooking, washing, and tidying up, with pauses for the dispensing of smacks and kisses to her rambunctious offspring.

Aunt Gen's voice was as loud and brassy as a fire alarm. She'd grown up on the top floor of a South Brooklyn tenement, and what with shouting up the five flights of stairs every day, it had naturally developed her lung power. She was an impulsive, kind-hearted woman, but her kindness was as haphazard as her household: you could never predict what would come flying through the door next.

All things considered, a visit to Uncle Al's was a strain on the nerves, and what it would be like under the added stimulus of Thanksgiving wasn't hard to imagine.

One happy aspect of the visit was that we were spared the usual subway-and-bus itinerary. The day before Thanksgiving Aunt Gen's unmarried brother showed up in Bayside. He'd driven up in a brand new Buick from his home in Florida. His name was

Frankie O'Brien, and reputedly he was a bookmaker in Miami Beach—that is, he had no visible means of employment, and the fact that he was always turning up unannounced suggested possible crackdowns by the Miami police. A result of his present visit, however, was that he was loaning Uncle Al the Buick with which to drive us out from Brooklyn.

We waited in front of the house, I remember, for the car to turn the corner at Bushwick Avenue, and Roseanne entreated me not to behave as if it were my first automobile ride.

"My first?" I said. "I rode in a car long before you—that time I broke my arm and Dr. Drennan drove me to the hospital. Plus I've been in taxis with Aunt Tilly."

"One taxi, if I recall correctly." She tugged at her hat and stood next to me on the sidewalk.

There was no doubt that Roseanne had changed since her haircut. Perhaps high school had accomplished it—she'd been elected freshman class president, to the family's astonishment, and was getting excellent grades in her studies. She claimed she was elected president only because she was in a classful of idiots, but even that showed a suprising modesty. She still had wacky notions of a future career—currently she planned to emulate Amelia Earhart and become the world's leading aviatrix—but she didn't shoot off her mouth about it.

As for the famous haircut—in truth, it had not made her beautiful; the freckled face was as plain and unalluring as ever. But now she took pains with her appearance, brushing her hair, keeping her clothes in order, as though to be ready in the event that beauty, like an unexpected caller, should arrive. Roseanne still had the habit of bossing me around—it was a habit of long duration, after all—but she also would do nice, unexpected things in my behalf. Like the day she'd brought home a copy of *Treasure Island* for me from the library. It was the first novel I'd ever been given to read, and the result was that I now headed for the library nearly every afternoon on my own steam and stocked up on Stevenson, Kipling, Jules Verne, Howard Pease—I couldn't get enough of them.

"You think Aunt Gen's brother is actually a bookie?" Roseanne asked, with another tug at her hat. "I'll see if I can worm it out of him. Bookies ought to have neat stories to tell."

Dad and Margaret were still in the house, but Vinny and Daniel were at the curb, discussing the merits of various automobiles while they kept an eye fixed on Bushwick Avenue.

"Would you buy a Buick?" I heard Vinny ask Daniel. "I'd buy a Packard myself. More class to it."

"I'd buy me a Cord," Daniel said. "Have you seen those babies eat up a road? Nothing like 'em."

My brothers were getting as car-nutty as Dad and Uncle Al were. They could spend hours on the subject, and next to girls, it was their most frequent topic of conversation. Sometimes, listening to their talk of streamlined bodies and the rest, I thought they might have been discussing girls.

"A Cord isn't a practical investment," Vinny said. "It's more in the nature of a second car. If I already had a Packard or Studebaker in the garage, then I might give it thought."

We waited in front of the house in our shined-up shoes and frayed Sunday clothes, and the one subject that nobody brought up was the one that was most on our minds: Catherine. If the setback at Greenvale had taken away her high expectations, it had robbed us of ours as well.

Before the setback we had been able to talk of her absence, because the end of it appeared to be in sight. A year to wait, six months, perhaps not even six. December, the coming of Christmas, surely no longer than that. But the trail of bright expectations had led us deeper into the woods, rather than out of them. The exit path was no longer in sight, and so we floundered on through this bewildering forest, unwilling to speak of it. To do so might confirm that each of us kept hidden the fear that Catherine was lost to us for good.

"I'm glad we're going to Aunt Gen's today," Roseanne said. She shifted her purse to the other arm and glanced down Warbisher Street toward Broadway. A lone trolley went by in a faint hiss of sparks.

"I wonder if there'll be Christmas decorations this year," Roseanne said. "I mean, if there'll be as *many* decorations," she corrected herself.

I turned and frowned at her. "Why wouldn't the stores be decorated like always?"

She scraped her shoe over the pavement. "I don't know. . . . Maybe it's not important, anyway."

I glanced up Bushwick Avenue for sight of the Buick. "Maybe so . . ." Rudyard Kipling, Robert Louis Stevenson, Charles Dickens—what I liked about novels was that they could carry you off to another world. Reading was like climbing on board the trolley for the ride to Aunt Tilly's on Saturday—even better, because novels whisked you farther away than any trolley, far beyond the reach of Christmas and two pale-green inches on a map.

I said, "Maybe I'll go in the house and get a book to bring to Uncle Al's," and started up the walk.

The front door opened and Dad came onto the porch, followed by Margaret, who was decorously balancing a cake box. She'd baked a pumpkin pie the night before, "Because Mom would want us to bring something to Aunt Gen's." The pie had come out slightly burned—but not enough to make it inedible, we'd assured Margaret.

"Any sign of Al yet?" Dad yelled from the porch, as he locked the front door.

"Not yet," Vinny yelled back. "It's twelve thirty. He's late."

Margaret and Dad came down the steps, and there was a shout from my brothers—a gleaming midnight-blue sedan could be seen rounding the corner. Dad hastened to the curb, and, lined up with Vinny and Daniel, the three of them gaped in admiration.

"Get a load of the chrome headlights," Vinny said, waving his hand.

Dan gave a low whistle. "I like the line of the fenders. That's some buggy, all right."

"Give me a Buick anytime—they lead all the rest," said my father with a firm nod. The Buick plowed down the street in a display of speed and power, and he shouted, "Watch it, Al, you're not driving a beer truck."

For a moment as I watched, the midnight-blue hood was replaced by the white of an ambulance, and I could hear the far-off scream of a siren. But then the sedan parked smoothly at the curb and Uncle Al's face grinned owlishly at us from above the steering wheel. Bobbing next to him on the seat were two red-thatched heads, which belonged to my twin cousins, Brendan and Billy. Immediately they opened the car door and scrambled onto the sidewalk.

"BRENDAN! BILLY! GET BACK IN HERE," Uncle Al roared at them in a voice that could shake telephone poles. Living with Aunt Gen had obliged him to develop some impressive lung power of his own. He reached out the door to shake Dad's hand. "What d'you think of Frankie's little crate, eh, Jimbo?"

My father ran a hand over the gleaming blue fender, while Vinny and Dan stood in the street and inspected the headlights and grille. "She's certainly a beauty to look at," Dad said.

"BRENDAN! BILLY! GET OFFA THAT GODDAM TREE," roared Al.

My cousins were attempting to shinny up the tree in front of the Johnsons' house. They jumped down and proceeded to chase each other in circles on the sidewalk. Uncle Al turned back to Dad and asked, "Still keep your driver's license up to date?"

Dad gave a sheepish grin. "Of all the fool acts of my life—yeah, I went and renewed it last year, faithful as ever."

Pushing over on the seat, Uncle Al gestured at the steering wheel. "How'd you like a turn at the wheel, pal? Maybe it wasn't so foolish."

"Al, I couldn't. A brand new car, I wouldn't dream of it."

"Get in, I'm telling you. Look, Frankie won't mind."

"No, Al, really—" Shying away, Dad continued his protests, but then my brothers, taking him by the arms, escorted him around to the other side of the car. "C'mon, you'll go great," they urged, and finally he agreed to at least get behind the wheel. His big hands clasped it in a mixture of awe and trepidation. "Only down to Broadway, then you take over," he said anxiously to Uncle Al, practicing with the gear shift and studying the knobs and dials on the dashboard.

"Okay, everybody pile in," Uncle Al bellowed. "BRENDAN! BILLY! YUH HEAR ME? GET IN THE CAR."

Vinny sat up front with Dad and Al, and the rest of us crowded as best we could into the rear seat. We squeezed in Brendan and Billy, and their hands grabbed the cake box, which Margaret had to hold valiantly aloft.

"I gotta go to the bathroom," Brendan shrilled, jiggling up and down.

"HOLD YOUR WATER OR I'LL BRAIN YOU. Turn on the ignition, Jimbo."

Carefully my father switched on the motor, and, with many anxious glances and instructions from Vinny and Dan, he backed from the curb and steered down Warbisher Street.

"Handles like a baby," he said in delight. "But you take her when we get to Broadway, Al. With all our woes, I guess I don't need to go busting up a new Buick."

Al slapped an arm over his shoulder. "Listen, you're doing the best thing, spending Thanksgiving with us. Gen wants you to start planning for Christmas too. What kind of Christmas would you have otherwise? None, is the answer."

The Buick glided around the corner onto Broadway, and the sound of the ambulance siren rang in my ear.

When we reached the ramshackle frame house in Bayside all was quiet in the front yard—for a few moments, that is. Then out the front door and from around the side of the house the cousins appeared, a red-headed army of invasion clamoring across the yard. They swarmed around the Buick, climbed onto the running board and fenders.

As we gingerly stepped onto the sidewalk another carrottop streaked out the door with a holler. It was Michael, and in pursuit of him was a large figure in a wrapper, hair curlers, and carpet slippers.

"I CAUGHT YOU. I SEEN WHAT YOU SWIPED," screamed Aunt Gen, chasing Michael across the yard. The hair curlers bobbed, the wrapper streamed in the breeze. Pursuing Michael to the oak tree, she stalked skillfully around the trunk, gave a blood-chilling yell, pounced, and caught him up by the hair.

"AFTER-DINNER MINTS ARE FOR AFTER DINNER," she screeched, wresting a candy box from Michael and fetching him a clout on the ear.

Turning, she spied us on the sidewalk and emitted another piercing shriek. "Oh, God, I ain't dressed yet. Lookit me in my wrapper and curlers. Oh, what the hell, you seen me like this before." And pulling the wrapper closed, she advanced graciously toward her Thanksgiving guests.

"Hiya, Jim. Margaret, Dan." She went from one to the other of us, offering hugs and kisses. "Did Al tell ya I won a free turkey at RKO? They called out my number from the stage, and, oh, God, I raced up there, no girdle or stockings or nothin'."

On me she bestowed a particularly vigorous embrace. "Poor Robbie, so skinny and frail," she said, grabbing me up in her arms. Her eyes moistened and she blinked. "Ah, it's no wonder, without a Mom to look after him, God, it wrings the heart out of me. No!" She put me down firmly, led the way through the junk-littered yard, the cousins darting and jumping in her wake. "No, we're only having happy thoughts today. No tears or long faces," she vowed, clumping up the steps. "Oh, God, the goddam turnips is burning. I can smell 'em!" With a shriek, she bolted out of sight to the kitchen.

It was an hour or so later, amid a deafening chorus of whistles, catcalls, foot-stompings and cheers, that Aunt Gen carried the huge golden-brown turkey into the dining room. She had exchanged the wrapper by then for a wine-red gown that was torn under the sleeves and afforded generous glimpses of bare flesh and pink undergarments as well. Her hair, fiery sunset, gave no indication that curlers had attempted to restrain its turbulence.

My aunt struck a gay vaudeville pose in the doorway, the platter of turkey upraised in her hands, and bellowed, "Anybody hungry?"

Uncle Al noisily pretended to blow a trumpet. Then, as the platter skidded sideways, "Christ, Gen, you're dropping the goddam bird."

"I got 'er. She ain't skidding off." Struggling, as if on ice skates, she succeeded in righting the platter, and gave the turkey a shove back into place.

"Ya nearly dropped it," said Uncle Al.

"Well, I didn't, did I, so quit beefing."

"Genevieve, you're some card," shouted her brother, Frankie O'Brien, from one end of the table. His hawklike face was nut-brown, his hair had a patent-leather gloss, and he was attired in a canary-yellow sports jacket, sharkskin trousers and two-tone black-and-white shoes.

"I want a breast, I want a breast," Kevin sang, beating his fork on the table. This quickly inspired a chorus of fork-thumping and cries of "Breast! Drumstick! Leg!" from the other cousins.

"Quiet down, this ain't the monkey house at the zoo," bawled Aunt Gen, and set the platter safely on the table. Actually, two tables had been pushed together—one slightly lower than the other—and covered by two nonmatching cloths that overlapped at the juncture where the ends met. Seats of every variety— kitchen and dining room chairs, stools, a stepladder, a bench from the backyard—had been assembled for us to sit on, and these, too, were of varying heights, which gave a slanting, lopsided look to the gathering.

Aunt Gen blew an errant strand of hair from her flushed face. "It's some trick cooking two separate birds. I hadda do one last night and one this mornin', and now I gotta warm up the other again. I guess nobody's got a big enough oven for two birds."

"Nobody except you, old girl," bawled Uncle Al, whacking her on the backside with the carving knife. "Turned out seven red-haired sons from that oven of yours."

She laughed and cuffed him on the head. "You oughta know, lover boy. You put 'em in there."

"Ain't she a card?" shouted her brother. "I tell you, she's a whole deck."

Uncle Al carved the turkey, and from the kitchen came a staggering array of bowls and platters to accompany it—turnips, mashed potatoes, cauliflower, creamed onions, giblet gravy, stuffing, cranberry sauce, and assorted relishes. When all the bowls and dishes had been set out, Aunt Gen grinned at my father and said, "Well, don't you get it?"

Dad was next to Uncle Al, near the head of the crowded table, yet despite the press of faces and outreaching arms, he seemed to be sitting all alone. "I'm sorry, what was that?" he asked.

"The creamed onions, the turnips and cauliflower—it's exactly what Cath used to serve on Thanksgiving. Even the watermelon rind," Aunt Gen said.

My father picked up his fork. "Yes. I hadn't realized."

"I prepared everything the same. Poor Cath, God pity her today . . ."

Brendan put down his turkey leg. "Where's Aunt Cath? Why isn't she here today?"

"God, there I go bringing it up again. Sorry, Jim." She tucked Brendan's napkin in his collar and explained, "Aunt Cath can't be here today, she's in a tuberculosis sanatorium. Let me give you some gravy, angel. Dig in, folks. Plenty for everybody."

No sooner had the first turkey been plucked clean, than the second, won by lucky number at RKO, was brought in for carving. In his role as host, Uncle Al kept up a steady flow of talk, interrupted by lionlike roars at his sons. "How 'bout a hunk of wing, Frankie? BILLY, STOP DUMPING YOUR POTATOES ON THE FLOOR. Jim, can I interest you in more potatoes and gravy? QUIT THAT, SEAN. YOU'LL POKE YOUR BROTHER'S EYE OUT WITH THAT FORK. Say, Jimbo, remember the Thanksgiving we talked the cops out of a turkey? They was handing them out at the station house, but you had to—I SEEN YA, KEVVIE. YOU PUT TURNIPS IN BILLY'S POCKET. TAKE 'EM OUT— have a ticket to get one. So you and me go waltzing over to the desk sergeant and—I SAID TAKE THEM TURNIPS OUT OF BILLY'S POCKET—give him a song and dance about we got nothing to eat but oatmeal at home. Remember, Jimbo?"

"Yes, I remember," Dad said quietly. "Robbie, you're not eating your turkey."

"Yes, I am," I said, stabbing at the meat. *Don't you get it, Jim? I cooked everything the same.*

Then it was time for dessert and Aunt Gen carried in three

mince pies in addition to Margaret's pumpkin pie. She slashed at the pies with a knife, the flesh shaking on her upper arm.

"The pumpkin pie is burnt," Sean announced, pointing at the blackened crust.

Aunt Gen slapped at his hand. "No, it ain't. It's just overdone a trifle. Of course nobody bakes pie like Cath. Perfect, she used to turn 'em out."

Uncle Al was handing out coffee. "Genevieve, do me a favor, please."

"Yeah, sweetheart?"

He poured coffee, slopping it over the cup. "Kindly stop referring to Cath in the past tense. You been doing it all through dinner."

She looked up at him. "Past tense, what're you— Oh, God." Her mouth fell open and a hand clapped to her face. "Oh, God, you're right. I been talking as if—" She shot a worried glance in my direction. "Would you care for some ice cream with your pie, Robs?" she asked with a bright smile.

"Yes, thanks," I said.

"It's right in the fridge, Al," she called back over her shoulder as she clattered to the kitchen, "Tell me about the plans for Christmas."

Uncle Al was still occupied with the coffee. "Give me a chance to, will ya? Jim, like I started to mention in the car—"

"Nobody's eating the pumpkin pie," Sean advised.

"SHUT UP, BIG MOUTH. Like I was saying, Jim—"

My father lifted up his plate. "I'm eating the pumpkin pie. Furthermore, it's delicious, Margaret."

Aunt Gen came back with a half-gallon carton of vanilla ice cream and proceeded around the table, spooning the ice cream onto each slice of pie. "Did you explain our plan, dear?" she asked. "See, Jim, we thought we'd have you here for Christmas. Robbie and Roseanne can come out a couple days ahead, it'll be easier on 'em, no sad memories or nothin'. Then the rest of you can come out on Christmas morning, and we'll open presents together. . . .

My father went on eating his pie as if he hadn't heard.

"I know what your hopes were—that Cath'd be home by then," Aunt Gen continued, holding the ice cream spoon poised over the carton. "Let's face it, Jim. You'll have no Christmas at all with that empty chair staring at all of you."

Dad looked up at Aunt Gen and said, "We don't mind the empty chair. We like to be reminded of Cath's presence." He turned to Uncle Al in an effort to switch the conversation. "Talking of old times, Al, remember the coal we used to swipe from Delaney's at Christmas? Enough to keep the stove warm for Mom until New Year's."

Uncle Al nodded fondly. "Say, Mom was some old girl. That Christmas after Pop died, we had nothing—remember? She still hung up stockings for us. Filled 'em with walnuts."

"Yeah, and remember how we never could sleep those nights before Christmas?" Dad reminisced. "Al and me used to share a cot in the kitchen," he explained to the rest of us. "Me, I'd lie awake half the night, worrying and stewing."

Ice cream dripped from the spoon in Aunt Gen's hand. "Worry about what?" she asked.

Dad gestured awkwardly. "I—I had this fear that something would go wrong—that Christmas wouldn't come. I don't know."

"Not come?" Uncle Al challenged. "What could stop Christmas? That was screwy, Jimbo."

"Guess so." My father nodded. He rubbed a spoon along the tablecloth. "I guess kids get screwy notions."

I listened to what he'd just said, and a sense of closeness to my father beat at my chest. Long ago he too had known fears about Christmas. I looked toward him from the opposite end of the table.

"I know what you mean," I said. "It's a feeling about Christmas . . . that has to happen inside you."

My father looked at me, but before he could reply, Brendan shouted, "Mama's dripping ice cream on Kevvie's head." And as Aunt Gen grabbed a napkin and wiped at the carroty mane, four-year-old Billy turned to me and asked, "Why are you coming to us for Christmas? Aunt Cath's not dead yet, is she?"

In silence we drove home to Brooklyn through the darkness.

Uncle Al offered Dad another turn at the wheel of the Buick, but my father didn't avail himself of it. He sat stiffly between Al and Daniel in the front seat and gazed ahead at the darkness and the road lights glimmering in it.

We pulled up in front of the dark brown-shingled house. No lamps had been left on; that was a chore Catherine had always attended to. We climbed out of the car, and Dad thanked Uncle Al for dinner and the ride, and we waved goodbye at the disappearing red glow of the taillight. Then, walking ahead of us, my father marched up the porch steps and unlocked the door. He stepped into the hall, switched on a light.

When we filed through the door he stood with his back facing us. He swung around, and I had never before seen the expression that flared on his face.

"We're spending Christmas together," he said, clenching his fists. "All of us together. Nothing, nobody, is going to split us up. That's my job to see about."

Then, his hands fumbling, he took off his coat and hung it in the closet.

When Dad got home from work the next night he held a family council. He waited until supper was over and Roseanne had cleared the table and stacked the dishes in the sink. Only Vinny, who was at work at his night elevator job, was absent. The rest of us sat on the sagging furniture in the living room—Daniel, Margaret and Roseanne on the sofa, and I on the hassock in the corner. Dad stood in front of us, like a speaker at an assembly, and it was obvious that he had rehearsed what he wanted to tell us. But he wasn't a public speaker, or an actor who could deliver lines effectively.

"I've been thinking about Christmas and what's best for us," he began. "For a time it looked as if Cath would be here to enjoy it with us, but, as you know . . ." The sentence faded, and he moved his hands awkwardly. "What I'm trying to say is that all of us need this Christmas. We can't let it slip past us. It's important to us as a family that we don't let that happen."

He reached into his coat pocket and took out a letter. I recognized the handwriting on the envelope, and on the sheet of stationery, with Greenvale printed on it at the top, that he carefully unfolded.

"Your mother wrote me this letter in October, before the setback," Dad told us. "The doctors had given her a good report, and I guess it encouraged her way out of proportion. Let me read what she wrote."

In a voice that struggled to be firm and steady Dad read us Catherine's letter about Christmas. *Dear Jim,* he read. *I just came from the main building and my weekly checkup, and I really think it might only be a month or two before my discharge. According to the X-rays, my lungs are healed, so it can't be much longer. I might be home in time for Christmas.*

He paused and gripped the sheet of closely written paper. *I've dreaded the thought of Christmas,* he read on,—*not for myself, but for my Indians—their first Christmas without me to help make it happy. God couldn't give me a finer present than to let me come home in time to celebrate with all of you. But if it happens that I don't get home, I want all of you to go ahead and have the best and merriest Christmas ever. In that way I'll have it too, wherever I am. Promise me, Jim.*

My father folded the sheet and put it back in the envelope. "So that's how she felt about it—and I did write and promise her. Then the setback came." He moved over to the dining room arch. "Tell you the truth, I'd been thinking about Christmas long before Cath wrote me her letter," he went on. "Back in July, when the doctors' reports were first encouraging, I began to hope she might be home by December. I kept quiet about it—I didn't want to raise your hopes too much—but what I did was to ask Mr. Carlson for more extra work at the office. It's only amounted to a few hours overtime each week, plus working the Fourth of July and Labor Day, but I've saved every dime of it, like I used to do for Hanna's envelope. And if Childs gives us a Christmas bonus this year we'll have some money to spend."

He stood in the archway and looked toward Catherine's empty chair. "We should have stayed here for Thanksgiving. Going to Gen's ended up wrong, despite her kind intentions." He turned to us. "Okay, then—we won't make the same mistake. What are we planning for December twenty-fifth? Let's hear some suggestions."

Roseanne got up and went over to the window. "It was Mom who made Christmas, wasn't it?" she said slowly. "This year it'll have to be us."

"We'll have to start planning," said Margaret, smoothing her dress as she rose from the sofa. "Christmas dinner, whether to invite anybody, what decorations to have— With my connections at Woolworth's, we'll be able to buy decorations at below cost— more than we ever could afford!"

"I wouldn't brag about your connections at Woolworth's," Roseanne said. "A lot of their stuff is cheezy, anyway. We could design our own decorations."

"Dad?" Springing up from the sofa, Daniel crossed to the arch, where my father stood, the letter still in his hand. "I don't see that there's any problem," Daniel said. "We can do it fine by ourselves. We'll each be responsible for a different job. Margaret, the dinner, Vinny, the tree lights—"

Dad rolled his eyes in mock alarm, "Poor Vin, another year of fiddling with those strings."

"I'll help him."

"You'd . . . want to take it on?"

"Why, certainly," Margaret said. "Why wouldn't we?"

Dad looked at the letter, put it back in his pocket. "I—I didn't know how you'd feel."

"I'll trim the tree," Roseanne said excitedly. "I'll use popcorn instead of tinsel, it's very traditional." She ran over to the corner where the Christmas tree was always placed. "Strands of popcorn and lovely, shining balls, silver and blue. Won't it be beautiful?"

"I'll help you," I said. "I'll paint a big cardboard backdrop for behind the tree. A Bethlehem scene—the three wise men on their camels, and the stable on a hill."

"And, Robbie can help me find a tree. We'll hunt one out as craftily as Cath ever did," Dad said, gesturing expansively. "I knew I could count on you. We'll keep our promise to Mom, you bet we will."

"We'll begin this very instant," suggested Roseanne. "Let's get some paper and pencils and make up lists. The thing is to be as organized as possible."

The plans for Christmas began that evening. Nobody asked why it was so important, or what we hoped to obtain from our efforts. We simply went ahead, as if we were preparing for the best Christmas of our lives.

Christmas cards, decorations, gifts, the menu for Christmas dinner—there was no end to the lists we made out. We decided to invite the Moser family to dinner, if they wanted to come, and to buy presents for each of them. On the first day of December Dad brought home an Advent calendar, and we placed it on the dining room sideboard. The calendar became a symbol of our goal. A Bavarian village scene was depicted across the front of it—gnarled houses, church steeples, quaint old shops—and it had twenty-four tiny windows to open, one for each succeeding day of Advent until Christmas Eve, when the last window would be opened. Every night from then on we made a ceremony of opening another window and counting how many were left. Twenty, nineteen, seventeen . . .

We shopped for Christmas cards, brought boxes of them home, sat around the dining table after supper, addressed and stamped the envelopes. Dad worked overtime each night, and came home with mysterious packages, which he hid stealthily in the front bedroom closet. One of the gifts my mother had always sent to friends and relatives was gingerbread cookies. Now Margaret took on the task, and, after several disastrous attempts, turned them out by the batches. Vinny, who had the least free time to spare, spent it fixing up the crèche in the cellar. I got some sheets of white paper, pasted them together, and, with my water colors, painted a backdrop of Bethlehem for behind the tree.

The activities and preparations mounted, enthusiastic letters went off to Greenvale describing it all, and the days and nights of December flew by. Ten windows to open in the Advent calendar, eight, five . . . and finally one.

One window left . . . the night before Christmas Eve . . .

and I sat in the living room, attempting to figure out what was wrong. School had been let out early that afternoon, and Sister Jerome had permitted the class to have a party. No more school for ten days—I'd hurried home on light feet, turned my face to the sky, and prayed for snow.

Just before supper Margaret had sent me to Bohack's for extra milk, and there, strung along Broadway, the store windows had glistened and shone with tinsel, holly wreaths, cotton snow, and twinkling lights. *Season's Greetings* was strung across the back of Rausch's jewelry-store window, and the Waterman pen-and-pencil sets each bore a red satin bow and sprig of mistletoe.

And nothing had happened.

The table in the dining room was a thicket of lights and strings over which Daniel hunched diligently, uncoiling the lengths, testing the bulbs. In the kitchen Margaret was baking more cookies. Boxes of Woolworth's tree ornaments were piled on the sofa, and seated cross-legged on the carpet, Roseanne was threading strings of popcorn. Christmas music floated softly from the radio.

She held up a string of popcorn and regarded it critically. "I have an idea it'll look crummy," she said. "What's your opinion?"

"Oh, come, all ye faithful," sang a choir on the radio. "Joyful and triumphant . . ."

"It looks fine," I said.

"I'm not so sure. When you go out with Dad for the tree you'd better bring tinsel home. How do you like the way I hung the cards?"

"Come ye, O, come ye, to Bethlehem . . ."

Christmas cards were scotch-taped over the living room arch and along the wall moulding, where they made bright, fluttering dabs of color. The backdrop of Bethlehem was already thumb-tacked to the wall, and as soon as Dad came downstairs I was going tree-hunting with him.

"Sing, choirs of angels, sing in exaltation . . ."

A house, I thought, should change at Christmas. Each ring of the doorbell should be as though the Magi were seeking admittance, each room should be filled with expectation, a promise of the Christ child's coming. Ornaments, decorations, tree lights, gingerbread cookies baking in the kitchen, a backdrop of Bethlehem —what was missing in our house? What had we left out?

"The cards look nice strung up like that," I said to Roseanne.

"Yeah," she answered, fiddling with the popcorn.

The room suddenly felt cold, the music cheerless. I went to the hall closet and got out my jacket and cap so that I'd be ready to leave with Dad. I pulled on the jacket, debated whether to put on my rubber boots. I might as well, it still might snow.

"It's eight o'clock," I called to Dad up the stairs. "We'd better get started or the good trees'll be gone."

His voice boomed down cheerfully, "Be right there, fella."

I sat on the bottom step, shivering in my jacket and cap. Decorations didn't count, or music playing, or the scent of cookies baking. It was so cold in the house, despite our efforts . . . and store windows couldn't make Christmas happen either. . . .

I stood up at the sound of my father's steps, and his jaunty grin swung toward me.

"Ready, Rob? Let me get my coat on." I followed him to the closet, and he put on the worn herringbone coat. "Wearing your snow boots, I see," he commented, reaching for his hat. "I doubt if the weather tonight will oblige you."

"It might," I said. "It still might snow."

He grinned and cupped my chin. "With faith like that, it'll have to snow. Just what we need for Christmas." His hand felt along my shoulders. "Robbie, you're shivering."

"It's the house—it's a little cold."

"Well, shall we be off?" he asked briskly. "Mom wrote me about this Italian fellow up on Bushwick near Aberdeen who had great trees last year. Let's try him first, shall we?"

We went down the porch steps, and my father's long legs covered the sidewalk in purposeful strides. "You Indians are doing a whale of a job," he said. "Margaret's turning out cookies as though her life depended on it, and that backdrop you painted for the tree . . ."

"I didn't paste the sheets together evenly."

We walked up toward Bushwick Avenue, and there were

Christmas lights in most of the windows. The windows framed scenes of family activities in the living rooms, and a round white moon floated carefree in the dark sky. Stars were out—some, at least. A dusting of stars. I moved closer to my father and took his hand. The sky gave no sign of snow.

"Well, the big day is almost here," I said. "I have this feeling we'll find a terrific tree. Mom always checked to see there were no holes between the branches."

"Yes, and thick enough at the bottom."

We proceeded along Bushwick Avenue, past the Christmas lights twined on iron fences, and the evergreen wreaths that trembled in doorways. A steady flow of cars rolled along the wide thoroughfare, their headlights yellowish blobs in the darkness. We waited at a corner for the traffic light, and Dad nodded at a gleaming black sedan that was pulled up in front of the light. "Lincoln," he said. "Cost you two thousand for a buggy like that."

"No fooling." I whistled at the princely figure and watched the car speed away. We passed under a street lamp, and in the harsh white glare Dad's face was haggard, his coat cuffs half worn through. "It's absolutely my favorite day of the whole year. Nothing can beat Christmas," I said, holding onto his hand.

We stepped down and crossed to another curb, where I'd pretended to tie my shoelace that day of the ambulance last spring. *Pretend,* I thought . . . Roseanne, Margaret, Vinny, Daniel—we were all pretending to get ready for Christmas. It was only pretending, that's what was wrong.

Dad patted his breast pocket. "They handed out the Christmas bonus today—first one in six years. I bought Margaret a twin sweater set. Peach."

"She likes the color of peach," I said.

"I'm not sure where he'll use 'em—maybe on Snake Hill—but I got skis for Dan. Think he'll like them?"

"Oh, he'll go wild for skis."

"Robbie?" Dad's hand tightened on mine. "Tell me honest. Are we doing okay?"

"Why, yes," I said. "We've never worked so hard or made more decorations."

He walked in silence for a moment. "You're not all trying to fool me? I watch you, and something's missing from all of it. Tell me the truth."

"I—"

We had reached Aberdeen Street where the trees were supposed to be on sale. The corner sidewalk stretched bare and empty in the reddish glare of a neon sign. There were no trees anywhere.

"Mom said this Italian fellow had a stand," Dad said. "Bushwick and Aberdeen, she wrote."

I glanced up to check the street sign. "It's Aberdeen, all right. Maybe he just isn't coming this year," I said.

Dad's eyes were pinned frantically on the empty stretch of sidewalk. "Maybe not."

I pulled on his arm and suggested, "Let's go down to Broadway. There's always stacks of trees at the Halsey Street El stairs, and every fruit store sells 'em. Dad, listen, I'm sure we—"

But my father wasn't listening. He was staring across the sidewalk at something that had caught his attention—a lamppost, a line of cars, and in the back window of one, a clumsily lettered sign, *Special for Xmas*. Dad stared across the pavement, and his face winked on and off in the light from the neon sign.

"Dad?" I said. "If we go to Broadway—"

He turned around and whacked me on the shoulder. "Run home and tell Margaret to pack," he said. "We'll need sandwiches, and blankets in case it's cold." He kept grinning and whacking my shoulder. "Hurry, Robbie. Tell her hot coffee too."

"I don't—"

He gripped my shoulders hard. "It's not a tree we need. Skis and sweater sets—that's not what all of you want, is it?"

"But—"

"Run. Hurry and tell Margaret to pack. I told you I'd take care of things. Faith, isn't that what I said?" He gave me another whack, and I sprinted off.

I turned back at the next corner and watched him cross to the curb where the old car with the for-sale sign was parked.

I ran home without a stop, not even for a traffic light, and burst shouting into the front hall. "Dad says to pack. We're to take blankets."

Roseanne looked up from her strands of popcorn, Daniel came forward from the dining room. "What are you talking about?"

"Where's Margaret, she's to fix sandwiches. *Margaret,*" I shouted toward the kitchen, "Dad says—"

Daniel spun me around, grabbed my shoulders. "Will you tell us what's going on?"

I gaped at him, dumb-mouthed, and he shook me some more. "I—I'm not sure," I stammered. "But Dad—there's this old car for sale—"

It was eight years old, a 1928 Chevvy, with drooping headlights and motor that gasped and rattled and gave off other strange noises and caused the entire frame to shake in an alarming manner. The rear windows couldn't be made to close, leaving a half inch at the top for the December air to swoop in and set our teeth chattering. The upholstery was in tatters, but rosebud vases flanked the rear seat, and the dashboard paneling shone richly. It was a steal for the fifty-dollar asking price, Dad said, when he chugged up Warbisher Street at the wheel.

"Are you packed?" he demanded. "Is Margaret making sandwiches? Don't forget blankets—the rear windows won't close."

"Where are we going?" Roseanne asked.

"*Where?* Why, to Greenvale of course," answered my father, as if the question was unnecessary. "Let's see—Vinny'll be home in an hour, and I'll have to call the sanatorium to get directions.

We left Warbisher Street before midnight. Vinny and Dan sat next to Dad in the front seat, consulting road maps, checking routes. All the next day we drove along highways, past the cities of Albany and Troy, and chugged up mountain roads, past towns and villages spread out like miniatures below. We stopped innumerable times, at the sides of roads to rest the motor, praying that it would not fail, at gas stations to refill the tank and ask directions. We passed farmland buried deep in snowdrifts, white church steeples, railroad crossings, barns and silos. And late that evening we reached the village of Greenvale.

We drove up the steep hill and through the sanatorium gates.

Dad parked the Chevvy on the horseshoe drive and we stepped out on the snow-rimmed asphalt.

The wind blew, no moon was out, and the buildings were dark shapes under the tall pine trees. The ground sloped through the trees to a faint-glimmering lake in the distance, and at the head of the drive the main building loomed up, dark and silent, except for a few shimmers of light in the upper floors. Darkness enveloped the big glass-enclosed porch that girdled the lower floor, at one end of which were stone steps and an entranceway.

"You—you'll have to wait here, except for Vinny," Dad said, stamping his feet in the cold. "Those are the regulations."

"I'll stay with the others," Vinny said, and put his arm around my shoulder.

We stood in the driveway and watched Dad go up the steps to the entrance. There was not a sound in the blackness until, far off, a loon cried mournfully. The entrance door opened and Dad went inside. Then, in the dark stillness, we heard another faint sound, and the porch lights switched on.

The lights switched on, and there, knocking on the pane, was a figure outlined against the light. She'd been waiting there, but the darkness had hidden her from us. It was only the darkness that had concealed her. She motioned us to come nearer, and radiance lit her face.

We ran to the porch and grouped ourselves below the windows. The ground became our living room, the snow was our carpet. We looked up at Catherine, and hope, which was Christmas, came at last into our hearts.

10

Happiness

The question of future trips to Greenvale was settled on the journey back to New York. There were to be no more trips; the car broke down.

Christmas Eve we spent in a farmhouse down the hill from the sanatorium, where rooms had been arranged for us. We attended Christmas Mass early the next morning in the village church. We talked to Catherine on the crank phone in the general store, and then we rode up the hill again for a final visit under the porch windows. Dad and Vinny went inside and carried our goodbyes to her. When they came out again we climbed into the Chevvy, it circled the horseshoe drive, and we waved from the car windows until the entrance gates were far behind and the ribbon of highway unfolded its long length between the wooded hills.

Stops for hamburgers and gasoline, wrong turns, map consultations—the ride home passed without event until, a few miles north of Albany, the rattle of the motor turned loud and alarming. It gave out a violent clanking, a curl of steam hissed from the radiator, there was a swaying lurch, and the Chevvy staggered to a mulish halt at the side of the highway.

As the family engineer, Vinny got out, folded back the hood and inspected the motor thoroughly. All he could report was that the motor didn't seem to be functioning.

"It's the main gasket, I think," Vinny said. "I think we blew it."

Dad got out and whacked at various parts of the motor to no effect; he got behind the wheel, pulled at the ignition knob until it nearly came off. Finally Dan and Vinny went racing to a gas station a mile down the highway.

"Don't panic," Dad advised the rest of us as we waited for assistance. "Everybody keep calm. No call to panic."

It was needless advice, really, for in the happy, euphoric mood that enveloped the broken-down Chevvy, panic could gain no foothold. We could have been stranded in Siberia, it would not have mattered.

Presently Dan and Vinny chugged back along the highway in a tow truck with a mechanic. He gave the stricken vehicle one brief examination and advised Dad to look into train and bus schedules if we wanted to reach New York.

"This old heap's had it, mister," he said. "Busted your main gasket, plus the crankshaft's ready to go. Surprised you got this far in it."

My father reached out and patted the exhausted hood, as if to reassure it. "Never mind, it did fine by us," he said.

"Cost you five bucks to tow it away."

Dad slapped him jovially on the back. "I'd have you tow it right to Brooklyn if I could," he said, and we understood exactly what he meant. The old secondhand Chevvy had accomplished what nothing else had been able to do: it had conquered two unspannable pale-green inches on a map. It had taken us to Catherine, permitted us to see her again and to know for ourselves that she was truly alive, rather than some fading ghost of memory. Catherine was alive, and we had seen it for ourselves, her face radiant at the sanatorium window, her eyes glowing at the sight of us. No matter how long her recovery took, no matter what the setbacks, we had that to sustain us now.

Dad counted out five dollars from his wallet. Blithely he handed the bills to the mechanic. "Just about bus fare left, but I'll tell you something," he confided with a grin. "A thousand dollars couldn't have bought this trip for my family—no, sir."

Not ten thousand dollars, not a dozen cars breaking down! We had been to see Catherine. We had lost faith that she would get well again, and it had been given back to us. Not a hundred thousand, not a million dollars, could have purchased a more shining or desperately wanted gift.

226

"No, sir, it's the best money we ever spent," Dad said to the mechanic and told him about the purpose of the trip.

Burly in a plaid mackinaw and grease-smeared overalls, the man shifted his boots and studied the dollar bills. "What the hell, climb in, it's Christmas. For this amount I don't see why I can't tow you to the bus station."

"We wouldn't want to inconvenience you."

"What the hell."

In such elegant style, then, did we pull up to the Albany bus depot, some of us grandly installed in the hoisted-up Chevvy, while others hopped down from the tow truck itself. The scene attracted no small amount of attention, and when Roseanne impulsively kissed the hood of the Chevvy as the mechanic towed it away, I half expected a round of applause.

"Goodbye," we called after the tow truck, "goodbye . . . ," until it turned the corner. Ignoring the curious stares, we marched into the depot.

We rode home on a Trailways bus. It sped smoothly along the snow-edged highway, it dipped up hills and down, made frequent stops at crossroads and Hudson Valley towns, and never had any bus carried more recklessly joyous passengers. We sat bunched together in the rear seats, Vinny and Dad, Margaret and Daniel, Roseanne and I. We sang carols, called to one another, changed seats, visited noisily back and forth, and boomed, "Merry Christmas," at each new passenger who came down the aisle.

"Merry Christmas," they acknowledged back, struggling down the aisle with gaily wrapped boxes and packages.

Our main gift, what we had been given this Christmas, contained no wrapping or ribbon, and it could only be seen on our faces, and understood only if our faces of yesterday could have been seen, taut and strained, desperate and striving.

"Merry Christmas," we called to the other passengers, "merry Christmas," with boundless joy.

The bus didn't reach New York until after midnight, and there was a wait for a subway train, so that another hour passed before we finally paraded up Warbisher Street. Thronging into the front hall, we turned on all the downstairs lights, shouted "Merry Christmas" at the walls and furniture, and swore that we weren't in the least fatigued.

Dad brought out our gifts and we opened them in a tumult of excitement—skis for Daniel, a sweater set for Margaret, books for Vinny, a luster pearl necklace and matching bracelet for Roseanne. And for me a Waterman pen and pencil set which set me to blubbering.

Afterward, Margaret fixed hot chocolate, and the conviviality continued around the table in the kitchen. Then, like the gradual winding down of a phonograph, the talk began to slur. Eyelids drooped, heads nodded stupidly, and I could not recall how I reached my bed or who had carried me up the stairs.

When I awoke the next morning the usual sense of panic and loneliness gripped me. But then I remembered what had taken place, and I hopped from bed and quickly dressed.

I was to meet Aunt Tilly for a holiday outing that day, and I hurried downstairs and phoned the apartment on Clark Street.

"Did I wake you, Aunt Tilly?" I said. "I'm sorry if I woke you. It's Robair."

"*Mon cher,* where have you been?" she cried. "Phoned the house countless times yesterday—no answer whatsoever—I grew frantic with concern."

"We went to Greenvale. A secondhand Chevvy Dad bought with his Christmas bonus," I babbled. "It broke down outside Albany on the way back."

"Secondhand Chevvy? Albany? Whatever are you—"

"We saw Mama, Aunt Tilly. We stood outside the sanatorium and saw her at the window with our own eyes. She waved to us and we waved back. We *saw* her."

"Oh, Robair," bubbled the ginger-ale voice. "What happiness!"

"Yes, Aunt Tilly," I answered, gripping the phone tightly. "Yes, happiness, truly."

And though it was to take another year and a half before my mother came home, there in the hall, on the phone with Aunt Tilly, the worst of the ordeal was over, and with it had ended another part of my childhood.

228

Part Three
_____

11

Arrivals and Departures

Outside the bedroom window the street lamp flicked on and a finger of light crooked down the alley, fusing with the May twilight. Daniel was buttoning his shirt at the bureau mirror, getting ready for a Saturday-night dance at Fordham University, where he was a freshman. He went over to the closet for his trousers, and I took the opportunity to gander at my own image in the mirror.

It was an unnerving sight, which I doubted I'd ever get used to.

Two more birthdays had gone by, I was thirteen, and all in a year I'd skipped a grade at St. A's and added five inches to my height. Five whole shooting-up inches—and if it didn't stop soon I'd be a freak in the graduating class. I hadn't counted on receiving *more* than my share of the Connerty height.

Garbed in my underwear, I studied the sorry reflection that the wavering mirror gave back. Look what I'd turned into, a gangle of pipestem arms and legs, ribs sticking out, plus a shadow on my upper lip that wouldn't wash off. What must Catherine have made of the birthday snapshots I'd sent to Greenvale? Pictures of a potential freak!

"I swear I'm taller than last week," I said to Daniel. "I think I'm just gonna keep growing."

"Don't worry, kid. You don't qualify for Barnum and Bailey's yet."

He stood behind me, Handsome Dan, combing his black hair. Girls rang him on the phone, besieged him with party invitations, some girls even waited outside the house on the chance that he'd come out—and all of it Handsome Dan treated with casual disdain. It was the secret of his attraction, Roseanne maintained. Whatever the secret was, it was sensational.

"Out of the way, you're blocking the mirror," he said, talking from the side of his mouth like Humphrey Bogart. In addition to attending Fordham, Dan worked five nights a week at the newsstand of the Taft Hotel, and the tales he told of the female guests were enough to make your eyes bug out.

I sat down on the cot, rubbing at my upper lip, and studied the way he slicked back his hair. What was a reliable cure for a cowlick, would somebody please tell me? "Already, I've outgrown this cot," I said. "If I forget to pull my feet up when I sleep, they dangle off the end."

He selected a black knitted tie and knotted it expertly in a double Windsor. "Cheer up, kid. Soon as Vinny gets married, you can have his bed."

"By that time I'll have outgrown normal-sized beds," I moaned.

Dan hurrying off on dates, Vinny getting married—the house was filled with comings and goings lately. Arrivals and departures —a perfect Grand Central Station of activity. Actually, Vinny was only engaged to be married, and not even formally yet. It would be a long while before he was able to afford a ring for Peggy McNulty, but even so it was a major event.

What prompted a person to suddenly decide he wanted to marry a girl he'd known all his life? Peggy McNulty was a neighborhood girl, who for eight years had been a member of Vinny's class at St. A's. After graduation he'd hardly ever seen Peggy. It was true that he often ran into her at church on Sunday, but he hadn't paid attention to her beyond nodding or mumbling hello. What had happened to change his mind?

According to Roseanne, it was the outfit Peggy McNulty had worn to church last Easter Sunday. There she was on the church steps after Mass, all done up in a frothy hat and dress and Vinny had sort of blinked and stared at her. They'd commenced talking on the church steps, then he'd told us not to wait for him, he was walking Peggy home—and every Sunday after that he'd walked her home. Next thing, he was sitting in the same pew with Peggy at Mass, then taking her out on dates, and at New Year's he brought her to Greenvale to meet Catherine.

It was all due to the new outfit Peggy had worn, Roseanne claimed. It had caused Vinny to view her in a different light. And maybe that was correct, because it reminded me of another dress and the magical effect it had worked on Dad. *Poor Easter dress, poor lilac dress that got wet and ruined in the April rain. . . .*

Vinny wasn't planning to marry Peggy until he finished college —which would take another two years—and landed himself a decent job. And of course nothing as important as a wedding would take place until Catherine came home.

I sat on the cot, thinking of all the comings and goings, the new things happening, the changes that couldn't be stopped, any more than I could have stopped my body from growing five inches. Vinny wasn't the only member of the family with marriage plans, I'd learned last week.

Last Saturday I'd been the only one home to hear Margaret's startling conversation with Dad. Supper was over, Dan and Vinny had left for their respective dates, Roseanne was out, and Dad was at the dining table, lingering over his coffee.

Margaret had come in from the kitchen and poured him another cup. From where I lounged on the living room sofa with a book—*A Study in Scarlet,* my first Sherlock Holmes—I could see her at his chair, hesitating, as if she had some business to take up with him. He'd spread out a newspaper on the table and was reading it and sipping the coffee. Margaret smoothed her apron, twisted her hands, and finally said, "Father, may I talk to you a moment?"

"Yes, what is it?" Dad asked. He looked up from the paper, and I slid down on the sofa in an effort to remain unnoticed. Passing unnoticed wasn't so easy, with five gangling new inches of arms and legs.

"Sit down, Margaret," Dad said, as my sister continued to twist her hands. "Is there some trouble?"

She sat in the chair across from him and vainly attempted to quiet her hands. "Not trouble—it's nothing like that."

"Margaret, you can speak freely to me."

"Yes, of course." She bowed her head, shifting her eyes to the carpet. "I—next Sunday there's a concert at the Academy of Music," she got out. "And I—that is, someone has invited me to attend."

My father sat back and smiled at her. "Well, won't your mother be tickled to hear about this. She keeps worrying you're chained to the house too much. Who's the lucky young man?"

The question only served to increase Margaret's agitation. Her hands might have been kneading flour, so agitated did they become. "He—well, he isn't what you'd call a young man, Father."

In a burst of intuition, even before my sister pronounced the name, I knew who it would be. No, it couldn't be true—yet why not? Who else had Margaret been in contact with, so impressed by his gentlemanly ways? Who else at Woolworth's wore both coat and tie while laboring among the counters and aisles? I almost dropped my book at the thought of having divined the truth.

"What's his name?" Dad inquired.

"He—that is—" Speech failed her for an instant, then she said in a nervous rush, "I don't believe you've met Mr. Fergus, the floor manager at Woolworth's, Father."

"Who?"

"The floor manager—Mr. Fergus, his name is."

Dad frowned, trying to remember. "I seem to recall stopping by the store one Saturday . . . short fellow, thinning hair?"

"Yes, that was him."

"Isn't he a good deal older than you?"

Margaret immediately began to bridle. "If you're going to criticize him unfairly—"

"Easy there, Marg." Dad reached out and took her hand. "I didn't mean it as criticism. I remember how polite and courteous he seemed."

My sister plucked at her apron. "He'll be forty-one in September, and he's shorter than me, and nearly bald." She raised her face and looked at Dad. "He's also very kind and good. When Mother went to Greenvale it was Mr. Fergus who arranged my hours so that I could keep working. As the months went by, he never failed to inquire about Mother or to show me every consideration. He's a perfect gentleman, Mr. Fergus is. As for his age . . ."

"Tell me about it," Dad urged gently.

"Sometimes . . . I don't think there's any difference in our ages," Margaret said. "Mother's been away for two years—I haven't minded my responsibilities or begrudged any of it . . . but sometimes I've felt older than anybody, Father. Older than Mr. Fergus or Aunt Tilly or anybody."

He nodded and tightened his hand around hers. "You never complained about it once. When I think of how generous and unselfish you've been— Listen, Margaret," he said, "listen to me. Your mother hasn't had a setback since last fall. When I was up there in March the doctors assured me we'll have her home by summer at the latest. You'll be free then. You can go out on as many dates as you want and be a young girl again—"

"Mr. Fergus—Howard, that is—is a person to admire. I've admired him for a long while. He . . . lives all alone."

Dad rose from the table. He stood next to Margaret, put his arm on her shoulder. "I'm sure he must be very fine if he's earned your admiration. Go to the concert with him, by all means."

"May I . . . invite him to dinner before the concert?"

"Is that what you'd like?"

"Howard lives in a boardinghouse, you know, like Charlie Cronin. He seldom has the chance to enjoy a home-cooked meal."

"We'll be honored to have him," Dad said. "And after Cath gets home you can go back to high school and not worry about cooking or housekeeping—"

Margaret stood up, her hand rubbing the table. "I don't think I'll be going back," she said awkwardly. "Mr. Fergus, Howard, has more or less intimated . . . Your coffee's cold. Shall I pour you another cup?"

Dad nodded absently, looking at the table, and she took his cup and crossed to the swinging door with it.

"Of course," she amended, turning to him from the door, "everything must wait till Mother comes home."

The door swung shut, Dad slowly sat down at the table again, and in the living room I went back to reading *A Study in Scarlet*.

235

Vinny and Peggy McNulty, Margaret and Mr. Fergus—comings and goings, so many new things happening, and yet the refrain was unchanged for all of us: *till Catherine came home.*

Daniel pulled on a sports jacket and took a final inventory in the mirror. Glen plaid jacket, gabardine slacks, saddle shoes—as soon as I had money for clothes I was going to dress like Daniel. I rubbed my lip and asked, "Who's your date tonight?"

He leaned toward the mirror, gave his knitted tie a final tug. "Ginny Rice, a swell little dish from Marymount. If you don't quit fiddling with that peach fuzz, you'll wear it off."

I lowered my hand self-consciously. "I wouldn't be surprised if I have to shave soon."

"Got hairs anywhere else yet?"

"Two." My voice gave an uncomfortable squeak. "The last time I looked anyway."

Daniel grinned at me from the mirror. "Hey, Mom better hurry home or she won't have a baby anymore. Here you are, graduating a year ahead—and next fall you'll be going off to Regis."

"Only if I'm accepted," I reminded him dolefully. Regis was a boys' high school in New York conducted by the Jesuits. It was a scholarship school and admission was solely by competitive exam. Every parochial school in the five boroughs sent their top students to compete for the honor of a Regis scholarship. Sister Raphael, who was our eighth-grade teacher, had expressed doubts about me—"I don't trust individuals who stare out the window in a woolgathering manner"—but I'd been one of the three boys chosen from the class to take the exam.

"I probably won't make it, though," I confided to Daniel, rubbing my upper lip again. "We took the exam in March and still haven't heard yet. It isn't too promising."

"Well, I admit you don't look too promising, laying around in your underwear like that." He checked his wallet, keys, got a comb for his pocket. "What are you doing up here, anyway?"

"I came up to take a bath . . . I *think.*"

"*Think?* That's a brainy statement for a Regis quiz kid."

"When Roseanne gets home," I said, "we might go to Loew's Gates. She's late tonight."

Since last September Roseanne had been working on weekends at the Catholic Children's Center in Greenpoint. One of the nuns at Bishop McDonell High School had recommended her for the position. It paid five dollars a week, but that couldn't have been Roseanne's reason for taking it. She could have earned more working part time at Woolworth's than toiling with swarms of unruly children for a few dollars a week. Yet something had drawn her there nevertheless.

"Well, kiddo," Dan said, sticking a toothpick in his mouth and swinging to the door. "I hope you remember whether you planned to take a bath. I can see how it might tax your mind." He aimed his index finger at me, pulled the trigger and went into the hall. A moment later his shoes rat-tatted down the stairs.

I drifted over to the window and looked down the alley toward the corner of the Fritzles' yard that was visible from the vantage point. The view didn't include the new fence the Fritzles had put up—after the old fence that I'd never climbed had gotten blown down in a storm the previous December. Now I'd never get to tackle it. The new fence was made of wire, unsuitable for climbing, and besides, it reached no higher than my chin—where was the challenge in that? Vinny, Margaret, the Fritzles' fence . . . so much was changing.

I leaned against the window and wondered if adding five inches to my height all in a year had joggled my brain. I made little sense anymore—the business about taking a bath, for example. I'd come upstairs after supper with the definite thought of taking a bath. But somewhere or other the thought had been mislaid, like a safety pin that you put down for a moment and can't find again. My trouble at thirteen was that a million thoughts kept colliding in my head in hopeless tangles. It was the same with the squeaks in my voice, the fuzz on my upper lip; I had no control over my thoughts anymore.

I reviewed my peculiar behavior today as another example of lunatic behavior. It was Saturday, and I'd gotten up with the usual thought of taking the trolley to meet Aunt Tilly and go to the city. A Renoir exhibit had opened at Wildenstein's, which we both were anxious to inspect.

Okay, a Renoir exhibit that I wanted to see. Perfectly fine prospects—but what had I done instead? Called up Aunt Tilly and told her I had a sore throat.

"Poor Robair," she'd sympathized. "It's all the growing you're doing. It lowers the resistance."

"See, I woke up with this funny scratchiness in my throat, and when I swallow, it hurts."

"Oh, you must stay indoors," she urged. "What a pity—I'd looked forward all week to the Renoirs."

"Don't let me stop you from going, Aunt Tilly," I'd said. "I'd hate for you to miss it on my account."

The bubbly laugh. "We'll save it for another time, *mon cher.* Let's see, I'm going to Greenvale to visit your mother next weekend—no, the following—"

"Gee, Aunt Tilly, I'm sorry about my throat. From the way it hurts, I wouldn't be surprised if it's an infection."

"Perhaps it's cause for a doctor."

"Oh, I don't think so. I'll drink hot lemonade and stay in bed."

"I mustn't keep you on the phone. *A bientôt,* Robair."

Lies, terrible lies. Why was I behaving like this to Aunt Tilly? Even worse was the next thought that skidded into my brain. "*A bientôt,* Aunt Tilly," I'd said, realizing as I hung up the phone that the reason for my lies was that I could go to the city by myself.

Which was exactly what I'd done. Concealing the phone call from Margaret and Roseanne, I'd left the house exactly as if I was headed for the trolley stop and the ride to Clark Street. And I'd taken the subway to the city.

New York was familiar territory after all the visits, and I'd wandered around the midtown area by myself, looking at this and that, making sure to keep away from Fifty-seventh Street and the art galleries. Aunt Tilly might have changed her mind about going to Wildenstein's, and it would hurt her to know that I'd lied. Still, it was fun to stroll around the city alone for a change.

Mostly I'd gone into bookstores, Brentano's and Scribner's and the smaller shops on side streets. It fascinated me to handle and look at the brand-new books that were arranged in plentiful stacks on the counters. I'd only known library books until recently, those scarred, soiled volumes in dull bindings with dog-eared pages and scribblings on the flyleaves. By contrast, a new book was like a new country, fresh and untouched, the binding encased in a shiny illustrated jacket that displayed the author's picture on the back. *The Rains Came,* by Louis Bromfield, *All This and Heaven, Too,* by Rachel Field—on this Saturday tour of bookshops I'd lingered over the authors' photographs, thoughts zig-zagging in my head.

I didn't know exactly where I'd gotten the idea, but I wanted to be a writer. Not that wanting counted for anything. I'd wanted to be an artist—and how long had that lasted? Not much longer than it had taken to use up Aunt Tilly's water-color set. Getting A's in composition papers at school didn't make a person a writer. Might as well want to be president of the world, or the next Pope in Rome. If you're looking for a good idea, forget all those big notions. Put the books and authors' photographs back on the counter and hit the streets, buddy.

I'd left the bookstores behind and sauntered up to Rockefeller Center. Strolled through the RCA building, sat on a bench near the outdoor fountain in the sunken plaza, thoughts still leapfrogging in my mind. It was great being in the city on my own—spending every Saturday with Aunt Tilly was getting tiresome. Never stopped talking, and those dyed red curls and fluttering scarves—her appearance verged on the eccentric. I'd started making lists of word meanings to memorize, and "eccentric" was a recent addition to the list. "Departing from conventional custom; differing conspicuously in behavior or appearance"—it described Aunt Tilly perfectly.

No, it didn't describe her in the least. I was ashamed of that last thought. I got up from the bench in Rockefeller Plaza and hurried away from such unworthy thoughts. What time was it? Two thirty. I stood in front of the statue of Atlas and debated whether to phone Aunt Tilly. Pretend I was calling from home, invent some story about my throat feeling better, and did she want me to meet her, after all?

No sooner had this newest thought presented itself than it was instantly replaced by another. Because coming toward me down Fifth Avenue was a woman in a lilac print dress. Her hat wasn't pink, but the dress was almost a duplicate of Catherine's.

She went past me with that same lilting stride, the sidewalk swayed crazily, and I wanted to call out to her. Then another thought seized hold of my addled brain: steal some money and catch the next bus to Greenvale. The wait was growing too hard again. I needed to steal some money and—

Theft! For an actual moment the thought of stealing had entered my head. I visualized my photograph, not on a book jacket but on page three of the *Daily News*. Thirteen-Year-Old Caught Stealing in Rockefeller Center. What sort of maniac was I turning into? Another entry for my word list rocketed in my brain. "Depraved: morally debased, corrupt . . ."

It had been more than enough confusion for one day. Hastening away from Rockefeller Center, I'd sped down the subway stairs and back to the safety and calm of Warbisher Street as fast as the train would deliver me there.

And here I was, mooning at the bedroom window in my underwear, fiddling with the fuzz on my lip, forgetting entirely about bathing. I felt along my lip and another urge leaped at me that I couldn't resist.

Stealthily I pulled down the window shade, went over, checked the hall, and closed the bedroom door. Standing under the ceiling light, I pulled down my shorts and looked between my legs.

Oh, God, oh, God, *three* black hairs—and more by tomorrow, no doubt. I'd be hairy as a gorilla inside of a week! If Catherine didn't come home fast there'd be nothing of the old Robbie left!

The front door slammed downstairs, and I quickly pulled my shorts back up. I ran to the window shade, yanked at the cord, sent the shade flapping and flying around the roller.

"Roobbbie," Roseanne called up the stairs. "Rooobbbie, are you up there? If you're still interested in a movie . . ."

I hopped into my trousers—no more knickers—and pulled on my shirt. On my way into the hall I banged straight into the door.

Hurry, Catherine—my shoes tapped out a message as I jogged down the stairs. *Hurry, before it's too late.*

At school two weeks later Sister Raphael rapped on her desk for silence. Chatter always broke out after morning prayers, but tomorrow was Memorial Day, and the prospect of a holiday had increased the noisy din.

"Silence," said Sister Raphael, white knuckles rapping on the oak desk. "I want instant silence." Actually, it took several moments for the room to quiet down, despite the baleful stare that Sister fixed on us. She hooked a thumb in her belt, which caused the rosary that hung from her waist to clank. "The results of the Regis High School examinations have been received," she announced, and thrust up her hand to still the excited response. "A member of this June graduating class has brought honor to St. Aloysius, I'm pleased to report," Sister Raphael intoned.

There was no stopping the buzz of speculation that swept the room. Heads pivoted around and attention focused on the three class members who had participated in the Regis competition. Johnny Zinsser, Edward Marsola, and myself. Sister Raphael's next remarks nearly tipped off the winner's identity.

"I regret that the recipient of this honor has been so tardy in distinguishing himself," she said, flicking back her veil. "In fact, when he joined this class he gave every evidence of being an idler, an out-and-out dreamer."

Well, of course nobody had to puzzle over who was the official class daydreamer. The suspense was over, and all gazes leveled at once at me.

"Robert Francis Connerty, please rise and accept our congratulations," barked Sister Raphael.

I stood up, or rather I unfolded my ungainly frame from the small cramped desk at the back of the room. "Thank you, thank you," I mumbled to the spatter of applause.

Sister Raphael regarded me bleakly. "I cannot guess how you

managed it," she confessed. "Most of the time in class you appear semiconscious at best. Take heed, Robert Francis," she warned. "Late bloomers are risky propositions. You may sit down."

With those glowing words of endorsement my moment of glory was over. I took my seat again, and Sister Raphael plunged the class into a rapid-fire grammar review for the forthcoming Regents' exams.

"Participial phrases," she trumpeted. "Mary Agnes Costello, give me a sentence with a present participle used in a phrase. Quickly!"

"Er . . ." As though discharged from a cannon, Mary Agnes Costello shot to her feet. "The girl, running down the street, met her father."

"What is the participle, please?"

" 'Running' is the participle."

Catherine, did you hear? A scholarship to Regis—the only boy in the graduating class to win. Did you hear that, Catherine?

"John, what does 'running' modify?"

Up leaped John Ryan, hands at his side. "The participle 'running' modifies the noun 'girl.' "

"Dolores Kane," barked Sister Raphael. "Give us a sentence with a past-participle phrase."

Did you hear, Catherine? I asked silently from my desk.

When class was dismissed that afternoon I hurried along the alley that separated the school building from the church and went up the steps of the side entrance. Ever since I'd skipped to the eighth grade in January I had recited a special prayer each day— in the morning when I got up, in church after school, at night before bed. It wasn't a formal prayer, I'd made up the words myself, and they were subject to change. But the message remained unaltered: that Catherine would be home in time for graduation.

I knelt at the garish main altar of St. A's, amid the gloomy frescoes and stern-visaged saints, and repeated the prayer over and over. I lit a candle at St. Thérèse's statue—she had given aid to me once—and then I raced home to write to Greenvale about the scholarship.

Sister Raphael announced it in front of the whole class, I informed my mother, hunched over a sheet of paper at the dining room table. *She said she couldn't guess how I won it, and that late bloomers are risky propositions. However, what I say is, better late than never. Right?*

I searched in the sideboard drawer for the book of stamps that Dad kept there. The accumulation of objects in the drawer had continued to grow—gas- and phone-bill receipts, circulars, more gift-wrap paper and ribbons and string. Rummaging for the stamp book, I lifted out the La Valencia cigar box in which Margaret now stored the family snapshots. There was only a small stack of them; the earliest was of Roseanne in her graduation dress, two years ago. The old snapshots were gone, that's all. Gone and disappeared—and who could say where? I put the cigar box back in the drawer.

I couldn't find the stamp book, so I took the letter and went loping down to Broadway to the stamp machine in Montuori's drugstore. I pasted on a stamp and dropped the letter in the mailbox on the corner, skiddled back up Warbisher Street—and as I came in the front door the phone was ringing. It was Aunt Tilly, and I told her right away about the scholarship.

"To be accepted by Regis, what distinction," she enthused. "Late bloomer, indeed. I shall seek out this Sister Raphael at graduation and correct her faulty impressions."

"I already wrote Mom about winning. I just got back from mailing the letter."

"Did you, Robair? How proud she'll be. . . ." The ginger-ale voice faded for a moment, then shifted to a different topic. "Speaking of letters, *mon cher,* have you by any chance looked at today's mail?"

It was an unexpected question for Aunt Tilly to ask, but I scooped up the morning's mail from the phone table, where Margaret still kept it. "It's right here on the phone table, Aunt Tilly. I've got it in my hand," I said into the phone.

Another pause. "By any chance . . . is there a letter from Greenvale?"

"You mean a letter from Mom?" I asked. "No. I looked when I came in from school."

"It would be typewritten," Aunt Tilly said. "The hospital stationery. A letter from the doctors."

A chill ran through me. "Just a minute," I said, propping the receiver against my chin while I thumbed through the batch of mail. Advertisements, the phone bill, a notice from church . . . "There's nothing from the sanatorium," I said, remembering the hooked rug and Mrs. Moser. "Why do you ask—is something wrong, Aunt Tilly?"

My aunt hastened to reassure me. "Nothing the slightest wrong, believe me, Robair. When I was up there last week your mother was in splendid health, the doctors were utterly confident. It's simply . . ." Her voice trailed off again. "You see, I received a letter today—a copy of one, really—the original would have been mailed to your father."

I shifted the phone to my other hand. "Please, Aunt Tilly. What was your letter about?"

She was reluctant to give me an answer. "Nothing of alarm, I assure you, *mon cher*. Such wonderful news about the scholarship. Would you ask your father to ring me when he gets in? Don't forget."

"I won't. Bye, Aunt Tilly."

I sat at the phone table, and the excitement over the scholarship drained out of me. The Christmas journey to Greenvale had given us faith for the long span of months that had followed. But faith was one end of a seesaw, and now the opposite end of despair swung up at me. Reports from doctors were to be feared, for what good news had they ever brought? News of delays, cautious statements and cheerless forecasts . . .

Dad was still working overtime at the office, and he didn't get home that evening until after nine thirty. He came in the front door, his eyes tired and red, and when I gave him Aunt Tilly's message he didn't seem to hear me at first.

"What letter?" he asked.

I stood with Margaret and Roseanne in the hall. "It was from the sanatorium," I told him. "A copy of a letter you were supposed to receive. She wouldn't tell me what it was."

His face creased and he went straight to the phone and called Aunt Tilly. The conversation that followed didn't make much sense or provide any information, not from what I was able to hear of it.

Dad started by telling Aunt Tilly that, no, he hadn't received a letter from Greenvale. "If you wouldn't mind reading me yours," he said, after which he kept listening and nodding his head. "Are you sure it says that?" he asked. "I don't understand. I assumed that any decision like that— Would you read me it again?" He listened intently, his mouth tight and anxious. "Before we do anything, we'd better check it out," he said. "I'd call the sanatorium right away, except they don't take any calls after nine. . . . You did? When?" Whatever was Aunt Tilly's reply to the question, it didn't relax the tension on my father's face. "I see," he kept repeating. "Still and all, I'd prefer to phone there myself in the morning. Yes, I know, Tilly, but—" He went back to listening again. "Sure thing, no problem arranging that," he said. "What time do you want Robbie to meet you? I'll tell him soon as I hang up."

He clicked down the receiver, got up from the phone table, and turned to Margaret, Roseanne and me. A mixture of emotions struggled on his face—a dazed kind of wonder, held back by caution and mistrust. "I don't want a lot of questions," he said to us abruptly. "The letter Aunt Tilly received today—I've got to talk to the doctors first, and I can't do that until tomorrow. I take it you've all had supper."

"Tuna casserole," Margaret said. "I've kept some in the oven for you."

"Fine, I could eat a horse," he said, heading for the dining room. "I'm sorry, but you'll have to save your questions for tomorrow." In the archway he stopped and turned back to me. "Robbie, your aunt's going to Calvary tomorrow. She's taking flowers for Memorial Day and would like you to meet her there. It's an easy trolley ride."

"Okay," I said.

"She'll be at the entrance gates at ten o'clock."

He started into the dining room, and I said dumbly, "I forgot to tell you. In class today Sister Raphael announced I won a scholarship to Regis."

"That's fine, Rob," Dad answered, and continued into the dining room.

That night I climbed into bed without reciting the made-up prayer about graduation. The words had gotten mixed up and lost in my head, like so much else had done, for so long a time.

I left the house the next morning before Dad was able to put through a call to Greenvale. It didn't matter; it was better not to know if the news was good or bad or whatever. To get to Calvary Cemetery from Warbisher Street by trolley wasn't a very complicated ride, and Dad had written out the directions for me. The Broadway trolley, then a transfer to the Greenpoint Avenue line, which skirted past the cemetery gates.

Aunt Tilly was waiting for me at the scrolled-iron gates. I hopped down from the trolley, stepped back as it rattled past, and started across the road. Aunt Tilly and I must have spied one another at the same moment, for she waved just as I caught sight of her.

She was standing at the side of the gatehouse, a bundle of flowers in her arms, and it lifted my spirits just to discover her there. Her pale gauzy dress billowed in the May breeze, and perched on the red curls was the floppy hat that had seen service on so many of our summer expeditions. Cars were backlogged along Greenpoint Avenue, trolleys clattered back and forth, but Aunt Tilly was heedless of traffic as usual. She dodged nimbly into the road, waving the flowers in salute. I started forward too, and we met on the trolley tracks in the middle.

"Ah, a perfect day for cemeteries," she greeted me. "Though why I should equate spring sunshine with gravestones . . ."

"Hello, Aunt Tilly." She was wearing sneakers, I noted.

"Let me look at you. Let me see how tall you've grown."

"Don't say that." I grinned. "Another inch and I'll be ready for a freak show."

"I've watched you grow, I've been present for all of it!" Smiling, she raised up on her sneakers and embraced me. The bundle of flowers pressed into my face, sweet and fragrant, and I thought of the timid, hesitant aunt of two years ago, hovering in the Clark Street lobby. Change had come to Aunt Tilly as well as to the rest of us. She had traded timorous handshakes in favor of public embraces on trolley tracks. Her lips touched my cheek and she whispered from the floppy hat, "Forgive me if I embarrass you, Robair."

"You don't, not ever," I said. She carried a shopping bag.

"You seem very happy for visiting cemeteries," I said. "May I carry the bag for you?" I asked.

"*Bien merci, monsieur.*" Shifting the bundle of flowers, she handed me the shopping bag, linked her arm through mine, and gaily approached the Calvary gates. With a smile and a nod for the gatekeeper, she led me along the main driveway.

"Tell me quite honestly, Robair," she chatted. "This costume of mine, the sneakers and the tea-party gown, is it outlandish?"

"No, Aunt Tilly."

"You would not call it an eccentric combination?"

"Certainly not," I assured her. "You, eccentric? Never, Aunt Tilly."

"Occasionally I have qualms about it," she confessed. A brief sigh took care of the qualms, and she turned her attention to the scene at hand. "Of course Calvary has none of the charm of Père-Lachaise in Paris, though it does own a certain dignity. I've never seen so many Memorial Day visitors."

Wreaths made splashes of color among the rows of gravestones, and everywhere the gray monotony of vaults and mausoleums was relieved by the spring hats and coats of the visitors, who flocked along the paths or knelt planting flowers at the graves. They moved among the memorials of death with an odd sort of contentment, and I remembered Catherine's lighthearted excursions to Calvary, the picnic lunches, the tales of bygone Fitzgeralds, McAllisters, Duffys and O'Neills. I had kept away from Calvary for two years, but in nightmares I had visited it often, and had seen a black hearse paused at the hillside where the Quinlans lay. The letter from Greenvale—what news did it contain?

"You are silent, Robair."

I took a deep breath. "No, I'm fine."

Aunt Tilly gestured at the graves and statuary that stretched before us, and we trudged along. "How strange that none of our great painters chose to depict cemeteries in their work. A definite omission—perhaps you will correct it, *mon cher*."

"It—it's an idea," I said.

"Though lately I've suspected that you are headed for a different career," she chatted on. "Yes, clearly—the absorption in books and the printed word . . . Robair, are you feeling all right?"

"I'm okay."

"How wonderful about the scholarship. Regis, you know, is situated only a few blocks from the Metropolitan. We can meet there now and again."

"Yes."

We turned into a side path and trod past rows of weeping stone angels and sorrowing Madonnas, and I remembered that this was the route my mother had always taken to reach the Quinlan graves, following along this path until it opened again onto the drive. *Poor lilac dress, ruined in the rain. . . .*

The pathway ended and the drive was directly ahead. We walked along the winding asphalt under the border of trees and followed the turn of the drive to the right.

"Here we are," said Aunt Tilly, stopping as the slight rise of a hill came into view. She lowered the bundle of flowers and contemplated the hill slope with untroubled regard. "Papa chose a charming vista, don't you agree?" she asked. "That cluster of willow trees, the curve of the road . . ." When we reached the grassy incline she lifted her skirt and started up it. It was only when she reached the top that she saw I had not accompanied her. "Robair?" she called.

I stood below in the drive and closed my eyes against a vision of a black hearse . . . undertaker's men lifting out a coffin. I had been right in keeping away from this place. Why had Aunt Tilly asked me to accompany her today? What was in the letter from Greenvale?

"Robair, come help me with the flowers," she called, and I struggled up the hill with the shopping bag. Quietly she watched my progress. "Does it upset you coming here? It shouldn't, you know."

"I—I know," I said.

She led the way past the graves, a small, fragile figure in a gauzy dress, who might have been walking through a sunlit meadow, so tranquil was her manner. "Cemeteries, you must remember, are resting places," she chatted. "To rest in peace, with pain and anxiety gone—I don't find it a frightening prospect. Though, of course, when you are young . . ."

We reached the Quinlan plot and she stopped in reverence. From behind her I read the three names that were carved on the granite headstones: JOHN JOSEPH QUINLAN, JAN. 5, 1880, NINE DAYS ON EARTH . . . JOSEPH PATRICK QUINLAN, 1857–1914 . . . ROSEANNE O'HIGGINS QUINLAN, 1851–1916 . . .

Aunt Tilly put down her packages, folded her hands, and the floppy hat bent down in prayer. When she had finished she knelt on the grass and undid the wrapping from the flowers. "I bring anemones for my infant brother, though they don't last," she said, placing a small bouquet to the side. "And for Mama and Papa, the hardier nasturtium." She folded back the paper and held up two potted plants for my inspection. "Just look at the lovely deep shade of yellow."

I stood back from her, away from the granite stone. "I remember something you said here once," I told her.

"Something I said?"

"When you came here with us one time."

My aunt looked across the square of grass at me, both startled and pleased, and asked, "What could I have said that was worth remembering?"

My voice sounded blurred, coming from far away. "You said that we should always plant flowers. I don't know why I remember it, but I do."

"I said that?" She sank back on her knees and balanced a nasturtium plant in front of her. "How like me to forget. Thoughts skittering through my head, no better than June bugs." She gazed

249

at the plant for a moment, seeking an answer from it. "I suppose I was referring to my fondness for flowers." Delicately she touched the green stalk, the curling yellow petals, her eyes wide and seeking. "The world's a hard place, in need of flowers . . . perhaps I meant only that."

I stood at the edge of the plot and did my best not to look at the granite stone. Aunt Tilly put the plant down, rummaged in the shopping bag, and drew out gardening gloves, a spade, a small blue watering can, and slowly my eyes were pulled to the headstone. The black hearse, the undertaker's men—and now, very distinctly, I saw a fourth name carved in the polished granite, where the space was smoothly blank. Aunt Tilly spoke, and I swung around to her. "I'm sorry, what was that?"

She held out the watering can. "I was suggesting that, while I dig, you might get us some water."

Poor lilac dress . . .

"Yes, sure."

"There's a spigot down the hill. If you look for Judge Brennan's mausoleum, directly in front of it—"

"Yes, I remember it," I said. I took the watering can from her and ran down the hill. The spigot was easy to locate, just a few mausoleums down the drive, but my hand was unsteady and I had some difficulty holding the can under the tap. CATHERINE QUINLAN CONNERTY, I saw carved in the granite. I carried the can back up the hill, and the ruined lilac dress floated in front of me, blotting out the sky. *Poor lilac dress, ruined in the rain.* I stumbled along, and as I reached the Quinlan plot I tripped and fell, and the watering can went spilling from my hand.

With a gasp, Aunt Tilly jumped up and rushed over to me. "Robbie, are you hurt? What happened?"

I lay twisted on the ground and remembered the Fritzles' fence. "The doctors promised there'd be no more setbacks," I said frantically. "They told Dad that Mom's almost cured."

"Yes, yes."

"Then tell me. *Tell me, please.*"

"Robair, my poor—"

I pulled roughly away from her beseeching hands. "Tell me about the letter. *Tell me*."

Aunt Tilly knelt alongside me. "I shouldn't have brought you here. I thought if you could understand that life is taken away and given back equally—*given back*, Robair, don't you understand?"

I crawled away from her, away from the granite stone. "There can't be more setbacks. *Tell me*."

"The letter yesterday—it was a copy of the one on its way to your father," she said, the words rushing at me. "He was afraid last night it might be a mistake. I told him I'd called Greenvale and spoken to the doctors, but Jim was afraid to believe it, just as you are afraid now."

I looked dumbly up at her. "What? What?"

"Jim talked to the doctors this morning. At this moment he's telling your brothers and sisters—" Her hand touched my cheek. "Catherine's coming home," she said. "I asked for the privilege of telling you myself."

I felt my heart hammer wildly. "For sure, is she? Only tell me if it's for sure."

"Yes, the letter said so. For sure. Oh, Robbie, I've been of use. It hasn't been wasted."

Then, gathering me in her arms, kneeling alongside me in the grass, the water soaking the gauzy dress, Aunt Tillybird stroked my hair and said, "It's all right, sweet Robbie. Don't be ashamed— no one's too old to cry."

The next week, in time for my graduation, Catherine came home to us.

On Friday my father rode the train alone to Greenvale, and on Sunday morning a taxi turned into Warbisher Street. We stood gathered on the porch in our Sunday clothes, Vincent, Margaret, Daniel, Roseanne and I, and the house inside was cleaned and swept twice over and more. Aunt Tilly was on the porch too, standing off to the side, and at sight of the taxi not one of us spoke or moved.

The taxi drew up to the curb, the yellow-and-black door swung open, and Catherine stepped out. It happened as simply as that.

Motionless too, she stared up at us from the curb, in her blue dress and ruffled white collar, and we gazed down at her, figures frozen on a landscape. Dad came around from the other side of the taxi with the suitcases, a hooked rug folded over one arm. He paid the driver, the taxi skimmed away, and the landscape changed. The frozen figures sprang to life and raced toward one another, colliding on the front walk in a turmoil of laughter, tears, shouts, and hands reaching blindly.

"My Indians," Catherine cried, blindly touching faces, reaching out, turning from one to the other. "I'm home," she kept saying. "Oh, my children."

I watched from the porch, half-hidden behind a pillar. "What is it, Robbie?" Aunt Tilly called softly, but I could not move my legs forward.

On the walk the tumult of embraces continued, then my mother pulled back and searched the cluster of faces. "Where's Rob? I don't—"

She saw me then, gangly and tall, the tag end of the parade. She started toward the steps, and I turned from the rail and ran into the house. I ran through the archway, through the rooms that had been empty and dark for two years. Strung over the kitchen door was a banner in her honor, which we'd made of old sheeting last night, with her name pasted on it in cut-out letters. I ran under the banner and through the swinging door, and there in the kitchen I waited for her.

She would know where I had gone. Catherine would know where to find me. I stood at the white table, and the years of waiting washed away, the lonely fears and shadows. It was over, and it didn't matter about the Valentine box. Catherine had come back, and it didn't matter. *What Valentine box?*

The door opened, and I pushed away the memory that thumped inside me like a drum roll.

"Welcome home," I said, and vowed that I would offer anything to keep her here always, safe and out of harm.

12

To Plant a Flower

She unpacked her bags, put her clothes away, put her hat in the closet, and it was as though she had never been away—and equally, as if we'd never had her among us before. She was like some fantastic, shining prize that had been unexpectedly awarded to us, undeserved, and so we dared not allow her out of sight. She was a prize that must be guarded and protected, watched over, lest she be taken back.

That first day of Catherine's homecoming we installed her, queenlike, in the living room, and took care not to press around her or tire her out with chatter and questions. We seated her at the dining table and served her dinner and did not allow her to rise from her chair or clear away the dishes. All afternoon the neighbors—Mrs. Fritzle, Mrs. Lauro, Mrs. Johnson—came to the door with greetings, and we permitted them only a glimpse of her. Charlie Cronin and Uncle Al and Aunt Gen came in the evening, but Dad let them visit no more than half an hour, after which he ordered Catherine up to bed.

And when she woke up on Monday morning she found that the other side of the bed was empty. Dad and Margaret had gotten up long before, and breakfast was ready, the table set, as she came into the kitchen.

"But, Jim," she said. "I was going to surprise you and fix pancakes."

"Never mind the surprise," Dad said, whipping out a chair for her. "Sit down and dig into some bacon and eggs. The doctors want you to have plenty of protein."

"But—"

"Here you are, Mother." Margaret rushed breathlessly from the stove with a platter of bacon and eggs. "Help yourself, please. Would you like coffee or tea?"

"Milk," Dad answered for her. "The doctors specified a quart a day minimum. Pour her a big glass, Marg."

"Jim, at least let me make some decent coffee for you. I'll make it with egg, the way Hanna taught me. It's delicious."

It was not permitted that she get up from her chair. We hardly ate breakfast ourselves, so busy were we dancing attendance on her, a perfect Irish jig of fetching and serving. Vinny and Daniel left for the city—"Don't get up, Mom. See you tonight!"—and Dad ignored her protests that he'd be late for work if he didn't leave for the subway in two minutes.

"Not till I see you settled upstairs," he said firmly.

"What are you talking about?"

"After breakfast you're supposed to rest. It's part of the schedule."

"What schedule?"

"The one I've drawn up for you, based on what the doctors recommended. Let's go, madam."

I trailed behind them as Dad led her up the stairs, where she promptly discovered that Roseanne was already at work making the beds and tidying the rooms.

"Here, let me finish that," said Catherine, reaching for the carpet sweeper. "Don't you have to catch the El for school?"

"Nonsense, Mother. I'll get a late slip. No trouble at all."

"Come," ordered Dad, escorting her down the hall to the front bedroom. "The doctors said rest periods are absolutely essential."

"Jim, I wouldn't pay attention to every *word* those doctors fed you. They can be awful fussbudgets, you know."

Refusing to listen, Dad marched her into the bedroom and was not satisfied until she was stretched out on the bed with her shoes off and the shades pulled down. The procedure was accompanied by a certain amount of muttering, but he calmly ignored it and consulted his watch.

"It is now eight thirty-one," he announced. "You're to rest for two hours and again in the afternoon from three to five. Margaret will shop for dinner on her way home."

254

The muttering from the bed had not ceased. "Just tell me this," said Catherine. "What exertions am I supposed to be resting from?"

"That's not the point." Dad leaned over the pillow and kissed her. It wasn't much of a kiss; his lips barely grazed her forehead. "Have a good day, Catherine. I'll be home by seven."

"Jim, listen to me—"

In the manner of an impervious physician, he beckoned to me from the doorway, where I was standing. "Rob, you're to come straight home from school and make sure your mother's taking her three-o'clock rest."

"Yes, sir."

"Oh, boy, listen to 'em," muttered the voice from the bed.

"Don't tire her out with a lot of talk either. She's to be left here alone, where there's peace and quiet. Is that clear?"

"Yes." I nodded soberly and followed him into the hall, closing the door firmly behind me. As it happened, however, I proved to be the weak link in the chain of command. Not that I didn't have every intention of carrying out instructions; in actual performance, though, I was somewhat less than effective.

That afternoon I chased home from St. A's without any stops or dawdling along the way. The moment I entered the hall I called up the stairs. "Don't worry, Mom, it's only me. Stay up there and rest, I'll look after myself."

I waited for some muttering, but a commendable silence floated down from upstairs. I turned and tiptoed toward the kitchen, taking care not to make any distracting noise. Then I pushed open the door and was handed a definite surprise.

Catherine was at the stove in the act of taking a pie from the oven. "My goodness, don't tell me it's three o'clock already," she exclaimed, using the potholder to carry the pie to the cupboard counter.

"It's a quarter after three."

"It can't be," she clicked, as if greatly astonished. "You see, I was just getting ready to go upstairs when Mrs. Fritzle knocked at the back door with this blueberry pie."

"It's Mrs. Fritzle's pie?"

"Wasn't it thoughtful of her?"

"If Mrs. Fritzle baked it," I said shrewdly, "how come I saw you taking it out of the oven?"

"That's a very good question, Robbie." My mother took a knife from the drawer and proceeded to cut the pie. "I was warming it up. I figured you'd want a slice when you came in from school."

The pie certainly smelled delicious, warm and fruity and fragrant. "You'd better go upstairs and start your rest," I said.

She took down a plate and transferred a fat slice of pie onto it. "I'm on my way, just let me pour you some cold milk first"—crossing to the refrigerator.

"You're not sticking to your schedule. Dad had a big talk with us about it. We all have to help with it, he said."

"Y'know, I always wondered what profession your father should have followed if he'd been able to go on with his studies." Catherine poured a tumbler of milk, carried it to the table. "I bet he would have made a swell doctor," she said.

"Every day when I get in from school, I'm supposed to check on you."

"Well, no one can say you're not. Now sit down and tell me how school went."

It wasn't in me to be strict or stern with Catherine. Besides, her presence in the kitchen cast a glow that I couldn't help basking in or wanting more of. That she was actually standing at the table talking to me had the quality of a dream, for how many times had I dreamed of just such a scene? She looked at me across the blue oilcloth, and nothing in her face had changed. It was the same face that I'd pictured and carried around with me. I pulled out a chair, sat down, and started on the pie and milk.

She turned and stared wistfully at the stove. "I'd love to get a nice supper started. What your father doesn't realize yet is that I'm perfectly well." She took off her apron, rinsed her hands at the sink. "I suppose I'll have to be patient and wait till he sees it for himself."

"I guess it wouldn't hurt if you didn't go right upstairs," I said, busy with the pie. I kept my eyes on the plate. "At school today we practiced the graduation march, with the piano playing 'Pomp and Circumstance,' and everything."

"You did?" Catherine sat opposite me at the table. "For two years I've waited for this. Oh, tell me about it, Robbie."

We began to talk, one sentence leaping ahead of the next, jumping from one topic to another, and it was after four thirty before Catherine finally went upstairs. She came down again at five thirty and didn't attempt to help with dinner, though the urge was great. She sat in the living room with magazines and the radio playing, while Margaret and Roseanne busied themselves in the kitchen.

"Well, how's the patient behaving?" boomed Dad when he arrived home at seven. "That's the girl, Cath—don't get up, stay right on the sofa. Robbie, did she take her afternoon rest?"

"Oh, sure," I said.

He turned and beamed at her. "First complete day home—you're probably all tired out. After dinner I'm marching you straight upstairs to bed. Now, isn't that the sensible thing?"

"Yes, Jim," my mother said gamely. "I'm sure it's what's best."

The swinging door opened and Margaret trilled, "Dinner's ready. You can come to the table."

"Easy now," Dad said, hurrying over to the sofa as Mom moved to get up. "Here now, take my arm. Lean on me if you have to."

"Thank you."

"Am I going too fast for you?"

"No, Jim."

It went on like that for the rest of the week. Each morning Dad was up ahead of Mom, and Margaret had breakfast ready by the time she came down the stairs. Roseanne made the beds and did the cleaning and shopped for groceries in the afternoon. Supper remained Margaret's province, and as soon as it was over, Dad led the march upstairs to an early bedtime. She was our prize, to be guarded, protected, watched over, and kept away from life.

But most prizes of great value are not easy to look after, we soon were made aware. On Saturday, when Dad woke up, it was his turn to discover that the other side of the bed was empty. Still in his pajamas and noticeably alarmed, he hurried down the stairs. He didn't need to get all the way down, because he could see Catherine seated at the phone table in her hat and the blue dress with the ruffled collar. Her mouth was set grimly and a suitcase was at her feet.

"What's this all about?" Dad demanded, pajamas flapping at his bare feet.

Without replying she picked up the phone.

"Who are you calling?"

"Long distance."

"What are you talking about?"

"I'm going back to Greenvale."

"The train's not till five."

"I'm taking a bus, or I'll walk if necessary."

"YOU'LL PUT DOWN THAT PHONE." It was then that Dad began the shouting, which brought the rest of us, startled and sleepy-eyed, to collect on the landing.

At sight of us the shouting stopped, and summoning his physician's manner, Dad descended the rest of the stairs. "Put down that phone and explain this outlandish behavior," he ordered Catherine.

She banged the phone down, and stood facing him, sparks in her eyes. "You have me so rattled I can't even dial."

"Take off your hat and give me that suitcase."

She seized the suitcase and held it protectively. "No, I won't. I'm going back to Greenvale. If I'm still to be treated as a patient, I might as well have some company."

There was a tense silence, with my parents exchanging angry glares.

"Catherine, you're being deeply unfair," Dad said.

"Oh, am I? Well, isn't it how you treat me?" she asked. "Lie down, get up, take it easy, lean on my arm."

Dad reached as if to tie his bathrobe, then realized he had neglected to put it on. "And how would you recommend we treat you?"

"By letting me have my job back," she answered, hugging the suitcase. "I suffered through two years of wanting it back, and now you've taken it away. . . ." She shook her head, trying to find the words. "I want to look after my family, Jim. I want to cook your meals and clean the house and have you complain when there's no white shirts. I want to be up early and get breakfast ready, stacks of pancakes and three kinds of eggs. I want to sit and laugh with you and be a part of you, not some mollycoddled fool, fussed over and waited on like a poor invalid."

Dad stood looking at her. "We want to keep you well and strong," he said. "So you never have to leave us again."

"I know you mean well, and you've been so faithful about it, but don't you see?" She lowered the suitcase and gestured imploringly. "The doctors discharged me, Jim. Released me as cured. They sent me *home*, not to some family sanatorium run by you."

"So you've packed, and you're going back there."

She looked down at the suitcase. "You ought to be able to guess it's empty. I'm not going anywhere. Fire and flood couldn't drive me away. It—it's just I wanted some way of showing you . . ." She turned away. "The children are looking, and I promised never to let them see what—" She put a hand to her face.

Dad went over to her. "Now, Cath, no use being upset. I guess we have been overdoing it." He patted her shoulder, then drew his hand back. "Say, listen," he said, "I keep hearing about these batches of pancakes you intend to make, but I sure haven't tasted any yet."

Catherine sniffled untidily. "Well, who's given me a chance?"

"What's wrong with now? It's morning, isn't it? It's breakfast time." He gestured at the stair landing, his doctor's etiquette abandoned. "As you can see, we're all up, and we're as hungry as horses."

Catherine glanced up at her Indians ranged on the landing and sniffled again. Then she whipped off her hat and coat, threw them on the table. "Ten minutes—no, give me fifteen. Go get dressed," she commanded. "I'll have a stack ready when you come down."

"Buttermilk," Dad said.

"No, blueberry," she laughed, and hurried through the archway. "I just happen to have some berries."

Dad looked after her for a moment and shook his head. Then

he turned to us on the stairs. "Well, what are you standing there for? Don't any of you want some pancakes?" he demanded with a grin.

Catherine turned out stacks of blueberry pancakes that morning. She made the beds, brandished the carpet sweeper, made out her grocery list, and went shopping for weekend bargains at Bohack's. She was bustling around the kitchen when we came down the next morning. We were a family again, she had taken her place at the center of it, and the only question was who was made happier by it, her family or herself.

Hanna came back on Thursdays, and there was a joyous reunion between the two friends. At the end of June Catherine proudly attended my graduation exercises at St. A's—I won a medal for excellence in English, which floored Sister Raphael altogether—and after the ceremonies the first big party in two years was held at the brown-shingled house. Catherine had prepared salads and platters of sandwiches, there was a cake with my name on it, a bowl of fruit punch, and quarts of ice cream from Schlack's. Charlie Cronin came, Mr. and Mrs. Fritzle, Uncle Al and Aunt Gen, and my seven red-haired cousins laid siege to the backyard.

The summer passed in golden contentment. On weekends there were outings to Rockaway Beach, a boat ride to Bear Mountain, picnics in Highland Park. Catherine invited Mr. Fergus to Sunday dinner, which left Margaret in a happy daze for a week, and the next Sunday Peggy McNulty and her entire family came to supper. There were quiet evenings on the porch, lazy mornings, a succession of summer days that passed in so perfect and flawless a happiness that it seemed as if nothing had ever been wrong or out of joint . . . until, in September, this was proved wrong.

Oddly, in the course of that peerless summer, in the midst of deep, contented dreams at night, there sometimes stole into my unconsciousness interrupting visions of the black hearse and the undertaker's men. In these recurring dreams I followed the men up the cemetery hill to the upturned earth. I would wake, half-conscious, the black vision still floating across my mind. The hearse, the upturned earth. . . . No fear, time had led me safely past all that. Reassured, I would drift into peaceful sleep again. Then in September I learned that these dreams didn't altogether belong to the past.

Life, Aunt Tilly had said, was given and taken away in equal measure, and in September the truth of her statement was made cruelly apparent. Two days after I had begun freshman term at Regis High School my aunt was struck down by an auto in front of the Metropolitan Museum of Art. The witnesses at the scene later reported that she had stepped out from behind a bus at the moment it was pulling away. Cut off from view, she darted into the street, apparently without thought to the traffic light, and an auto that was speeding southward on the avenue was not able to stop in time. Aunt Tilly was struck down while, two blocks from the scene of the accident, I waited in line at the Regis bookstore to buy Latin, algebra and biology textbooks. I never heard the ambulance scream by that carried Aunt Tilly to Lenox Hill Hospital, where she died a few hours later.

No one in the family understood why she had chosen to visit the museum on a school day, rushing over there after class was finished. But I knew what she had hastened there to find. Autumn and school had started, and she had left her prison, taken a bus, and hurried toward the museum in the hope of finding summer there—and perhaps a chance meeting with me.

Instead she had embarked on her own journey to Calvary.

Riding to the cemetery in the black limousine, I saw Aunt Tilly at the ship's rail and remembered the cluttered apartment and the empty bottle that she'd hurled into the trash basket behind the kitchenette screen. Birds were not such fragile creatures. . . .

The limousine swung through the Calvary entrance gates, and I sat on the jump seat and told myself that cemeteries were resting places and Aunt Tilly would be glad to be at peace, with pain and anxiety gone. But there was so much about her I didn't understand. The brandy bottle, and her talk of "being of use," and the "last chance" she had spoken of that day we'd bade *bon voyage* to the *Normandie*.

Down the center drive the limousine slowly traveled, past the rows of graves and weeping stone angels, and in the back seat Daniel said, "Poor Aunt Tilly, all her life she never did anything."

Catherine, garbed in black, eyes red and swollen, her face white and taut, turned to my brother. "What did you say?" she asked. "Never did anything?"

Daniel pressed her hand. "I'm sorry, I didn't mean to sound unkind. She had such a poor sort of life. . . ."

"Yes, she died poor," my mother replied. "A few hundred dollars in the bank—and do you know why?" She looked at us in turn, at Margaret and Roseanne seated in the back of the limousine, at Vinny up front with Dad. "Never did anything? I wonder where you think the money for Greenvale came from," Catherine said. "If Tilly hadn't helped out with the expense . . . *Nothing*, indeed. She gave me back to you."

So that was the last chance, the chance to be of use. I looked ahead at the floral car and counted the few sprays of flowers. A few hundred dollars in the bank, a burial policy . . . and made out in my name, a life insurance policy for a thousand dollars. And who would pay any of it back?

We followed the coffin up the hill and stood at the open grave. The priest began the burial service, and I thought of something I had never spoken of to my aunt. I had never said it, not once, though in my heart I had felt it. The priest sprinkled the coffin with holy water, and I planted the kind of flower my aunt would have wanted on her grave. Perhaps it was what she had meant to teach me.

Aunt Tillybird, I love you, I whispered to the green grass and spaded-up earth. *I love you, Aunt Tilly.*

Part Four

13

The Leavetakings

Catherine came home, and her children grew up and went away. In that manner could the rest of this story be told, for in essence it is what happened. The growing up had started before Catherine's return; the going away was the natural outcome of it, hastened along by the outbreak of war. Yet perhaps that does not complete the story, after all—for not all of Catherine's children went away.

There was one who remained on in the brown-shingled house, unable to leave.

Vinny, Margaret, Daniel, Roseanne—it took five years before their places at the dinner table were left empty, yet, looking back, it seemed to happen overnight, in one exiting. Perhaps it is because I remember so vividly the night the turning point came, when a signal seemed to sound—a bugle, Dad called it—that summoned my brothers and sisters away.

A bugle, but none of us heard it very clearly. It called a reveille over the gabled roof just a year after Catherine's return, and, in looking back, I wonder now if it was she who heard it first. That morning in September when she went into the yard to hang up a basket of wash, did she hear it then?

It was 1939, the Saturday before Labor Day, and the next week would mark the first anniversary of Aunt Tilly's death. I tried not to think about that too much, because when I did my thoughts tended to get scrambled and my hands took to dropping things. Like right this minute, knocking a spoon off the white table in the kitchen for no apparent reason.

"What was that?" Catherine asked from the sink, where she was rinsing off the breakfast dishes.

"Old butterfingers here," I said, bending down to retrieve the spoon. I was still skinny and sprouting, but a new feature of my appearence was horn-rimmed glasses, which I'd acquired in April. Extreme nearsightedness—and what caused it, Dad said, was my ceaseless and owlish reading of books.

Propped against the sugar bowl as I sipped my allotted morning cup of coffee was a notice from Regis High School. It announced the opening of school the week after next. *Student Assembly, Monday, September 11, 8:30* A.M. *Promptness Required*—if that didn't sound like the Jesuits.

I didn't really mind going back to school—freshman year I'd ranked ninth in a class of two hundred—but I was loath to bid goodbye to summer. I'd had my first full-fledged job this summer, pushing an ice-cream cart around Highland Park. The minimum age for city park employees was sixteen, but I was six feet tall, the squeak had gone from my voice, leaving it a startling baritone, and the concession manager at Highland Park hadn't even asked about my age.

The job had kept me outdoors, and the weather all summer had been ideal—almost no rain, just a flock of sunshiny days, with a cooling breeze from the reservoir to ease the heat, and girls on the park benches to liven up the afternoon hours. (Herb Lieberman, who worked the hot-dog cart, claimed you could tell the virgins from the nonvirgins by the way they crossed their legs. Nonvirgins crossed their legs higher up, Herb claimed. If so, Highland Park was a veritable mecca of nonvirgins, though naturally it was nothing that you could absolutely prove.)

On my days off from the park, there had been money in my pocket and wonderful pursuits to spend it on, such as the New York World's Fair. Flushing Meadows, where the fair was located, was only a half hour's subway ride from Warbisher Street, and what a place it was. The Trylon and Perisphere, Billy Rose's Aquacade, General Motors' Futurama, Steinmetz Hall, the parachute jump. Daniel, who was employed at the fair as a guide, natty in a blue jacket and white trousers, could get me free passes on weekdays, as well as discounts on most of the rides. Most of my days off had been spent at Flushing Meadows, right up until the previous week, when my job ended. And now this glorious knockabout summer was going, going, gone. *Monday, September 11, 8:30 A.M., Promptness Required . . .*

"It doesn't seem to bother you, I notice," I said to Catherine, who was stacking dishes on the drainboard.

"Robbie, you can't have nothing but coffee for breakfast. Let me soft-boil you some eggs."

"Here it is, a perfect summer almost over—" I pushed up the horn-rims, the frames needed tightening. "—I get my assembly notice today, tomorrow Dan finishes up at the fair, and you go right on with your dishes."

She wiped her hands on a towel. "You won't mind once you're back at school."

I sipped my coffee and announced broodingly, "Time is our enemy, didn't you know that? Good times go by in a flash, and when it's bad it drags on forever. Time, our enemy."

"You read that in some book," Catherine said, going over to a basket of wash on a chair. "At least fix a bowl of cereal for yourself. I've got to hang out this wash."

I watched her carry the basket to the door and thought what a miracle it still seemed, her presence among us. It still caught me unawares—coming in and finding her there, busy at her tasks, humming a snatch of a song, turning around in delight, as though the sight of you was exactly what she wanted for that particular moment to be made perfect. Even after a year the miracle had not worn off; there was still the sense of a shining gift having been returned to us, which must never again be taken away.

Not taken away, as Aunt Tilly had been, I thought, stirring my coffee. There, too, time was an enemy. If she had lived another year, how she would have enjoyed the fair, touring the foreign pavilions in her floppy hat and canvas shoes. *Ah, Robair, regardez là.*

The screen door banged shut, and through the screening I watched Catherine go down the back steps and deposit the wash basket in the patchy yard that, despite Dad's renewed ministrations, still refused to yield more than a clump here and there of spiky green grass. *Aunt Tilly, what does it matter, the thousand dollars in the bank? I'll never want to spend it, I think.*

In the yard, as Catherine reached for the bag of clothespins that hung from the line, a voice spilled over the fence. "Mornin', Mrs. C."

It was Mrs. Fritzle, in hair curlers and wraparound, busy at her own wash line. "I see you're gettin' a head start on the weekend." She grinned.

"Such perfect drying weather, I figured I might as well," my mother called back.

"I can't believe Labor Day's on top of us. Where'd the summer go to, where'd it disappear?" Mrs. Fritzle pinned a damp, wrinkled sheet on the line, and sent it jiggling forward. "I guess you got big plans for the holiday."

Mom laughed and fastened a white shirt on her line. "With a family at our stage, you don't make plans. Vinny's girl is at the Jersey shore with her parents, so he's heading there when he finishes work tomorrow. Some girl's invited Dan out to the Island . . ."

"That's how it is when your kids start growing up." Mrs. Fritzle nodded sagely. "I wouldn't wish being childless on nobody, but I don't envy you that part of it. Watching your children leave, I mean."

My mother sighed and bent over the basket. "That's what you raise 'em for, I guess, to go out on their own. It's what the whole job is about."

"Yeah, I suppose . . ." Our neighbor absorbed this philosophy in silence for a moment. *Whoosh* went her clothesline—a pillowcase sailing out. "Say, ain't it terrible about the headlines?"

"What headlines?"

"You didn't see the papers this morning or hear it on the radio?"

"Our radio needs new tubes. Why, what's up?"

In the kitchen I went to the cupboard to pour some Rice Krispies in a bowl. I watched Mrs. Fritzle make her way over to my mother at the fence, her hair curlers bobbing. "Mr. F. was on the night trolley run. He brung home a *Times* extra," she declared.

"Big headlines—Hitler's invaded Poland. Marched his troops right in."

Catherine stared at her. "Oh, that's bad, isn't it? That terrible man."

"I guess it ain't good." Mrs. Fritzle scratched at her curlers. "Speakin' of news, did you get that Bohack's circular advertising the meat sale?"

But my mother wasn't ready for other topics. She reached into the wash basket for another shirt. "I—I suppose it means war," she said quietly.

"Mr. F. claims it'll happen any minute—an' it won't be over in no hurry. About the meat sale, Mrs. C. . . ."

My mother lifted the shirt from the basket, reached up to fasten it on the line. Her gaze lifted to the blue summer sky that stretched in perfect tranquility over the rooftops, and I was reminded of another time when she gazed up in similar admiration at a perfect April rainbow. Slowly I crossed to the door.

"They got chicken fryers at Bohack's, seventeen cents a pound," Mrs. Fritzle chatted on. "Rump roast, leg of veal—If you want a look at the circular, I got it inside."

My mother gazed up silently at the blueness. "It's such a beautiful sky, don't you wish you had a picture of it to keep always?" she asked, and I stood at the screen door, as though to protect her from the dangers of perfect skies. But the next instant she pinned the shirt to the line and gave it a vigorous push forward. "Well, he'd better not come near me," she said.

"Who?" inquired Mrs. Fritzle.

"Hitler," said Catherine, and it didn't appear that she needed protection at all. When she came back into the kitchen—with the basket empty, yet carrying it as if the weight were heavy—her mind seemed chiefly taken up with the meat sale at Bohack's. Mrs. Fritzle had supplied her with the circular, which she was studying intently.

"Poland invaded—well, we've been expecting it," I said.

"Seventeen cents a pound for fryers. Sounds like a good idea for Sunday, don't you think?" She propped the basket on a chair.

"I know the way my Indians go after a platter of cold fried chicken."

"But there won't be many of us home on Sunday," I said.

She turned around from the cupboard. "What do you mean?"

"Well, Vinny and Dan will be away, Margaret's going to the fair with Mr. Fergus—"

"Howard," Mom corrected. "We shouldn't keep calling him 'Mr. Fergus.' "

"Howard, I meant—and isn't Roseanne going on some picnic with the shelter?" I went on.

"Rosie will be busy, too?"

"I'm almost sure." Roseanne was working full time this summer at the Catholic Children's Center helping with the program of activities. She left the house early every morning, returned late, and we had seen little of her at home. "There'll only be me, Dad and you for Sunday dinner," I finished up.

Catherine's mouth was a round O of surprise. "Well, can you tie that?" she said. "Discussing the very subject with Mrs. Fritzle a minute ago, and here I start planning a big dinner, like none of my children were going anywhere."

"Only you, Dad and me."

"I already heard you, Robbie. You don't have to repeat it." Catherine stood musingly at the stove, hand cupping her chin. "When are Vinny and Dan planning to take off?"

"Tomorrow night, I think. Soon as they come home from work. Some friend of Dan's is going to drive him to Southampton."

"Still, I don't guess they'll have to leave the very second they get home," Catherine mused. She swung around to me excitedly. "I know what we'll do—switch Sunday dinner to tomorrow night. Margaret could invite Mr. Fergus over—"

"Howard."

"Yes, Howard." Mom's face brightened noticeably as plans began swiftly to form. "If we're having fried chicken I can't not invite Charlie Cronin," she said, getting a pad and pencil from a cupboard drawer. "Let's see . . . corn on the cob goes nice with it . . . cucumber salad . . . oh, and peach pie for Charlie, it's his favorite dessert." The pencil scurried over the paper, making a grocery list. "We'll want pitchers of iced tea. If I hurry, Ferretti's might have some fresh mint left."

She tore off the shopping list, started for the swinging door. "I'll go down to Broadway right now, before the stores get too crowded."

I followed her into the dining room. "No one in the whole world is like you," I said. "Hitler just invaded Poland—it might mean war—and you're planning a party."

"Not a party—just the family getting together." She pondered her statement a moment. "Maybe that's all the more reason to," and looping her pocketbook over her arm, she sailed down the front hall, as tranquil as the morning blue sky.

"Wait, I'll come help with the bundles," I called.

She turned, smiling, as I bounded toward her. "You know, Robbie, I'm not about to disappear. Sometimes I think you don't really believe I'm home for good, even after a year."

I pushed at the horn-rims. "I know you are," I said. "I've left you every day to go to work in Highland Park."

"And raced home so anxiously every night. . . . I'm in fine health, you needn't worry."

"I don't," I said, "but I'll help with the bundles just the same," and I galloped ahead of her down the porch steps, where the ambulance attendants had carried the stretcher that I still could see.

By five thirty the next afternoon, when Charlie Cronin and Mr. Fergus—Howard, that is—were due to arrive, the house was in a state of crisis, caused by the ceaseless preparations that had been going on since Catherine had marched home with her frying chickens.

She was in the kitchen, dipping chicken legs and breasts in batter, hurrying to get the last batch fried. Quarts of hot tea spiced with lemon and mint were cooling in bowls, the cucumbers were sliced and in the refrigerator, and a big dented pot boiled on the stove, waiting to receive the ears of corn.

It was hot, and flies zzzthed around the living room, because of a hole belatedly discovered in the window screen. I was chasing after the pesky intruders with a fly swatter while Dad attempted to mend the window screen without having to haul it down to the cellar.

"So much junk piled down there, can't find the space to turn around in," he grumbled, measuring a patch of screening to fit over the hole. "Why aren't we at the beach, cooling off?" he demanded. He'd put new tubes in the Emerson, but there had been no more bulletins.

Dad's reactions to the party, when he'd come home from work the night before and discovered Catherine up to her elbows in pie dough, hadn't been overly favorable.

"What're we doing giving a party?" he'd asked.

"Well, not exactly a party, Jim. By the way, we mustn't forget to call Charlie and invite him."

"How come Charlie's invited?"

"Well, fried chicken and peach pie, his two favorite treats . . . Jim, I hope you won't mind fish cakes and canned spaghetti for supper tonight. With so much to get ready for tomorrow . . ."

Dad had waved the evening newspaper at her. "I guess you haven't bothered to read the headlines. All hell's breaking loose in Europe, but Elsa Maxwell here is busy with a party."

"Now, calm down and listen to me."

My father'd drawn himself up indignantly. "I haven't forgotten how you went skylarking through the Depression, Catherine. I guess a war is even more right up your alley." And with that salvo, he'd slammed out of the kitchen.

"Goddammit," he cursed now, pricking his thumb as he cut the patch of screen with shears. "Where the hell's that Mystic Tape? Where'd I put it?"

"I'll find it for you," I volunteered, temporarily abandoning the flies. "I know you had it, I saw you with it."

Vinny was upstairs showering, and Daniel, who had just hustled in from his last day at the fair, was in the hall, having a complicated phone conversation with his friend Steve Dowling. It concerned the ride out to Southampton, which Steve Dowling was against delaying until later in the evening. "Look, if you leave now you'll hit all that heavy weekend traffic," Daniel was saying into the phone. "But if we leave at ten or eleven— Honest, I can't get away any earlier, Steve. It's one of these family deals."

I snatched up the roll of Mystic Tape from the phone table and ran back to Dad with it. "Here's the tape—I found it."

"Goddammit, why aren't we at the beach?" he moaned, taking the tape and wiping at his forehead.

In the dining room, Margaret was arranging flowers. Or rather, she was rearranging, for about the ninety-eighth time, the slightly wilted bunch of marigolds she'd brought home to serve as a centerpiece for the table.

From the moment Mom had told her about it, Margaret had been an enthusiastic endorser of the party. "We'll make a formal occasion of it," she'd said. "A floral centerpiece, candles, perhaps —they add such a distinguished touch. Howard will be delighted to come. Oh, I'll leave work early and help with the arrangements. We'll really do it up."

Margaret was working full time at Woolworth's again, and devotedly saving money for her wedding. As far as she was concerned, it ought to have taken place months ago, but Howard Fergus was not a man easily talked out of his convictions. Last year, after Mom's return, he had insisted that Margaret go back and complete high school. "True, your career is to be that of wife and homemaker," he'd said. "But what if tragedy deprives you of both? A man in his forties must face the threat of a heart attack, circulatory failure, bleeding ulcers—"

"Stop. Without you, Howard, I shouldn't want to go on."

"My dear, what if I leave small ones behind, and you without a high-school diploma?"

"Yes, of course, how unthinking of me. I'll enroll at once."

It was a unique experience, listening to a conversation between Margaret and her intended. She had found a perfect match in Howard Fergus—they both spoke in stilted phrases that seemed to them as fresh as daisies. In any event, she had completed her senior year at Girls' Commercial and was currently poring over bridal magazines and home-decorating guides in preparation for a spring wedding.

She stood back from the dining table and viewed the arrangement of marigolds. "A centerpiece requires graceful blooms," she fretted. "Camellias or gardenias. These marigolds look as if I'd just picked them in the woods."

"Oh, for crying out loud, what's wrong with that?" asked Roseanne, who also was at work in the dining room, engaged in some last-minute silver polishing. "Howard doesn't go around drooling about centerpieces, I hope."

"No, but he's practiced in observing detail. It's a necessary requirement for a merchandise executive."

"Merchandise executive. I love that."

"If you imagine that Howard intends to spend his life as a floor manager"—Margaret fussed anew with the marigolds—"you're very much mistaken. He intends to rise."

"Like what, a cake of yeast?"

"I won't dignify that last remark with a comment," said Margaret. "Of course, I could ask just what exciting males you've met at the Catholic Child Center. None, so far as I can see."

"I wouldn't say none, exactly." Roseanne brushed back the unruly fringe of bangs. "Tom Donovan, one of the case workers is not only handsome but unmarried too. Naturally I'm just a seventeen-year-old kid to him."

She rubbed diligently at Grandma Quinlan's silver bonbon dish. She had managed to pry herself loose from the shelter at a reasonable hour today, but last night she hadn't come home till supper was half over. Dad had dressed her down good and proper for it. "I don't like you at the shelter," he'd said. "For one thing, it's located in a mighty rough section—it's not the right neighborhood for a young girl like you."

And Roseanne had said quietly, "Isn't it funny? It's the only place I've ever found that was right."

In the living room Dad fitted the mended screen back into the window, and I held the fly swatter poised over the Emerson. Down, I swatted with lethal aim. A zzzthing sound—escaped!—and the next moment a loud shriek rang out from the dining room.

"Eek, Robbie," squealed Margaret. "Hurry, quick, it's attacking the marigolds."

Brandishing the swatter, and with a push at my horn-rims, I

charged toward the dining room for more combat, then as I reached the table the kitchen door opened, releasing a cloud of steam. Catherine stood there, apron damp from the heat, hair disarranged, but with a look in her eyes that suggested she'd a moment ago been visited by angels.

"Roseanne, you didn't tell me," she said. "You waited for me to find it on the cupboard shelf where I'd kept the other one."

She gazed incredulously at my sister—clasped in Mom's arms was a sparkling Waterford pitcher. "You went and replaced it," she said. "You didn't need to."

Roseanne's head was bent over the silver candy dish and she didn't look up. "But I promised to," she said. "I wrote you at Greenvale about breaking it and promised to buy you another."

"And I wrote you not to be silly, it wasn't necessary." Catherine ran a hand over the sparkling cut glass that gave off flashes and glints of light. "I believe it's the very same design. The same size and design. Roseanne, you shouldn't have gone to such expense."

My father came into the archway. "What's this all about?" He saw the pitcher and drew back. "What—?"

"Roseanne bought it to replace the other," Mom told him. "She put it up on the top cupboard shelf and waited for me to find it."

Roseanne looked up from the candy dish with embarrassment. "I've had the money saved for months," she said. "It was getting the right pitcher that caused the delay. I went to Wise's, you know, that fancy china and silver store on Fulton Street? Well, they had to order one from Ireland, and it only arrived this week."

"Well, Rosie," Dad said softly. "What a fine thing to do."

My mother placed the Waterford pitcher on the table as reverently as if it were the Holy Grail. "It's beautiful," she said. She brushed at her wrinkled apron, tried to smooth her hair. "Look at me, all messy from the kitchen. I—I can't take you in my arms like I want, Roseanne."

Roseanne lifted her face up and looked at Mom. "Yes, you can," she said. "You can take me in your arms."

It was exactly what Catherine did. She went over to Roseanne's chair and put her arms around her. She cradled the plain brown hair against her apron, and her voice was filled with wonderment. "Children . . . oh, they're the best gift there is," she said. "I'm so glad that we're all together today. It's hardly happened once the whole summer long." She glanced over at the table set for dinner, and then at Dad. "That's why I planned it all," she said. "Time passes so fast, the days hurry along so. . . . Yesterday when I hung up the wash, Jim, the sky was so blue and perfect. We mustn't waste a moment of it, I thought."

She stroked Roseanne's plain brown hair, smoothed the bangs. "We'll always remember this day, because of the wonderful thing you did," she said. "Always, Roseanne, you hear?"

Right then, as though on stage cue, the front bell rang. As I raced to answer it, I could not have known there would be another reason to remember this day—for, what we unknowingly were celebrating, in a sense, was the last gathering of its kind in the brown-shingled house.

It turned out that there was no shortage of flowers at the party. Resplendent in a white ice-cream suit, pink-striped shirt, Celluloid collar and black-and-white shoes, Charlie Cronin stepped into the hallway with a giant bouquet of chrysanthemums, which he presented to Catherine.

"For the Queen," he intoned with a bow. "Or should I let her believe it was the fried chicken and peach pie alone that drew me here?"

As always, Charlie's presence turned my mother into a fluttering, gushing maiden. "Oh, Charlie, my heavens," she fussed, sniffing the gaudy bouquet, "here I've let you catch me in my apron again. I promise a more attractive frock at dinner."

"'Gracious,'" Dad imitated her, "it's frocks we're wearing to dinner."

"Now, Jim, fix Charlie a drink while I put these gorgeous mums in a vase."

"Lemonade?" Dad suggested, keeping his face perfectly bland. "Or would you prefer sarsaparilla, Charlie?"

"You'll find a bottle of Jameson's on the hall table," said Charlie, ending the nonsense. "A splash of water and an ice cube or two will do fine."

No sooner had Mom carried the vaseful of chrysanthemums into the living room than she was called on to cope with additional flowers. These, however, were blossoms of a different variety—Howard Fergus arrived, ushered in by Margaret, and in his possession were the pick of a recent Woolworth's shipment from Japan—a dozen wax roses.

"Very high-quality wax," he explained to Mom. "Be sure to avoid radiators, dust them regularly, and they'll keep indefinitely."

"Yes, you'd have to remember to dust them," Catherine agreed, somewhat rattled. She held the wax blooms to her nostrils, lowered them quickly, aware that no scent was possible. "And of course they'll never need water."

"The main precaution—no radiators."

"Yes, Howard, I'll be very strict about it."

By then Vinny and Daniel had come downstairs, and after Mom, Roseanne and Margaret had repaired to the kitchen to get dinner ready, the men settled in the living room. The afternoon sun blazed in through the windows, jackets were taken off, drinks distributed and replenished, and the crisis in Europe was discussed from varying viewpoints. It was Charlie's opinion that it would all blow over and that even if it didn't, the World Series games would be held as scheduled. Dad's conviction was that whatever the developments in Europe, President Roosevelt would "keep us out of it."

"On the subject of England, let me quote the wisest lady who ever breathed," said Charlie, referring to his deceased mother. "The late Sarah Dorsey Cronin used to say, let the whole damned island sink beneath the waves, pay 'em back for the centuries of tyranny over Ireland."

"Your mother had a colorful turn of phrase," Dad said.

"She was a wit."

Thus the talk went on with only minor interruptions of its leisurely course. At intervals Margaret appeared in the arch to announce the imminence of dinner, Daniel went back to the phone to check on whether Steve Dowling had as yet departed for Southampton—no, Steve hadn't—and Vincent brought out some snapshots of Peggy McNulty to pass around, while I entertained reveries of future scholastic triumphs at Regis High.

I sat, as usual, on the hassock in the corner, my legs jutting out like hockey sticks. I loosened my collar in the heat from the dwindling sun and decided maybe it wasn't so bad that summer was ending. Sophomore year at Regis I'd rank first in my class. *Why did I insist on being first?* Because I'd always been last—I supplied the answer. First in my class, and during the winter I'd read a hundred novels—*War and Peace, Lord Jim, Moby Dick* . . . and when I came home each afternoon Catherine would be there to greet me. No more empty house of fears, never again, all of that was finished. As Mom had said yesterday, there was no need for worrying. Put my worries away, that's what I'd do. Store them down in the cellar, along with the other articles for which there was no longer any use.

My thoughts drowsed on, until suddenly a remark of my father's jolted me awake. Vinny's snapshots were still being passed around and commented on, and I heard Dad say, "I'll tell you this—I got perfect results with that first Brownie of mine. It was a shame I had to go and break it."

For some reason his words prodded at me. Then Charlie Cronin asked, "Y'mean the Brownie you bought when you married the Queen? I thought you still had it, Jimbo," and Dad said, "No, that first one got broken. It meant the end of my picture-taking for a time."

I listened and the words ballooned out. "Broken?" I said from the hassock. "You always had the same Brownie, I thought."

Charlie grinned at me from the morris chair. "It seems the violin has awakened from his daydreams. Which reminds me, Jimbo—"

I got up from the hassock, pieces sliding together . . . *of what?* "You *broke* the first Brownie?" I repeated, trying to reach hold of something that was agonizingly close.

Dad took a sip from his whiskey and ice. "I'd had that camera since I married your mother. Took years' worth of pictures with it. The honeymoon and the first snaps of Vinnie . . ."

Charlie steered off in another direction. "Sure, I was with you when you bought it—a discount store on Nassau Street," and then Dad was passing the snapshots back to Vinny.

"Those are excellent, fella," he said. "If I may remark, Peggy's a humdinger in a bathing suit."

The pieces were slipping apart, I was losing hold of them. "The first Brownie—when did you break it?" I tried to prompt my father.

"What's that, Rob?"

"I asked—"

"Color photography is the coming thing," spoke up Howard Fergus. "The Kodak exhibit at the fair is proof of that. According to one of the guides at the exhibit, there's this new low-cost color film—"

"Dad, listen," I said, then Margaret appeared in the archway. "Dinner's ready," she called, and the pieces broke apart, like glass, like the Waterford pitcher. *When had the Brownie been broken? Why was it so important?*

We assembled at the dining table. Glasses shone on the damask cloth, silver gleamed, the wax roses clumped up from a bowl in the center, a hasty replacement for the marigolds. The table was crowded with extra chairs and I had to squeeze in between my brothers down at the end. Dad, pulling out his chair at the head of the table, clucked at me in commiseration.

"That's what comes of being last in the parade, even though you're nudging six feet," he said. "Well, at least you don't need phone books under you anymore."

"That's right," I said, the pieces about the Brownie floating away, like a paper sailboat over a waterfall's edge.

Platter upon platter, the meal was brought in, with a round of applause for each new entry. The fried chicken was cold and crisp, the corn golden and buttery, the cucumbers in the salad were sliced wafer-thin, and frosty glasses of iced tea were served from the Waterford pitcher. We sat in a circle around the table and passed plates back and forth. The gnawed corn cobs and chicken bones piled up, and Catherine, in a flowered print dress, kept hurrying to the kitchen for reinforcements, while Charlie maintained a flow of tribute to her culinary skills . . . and all that while, as we ate and talked, outside the windows, unnoticed, the sun went down, the light steadily deepened until, by the time the peach pie was carried in to another salvo of applause, it was dusk, and darkness edged the windows.

More iced tea was served in the living room, and after the table was cleared and the dishes stacked, Catherine brought in her sewing basket and joined Dad on the sofa. Margaret and Howard carried chairs out on the porch, and Dad got up and turned on the Emerson. A Victor Herbert medley played softly, and I sat listening on the hassock and resuming my reverie about school. I made a mental note to start taking cold showers in the morning as a preparation for the rigors of Jesuit training. Give up daydreaming, I continued the inventory. Get top marks in order to win college scholarship. Become famous author, live at Plaza Hotel . . .

As I went on in this vein, the music on the radio abruptly faded out. One moment a lavish swirl of strings, the next, silence.

"But Jim just put in new tubes," Catherine said, glancing up from her sewing. "That was such pretty music too."

"New tubes aren't always enough for this baby," Dad said, bending over to examine the Emerson, which of late had been wheezing regularly into silence. Usually a deft bang or two was enough to reactivate the sound, but not this time, however.

Vinny, in his capacity of family engineer, began fiddling with the wires and tubes at the back. "You know, television's going to replace radio some day," he said, probing with his hands. "Hey, these tubes are working. We ought to—"

There was a sputter, and the voice of a radio announcer suddenly came on. "We interrupt this program to bring you an important announcement from London," the announcer said.

Catherine lowered her sewing, Dad stood listening, and in the morris chair, Charlie Cronin reached over to rest his iced tea on the side table. There were more sputters, a series of bleeps, and then another voice came on.

"Good evening, this is Edward R. Murrow," the clear but rough-hewn voice reported. "I am speaking to you from London, where earlier today Prime Minister Neville Chamberlain called together an emergency meeting of Parliament. As yet no official announcement has been made, but there is no question that the business of the emergency session will be to declare a state of war between England and Germany."

The windows were dark. Daylight had gone, and in the brown-shingled house another part of our lives was ending.

No one spoke, as a recording of an interview between Murrow and Chamberlain was broadcast. The Prime Minister's clipped, quavering tones filled the room, and we strained forward to listen in disbelief. Dad crouched over the Emerson as if he thought it might lapse into silence again, and Daniel stood motionless in the archway. Outside, somebody was running up and down the street, shouting excitedly. Chamberlain's interview ended, and Edward Murrow came back on. He spoke tersely of air-raid shelters, enemy air attacks, and the evacuation of children which was already in full-scale operation in London.

Margaret and Howard rushed in from the porch. "Someone outside was shouting war's been declared," Margaret said. "Is it true?"

"I guess it'll soon be true," Dad said. He turned the knob on the Emerson, shutting off Murrow's description of air-raid drills, blackouts, and enemy alerts. "Thank God, we'll have none of that here," my father said grimly. "We'll stay out of this one. We learned our lesson in '18."

Charlie Cronin reached for his iced tea. "I'm with you, Jimbo. Considerin' the record of English tyranny against Ireland, His Majesty's Government be damned. Sarah Dorsey Cronin said it right."

Dad lit his pipe nervously. "Don't worry, Roosevelt will keep us out. Strictly nonintervention, he's stated it over and over."

Vinny shoved his hands in his pockets. "I don't know, Dad. I don't know. When you listen to what those people in London are facing . . ."

"I wouldn't trust Roosevelt, Jimbo," Charlie warned. "The foxy devil—I'd trust him as far as I could throw an elephant."

On the sofa Catherine had resumed her sewing. "The big bully," she said after a moment.

"Well, now, Cath," Dad said. "I've heard FDR called a number of things, but nobody's ever—"

Mom's needle maintained its steady rhythm. "I tell you, he got me so mad in the yard yesterday when I looked at that lovely sky. Hitler, I mean."

Amazement spread over my father's face as he absorbed this latest of her musings. "Let's hear that again," he said. "*Hitler* got you mad yesterday?"

"Yes." She nodded firmly. "I looked at the sky and could almost see planes roaring across . . . and when I realized this family hadn't had dinner, all of us together, the whole summer long—"

"I see," Dad said. "So it was Hitler who inspired this get-together."

"Oh, it's glorious," Charlie cried, toasting her with his iced tea. "The Queen has declared battle. She's called out the Guards."

"Well, somebody's going to have to stop him. A lot of people, maybe," Mom said, taking care with a stitch.

Dad looked at her and his face slowly flushed red. "A lot of people, but not us, Catherine. You enjoy a fight, that's the truth of it. That damned Irish belligerence. Do you know what a war would mean to this country? To this family?"

"Jim, I only meant—"

"It's perfectly clear what you meant. God, Catherine, is there no end to it?" Dad railed. "You sit there calmly sewing—"

Roseanne spoke then. She had gone over to the archway, and her voice was so quiet that at first she couldn't be heard. "It's a question of choice . . . a-and responsibility," she said. "Of what each person is responsible for." She came forward, and her voice grew stronger. "Coming home from the shelter this week, there was a big lout pushing around some little kids. Shoving them around, slapping them. Was I simply to ignore it? Just walk on, as if nothing—" She saw Dad frowning at her and turned quickly away.

"Wait a minute, Roseanne," he said. "What's that mark on your cheek?" She tried to shield her face, but Dad went over and turned her toward him. He brushed the brown hair back from her cheek. "It's bruised—someone hit you," he said. "What happened?"

My sister stammered. "Honest, Pop, it's nothing."

"I asked what happened?"

"Monday, it happened," said Catherine from the sofa. "Roseanne went to the aid of those children. It was foolhardy of her, and she was knocked down."

Dad spun around. "You knew about this and didn't tell me?"

Mom put down the curtain she was hemming. "I knew you'd only be worried and upset, and Roseanne assured me she'd be more careful in the future."

Dad looked at Roseanne. "Some hoodlum hit you. You tried to help some kids and that was your reward."

My sister returned his look. "I guess sometimes you have to get hurt," she said, her voice low and hushed.

Dad's eyes flared angrily. "I don't want you at that shelter anymore," he said. "It's doing something to you—leading you off somewhere. You're only seventeen, a girl still." Then, his anger going, he pulled her into his arms. "What am I saying? I'm proud of you, Rosie. You kids are growing up so fast and getting so far ahead of me . . ."

After that everything seemed to happen at once. The phone rang, and it was Steve Dowling. He wanted to let Daniel know he hadn't left for Southampton yet, and if Dan could be ready in fifteen minutes . . .

"Sure, just let me toss a few clothes in a bag," Daniel said. He hung up the phone, sprinted up the stairs. Halfway up, he turned to Mom and Dad. "You don't mind if I take off, do you? If I can avoid that long train ride tomorrow . . ."

"Of course, go right ahead," Dad said.

Daniel yelled down to Vinny, "Hey, maybe you could catch a late bus for Jersey. Steve could drop you off in the city."

Vinny hurried to the bottom of the stairs. "Gee, if Peggy was listening to the news, maybe she's worried about me."

"Why should Peggy worry?" Dad asked. "There'll be no war for us."

"Well, you know," Vinny said, turning to him. "Me joining the R.O.T.C. last year at college."

Dad stared at him a moment. "Surely the young lady doesn't imagine you'll be marching off tomor—" He stopped, as though visualizing in his mind's eye the closet upstairs, the sports jackets and summer suits and corduroy trousers and, crowded among them, on a hanger, the Army uniform that Vinny had been wearing to his R.O.T.C. training class since his enlistment in the program last October.

Vinny smiled. "Oh, Peggy's no alarmist, Dad, but she'll be glad to see me. I can get a late bus from Times Square. I'll call her from the terminal."

"Well, step on it if you want a ride to the city," Daniel shouted from the upper landing. "Steve'll be here in five minutes."

My father patted Vinny's arm and urged him up the stairs. Dad turned and came back into the living room. He went past Charlie in the morris chair and over to the front window. Laying aside her sewing, my mother got up and started toward him. Then he spoke.

"Listen to how quiet it is on Warbisher Street," he said, staring out the window. "Funny, I could swear just now I heard a bugle blow."

Catherine stood behind him at the window. She clasped his arm and pressed her face against his shoulder. "I don't hear any such thing," she said. "Cheer up, Jimbo. We've had such a good evening together. Don't always go worrying about tomorrow."

Dad turned to her and put his hands on her shoulders. His hair was turning white at the sides, I noticed. It wasn't gray anymore, but white, and I didn't understand how I had failed to notice it before. "Well, Cath," he said. "I'm glad you got mad at Hitler and went and had your party. But it looks like it's over now, doesn't it?"

14

Never Again

___

It was not the last party to be held in the brown-shingled house. It wasn't really even a party, Catherine had said. But of its kind there would be no more. Never again were all of us to circle the dining room table, in the same manner, as sisters and brothers, father and mother, a family living and sharing together under one roof.

I search my memory, like a rider beating a flagging horse, and I cannot pluck from it another time when all seven of us were gathered at the oak table again. What of Thanksgiving that year? I ask myself. Christmas? I search back and recall that Uncle Al, Aunt Gen and the red-haired cousins came to Warbisher Street that Thanksgiving. ("Didn't I always predict Cath'd be servin' her own turkey again?" clanged Aunt Gen. "Sweetheart, I always knew you'd make it back.") But Vinny was missing from the table —he was at the McNultys' for dinner—and Daniel was spending the weekend at the Army-Navy game.

What of Christmas that year? Surely at Christmas the whole family— But no, another event intervened. Margaret was married at Christmas. The war in Europe and Howard's surprising talk of enlisting, should the United States become involved, drove my sister to advance her wedding date and heed no arguments opposed to it. And so the day after Christmas, in an ivory satin gown and tulle veil, and carrying lilies, Margaret walked down the aisle of St. Aloysius's on Dad's arm. The organ played *Lohengrin*, candles lighted the altar, and it was all as she had once dreamed it as a little girl watching the Saturday weddings from the back of church. Margaret was married and went off to the Poconos for a honeymoon with Howard Fergus, and her chair at the dining table was permanently assigned to me.

War, and the march of life itself, intervened in the family gatherings, and so my father was not all that wrong to have heard a bugle in the September-evening quiet of Warbisher Street. Pearl Harbor and the war service of both my brothers were not so very far distant.

War. We had fought all manner of wars in the years that lay behind us. The Great Depression was a war, decimating Dad's pay envelope and the food on the table. Illness was a war, depriving us, very nearly forever, of our mother. The act of growing up, as I was to learn, could be the fiercest of wars all by itself. But on that September evening in 1939 a war began, which, in its slow, steady advance on the brown-shingled house, was to sever the links that formed the family circle.

Catherine had come home, and now her children went away—all, that is, save one.

"Goodbye." We waved from the porch as Steve Dowling's fire-engine red convertible bucketed down the street, bearing away Vinny and Daniel in the open black-leather seat.

"Have a good time." We waved goodbye.

Margaret had left to walk Howard to the subway, and the other person missing from the gathering on the porch was Charlie Cronin.

"Say, where's Charlie?" Mom asked suddenly. "Why didn't he come out with us?"

The answer was readily apparent when we went back inside. Charlie was sprawled in the morris chair, sound asleep.

"You can't figure it out?" Dad asked. "I'll give you a hint, Cath. How many glasses of iced tea did you feed the old buzzard?"

"Two or three, I suppose, but my lovely mint tea never hurt—"

"What about lovely spiked tea?" Dad asked. "I take it you failed to notice Charlie's numerous trips to the Jameson's on the sideboard."

Charlie reclined inertly in the morris chair, head tilted over, snoring vigorously. Catherine went over and looked at him sorrowfully. "Poor Charlie, without a good woman to look after him."

"Whassit? Whass happen?" Suddenly the sprawled figure

lurched forward, swinging his arms combatively.

"You fell asleep, Charlie," Mom said. "Let me give you a hand."

"Stand back. Nobody helps Cronin." Arms flailing, Charlie hauled himself up without aid. He teetered back and forth, his voice thick and blurred. "My apologies to the Queen. Fear I have disgraced her hos'tality. Thirty-two years been livin' alone. . . . Buried my mother an' moved to a roomin' house. . . ."

"Robbie and Roseanne will walk you to the trolley," Mom said, helping him on with his jacket.

"The Gates Avenue trolley, so you won't have to transfer."

"Lissen 'a me, Cath Quinlan," Charlie said. "Twenty-two years ago I buried Sarah Dorsey . . . and only one woman since has been her equal. Unnerstan'? Only one woman since."

"No, there was someone else," Mom said, shaking her head. "I'm sure there was. But you weren't able to find her, and I wasn't able to help."

Then Roseanne and I were helping Charlie down the porch steps and walking him to the Gates Avenue trolley. Roseanne was wonderful at it, talking to Charlie, guiding him carefully from curbs and out of the path of trash cans and lampposts, never relaxing her vigil for a moment.

"You're doing fine," she kept assuring him. "Breathe the nice fresh air, it'll make you feel better." And when we reached the Gates Avenue trolley stop, and a trolley clanged out of the darkness to a halt, Roseanne insisted on helping Charlie on board to a seat near the front. "If you could see that he doesn't fall when he gets off," she said to the motorman.

"Goodbye, Charlie." She waved at the slumped, solitary figure. The trolley clattered away, and the sparks shooting from the wire overhead made me remember the day of my first trolley ride, when I'd gone to meet Aunt Tilly at the apartment on Clark Street. Roseanne waved after the lighted interior and I thought of how I'd never said goodbye to my aunt. Never had the chance to, but suddenly I was glad of it. All night, it seemed, the air had been filled with goodbyes.

Roseanne and I started back home along Broadway and I said, "I don't like goodbyes much, do you?" I loped along next to her, past the El pillars and silent closed-up shops. "When you say goodbye, it puts an end to something. Finishes it—you know?" I took big firm strides over the pavement, feeling grown-up and knowledgeable. "If you skip the goodbyes, then nothing really has to end."

Roseanne peered ahead into the darkness. Except for a delicatessen or two or an occasional dimly illuminated saloon, the street was dark and deserted, the El pillars black shapes looming up to the El tracks overhead. "Remember when we used to skate along here after school every day?" Roseanne said. "It's changed a lot since then."

"Broadway's changed?" An El train rattled by on the tracks above and I gestured at the familiar line-up of shops. "Seems to me it's the same old street as always," I said. "Same stores and windows. Hymie's and Schlack's and Rausch's Jewelry. I bet if we looked, the same Waterman pen-and-pencil sets would be in the window."

Roseanne walked silently along for a moment. She reached up to trail her fingers along a barbershop awning. "Nothing seems quite the same anymore. It's like it's all suddenly happening. Both Vinny and Margaret will be married soon . . . the war starting in Europe. All through dinner tonight I kept thinking it'll never be the same again." Lightly she trailed her fingers along the awning, then asked, "Robbie . . . do you think I've changed?"

"Yes," I said, looking at her as though she were a person separate and apart from my sister. "Yes, you really have—you're turning out the best of us, I think. The work you do at the shelter, and tonight, the way you helped Charlie Cronin . . ."

"I work at the shelter because it makes me feel happy," Roseanne said. "That's all." We walked under a street lamp, and the light suddenly picked out her face. She brushed at her bangs in that habit of hers, then she said, as if the thought of it was bewildering, "Sometimes I think I want to help everyone in the world. Isn't that crazy of me? But I think I'd want to."

Everything changing . . . I hiked along next to my sister debating whether change had really come to me. Tall, but not really tall—a boy still, a small boy, despite the gangling height. I shoved

288

my hands into my pockets. Nothing inside me had changed or gone away. It was all still happening, the ambulance that took Catherine away, the pictures in the Valentine box . . . the ambulance screaming . . . *What had Dad said tonight about the Brownie? What did it mean?*

"Here I've been going on about myself," Roseanne said, "and we haven't uttered a syllable about you. The scholarship to Regis, way at the top of your class last term. Think of the future in store for you! A famous writer—I fully expect it."

I pushed up my horn-rimmed glasses and attempted to keep my ridiculous baritone firm and grounded. "Oh, I'll get famous right here on Warbisher Street and stay with Mom and Dad. I'll make it all up to them."

Roseanne stopped and turned to me. "Make up what to them?"

"Oh, I don't know," I said lightly. "Look how good they've been to us. Especially to me, the last of the litter. Think how hard it must have been when I came along. No money, and Mom's health failing."

Roseanne frowned at me. "Who said Mom's health was failing when you were born?"

"I heard Dad mention it once."

"I never did. Having you was no hardship to Mom—or Dad. I'm sure they never regarded it as such."

"No?" I shrugged and made as if to dismiss it. "Anyway, they've been good to me and why shouldn't I make it up to them?" I was silent a moment. "I mean, look how much Aunt Tilly did for me, and I never had the chance with her."

"Robbie, you're way off base," Roseanne said. "I don't understand how, but something's mixed you up. . . ."

"You see?" I joked, laughing in the darkness. "I'm one of those people you need to help. A brooder, see, filled with dark thoughts. Hey, I know! If we're both so changed, let's race up Warbisher Street and see who wins. On your mark, get set, goooooo."

With that, throwing my head back and pumping my long legs over the sidewalk, I sprinted up Warbisher Street, past the trees and porches and lighted windows, toward the house that waited, and would always be waiting, for me.

Part Five
_____

15
The Ghost Child

From the bedroom that I now occupied alone, and that also served as my workroom, I heard the quick *brrnng* of the front bell which signaled the postman's arrival. It was June, ten years later. The cot in the corner had been folded up and stored in the cellar. In its place was the desk at which I was sitting. In 1944, after Dan was married, I'd inherited his bed permanently.

Daniel lived in Washington and was a doctor—a surgeon. During the war he'd been a Navy lieutenant on a hospital ship in the Pacific, and the experience had led him to enroll at Georgetown Medical School after his discharge. He'd chosen Washington because he'd met his wife there during the war—Marijane Walker, a debutante, no less, whose father was a federal judge. The war had also been the determining factor in Vinny's career. As an overseas Army engineer he'd built bridges and roads all the way from North Africa to the Rhine. One of his fellow officers owned a small highway construction company in Los Angeles and had invited Vinny to join him as a partner. Vinny, Peggy and their three sons lived in California now.

I took a sheet of white bond paper, inserted a carbon and a yellow copy sheet, and rolled them into the typewriter. Nine thirty was my starting time at the desk each morning. If I was going to be a writer, it had to be a full-time effort, with the fresh hours of the day given over to it. I'd gotten my Master's in English at Columbia the year before and a job teaching Freshman English to the night students at St. John's in Queens. It enabled me to earn enough money so that I could spend the rest of my time at the typewriter in this room.

I contemplated the blank sheet of paper and waited for footsteps downstairs to answer the postman's ring. It would be Catherine who'd answer; working on his projects in the cellar, Dad seldom heard the doorbell. Since his retirement from Childs in January he'd reorganized the cellar, piled all the junk at one end, cleared out the other end for a workshop. He'd built a table and shelves, acquired electric power tools and kits, bought himself a stack of do-it-yourself manuals, and embarked on a campaign of repairing and refurbishing the house. He spent his mornings at these tasks; afternoons he went out for what he described as his "constitutional." It often included meeting Charlie Cronin at a pool hall.

Light, hurrying steps—the years had rendered Catherine no different. She still sped to answer the postman's ring, as though he were bringing marvelous, unimagined tidings. I heard the asthmatic wheeze of the door being opened. Hinges wanted oiling—another job for Dad.

The Hunter, I typed neatly in the center of the white bond paper. *A Short Story by R. F. Connerty.* In the bottom right hand corner I typed my address, *24 Warbisher Street, Brooklyn, N.Y.,* and in a sudden surge of expectancy added my phone number as well. This was in case a magazine editor, impatient to buy the story, might want to contact me by speedier means than the mails. Wild reckless hope was the main sustenance of unpublished writers. A silly optimism, to confront the manuscripts that kept bouncing back with the alacrity of bad checks. One day, one day for certain, a check would arrive, or the miracle of a phone call . . .

I separated the carbon and copy sheet, prepared another set, and rolled it into the typewriter. It was a Royal portable, which I'd bought with some of Aunt Tilly's money back when I was an undergraduate at Columbia. I'd made a rule that the legacy wasn't to be spent—not a dollar of it—on ordinary expenditures such as textbooks or lunches, or on tuition, unless I failed to win a scholarship. But the scholarship to Columbia had come through, and a part-time job in the bursar's office had covered my other expenses. Aunt Tilly's legacy had gone for more grandiose purchases: tickets to Carnegie Hall and the Metropolitan Opera, and, after graduation, a student tour of Europe. I was sure my aunt would have been delighted by this latter purchase. Rome, Paris,

London—all the cities to which she had wanted to take me . . . and her spirit had traveled with me every glorious mile. No good-bye to Aunt Tilly—she had stood at my side in St. Peter's Square, crossed the Ponte Vecchio, dodged the traffic in the Place de la Concorde— *No, not the traffic, a car striking her down* . . .

I rolled the paper into the typewriter and prepared to type the opening paragraph of the story . . . and in some other part of my mind I waited for the sound of the front door to close down-stairs. Catherine would have gone out to remove the mail from the letter box, sorted through it, come back across the porch . . .

I typed the opening paragraph. *He crouched at the end of the pier and breathed the good true smell of the pines.* Good opening sentence, sounded like Hemingway, lean and sparse. Actually, if my own name hadn't been affixed to the last few stories, I wouldn't have blamed an editor if he'd gotten the two of us mixed up. Imagine, giving a magazine the opportunity of launching an-other Hemingway. It buoyed up my hopes, and I typed on. *Some smells were honest and true, and some were not. Pines were true, as were bread baking and the rough red peasant wine the Span-ish called—* There is was, the soft closing thud of the door down-stairs. Catherine returning from the porch with the mail.

I stopped typing, read over the paragraph, and the buoyancy vanished. I wanted to tear the pages from the roller and crumple them in an angry ball. Pure junk. Why did I write about pine trees and good true smells when only once in my life, on the Christmas trip to Greenvale, had I ever known the scent of pines? Why a story about fishing in the woods when I'd never fished anywhere, not even in Brooklyn's Sheepshead Bay? Utter foolish tripe!

What I ought to write about was sounds. Doors thudding, clocks ticking, faucets dripping—the muted sounds that could re-verberate like rifle shots through a house that was silent and aging. I had become a master at identifying such sounds, faint and dim, yet breaking like thunder over the empty rooms. I could write from experience of what happened to a house when most of a large family had moved away. The rooms stayed the same, each piece of furniture in place, yet nothing about it was really the same. Discarded rooms in a house that had . . . fallen asleep, like a castle in a fairy tale. A house that stirred to life only with the arrival of visitors—children especially, so that once more the rooms could ring with their shouts and laughter, and the stairs vibrate from the hectic tattoo of their feet. Like a fairy-tale house, children found it wondrous to explore. For them the shadows did not exist.

I sat at the typewriter and remembered Christmas the year before and Dan's three youngsters at the dining table, shining-faced and eager. "I like your house, Grandma," four-year-old Christopher had proclaimed. "Tell me again who lives here."

"Well, Grandpa lives here"—Catherine bustled around the table, distributing vanilla ice cream—"and I live here . . . and Uncle Robbie . . ."

The small face had turned to me with questioning eyes. "Uncle Robbie, why do you live here? Why aren't you married, like Momma and Dad?"

A smile. Slightly forced, a treat-it-as-a-joke smile. "Well, give me some more time, huh, Chris? Haven't gotten round to it yet."

"Uncle Rob's still a young fella," Dad had explained. "He's got everything ahead of him."

"He isn't young, Grandpa. He's old—aren't you, Uncle Rob?"

"Well, I could be younger, I guess."

"Anyway, this house is nice. If I was you, Uncle Robbie, I'd live here forever."

"Maybe so, Chris."

And after the visitors had departed, the rooms had gone back to their slumber.

Why couldn't I write of that? Of living in a discarded house, which each day grew more cut off and isolated; living on there and trying to make up to the two good souls who shared the emptiness . . . Make up *what* to them?

"Robbie," Catherine called from below, rousing me from my reverie. Her voice brimmed with excitement, her eager steps sounded on the stairs. As I got up from the typewriter, she burst in, a letter clutched in her hand.

"Forgive me for interrupting your work, but—" She smiled and waved the letter. "It's the best news."

The writer in me spoke first. "I haven't sold a story?"

"Even better—at least, I think you'll agree." Catherine couldn't contain her excitement. "It's been so quiet lately, haven't you felt it?" she babbled. "Just think, five years ago this June."

"Slow down, Mom. Who's the letter from?"

"I must tell your father about it." She thrust the letter at me, started into the hall, turned back. "It's from Roseanne—she's coming home next week. Five years, Robbie, and she'll be right here in this house. Can you believe it?"

She hurried off to tell Dad, and I stared down at the letter, almost unable to believe it. Five years . . .

Her name wasn't Roseanne anymore.

Five years ago she had been a senior at college, a few months away from graduation. Hustling home one night from my classes at Columbia, late as usual for supper, I'd come into the front hall, face stinging from the cold March wind. The war was still on, Daniel had recently been shipped overseas to the Pacific, and two service flags hung proudly in the front window. The hall was unusually dim, I remember, because of the 30-watt ceiling bulb Dad had installed as an example of our "wartime restrictions." Strict adherence to food rations, blackout curtains for air-raid drills, minimum fuel usage—exactly as if we were citizens of London. Dad was block captain of the neighborhood Civil Defense unit and talked of quitting Childs and getting a job in an aircraft factory. He had embraced the war effort wholeheartedly and was in constant correspondence with his two overseas sons, discussing strategy and the latest battle maneuvers.

Or perhaps it wasn't the 30-watt bulb that caused the dimness in the hall. By then, I think, the house itself had started to dim . . . the shadows crooking long fingers from the stairs, the quietness lapping around, like water against pilings. And my self-appointed role in this dimness was to act as an agent of cheer. Vinny and Dan were both in combat zones, and my task was to ease my parents' anxiety.

So I banged the front door shut, ignored the beckoning shadows, and called into the dining room, "Save any supper for me? Listen, what a funny incident on the subway tonight. These two drunk sailors—"

In the dining room I came upon a tableau that stopped me short. Dad was at the sideboard, his air-raid warden's helmet strapped on in preparation for the weekly meeting of block captains. Catherine was at the table, motionless, holding a spoon and a bowl of rice pudding. Margaret, who was visiting us, sat dabbing at her eyes. And facing them all from her chair was Roseanne, her expression tentative and uncertain.

"It's perfectly beautiful," Margaret said tremulously. "It's nothing less than inspiring." Margaret had moved away from Brooklyn last year. Lo and behold, her predictions about Howard's career had been correct: a Buffalo department store had plucked him from the aisles of Woolworth's and installed him as executive assistant manager in charge of personnel. However, Margaret's new existence in Buffalo was lonely, and since no children had blessed the marriage yet, she came home to Warbisher Street for periodic visits.

"I tell you, it's inspiring," she said again, with another dab at her eyes.

Roseanne laughed nervously. "I'd as soon you didn't refer to it as inspiring, Marg. It's probably the prize fool decision I've ever made and I'm sure to be kicked out in a week."

I stepped toward the dining table. "Kicked out of where? Somebody please enlighten me, if you don't mind."

"Oh, Robbie, I'm sorry." Roseanne got up and came over to me. "I hadn't intended to announce it tonight, but we started talking about my plans once I graduate in June, and . . ."

"And what?"

"She's entering the convent," Catherine said. She held the spoon over the rice pudding. "After graduation she's joining the Missionary Sisters of Marywood—and it's the finest thing I could think of for her to do."

My father was obviously too stunned to speak. Roseanne went over to him. I had not been alone in my role of cheerer-upper. "Pops, I meant to tell you sooner—I've been mulling over it for weeks, but I never could find the right words," she said.

Dad moved slowly away. "Well, you took us by surprise, that's for sure," he said. "A missionary nun, eh? I might have guessed it'd be something out of the ordinary. No parish convent for you."

Roseanne brushed at the unruly bangs. "Marywood's an outstanding community of nuns. They operate clinics and child shelters throughout Latin America. Some of the sisters are doctors, surgeons, Ph.D.s in social service. It's none of this *Going My Way* cutesy business."

Catherine started portioning out the rice pudding. "Why, it's a wonderful order, those missionary sisters. They work without charge among the poorest people in Brazil and Colombia. I sent them a donation last year."

"How much?" Dad asked.

"Five dollars."

"You're always sneaking donations on me, Cath."

"Well," she countered, "now we'll be donating our daughter. Tell her how proud you are."

There was no reply and Roseanne said, "Dad, I can delay it, if you want. I'm due to enter the novitiate in July, but I can put it off till next year."

"Nonsense," Catherine declared. "Once you've decided something, thing to do is go straight ahead with it." She fumbled with the rice pudding. "The minute I knew I wanted to marry your father, wild horses couldn't have stopped me. You be that way, Roseanne. We'll salute you for it." Her hands tightened on the bowl of pudding. "Won't we, Jim?"

"Yes," my father said slowly. "Of course we will." Then my sister was in his arms.

It was settled and over with, and in a few days' time it seemed as if we'd always known that Roseanne would enter Marywood. Dad and Mom accompanied her to the motherhouse in Rhode Island when she formally applied for admission, and her departure was talked of and discussed with easy manner, except by me. Somehow I could not talk about it with Roseanne, which was strange, for there had been no constrictions between us for years, perhaps not ever. But on the night before she was to leave in July she came into my room.

I hadn't been able to sleep. It was hot and airless and I lay in Dan's former bed, waiting for the first light of dawn to touch the ceiling. I gazed through the dimness and saw Roseanne in the doorway.

"Can't sleep? Neither can I," she said, and came and sat on the edge of the bed. "Robbie, please be happy for me," she asked.

"I am. Honest."

"Honest, you're not." She smiled. "You know, one of the reasons I kept delaying this was you, old brother. We've always had each other to hang onto, even when I was batting you over the head. Vinny and Dan are gone—and now you'll really feel left behind."

"No, I won't," I assured her. "Listen, I'm the youngest—it happens in families like ours. I'm doing fine."

Her face loomed above me in the darkness. "What was it I used to call us? The tag end of the parade? Well, I have news for you. It's my personal mission to see that you march at the head of the parade. Nuns do a lot of praying, you know. I intend to take up your cause with God."

"Do you?" I asked. "Be sure to let me know what He says."

"Robbie"—she touched my arm. "At least a little happy for me? Please?"

During her last week at home Roseanne's friends from high school and college had come with gifts to wish her well, and the next morning, on her way to the city with us, she asked to stop off at the Catholic Child Shelter, where all of her future had begun. She'd promised a last visit, she said.

I waited in the taxi with Mom and Dad while Roseanne rang the bell at the door. Suddenly they flocked out at her, children of every size and description, many of them black-skinned. Laughing, shrieking, clamoring to be near, they converged on my sister in noisy affection. She talked with each child in turn, and when she attempted to leave they followed her down the steps, reaching for her. Then a nun collected them and shooed them back inside, and the rest of the trip to the city I kept seeing this glimpse of my sister's other existence.

Dad and Mom were to go with her on the train to Providence,

but I stayed behind at the station. I hugged her wordlessly and said no goodbyes, and then she was on the train, waving from the window, and I turned and walked from the platform. That evening when they returned, my parents described the scene at the novitiate, the young girls bidding tearful farewells in the visitors' parlor.

"But not our Rosie," Dad boasted. "There was this long hall they had to walk down to the novices' wing. Rosie stayed chatting with us, then off she went down the hall and never looked back once. I tell you, she's quite a gal."

"Yes," I said, and went upstairs to my room.

Roseanne's period of noviceship at Marywood lasted for six months, and in December she was to take her first vows and be given her nun's habit. I traveled up to Rhode Island with Mom and Dad for the ceremony. The novitiate was located in the rolling countryside a few miles out of Providence. The spacious stone building stood at the crest of a snow-furrowed hill, and as we got out of the taxi, looking up, I saw Roseanne running toward us down the circular drive. She wore a black novice's dress and fluted cap, and on her face was a smile I had never observed before. Impatient with the drive, she bounded toward us over the snow, and I recalled another snowy hill we had raced over as children, toward a lighted porch window on Christmas Eve. But now my sister ran unencumbered and free.

"You came, Robbie," she exclaimed. "I didn't think you'd come, but you did. I'm so happy."

Then, in the novitiate chapel, from my seat in the upper gallery, I looked down at the procession of girls in the center aisle. They carried candles and were dressed in white, like brides. At the altar each would kneel and pronounce her vows and then receive the gray habit she hoped to wear for the remainder of her days. I looked at the line of girls and picked out Roseanne, so slender and erect, advancing so surely toward the altar, and I thought of the wrinkled white graduation dress that had hung from her closet door.

It was as though she wore the same dress, except that now it fell in smooth, serene folds, and it made me understand what had taken place. My sister of the movie magazines, plastering the glossy pages with kisses—"Ricardo Cortez, I adore you . . . Buddy Rogers, you're gorgeous"—had found God to love. It was the answer to what she wished to do with her life. Kneeling at the altar, she spoke her vows, received her nun's garments and became Sister Ann Clarita.

The ceremony was over and we stood in the visitors' parlor, where coffee and pastry were being served. She came toward us through the crowd, her long gray skirt swinging out, the white veil framing a glowing face that shone brighter than candles. She went to embrace Mom and Dad, and I carried my coffee to a table in the corner. She called my name and I turned around as she came toward me.

"I'm happy for you," I said.

I sat at the work table in the bedroom and read over the letter. After five years of training—a nursing degree at a Providence hospital, a Master's in Social Science from Brown University, a year of welfare work—Roseanne had been given her first foreign-mission assignment. With three other nuns, she was being sent to Bogotá, Colombia, to staff two child-care medical units maintained there by her order. "We'll work in teams and shuttle back and forth from the main unit in the city to the other in the mountain," she wrote. "From what I've read, the political situation in Bogotá is explosive, to put it mildly. Bandits, guerrilla raids—La Violencia, the Colombians call it. But, as usual, the poor are the victims. They are in desperate need, and so we must go to them.

"We are booked to leave from Idlewild a week from Monday," the letter continued, "but the best news is that we're to be allowed to visit our families over that weekend. Home to Warbisher Street, can you imagine? I'm afraid convent rule doesn't permit me to stay at the house, but I'm sure the nuns at St. A's will be happy to put up their former harum-scarum pupil. I'll be just around the corner, so I can spend every minute with you, put my feet up on a chair, have long talks, and catch up on family events."

There was a postscript to the letter. "Especially intend to catch up on Robbie," my sister had scrawled. "His letters have been exceedingly vague and noncommittal. If he tries to escape, hold him down till I arrive."

"Robbie," Mom called up the stairs. "Did you read the letter? Isn't it wonderful?"

I went out to the landing. "It's terrific."

"She'll be coming home," Catherine said, clutching the newel post. "She'll be ringing the front bell . . ."

Roseanne wasn't due to ring the front bell until a week and a half later, but the house went into a state of high excitement at once. Catherine kept reading and rereading the letter, and it was quickly apparent that some elaborate plan was taking hold of her.

"It's been so quiet around here lately," she kept remarking, which for her amounted to an extended complaint. It had never ceased to amaze me in the last few years, my mother's ability to be cheerful and seemingly content as she moved through the empty, echoing rooms of her once-active domain. A letter from Vinny, Margaret, or Daniel was enough to set her beaming; a trip downtown to the department stores, or even to her marketing haunts on Broadway, provided diversion and topic enough for lively conversation. Catherine was dauntless; nothing could make her lower her chin.

The neighborhood, as she had known it for thirty-one years, had all but ceased to exist. In place of the clutter of small owner-operated shops on Broadway loomed vast supermarkets, complete with deep-freeze bins, wire carts and check-out counters. Schlack's Ice Cream Parlor had shut down and been replaced by a gaudy pizza establishment, and Schmierman's bakery was presently the site of a laundromat that boasted two aisles of washers and driers. And there were other changes.

With the war's end the great building boom had started in the suburbs. Whole new towns, developments and residential areas had sprung up, and to them a mass exodus from Brooklyn had begun. Hardly a week passed that a FOR SALE sign was not displayed on one Warbisher Street porch or another, and into the vacated houses black families had moved. Catherine's voice did not take part in the whispered chorus of protest conducted by many of the remaining families. She was peculiarly astigmatic in regard to racial matters. She could find no objection in mixing black with white, and fell into easy conversation with these new shoppers at Bohack's.

The Fritzles next door had emigrated to Baldwin, Long Island, for, alas, another major change in Brooklyn had rendered Mr. Fritzle obsolete. The trolley-car lines, which once had formed a splendid transit network throughout the borough, were no more. Buses had replaced them, trundling smoothly along the avenues that had resounded with the clang of bells and the hissing sputter of sparks. Mr. Fritzle, pride of the DeKalb Avenue run, had turned in his motorman's badge and retired to pasture. The Reverend Theodore Calkins, a Baptist minister, and his wife were our new neighbors. Within days Catherine was chatting across the fence with the ebony Mrs. Calkins while both ladies hung up their wash.

She was undisturbed and my own continued anxiety over her and Dad's state served chiefly to puzzle her. Often, on the nights I wasn't teaching, I would suggest movie excursions to help combat what I regarded as the desolate evening hours at home.

"Say, there's an English movie playing at the Halsey," I would remark. Catherine had a penchant for English films—the picturesque settings and the stylish behavior of the actors caught her fancy. "Alec Guinness is starring in it. I thought you and Pop might like to go."

Catherine would finish stacking the dishes in the sink or whatever other task occupied her. "That'd be nice, Rob, but . . ."

"But what?"

"Well, I hope you don't think you have to rescue Dad and me from a lonely old age. Why, when I was at Greenvale, I figured I'd be lucky to reach fifty. Here I am, past sixty. Don't you be concerned about Pop and me, Robbie."

"I'm not, but . . ."

She would turn to me and shift the conversation. "If you'd really like to please us, then call up some girl and take her out. All day long working in your room . . . Where are the friends you used to see, the girls you dated at college?"

"My mind's on writing a decent story—and seeing that you and Dad are all right."

"Well, ease your mind on that last score. We're fine."

Undismayed, Catherine faced each new morning eagerly. If the empty rooms, the unused beds, the idle chairs and vacant places at the table pinched her heart, she gave no indication of it. Yet her very joy at the prospect of Roseanne's homecoming suggested that she concealed more than she would ever admit. And as the event grew nearer she struggled for some expression of her joy.

"Why didn't I think of it sooner?" she exclaimed on Sunday night, jumping up from the sofa. "She'll be gone for ten years. We ought to give a party for her."

"A party?" Dad said.

"A farewell party," she said. "On Saturday night. Dan and Marijane could come up from Washington. Too far for Vinny to travel, but I know Margaret would want to come from Buffalo. We'll invite Al and Gen and the cousins, Charlie Cronin." The party was already growing in size. "We'll round up some of Roseanne's friends. The people at the shelter, that Tom Donovan she worked with, and the girls from college."

She went in to the dining room table and began making out a guest list. She scribbled down names, and the list grew longer, and still more names were added. "The nuns from St. Aloysius's— and who was that sociology teacher at St. Joseph's she was so fond of?"

Dad took the list and studied it. "You've got close to forty names on this. Take a gander at the size of your dining room— you can't accommodate a crowd of that size."

"Very well," she said, surveying the small dining room as though it had turned into her adversary. "We won't use it. It's lovely June weather, and I've always wanted to give a party in the yard."

"The backyard? Are you out of your—"

"Why not? It'd be perfect, Jim. We could set up a buffet, hire chairs, string up lanterns! I'll serve cold fried chicken and a nice hot casserole. We'll make it for eight o'clock. I'll start contacting people tonight. We don't have much more than a week."

From then on, preparations for the party began in earnest. In his capacity of general house contractor and handyman, Dad set himself to complete the various tasks. Since January he had reupholstered the living room sofa, wallpapered two of the bedrooms, and refinished the dining room tables and chairs. Now he was determined to paint the kitchen and install the new wall-to-wall blue carpet he'd ordered from Sears, Roebuck. Catherine kept busy on the phone rounding up guests for the party, and chairs and lanterns were ordered from a caterer's. Each day some room in the house was selected for exhaustive cleaning. On Thursday, interrupting her labors, Catherine went marketing and ordered enough food to stock a restaurant.

Friday came, and I doubt if ever the house had been as tidied and spruced up for any homecoming. Roseanne was expected at noon, but long before that hour my parents sat waiting for the bell to ring. Catherine, in fact, rushed to the door half a dozen times under the impression that she'd heard it ring.

"Isn't it wonderful Dan and Marijane and the children are staying overnight," she said. "We'll bring up the cot from the cellar and there'll be exactly enough beds."

"House looks mighty spic and span," Dad said, viewing the blue wall-to-wall splendor in the living room. "Too bad all your guests will be out in the yard."

"Well, they'll have to go *through* the house to get to the yard."

Roseanne was to stop off at the convent with her luggage before coming to the house. When it got to be twelve thirty Catherine gave up rushing to the door at imagined *brrnnggs* and went to prepare lunch in the kitchen. Then Dad got edgy.

"I bet it's those gabby nuns at St. A's," he said. "They're probably talking Rosie's ear off. Keeping her there, without a thought to her family."

"Now, Jim, she can't waltz away without making a show of politeness," Mom said, mixing some deviled eggs. "Leave that milk

306

in the refrigerator alone. Roseanne wrote that what she missed most at Marywood was cold milk. They serve it on the warmish side, which I personally couldn't abide."

"Oh, hell," Dad said, slamming the refrigerator door. "Another ten minutes and I'll go around to the convent myself."

Privately I was relieved that my sister was staying at St. Aloysius's. The postscript to her letter indicated that she had probing questions to wing in my direction. My letters to her over the past five years had been filled with chatter about my courses at Columbia, the trip to Europe, movies and concerts I'd been to, but very little was included about myself or any problems I might be facing. Whatever sort of pale, watery life I had entered on, it didn't seem as if much could be changed about it. Certainly my writing career wasn't about to rocket skyward. Only this morning the manuscript of "The Hunter" had been returned by *The New Yorker* with a letter enclosed from one of the editors. *We enjoyed reading your parody of Ernest Hemingway,* it said, *but unfortunately we seldom have use for material of this kind. Thank you for thinking of us.*

Parody? What were they talking about?

Dad paced the blue-and-white tiles. "I respect and admire nuns for their good work, but they're the gabbiest women on earth," he gloomed. "I don't doubt they'll keep Roseanne trapped in the parlor till nightfall."

"Jim, it's not even one o'clock yet."

Roseanne's staying at the convent would lessen her opportunity for late-night quiz sessions with me, and there'd be plenty of others around to claim her attention. Dan and Margaret, and tomorrow night the party—

Brrnngg!

It was the doorbell. For a long instant neither of my parents moved. Dad was at the sink, getting a glass of water, and Mom was stuffing the deviled eggs. The *brrnngg* sounded again, and Catherine rested the fork in the mixing bowl; slowly Dad turned off the water tap.

As fleet as a young girl, my mother rose from the table and flew toward the hall, and Dad clumped eagerly behind her. From the living room arch I watched the door open wide, the sunlight flooding in.

"I forgot to take off my apron—I always forget," Catherine said. "Oh, Roseanne, how fine you look."

The face, framed in the black veil, still wore the glow I remembered from the clothing ceremony at the novitiate. The marvelous smile that had hurried to us over the snow was still present.

My sister fell into Mom's arms, reached out to include Dad in the embrace. "Five years. I can't believe I'm here," she laughed. "How are you both? Am I really home?" Her glance darted around the hall, to the stairs, the phone table, the arch, and there it lighted on me.

"I've fixed lunch," Catherine was going on. "Deviled eggs, tomato sandwiches, and milk so cold it'll rattle your teeth."

"It was the nuns at St. A's that delayed you, wasn't it?" Dad said. "They kept you in the parlor and gabbed away."

Sister Ann Clarita came toward me. "And how's my brother doing for himself?" she asked. And calling to mind the pig-tailed terror who had stalked me down alleyways and searched me out, I might have guessed I would not succeed in eluding her now, twenty years later.

It was at the party the following night that she took aim at me in my lair.

Japanese lanterns were strung across the fence and in the branches of the tree, like colored vessels of light bobbing on the sea of night. A buffet table stood at the rear, groaning with platters of fried chicken, bowls of salad, dishes of sweet pickles, homemade biscuits, mint candies, and a frosted cake. To the side of the buffet was the punch-bowl table, where I was stationed, ladling the wine-ginger-ale-and-fruit beverage into paper cups. An accordion was playing, courtesy of one of the nuns from the shelter, who sat on a folding chair and supplied music for the guests. The yard was packed solid—Uncle Al, Aunt Gen, the cousins, Charlie Cronin, Margaret and Howard, Dan and Marijane and their three children, the Reverend and Mrs. Calkins from next door, a dozen of Roseanne's classmates from high school and college. Most of the staff workers from the shelter had come, including Tom Donovan, who had brought his mother along. Having fetched fried chicken and salad for her from the buffet, he came over to me for some punch.

A handsome graying man of forty or so, he asked, "It's not too strong, is it? Mother's not too keen about hard liquor."

"It's wine mixed with ginger ale and fruit."

"Excellent, but only half a cup for her, I think," he said.

Carefully balancing the two cups of punch, he edged through the crowd toward the white-haired lady who sat removed from the other guests in a corner against the fence. She smiled as he presented the punch and patted the vacant chair at her left. He sat down with her and together they watched the party doings.

While the guests loaded paper plates with more helpings of fried chicken, Dan's children raced up and down the back steps and chased one another endlessly around the tree, which had once been our own diversion at parties. I saw Dad take Christopher and give him a piggy-back ride down the alley—another of our diversions. Catherine had her twin granddaughters in tow and was pressing cupcakes and orange soda on them. Charlie Cronin, to the accompaniment of the accordion player, was dancing a jig, and behind him Tom Donovan made his way over for more punch.

I tilted the bowl to ladle out what was left. "Sorry, it's just about gone. I can get you some Scotch, if you'd like."

"No, thanks, I've had more than enough already." He nodded at Roseanne, who stood under the tree encircled by guests, as she had been all evening. "It's quite a sister you've got," Tom Donovan said. "We hated to lose her at the shelter. Before she entered Marywood we hoped she'd become a permanent staff member. Terrific girl, your sister."

"We think so too."

He raised his paper cup. "Well, thanks for dredging up what was left." Edging back through the crowd to the white-haired lady, he sat down next to her again, and it seemed to me that they made a sad pair, sitting away from the laughter and talk.

The nun who had been playing the accordion launched into an elaborate opening chord, and Charlie Cronin, hand placed solemnly across his chest, began to sing in a cracked but impassioned tenor.

"Tell me the tales that to me were so dear," Charlie sang, "Long, long ago, long ago." First Dad and Uncle Al, then more of the guests joined in. "Sing me the songs that to me were so dear, Long, long ago, long ago"—until a chorus of voices broke over the yard, over the swaying Japanese lanterns and the night sky above them.

"Long, long ago," the guests sang, and I left my station at the punch table and shouldered through the crowd to the alleyway. Long, long ago, long ago—it was the perfect song for this yard, this brown-shingled house. Long ago, the days of the past, were its lifeblood. Memories floated up the stairs and hovered in every room, and the house drowsed in the past, rousing itself only for occasions such as tonight's party, or upon the advent of grandchildren at holiday time. Tomorrow Dan and Marijane would drive back to Washington; on Monday Roseanne would board her plane at Idlewild . . .

I didn't want to think about tomorrow or Monday or the days of the future. They would come soon enough, and I had no clue as to how I would deal with them. Think about the next story in the typewriter, think only of that—stories and writing and becoming an author. It was only when I sat at the typewriter that the past or the future didn't exist.

Behind me in the yard another round of song began, "The Rose of Tralee," led by Charle Cronin, and I hurried down the alley away from it. *We enjoyed reading your parody of Ernest Hemingway, but unfortunately . . .*

I rounded the sidewalk in front of the house went up the porch steps. I lit a cigarette and gazed out at Warbisher Street. It lay slumbering, too, in the quiet of the summer darkness, here and there a lighted porch glimmering in the border of trees. I blew out smoke rings and watched them widen, float away, and dissolve in the night air. I sat down on the steps and tried to make my mind as empty and floating as the rings of smoke.

"It's quite apparent by now," said a voice from the doorway, "that Mohammed will have to seek out the mountain." Roseanne came across the porch in a rustle of skirts. "It's such a lovely night," she said. "Only I wish we had a moon."

"We tried to order one from the caterer," I said, "but they were out of stock on moons."

She plumped down next to me on the steps. "In any case, you're cornered."

"What do you mean?"

"Ambushed. You know exactly what I mean."

"Roseanne," I said, to divert her, "it's unseemly for holy nuns to squat down on porch steps. Show some regard for your religious vocation."

My sister flicked back her veil, pushed up her long, wide sleeves. "I'll be squatting down a lot worse in a few days. Mud huts and hovels—or ducking bullets, more likely. *Los banditos,* you know."

"Is the situation that bad down there?"

"There are lots of poor people, you see, and some of them have taken to using guns. Bands of outlaws, full-scale attacks on the mountain villages."

"But you'll be in the city."

"Two days a week Sister Julitta and I drive a medical truck to the mountains."

"A bullet wouldn't dare hit you."

Roseanne laughed and clasped her arms around her knees. "Is that why you avoid me, Robbie—I'm so formidable? Attempt to get you alone for a minute and, my, how you disappear."

"Like smoke," I said. "Like smoke rings," and I sent out another hazy circle to float and dissolve in the darkness. Abruptly I squashed my heel over the cigarette. "I haven't avoided you. I haven't wanted any lectures, that's all."

"Lectures from me?"

"On the retarded development of younger brothers."

"Retarded? Actually, the word I'd use—"

"Cut it out, Roseanne. Just spare me your case-worker analysis and I'll be fine." I got up from the steps. "Excuse me, Sister Ann

Clarita, but shouldn't you be attending to your guests in the back-yard? I'll go back to them, if you like."

"Yes, go back," she said, as I started for the door. "Go back in the yard and have a good look at Tom Donovan. Or even Charlie Cronin, for that matter."

I stopped in the doorway. "Tom Donovan?"

She sat on the steps, her back toward me, the veil flowing down. "When we had staff parties at the shelter Tom often brought his mother along. He's extremely devoted to her. People used to say how admirable it was. Or tragic—depending on the viewpoint."

I looked at her from the doorway. "What's Tom Donovan to do with me?"

She rose from the steps. "Let's see. He drinks a lot, the way Charlie does. Tom isn't as noisy a drunk. He accomplishes it more quietly. I dated him a few times, so I know."

The song fest was still in progress in the yard. The chorus of voices rolled softly down the alley mixed with laughter and the grind of the accordion. "Drinking's not one of my problems."

Roseanne looked at me. "Back in high school I imagined I was in love with Tom Donovan. I wasn't, really, but it wouldn't have done me any good. In a sense, he was already married."

I stared at her and my hand began to tremble.

Roseanne went on. "How it happened, the closeness, the attachment, I never learned. Charlie's been holding a drunken wake for his mother for twenty-five years. How did it happen with him? Out of good things, I suspect. Vulnerability . . . something fragile inside the man. Or guilt."

"Please stop," I asked her. "Please don't go on."

"In your case, I think it's partly to do with guilt," she said. "When Mom went away to Greenvale—"

"*Guilt?* Why would I feel guilty about that?"

She came toward me and put out her hand. "Didn't you know that when there's a mishap to a parent, children usually blame themselves? They think if somehow they'd behaved better, or loved the parent more—"

I went to the porch rail and pounded it with my clenched fist. "I never felt any guilt. I assure you I didn't."

"I did," my sister said quietly. "So did Vinny and Dan and Margaret—I'd be willing to bet. Except that with us . . . the guilt didn't last. I even wonder if Mom's illness didn't help us to grow up faster, manage on our own more." She came over behind me at the rail. "But with you it did something else, Robbie."

"Did it?" I asked in a flat, dull tone.

"Stop that," she said. "I'm not talking to you as if you were a case history, and you know it. I want to help you, because . . ." She took my arm. "It's always been the two of us, and on Monday I'll be going away. Foreign assignments are for ten years, you know, and when I come back . . ."

I swung around to her. "What? You don't want to find me here? I suppose it would be disastrous."

"No, but it might be . . . too late," she said.

I stepped back from her. "You think I can't leave here if I want? You think I'm incapable of it?"

"Robbie, when I walked in here yesterday and first saw you . . ." She looked at me and the words trailed off.

"What?" I asked. "What?"

"I came in the door yesterday . . . and I found—"

"Yesterdays are what you found," I said. "Memories and echoes and empty rooms."

She shook her veil. "I found Mom and Dad . . . the sun spilled in the door and I saw how much white is in Mom's hair. But she and Dad were in good mettle. Then I glanced across the hall. There were shadows . . . and in the archway I saw a ghost."

I stared at her. "*What?*"

"A ghost child," she said, "whose heart was broken when his mother was taken away. I'm sorry if that shocks you—"

I backed away in revulsion. "I don't thank you for it. I don't really thank you."

"Then curse me for it," she flung back. "I don't mind what you do if—"

"Are you pinning the tail on the donkey?" I asked. "Is it the truth you want? Only the truth? All right. I can't leave here. I can't, that's all."

"Why not?"

"I think it's because I'm still afraid—" I stopped, unable to speak the rest of it.

"Of what?" Roseanne prompted.

"That she'll die," I said.

She stared at me. "Mother will die?"

"I'm afraid that if I go away, if I don't stay here and make it up—"

"Make *what* up? You said that once before. Years ago . . ."

"I don't know. I swear I don't." My voice rose. "And I'm afraid that if I stay here I'll begin to hate this house. I'll end up hating Mom and Dad along with it. Blame them for whatever it is I can't solve. Hate them in place of hating myself. It's already starting, I think."

I turned from Roseanne's shocked eyes and stood with my hands covering my face. The singing in the backyard sounded faint and distant, as though it were miles away. "I'm sorry," I said. "I didn't know till now what I felt. I couldn't bear it to happen, Roseanne. All of it to end with hating . . ."

"But you must leave," she said. There were steps, and I felt the fragile touch of her hand on my arm. "Dearest Robbie . . . it's not so impossible. It can be done. I know."

I lowered my hands. "I remember the day you left. You walked down those steps—"

"Oh, I carried off that part of it quite tidily," Roseanne said. "It was when I arrived at Marywood with Mom and Dad that the sticky part came. Having to walk from the visitors' parlor, leave them behind. I talked away, cheerful as a magpie, but all the time I thought, 'I can't do it, I can't say goodbye.'" Her fingers pressed into my arm. "But I did it," she said. "There's a long hall at the novitiate that leads to the novices' wing. I walked down it and didn't look back once."

I turned to her and smiled. "Dad talked about it when they got home. He seemed to think you had no trouble at all."

"Catherine knew better," my sister said. "Wait and see, she'll help you with it too. Thank God, we haven't parents who hang onto their children."

"*I* hang on," I said. "*I'm* the hanger-on."

Roseanne flicked back her veil. "Shall I apply my missionary techniques to the problem?"

I produced a wobbly smile. "If it's similar to the barrage you just put me through."

The skirts swirled and she was halfway to the door. "Have we a copy of *The New York Times* around?"

"What do we want the *Times* for?"

She started into the house. "The classified ads. If you're moving to the city, you'll need a room, won't you?"

"Wait a minute," I protested. "Let's not rush this too much. I give you my solemn oath I'll quit being a ghost, but—"

Laughter came from the doorway. "Solemn oaths, is it? Instead of taking the plane on Monday, I'll send a solemn oath to Bogotá."

"Roseanne, it'll take months before I can move. For one thing, I'll need money in the bank, plus a better-paying job—"

"I didn't know you'd spent Aunt Tilly's legacy," she said. "Is there none left?"

"Listen here, that money is only for special things."

"To exorcise a ghost—isn't that rather special? If Aunt Tilly could know she was the means of turning her nephew into a man, I don't think she'd object."

"You missionaries are a tough bunch."

"We expect results for our efforts," my sister said. "We're not paid in cash, you know. Or maybe you could call it a joint bank account with God. I put my earnings in, and if someone else is in need . . ."

She was making light of her vocation, but then her face, in the frame of white linen, became suddenly intent. "It's why I'm going to the missions, you know," she said. "I'll offer it to God, and in return He'll look after all of you."

"Roseanne?" I went over to her in the doorway. "You'll take care of yourself. You won't try to do too much in Colombia."

She laughed again. "If I can fly two thousand miles, you

shouldn't find a trip to the city so arduous. Let's start looking up rooms in the *Times*."

We couldn't find a newspaper in the house, and if we had found one, there wouldn't have been much opportunity to consult it. The singing in the yard had stopped. Then, "Where is she?" "Roseanne?" Then, careening through the kitchen door, Dan's twin daughters shouted, "She's in here with Uncle Robbie. We found her, Grandpa."

I followed her back to the yard, where the party was winding up and the guests were preparing to leave. Tom Donovan and his mother were saying good night to my parents. Mrs. Donovan turned to Roseanne.

"I know you'll do fine work down there," she said, clasping Roseanne's hand. "Sometimes I wish my Tom wasn't such a homebody."

"I guess we do what we're capable of," Tom Donovan said. "Don't forget to pray for us, Rosie." Then, taking his mother's arm, he guided her down the alley, slowing his steps to keep pace with hers. He carried a sweater over his arm, and at the end of the alley he stopped and arranged the sweater over her gaunt shoulders, and they went on.

"Roseanne, look. The moon's coming out," Catherine exclaimed. She pointed above the tree at the orange-yellow disk that rode through the night clouds. "You wished for a moon, and now you have one."

It was another half hour before the final guest—Charlie Cronin, of course—had departed, and we were a long time tidying the yard. As Dan and his family were to occupy two of the bedrooms upstairs, Dad brought up the folding cot from the cellar and set it up for me in the living room.

"The junk that's piled up next to the coal bin," he complained to Catherine as he carried the cot up the cellar stairs. "My end of the cellar's neat as a pin. All that old broken furniture and whatnot—when do you plan to get at it, lady?"

"Now, let me alone about that, Jim. I told you I'd take care of it one of these days."

"You told me that six months ago."

"Well, let me worry about it."

After the children had gone upstairs and the last of the lanterns were taken down and the folding chairs stacked, Dad and I walked Roseanne around the corner to St. Aloysius's. "Meet you in church for nine o'clock Mass," he said as she rang the convent bell. "Mom's cooking a big breakfast."

"Fine, Pop." An elderly nun opened the door, and Roseanne started inside. "Rob, don't forget to pick up the *Times* tomorrow," she called before the door shut behind her.

"What does she want with the *Times* so much?" Dad asked.

"Sort of a project," I said.

We went back along Bushwick Avenue, turned in at Warbisher Street, and I kept my eyes fixed on the bright summer moon as though it were leading the way through a forest that had been impassable for me before. I remember how quickly I fell asleep on the cot in the living room that night, almost the instant I stretched out under the sheets. The *Times* tomorrow, I jotted sleepily in my mind, and it seemed at last that I wasn't concerned only with yesterdays.

If, in a last-ditch effort at delay, I had neglected to buy the paper the next morning, Roseanne was ready for such tactics. She appeared at church with the *Times* under her arm, and when breakfast was over, and Dan was carrying his bags to his car at the curb, and Catherine was wrapping cookies in the kitchen for the twins to munch on on the journey, my sister cornered me on the sofa with the real-estate section.

"Let's see, where's the furnished-rooms column?" she mused, paging briskly through the classified ads. "You can't afford an apartment yet, so you'll want a room. Here we are." She folded back the page at the column that was headed at the top, *Furnished Rooms.* "How much you think you can spend? Most seem to run ten a week."

"Well, I'm earning about fifty a week at St. John's."

"Here's one for eight." Reaching into her nun's reticule for a pencil, she proceeded to make check marks alongside the likelier prospects.

The plane for Bogotá left from Idlewild Airport at two the next afternoon. Dad and Mom and I rode out to Queens in a taxi with Roseanne and met the other three nuns who were to accompany her on the flight. They were in the passengers' lounge with their own families, and we assembled in a group in a corner of the lounge. A loudspeaker voice blared out information about take-offs and landings, and in my pocket was the furnished-rooms column that Roseanne had clipped out for me. Earlier in the day I'd gone to the Bushwick Savings Bank and withdrawn the remainder of Aunt Tilly's legacy. I had closed the account, for to leave it open might provide me with a reason for staying in Brooklyn.

The loudspeaker voice went on, Roseanne and the nuns kept up a sprightly conversation, and I thought of Tom Donovan and his mother. I can't do it. I won't be able to, I suddenly thought. If I leave and something happened to Catherine . . . but then I looked over at my relaxed, smiling sister, who was to depart in a few moments on a two-thousand-mile flight to work in a mission for ten years. Look at her smile so easily and converse with the other families. Look at Dad and Mom fulfilling their part of it without distress.

The loudspeaker voice announced the Bogotá flight, and then we were standing with Roseanne at the passengers' ramp. A medical kit was slung over her shoulder and she carried an airline bag, which she put down to embrace Mom and Dad. *I can't leave,* I thought. *If I go, they'll be alone in the empty house.*

"Goodbye, dear." A quiver shook Catherine's mouth, which she quickly covered. "I understand they serve delicious food on these planes," she went on. "Write us when you get there."

"I will. Bye, Pops." Roseanne turned and put her arm around Dad. She hugged him silently and didn't speak.

"Old Rosie," he said, holding her tight. "I'm proud of you, old Rosie."

She turned to me next, and her arms held me for a moment. "When you write, remember to include your new address," she said. Then she hurried up the ramp with the other nuns.

"What's that about a new address?" Dad asked.

Halfway up the ramp she turned back and waved the airline bag at us. I called, "No fair. The rule's to keep going ahead."

"She said something to Robbie about a new address," Dad grumped. "I heard her distinctly."

"Jim, you're not waving," Mom admonished. "*Wave, she'll be out of sight in a minute.*" We watched the striding nuns' figures disappear up the ramp, then my mother turned her glance on me for an instant, and I understood that Roseanne had talked to her. Catherine was prepared to bid farewell to two of her children this day.

We drove home in a taxi, which was a rare treat, Catherine said, clasping and unclasping her pocketbook. I went to my room to work, but the typewriter wouldn't click out any words. What if I started another story and it, too, turned out to be a parody. Maybe I ought to forget Hemingway and good true smells and write about what I knew. Brooklyn, and growing up . . . the brown-shingled house and all the things that had happened here . . .

The late afternoon sun stretched across the floor, went away, and was replaced by shadows that crooked long fingers at me. Outside the door the echoes and emptiness waited, and I felt my resolve ebbing away like the last rays of the sun. *I'd never be able to do it.*

"Robbie," Mom called up the stairs. "Supper's ready."

I got up from the typewriter and went down into the lapping quietness below. I couldn't leave, because something was unfinished.

I took my place, Vinny's old place, at the table in the dining room and listened to Mom and Dad talk about the airport and Roseanne's departure.

"Twelve hours the flight takes," Dad said. "Can't almost conceive it could be so quick for that long a distance."

Catherine set down the chicken casserole. "The wonders of aviation. Doesn't seem credible."

I ate my supper, the minutes marching past. Twelve hours . . . Roseanne's journey was nearly half over.

Catherine brought in dessert, sliced peaches, and spooned them into dishes.

"Dad, I've been meaning to ask you," I said. "That stuff down in the cellar—is Dan's old suitcase from the Navy there?"

He looked up at me. "Why?"

"I've been thinking—I might have use for it."

He took a dish of peaches from Mom. "Well, good-quality leather like that ought to— You planning a trip, Rob?"

Twelve hours . . . and halfway there. "Don't fall over in surprise," I said, "but you know how I used to talk about moving to the city? It was always my big ambition."

"I haven't heard you mention it lately."

"Well, now, Jim"—Catherine passed a dish of peaches over to me—"maybe he's been thinking about it."

"Have you, fella?"

I picked up a spoon, put it down again. "Matter of fact, I have."

Catherine held out a pitcher of cream to Dad. "It wouldn't be surprising if Robbie wanted to take off on his own. All the others have. His turn has to come."

My father poured cream on his peaches. "I know it does. Just a surprise, that's all. When you planning on it?"

It was very quiet in the dining room. "Tomorrow," I said.

The journey for me was half over too.

The next morning, still mystified by the unexpected turn of events but cooperating with them, Dad dug out my brother's old suitcase from the accumulation in the cellar, and in the bedroom upstairs Catherine helped me to pack it.

She got out my shirts and underclothes, socks and ties, and kept up a flow of chatter. "It's good you're doing this, Robbie. Long overdue, actually. You've been too cut off from your friends and interests." She had difficulty folding the bathrobe. "Try to find a nice cheerful room."

"I've got a list to look at." I put the typewriter in its leatherette case. "Most of them are on the West Side."

"I took a ride up Riverside Drive once. It was lovely."

"I'll need a room where I can work at my writing."

"Yes, where it's quiet enough. Well, you'll find one."

The suitcase was packed. I carried it and the typewriter downstairs and got my raincoat from the hall closet, and Dad opened the door for me. "Well, good luck, fella. Your brothers and sisters have all packed—as Mom says, it's your turn, I expect."

Holding the suitcase in one hand, the typewriter in the other, I went out the door and down the steps. Behind me in the doorway my parents called goodbye, but I walked quickly down Warbisher Street and didn't call back to them.

I found a vacancy in a brownstone rooming house in the West Sixties in the city. It was on a street of brownstones, half a block from Central Park. The ad that Roseanne had checkmarked read, *Nr pk, quiet sgle, ideal for wrtr/profr. $11 wk.* A quiet single room, ideal for a writer or professor—I qualified on both counts!

The building was in the middle of the block. The brownstone stoop was swept and tidy; trash cans stood neatly ranged in the basement entry, and the brass knob on the front door was polished. I carried the suitcase and typewriter up the steps to the equally polished brass bell. If the landlady had specified a writer in the ad, perhaps she was kindly disposed toward the breed.

I rang the bell and in a moment the curtained door was opened by a large plain-faced woman. Her hair was twisted in a braid and her eyes were not unfriendly.

"Good morning," I said. "I'm a writer—and I've come about the room you advertised. Is it taken?"

She looked me over in silence. "A *young* writer, I think we must say." She opened the door wider. "Yes, the room is still available. You care to look at it?"

"Oh, I would," I said, and gathered up my bags and followed her into the hallway.

Her name, as I soon learned, was Mrs. Chovotny. She was a widow, her husband had been a music professor in Vienna, and they had fled to America, war refugees. He had died shortly after they had purchased the boardinghouse as a means of supporting themselves. The room that Mrs. Chovotny showed me was on the third floor, in the front. It was a sunny room, with a window that looked down on the other brownstones that lined the street. There was a table at the window large enough for my typewriter and papers, and a wash basin stood in a curtained-off alcove. The bed was narrow, with a hard, lumpy mattress, but I was used to spartan beds. I rented the room on sight, gave Mrs. Chovotny a week's rent in advance, and called up my parents to tell them that I was settled. That night I typed a victory letter to Roseanne from the room and printed my new return address on the envelope. I didn't sleep very well that first night, but I didn't lie awake either.

I opened a savings account the next morning and deposited in it what was left of Aunt Tilly's money—three hundred and forty dollars. I estimated that the fifty a week from the teaching job at St. John's ought to be enough for living expenses. If I ran short, or if there were emergencies, Aunt Tilly wouldn't mind if I used her money to help tide me over. She wouldn't mind helping me to become a man.

Mrs. Chovotny's brownstone, the room on the third floor, was my home for the next three years. New York City was a long hall, and for the next three years I walked down it and tried not to look back.

16

Lissy

Three years, and at the start, fifty dollars a week.

I ate in cafeterias and took my shirts to a Chinese laundry on Columbus Avenue. I washed my socks and underwear in my room. Three nights a week I traveled to St. John's to teach Freshman English, and on the other nights I went to cheap movie theaters on upper Broadway or bought second-balcony tickets to plays. In the mornings, from nine until two, I worked at my writing at the table near the window. I didn't turn out parodies anymore, unintentionally or otherwise, but the stories I wrote had an undefined quality about them; they were stories that anybody might have written.

On Sundays I took the subway back to Warbisher Street and spent the day with my parents. I didn't go the first Sunday—it was too soon to walk back up Warbisher Street. The next Sunday I went, and it was all right. Catherine served dinner, I talked with Dad in the living room, and when it grew dark I left to catch the subway. But on the following Sunday, as I sat with my parents at the oak table, the old struggle began, the pull to stay, and I didn't think I would be able to leave. I didn't go back to Warbisher Street for a month after that. By then it was November, and walking back to Sixty-eighth Street through the park one evening in a chill rain I caught a cold.

I awoke the next morning sneezing and with a sore throat. By evening a fever had started, and I phoned in to report absent at St. John's. I drifted asleep, and when I opened my eyes again I didn't know where I was. It was dark, cracks of light poked in through the green shade . . . but what was wrong with the window? The desk was wrongly placed: it belonged in the corner, where the cot used to be. Where was I, in what strange room?

The rooms of our childhood, once we leave them, follow after us.

The fever was worse, and when Mrs. Chovotny brought me aspirin and hot tea later in the morning, fever alternated with chills that shook my body.

"It is not good, how you look," she said. "The bedsheets are soaked, your body trembles."

By afternoon there was a rattling in my chest, and it was becoming difficult to breathe. I got out of bed, remembering Catherine's tortured breathing before the ambulance had taken her away, and called down to Mrs. Chovotny.

She hastened up the stairs. "Mr. Connerty, you should not be out of bed."

"Please . . . is there a doctor?"

She led me back into the room. "You are sick, Mr. Connerty. In Brooklyn lives your family, *nein?* I phone them, if you want. To be sick like this and alone . . ."

I got into bed. "No."

"You tell me the phone number and I call them."

I raised myself. "No, you mustn't. Is there a doctor I can call?"

"But Mr. Connerty—"

"I mustn't go home. You don't understand. I mustn't. If a doctor could come . . ."

She urged me back onto the pillow. "Down the street—I think I will try to reach him."

It seemed that a doctor lived a few doors down from the brownstone. He was away making hospital visits, but his answering service got hold of him and two hours later he came into my room and put his black physician's bag on the table. He took my temperature, held a stethoscope to my chest.

"A hundred and two and severe congestion, young man."

"The hospital, Doctor? Pneumonia?"

He prepared a hypodermic. "Influenza. There's a lot of it around. I don't think you're quite ready for the hospital, however." He gave me an injection of penicillin; that night he returned for another injection, and in the morning the fever was

324

broken. The doctor ordered me to remain in bed for the rest of the week.

I traveled to Warbisher Street the next Sunday and reported to my parents, "I caught cold last week. Nothing serious, stayed in bed a couple of days."

"You look pale and shaky for a minor cold," Dad said. "Think you've lost weight."

"It wasn't anything serious," I said.

"Besides, he's recovered from it," Catherine said. "All by himself too."

I knew, then, that I had crossed some invisible boundary and that the days in the city, the long walk down the hall, would be possible after all.

It was in the spring that my writing career—nonexistent, thus far—took an upward swing as well. Often on afternoons, after my work sessions were finished at two, I set out to explore the city. Sometimes I rode down to Chinatown, the Battery, or uptown to Washington Heights—areas of New York I was less familiar with. Or I headed for Central Park, chose a path and followed it to whatever street it exited on. Ambling on, I browsed in the bookstores I passed, window-shopped, ventured into shops and art galleries. The path I chose in the park one afternoon took me to Eighty-fourth Street, and I decided on a look at the Metropolitan. I wandered through the procession of galleries on the second floor, past Rembrandts, El Grecos, a Goya. . . . I stopped in front of the latter painting, which showed a boy in a red suit, and as I looked up at it, I remembered Aunt Tillybird.

We had once stood together in front of this very same painting. My aunt's red hair, the fur piece clasped around her neck, the velvet-ribboned eyeglasses raised to inspect the canvas—*Ah, Velázquez! Regard the flesh tones, Robair. Magnifique.*

Goya not Velázquez—Aunt Tilly was always getting her artists mixed up. I stood alone at the painting and remembered the summer afternoon in the lobby of the Plaza Hotel, the floppy hat and parasol, and the vow I had made that someday I would paint Aunt Tilly's portrait and take her to fancy lunches at the hotel. So clearly did I remember that afternoon I could hear in my mind the exact unctuous tone of the assistant manager's voice and glimpse again the hurt and embarrassment in my aunt's eyes as he asked her to explain our purpose in the lobby.

I looked up at the Goya and remembered that day with Aunt Tilly. It wasn't possible of course to take her to luncheon at the Plaza, but perhaps it wasn't too late to paint her portrait. Words could paint a picture as well as oils on canvas. If Aunt Tilly was important to me, perhaps readers would find her important. I walked away from the Goya . . . and then I was speeding from the museum. Down the great center stairway, out the doors, into Central Park. Not content with paths, I cut over fields, snaked down hills, hurdled shrubbery, and reached Mrs. Chovotny's brownstone in fifteen minutes flat.

That evening I failed to report for Freshman English at St. John's—forgot even to phone in my absence. I was at the type-writer, painting a likeness in words. I worked all night through and finished the story at dawn. "Oil on Canvas," I entitled it, and sent it off to a magazine. It was bought within ten days.

The morning the letter came from the magazine I rushed to the pay phone at Mrs. Chovotny's and called the brown-shingled house. "I sold a story," I told Catherine, the words spilling out in a jumble. "A magazine's going to publish it. They sent me a check for five hundred dollars."

"Oh, Robbie, how wonderful."

"Isn't it? Isn't it? Excuse me, I have to hang up."

Back upstairs to my room, and a letter to inform Roseanne of the news. *I sold a story. I can't believe it's happened. I'm sending part of the money as a donation for the mission. If it weren't for you, I wouldn't have moved to the city. I wouldn't have written the story. Now I can ask you to be happy for me. Be happy, you hear?*

Then down the stairs to the pay phone again. "Mom? It's me. I thought I'd call you again. I just wrote Roseanne. Did you tell Dad about the story? Dan and Vinny and Margaret will probably want to know too. Listen, I'll write so many stories, nothing can stop me now. You see, the thing is, I never thought it would happen."

I deposited the check in my account at the bank. I went to Fifth Avenue and bought gifts for my parents—Sulka ties for Dad, a French purse from Saks for Catherine. After I wrote out a check at Saks I wrote another for the missions and mailed it to Roseanne from the Rockefeller Center post office. Then I went into a florist's and ordered a large bouquet of white carnations. I hadn't been to Calvary Cemetery since Aunt Tilly's burial; I didn't know that I could ever go there again, but today my flowers would be at her grave. For this was what mattered most to me. More than the check for five hundred dollars, or the prospect of seeing my name in print, I had finally given back to my aunt something in return for what she had given me.

The next months flew past; it seemed that the end of the long hall was in sight.

Not all of my time was spent alone in the city. There were some friends from my undergraduate days at Columbia whom I saw with fair regularity—Bob Thompsen and Jerry Nichols, Bob Gottlieb and Dick Locke, Jack Lawlor, Jim Russell. They worked in advertising agencies, banks, law firms and brokerage houses, and were still unmarried, as I was. We toured the Third Avenue bars together, went to hockey games at Madison Square Garden, and on weekends there was the party circuit to travel.

There were always parties that Bob or Jerry or Jack knew of, and hardly a Saturday night passed that I wasn't bound for some apartment or other, standing in a doorway with Jerry or Bob Gottlieb. The trouble was, I lost track of the parties after a while, because they were all more or less alike. An apartment in the Village, the East Side, or up on Morningside Heights. Studio couches, hi-fi records, Picasso prints on the walls. Beer piled on ice in the sink, a table crowded with bottles of Scotch, potato chips and cheese dips, and a roar of talk as you came in the room, shouldering through the crush of faces, smiles, drinks, and cigarettes. "Hi, Jere, long time no see." "Wait a sec—I've got it. We met last month at whosit's. Right, right. Listen, I'likeyatomeet—"

Over the course of a year the parties got to be indistinguishable. The same faces and smiles, the same laughter and jokes and New York-type conversation. It was like a series of party scenes in different movies where the same extras turned up as guests. All of the Saturday nights the same . . . except for one night in March and the party I went to with Dick Locke.

It was a rainy night, and a year and a half had gone by since I'd moved to the city. I'd sold another story and was beginning to work on a novel, and when Dick Locke called about meeting him at eight, it didn't seem worth the bother of going out in the rain.

"Aw, come on, Bob," he urged on the phone. "There're supposed to be some sensational numbers there. I hate showing up at these things alone."

"I'm in the middle of a chapter."

"You've been at it all day. You'll go stale."

I sighed. "Okay, where'll I meet you?"

He gave me an address a few blocks north in the West Seventies, which meant that I could walk there from Mrs. Chovotny's. It was March, but not blustery outside; a quiet rain slanted down, turning the pavements into patent leather. Dick Locke was waiting in front of the brownstone; when he saw me he hustled down the steps of a basement entranceway and pressed the bell. A girl in a green dress opened the door, and as we entered a wave of noise hit us. Whether the girl was giving the party she didn't make clear—it was never made clear at parties like these just who the host or hostess was. In any event, she greeted us and went off, and Dick and I made our way down a hall, past a kitchen, and into a bedroom, where raincoats were piled on sheets of wrapping paper spread across a bed. A bathroom door opened and another girl appeared. It turned out she was from an agency and had met Dick at some public-relations affair. "Aren't you from J. Walter?" she shrieked, and they disappeared down the hall together.

I was on my own. Let's see, next stop, kitchen—beer in the sink. I went down the hall, turned at the kitchen doorway . . . and *click*.

There was a girl struggling with an ice tray at the refrigerator. Blond. Wide cheekbones, blond shining hair. A wool jumper, burgundy red, some sort of striped knit shirt. *Click.*

"Need ice in the living room," she explained, pulling at the tray.

"Here, let me help." I went to the refrigerator, gave the ice tray a yank. *Click.*

"Thank you." She pushed back the blond hair, rinsed off the tray under the faucet. *Click, click.* "If I can find some bowl to put it in."

"I'll get a bowl for you." I began wildly opening the cupboard doors above the sink. *Click.* "I'll find you one. I'll get you the moon if you want it. You want it?" I pretended to start away. "Wait right there."

"But you can't. It's raining," she pointed out.

I turned back to her. *Click.* "Well, I'll write my sister about it. She's very good with moons," I said. "My name is Robert Connerty."

"Hello," she said.

"Connerty, Robert," I said, "and I've never talked to anyone like this. In fact, I don't seem able to stop. It's compulsive—you'd better do something fast."

She looked at me for a moment. "I don't mind," she said.

Click.

Her name was Felicity Vole. The blond hair was from her mother's side of the family, Norwegian. The Vole was French—her father's side had emigrated to Quebec, then to the territory that had become Montana. She was from the town of Red Feather. That was its name. Actually.

I found out all about Felicity. After the party that night I took her to a coffee house on Broadway, and walked home with her afterward to the apartment on West End Avenue she shared with two other girls. I asked for her phone number and called her the next day. I didn't go out to Warbisher Street that day; I took Felicity to a revival of *Bicycle Thief* at the Thalia Theatre.

In the weeks that followed, the tumble of nights and days, I found out all about her.

She was the oldest of seven children, whose names in order of sequence were Evan, Miranda, Toby, Fabian, and the two youngest, Daisy and Fern. Red Feather, Montana, was a bustling metropolis of twenty-four hundred citizens, sixty miles north of Missoula, in the Rockies. In addition to bestowing unusual names on his children, Mr. Vole operated a hardware and sports-equipment store in Red Feather and worried about letting his oldest child come to the big city. (I wanted to write him not to worry.)

Felicity taught the fifth form at a girls' school on East Eighty-fourth Street. She had been in New York for two years, which almost matched my own length of stay, and she wasn't certain how much she wanted to stay in the East. (I wanted to tell her not to be in a hurry about leaving.) She didn't consider that she was pretty, and I straightened her out definitely about that. She was wrong, I explained. In the opinion of an unprejudiced male by-stander, she was extremely attractive. "In fact, beautiful," I said.

" 'Extremely' is one of your words. The other is 'actually.' "

"Something else about you too."

"What?"

"To a Brooklyn boy it's extremely exotic. You represent a rare, exotic species."

"What are you talking about?" she laughed.

"Oh, you're clever about it," I said. "You've adopted the ways of the city. Most people would take you for an urban type, but it's deceptive."

"What am I, then?"

"A country girl," I said. "Through and through."

It was true. It took some watching (by the end of the summer I'd done plenty of watching), but underneath the stylish surface, the Lord & Taylor clothes and Fifth Avenue polish, there dwelt a country girl who, in her mind, was still clambering up mountain ridges, streaking across meadows, and stepping over stones in a creek. She traversed the city streets in a smart cosmopolitan manner, but stop for a traffic light and watch those feet grow restless; come upon a clean stretch of sidewalk and watch that gait quicken. Go walking with her through Central Park, and she could not resist a field or a rock cluster to climb. It was useless. Off and away went the country girl.

And in winter (that first winter I continued the opportunity to watch her), she changed into another creature entirely. Let the first snow fall and a transformation instantly took place. Let the first white flakes swirl down and she could not restrain herself. Tramped in the snow, scooped it up by the handfuls, threw back her head to let the fleecy white fall upon her face. From then on—wool scarves, boots, tasseled skating caps—she dressed in daily expectation: she became a snow maiden.

She was extremely wonderful and there was no one like her. (No one. I was prepared to take oath. Testify.) "I've met this girl —she's fantastic," I wrote in my letters to Roseanne. "She's absolutely incredible," I told my parents when I asked if I might invite her to Warbisher Street for Sunday dinner.

"By all means, let's have a look at the young lady," Dad said. "I'm beginning to think it was a major step, your moving to the city, Rob."

"I knew it would be," said Catherine. "What shall I cook for Sunday? My rib roast's always reliable. Or roast lamb? I want it to be special."

It was special. For the first time I had brought someone home to Warbisher Street, and when I left that Sunday at nightfall I didn't leave alone, as in all the months past.

Her name was Felicity, but I called her Lissy. And she called me Robert.

"But nobody's ever called me that," I said. "It's always been Rob or Robbie."

"I like Robert," she said. "It's a good-sounding man's name."

Spring came again, and it was extremely impossible that a year had passed so quickly. April marked only the tentative beginning of spring, but I was prepared to welcome it ahead of time, and so, one Saturday afternoon, a week before my birthday I took Lissy to Central Park. It was cold and raw, a thin sun, but we brought our coffee outside to the cafeteria terrace and sat at a table that overlooked the seal pond. We sipped our coffee, which rapidly lost its warmth, and for once in Lissy's presence I wasn't bursting with talk. She did her best to stem the drifts of silence, and finally she asked, "What's wrong, Robert?"

"Nothing."

"Well, something is."

"Well, I can't decide what to do," I allowed. "About St. John's, I mean." In June I would finish another semester of teaching, and the chairman of the English Department at St. John's had advised me that if I wished to continue on the faculty I must start work on my doctorate, preferably by the fall. "I don't really want to teach," I said to Lissy. "Yet I sure as hell can't depend on writing for an income. Last story sold was six months ago."

"Then take the job the publisher offered you."

I had completed my first novel in January. While it hadn't been bought, one of the publishers it was submitted to had liked it enough to offer me a position as an assistant editor.

"I think you should take it," Lissy said. "Publishing's difficult to get into."

"I probably will, but the salary's only eighty a week."

"That ought to be enough."

"Depends," I said, and lapsed into another mulling silence. The fact was that underneath the silences I was getting increasingly nervous. I'd chosen the park for this afternoon, and each minute of silence was a wasted minute. I suddenly pushed up from the table. "It's cold sitting here, don't you think?"

"Robert, it's perfectly fine. I'm sure you'd like more coffee."

I stood marveling at her and shook my head. "You actually call me Robert. A real grown-up name. Come, I want to take you somewhere."

I took Lissy's hand and guided her through the Saturday crowds that were gathered in front of the lion and monkey cages, and headed along the winding path that led north. In the past year Lissy and I had come often to the park, and it hadn't taken us long to find our favorite place there. It was the hill at Seventy-ninth Street, the broad ridge of ground that sloped down to a meadowlike stretch of field below. We'd claimed it as our special place last spring when we'd first climbed it, and this winter we'd borrowed a sled and gone belly-whopping down the steep incline. I liked the hill because I knew that it put Lissy in mind of the ridges and slopes of Montana, towering though they were by comparision. It was necessary to seek out hills for my country girl's contentment in the city . . . or she might leave. In June, school would be over for her as well. What if . . . ?

The cold April air was stinging to the face. We walked under the bare trees, and I pressed Lissy's hand. Holding her hand wasn't enough; releasing it, my arm traveled to her waist. Curved lightly around her waist.

"I must say you're awfully pensive and quiet, Robert."

I'd mapped it all out, rehearsed it a dozen times in front of the mirror at Mrs. Chovotny's. Why was I so nervous? What was there to be so damnably nervous about?

"I know where we're bound," Lissy said, glancing ahead up the path. "The hill, of course, I should have guessed."

"It's cold. Let's step up the pace a bit. Okay?"

When we reached Seventy-ninth Street I broke away from her and started across the open ground. "Race you to the top," I shouted, dodging among the bands of children on the grassy sweep. Behind me I heard Lissy's laughter, and I dug in my feet and started up the hilly steepness. I ran upward, breath starting to come in gulps; I kept on, and it seemed to me that I'd been running, in one way or another, for a good part of my life. But then it struck me too that today I was running toward, rather than away from, something. Toward something, if only I could reach the top without falling. Tomorrows, instead of yesterdays . . .

I cleared the crest of the hill, and for a moment another, smaller hill flashed in front of my eyes—the hill at Calvary, studded with gravestones, that I could not climb again. Then, turning, I saw Lissy reach out her hand, laughing, as she neared the top, and I put out my hand and linked it in hers.

"I've been worrying," I said. "You can't go back to Red Feather this summer. Besides, there's no such place. You've made it up."

She leaned against me, catching her breath. "I showed you Red Feather on the map."

"You made up your brothers and sisters as well. Evan, Miranda, Toby, Fabian, Daisy and Fern, indeed."

"Shall I send for their birth certificates?" The air had turned her cheeks apple red.

"If I had children, I'd want to give them marvelous names like that, wouldn't you?"

The scarf fell from her hair. "I'm not sure."

"Then we'll have arguments about it. Will you mind having arguments?"

"Robert, what are—"

I reached out and brushed a blond strand from her forehead. "It's your fault, for calling me that. I'm extremely nervous and I can't think what I rehearsed to say. I've forgotten it all."

"I don't—"

I searched in my coat pocket and brought out the jeweler's box. Six hundred dollars for half a carat at Cartier's. I'd used up my savings and the last of Aunt Tilly's money. I thrust the box at Lissy. "It's for you. Here—if you want it."

"Robert—"

"Marry me, Lissy," I said. "I'll be a good man for you. Here, take it, or I'll think you don't want it."

The blond hair blew in the wind. "That party where we met— you asked if I wanted the moon," she said. "I never have wanted it, but it was lovely of you to offer it, Robert."

And she accepted the small black-velvet box from my hand.

We were married in Montana a year after our engagement. I went to work at the publisher's and stayed on at Mrs. Chovotny's. After buying the engagement ring I was too broke to get married; it took a year to save enough money—and after the honeymoon I'd be broke again.

We were married in the mission church of St. Isaac Jogues, which was in a neighboring town ten miles from Red Feather. It was the oldest church in the state, built a hundred and fifty years before by the first missionaries to come into Montana territory. It pleased me that it was a mission church. Roseanne could not be present for the wedding, but she was a missioner, and somehow the simple rough-hewn church was a part of her and bespoke her presence. From Bogotá she had sent the delicate lace mantilla that Lissy chose to wear as a bridal veil. It was June, a morning brilliant with sun streaming in the church windows, and I stood at the altar, Daniel alongside me as best man, and watched my bride move toward me. The sun made gold of her hair, and I could not take my eyes from her.

I was happy that wedding day as I had never been before. I was nervous and stammered out the responses; my hand shook as I took the thin gold band from Daniel, and I nearly dropped it as I slipped it on Lissy's finger. But I was happy, and inside me angels sang and played music. So short a while ago I had foreseen a stunted solitary existence, and now all of it had changed. I had found someone with whom to share my life, and gathered in the small church were the people of my life, come to celebrate this new beginning.

In the front pew were my mother and father, seated together to witness the going away of their last child. They'd traveled out to Montana by bus, taken ten days for the journey, and made numerous sight-seeing stops en route. It was the first time my parents had traveled west of New York State, and for my father it initiated a love affair with cross-country buses that would not easily be abated. Home improvements lost their urgency; no longer was he content to stay in Brooklyn and dream of open highways. The dream of owning a car was gone—it was too late for it—but a Greyhound bus was not a poor substitute. That initial excursion to Red Feather began a series of trips over the next years that took Dad and Catherine to Florida, Arizona, California, Washington, Wyoming and Canada.

And what I used to wonder about was whether these highway adventures would ever have occurred had I stayed on in the brown-shingled house. For my parents, too, my wedding was a beginning.

Vinny and Peggy were also present in the church, as was Dan's wife, Marijane. Margaret and Howard were there. Still childless, their efforts to adopt a baby had been fruitless—according to adoption regulations Howard was overage. On the other side of the aisle ranged the Voles. Mr. and Mrs. Vole as well as a generous helping of cousins and aunts and uncles filled the pews, while Vole children comprised most of the wedding party. Evan was an usher, Toby and Fabian were altar boys, Miranda served as the maid of honor, and appropriately, Daisy and Fern were flower girls.

Two families, I thought, as we turned from the altar. I belonged to two families now, and one day soon Lissy and I would begin a family of our own.

We drove—that is, my bride drove; a city boy, I was limited to trolleys and subways—to Glacier Park for the honeymoon in a car borrowed from Mr. Vole. We stayed for a week at the Many Glacier Lodge, a rustic wooden structure with outside balconies, bear rugs in the lobby, and stone fireplaces in the rooms. We arrived late at night, and in the morning a sapphire lake glittered below the window and high above were snow-capped mountain peaks. We rode up mountain trails on horseback—after the first ride I could neither walk nor sit down for several hours. We fished for trout in streams that were fed by glaciers, saw mountain goats and bears, and once, at the top of a far-off ridge, a giant horned moose was silhouetted against the sky. Dan and Marijane had extravagantly gifted us with a Rolleicord camera, and we took roll upon roll of foolish snapshots, posed against the mountains and flashing streams. At night after dinner we lay by the fire in our room, and I held my bride wordlessly close to me.

A week at Glacier Park, then we returned the car to Mr. Vole in Red Feather and caught a plane in Missoula for New York. We drove in a taxi from the airport to the apartment we'd rented on West Ninety-third Street, a block from the park.

It was a one-room furnished apartment, and it had been my idea to rent it.

"This way we can save till we can afford some decent furniture," I'd said when we'd gone apartment-hunting before the wedding. "You know I won't have two bucks in the bank. This way, whatever extra I make from my writing we can sock away, and in a year or two . . ."

Lissy's teacher's salary was as modest as my assistant editor's wage. "We could look for a cold-water flat and buy furniture at the Salvation Army," she'd suggested. "I wouldn't mind. Besides, the future will take care of itself. Why worry?"

"You sound like my mother," I'd laughed. "Which means that I must sound like my father. Well, one of us has to be cautious. We'll take the furnished apartment. Okay?"

"Okay," she'd agreed.

The apartment was in a building that had been made over from two adjacent brownstones and converted into minuscule one- and two-room flats. It had been my idea to rent it, and it was a mistake.

But what haunts my memory about those first months on Ninety-third Street was another mistake I made, in connection with the door keys. The apartment was on the top floor, a walk-up, and I remember going up the stairs the first day of our return to the city. Carried the luggage up the stairs, put it down in the hall, got out my key ring. The lock wouldn't turn, the door remained shut, and I fumbled among the keys.

I did it that first morning and for months to come. Not always, but it happened with regularity. Standing at the door, fumbling with the keys, searching for the right one.

It was Lissy who caught onto my error. One night after we'd been to the theater and I was fumbling as usual in front of the door, she took the keys from my hand.

"Which key are you using? It's the wrong one. Why, Robert, I believe it's your old house key from Brooklyn. You still try to use it."

"Can you beat that," I said, fitting the correct key into the lock and opening the door into the darkness beyond.

17

The Baby Carriage

A book is an orderly creation. It is divided into chapters, which guide the reader along, pointing the way, organizing the action into sequences that lead resolutely to the ending. Books are careful structures, the pieces planned and fitted together with skill. Life, however, follows no such orderly design. The contents are flung at us every which way: the action jumps, spins, ricochets dizzily from our grasp. Not all the pieces fit together; and as for the ending, it is beyond prediction, indeterminable. No matter what shrewd guesses we make, we can never, until the final moment, be sure.

And of all the chapters that life writes in its untidy scrawl the most bewildering and incomprehensible are the chapters marked "Childhood." By the time we are old enough to go back and read them the language has become unintelligible. We have forgotten it, we speak it no more—and even if we did, we would find that too many pages are missing. The chapters are incomplete, and so we are compelled to leave them behind and move on with our adult concerns. Life carries us forward, and in time we no longer remember what once was or was not.

But sometimes it can happen otherwise. Very rarely it can happen that years after the quest has been given up, by mere chance we stumble on those missing pages of childhood—and in a blinding moment, to our dazed astonishment, the pieces are fitted together.

So it was for me one autumn afternoon when, three years after I had married Lissy, I set out for Warbisher Street on an unexpected visit. It hadn't been planned; getting up that morning, taking the bus to work, I had had no thought of a subway ride out to Brooklyn. Roseanne would have said that perhaps a kindness of

338

God's had prompted me. If so, it was a double kindness, for if I had not gone—

But I leap ahead of my story. There are still three years to fit in.

The one-room furnished apartment was a mistake, though Lissy did her best to pretend that it was a triumph of thinking on my part.

"It's really very snug and homey," she said the first day when we arrived back from the honeymoon in Glacier Park. As I put down the luggage she clasped her hands, standing in the middle of the carpet, and inspected the small boxlike room. "It's very compact and efficient, and I like it."

It was cheap, garish and dismally furnished. A drop-leaf table of fake Colonial design stood at the window, which was hung with sleazy draperies of a nautical design. A Pullman kitchenette —two-burner stove, bar-size refrigerator—was squeezed into a corner, and the bathroom was no larger than a broom closet.

The rest of the furniture was equally forlorn. A maple armchair looked as though it belonged on some derelict porch. Next to it was a floor lamp with a steering wheel in its middle, carrying out the nautical theme. The cushions on the convertible sofa bed proved, when sat upon, to slither around like snakes, and when the sofa was opened out for sleeping, as we discovered that first evening, it extended to within an inch of the opposite wall.

"Easy," Lissy said. She made up the bed with brand-new percale sheets from her trousseau. "I'll stand on one side, you on the other, and we'll hand things across. Robert?"

I was staring at the remarkable prints that decorated the wall above the sofa. They depicted two enormous-eyed street urchins, each cuddling an enormous-eyed kitten. "The kids in these paintings certainly have big eyes," I said.

"Robert, if you'll hand me the pillows."

I got the pillows, which were stacked on the carpet, and handed them across the folded-out bed. "Well, I grant this place doesn't look as if W. and J. Sloane did it, but the rent's cheap. That's the main consideration."

My wife slipped the pillows into cases. "It's our first home and therefore precious to me. I don't—" As she handed over my pajamas she tripped on the low mattress and was sent sprawling. "Don't intend to—" I reached out, as across a chasm, and helped her up.

"Thank you. Don't intend to change a single thing."

It was the perfect truth Lissy was speaking: she didn't make a change in the apartment—for about a week. It was July, and she wasn't due to start teaching again until September. She had enrolled for some teaching courses at Columbia, but otherwise her days were free, and she announced that she intended to devote them to her new role of homemaker.

It was questionable, however, the amount of homemaking that could be devoted to a one-room furnished apartment. That first week Lissy washed down the dingy walls and cleaned the window until it sparkled. She arranged the kitchen cabinet—three shelves for the storage of all food supplies and cleaning equipment. She scoured the minuscule bathroom, hung guest towels on the rack. She waxed the floor and with a bottle of stain remover attempted to remove the spots from the carpet, and each evening she somehow contrived to prepare a delectable meal on the inadequate stove.

There was just so much waxing and cleaning and shelf-arranging to do, and when I came in from the office one evening I found Lissy busily sewing.

"I passed this marvelous yard-goods store on Columbus Avenue today," she said from the maple armchair. "You wouldn't believe the low prices," and she held up a length of sheer white material for my inspection. "Imagine, three dollars, and we'll have new curtains." An ovenware pot simmered on the stove, giving off delicious scents.

"I thought you didn't intend to change a thing."

"Oh, I don't, Robert. Except for the curtains," she added, and resumed sewing. "We can always use white curtains wherever we move."

"You know, Liss, we won't be moving for at least a year."

"I know, darling. I know."

The white curtains were a help to the window, and a few days later I noticed that the prints of the giant-orbed urchins were missing from the wall and had been replaced by some water colors.

"Dug 'em up in an old bookstore on Broadway," Lissy explained, standing alongside me to view them. "Like them, Robert?"

The water colors sounded a tiny note of cheer in the otherwise unredeemable dreariness of the apartment. If anything, however, they emphasized the dreariness.

Lissy's next recourse was to flowers—little bunches of daffodils in glass jars on the tables, the kitchen shelf; a bowl of pink roses when we had dinner guests on Saturdays. Little clumps of flowers, swallowed up whole by the room. Then, with the arrival of a large wooden crate from Red Feather, my wife hit her stride. The crate contained our wedding gifts, which Mrs. Vole had packed and shipped off weeks ago via Railway Express, but which had taken more than a month to reach Ninety-third Street. When I entered the apartment one Friday evening in August the startling transformation caused me to blink.

The stumpy drop-leaf table was set with a lace cloth, china plates, and a pair of elegant silver candlesticks. A crystal bowl gave luster to the scarred end table, and on the cobbler's-bench coffee table were an assortment of china and silver candy dishes, cigarette urns and ashtrays. Wrapping paper and excelsior littered the carpet, and Lissy was bent over the wooden crate, unpacking further treasures.

"Excuse me, I'm in the wrong apartment," I said.

She brushed some excelsior from a china tureen and held it up. "It's antique Spode," she said. "Aunt Yvonne's mother-in-law's grandmother brought it to Montana in a covered wagon. Isn't it lovely?"

"Give me that more slowly," I asked. "Aunt Yvonne's mother-in-law's grandmother?"

"And gave it to us as a wedding present."

"The grandmother?"

"No—Aunt Yvonne. She knew I'd always admired it. Look how

many gifts we received, Robert. I didn't realize there were so many. I found some I haven't written thank-you notes for."

After dinner Lissy resumed the unpacking, and the one-room apartment was slowly turned into a wonderland of silver trays and candlesticks, sugar-and-creamer sets, an ice bucket, Steuben glasses, china cake plates, silver teapots, hurricane lamps and cocktail shakers, all set out on display.

She unwrapped the final item, made space for it on the rather crowded coffee table. "Know what this is, Robert? I'd never seen one before, but it's a caviar server."

"It'll get lots of use," I remarked from the maple armchair, where I was correcting some printer's galleys. I glanced around the room. "Maybe we ought to hire a private patrol agency. If word gets out about the fortune in silver up here . . ."

"Robert, I'm not overdoing it, am I? I haven't put too much of it around?"

"Honey, it's all suddenly very grand."

She swept up the last of the excelsior from the carpet, dragged the wooden crate to the door.

"Are you sure" she asked, and something in her expression, as she surveyed the evening's handiwork, caused me to get up from the armchair and go to her. I had observed a similar doubtful expression on my mother's face as she had fussed over the appearance of a room. I'd seen Dad go to her and put his arms around her at such times, and now I slipped my arms around Lissy's waist and said, "It looks great. This dismal apartment, which I forced on us—and look how you've transformed it."

"I won't throw out the crate just yet," she mulled. "If I put it under the stairs in the hall, do you think anyone would take it?"

We dwelled amidst splendor for the remainder of the weekend, but when I came home Monday evening the splendor was being packed away. Once again the wooden crate was in the center of the room, and into it were going the silver candlesticks, the Steuben glasses and china bowls.

"What's going on?" I asked, closing the door.

Lissy looked up from the crate. "Dinner'll be ready in fifteen minutes." She picked up a candlestick, slid it into a gray bag, and packed it into the crate.

"What are you doing?"

She laughed and pushed back the shining blond hair. "Let's face it, the display was ridiculous. It made the apartment look worse, if anything. I was right not to throw out the crate."

"But you seemed so proud of it. As if finally the apartment had been made ours."

Lissy wrapped a crystal bowl in tissue. "I knew it was absurd as I was doing it. This weekend was like living in the gift department at Altman's."

I put down my briefcase and went over to the crate. "I don't think it was absurd or ridiculous."

"It was, though." She packed the crystal bowl, pushed back the shining blond hair again. "It's like you said, Robert. We didn't seem to have anything of our own here, and the wedding presents seemed to change it. My nesting instinct got the better of me, I guess." She closed the lid of the crate, pressed it down firmly. "Your mother says there's plenty of room in her cellar if we want to store anything."

"Dinner's in fifteen minutes?" I asked.

"Macaroni and beef. Not very special."

"Can it stay in the oven a while?"

"Why?"

I took off my coat, hung it in the closet. I took off my jacket, unbuckled my belt, pulled off my shoes. I flicked off the ceiling light and went to my wife. "It's not true we don't have anything of ours here," I said, and reached for her.

Later, on the pulled-out sofa, I held her tightly in my arms. "We have this," I said, "and *this* . . ."

There was a missing element, something vaguely absent from West Ninety-third Street, and it took me several more weeks to realize what it was.

It was a strange sort of building, however you looked at it. Many of the tenants were transients—at least, someone or other was always moving in or out of one of the apartments. Perhaps that was why we made no friends in the building, except for another recently married couple on the floor below. Apartment buildings in New York are not known for their friendly neighborliness, but here even the small talk in the lobby, the exchange of greetings in the halls, were at minimum.

The tenants for the most part were unmarried, solitary individuals, similar to the boarders I had known at Mrs. Chovotny's. They scurried off to jobs in the morning and hurried like lemmings up the stairs at night, closing the doors of the cell-like apartments behind them. As for the married couples, they were all middle-aged, except for Lissy and me and the Hillards downstairs. Some taken-for-granted normal component of life was missing from the building, and I didn't tumble to what it was until a few weeks before Christmas one Saturday morning when I'd gone marketing for Lissy at the A & P on Columbus Avenue.

It was a crisp clear morning, which made the walk home enjoyable. We usually had dinner guests on Saturday, and tonight my parents were coming. I was working on another novel and would spend the other weekend hours at the typewriter.

I walked along Columbus Avenue toward Ninety-third Street, enjoying the riotous swarm of children who flocked over the sidewalks and curbs. Girls skipped rope, boys tossed balls and chased one another between the parked cars, while the smaller children were occupied with dolls and push-toys on the stoops and entryways. The noisy shrieks and peals of laughter reminded me of a typical Saturday on Warbisher Street. I swung into Ninety-third, and when I entered the cubbyhole lobby of our building the noise abruptly dimmed and was replaced by silence.

That was it, of course. Wondering at my denseness, I hurried up the stairs, rounded the empty, quiet halls, and burst into our apartment on the top floor. "I know what's wrong with this building," I said as I came in. "How could it take me so long to figure it out?"

Lissy was at the drop-leaf table at the window, which did double duty as a desk and a dining table. She'd already finished her housework—a one-room apartment doesn't require much time to be put in order—and was busy with some project at the table, which she quickly put down as I strode toward her.

"There's something definitely missing here," I said.

She took the groceries from me. "Oh? What?"

"No carriages in the halls, no toys left on the stairs—"

She carried the bundles to the postage-stamp kitchenette. "In other words, no children."

I regarded her blankly. "You realized it long before me."

"Well, Robert, it's awfully quiet in this building, except for Saturday-night parties. I haven't once heard a baby's cry."

I went over and helped her unpack the groceries. "Forty apartments in this place and not a kid in one of them. It's incredible."

She put some meat in the refrigerator. "Don't worry, darling, it won't hinder us."

I unwrapped the bottle of Jameson's in preparation for Dad tonight. "How won't it hinder us?"

Lissy turned to me. "Don't forget, I've been married to you for six months. By now I'm slightly familiar with how your imagination works."

"Really?"

She put some cans on the crowded cabinet shelf. "You're a worrier, the silent variety, and when it combines with your writer's imagination, watch out."

I asked, "But what's it got to do with no kids in the building?"

Lissy reached up to the shelf. "Well, you might get the notion that the building's jinxed. We'll never produce a baby while we're here."

"It'd be just as well." I went to the closet to hang up my coat. "It'd be damned impractical. All the economizing, and we've only saved a little over three dollars so far."

Lissy folded her arms. "Then I'm mistaken. You're not impatient for a baby?"

"We'd be foolish to." I got out a hanger. "Too much else has to come first. Finishing my novel, getting a decent apartment."

My wife smiled. "Then why do you make anxious inquiries about my monthly periods, Robert?"

"I don't," I said, and reconsidered it. "Well, if I do, it might be from the opposite viewpoint."

She stepped toward me. "But when I tell you I've started my

period, you don't look relieved. You look disappointed." There was a silence, and she came over to the closet. "Darling, I'm not criticizing you. I think it's wonderful for a man to want children," she said. "My mother claims that Dad could hardly wait for me to get born."

"I haven't thought about it," I said.

"So many husbands regard it as an end to freedom, but I believe you want children as much as I do." She put her hand on my face. "I love you for it."

I shrugged. "I guess babies seem very natural when you grow up in a large family."

Lissy nodded. "Don't I know? At six, I was an expert diaper changer."

"Of course, it was different for you. You were the oldest," I pointed out. "You came at the head of the parade. When you're at the tag end like me . . ." My voice trailed off and I looked at her for a moment. "I suppose that's why I worry about getting a baby started. Yes, I suppose it is."

She looked puzzled. "What do you mean?"

"It's the Fritzles' fence all over again."

"Fence, Robert?"

I went slowly over to the window and told her of the long-ago incident involving the backyard fence. "You see, everybody'd climbed it except me. Dan, Vinny, even Roseanne," I said. "I was the last, and scared I'd never make it."

"What happened?" Lissy asked.

"Well, I tried one day and broke my arm in the attempt. I never succeeded, really."

"Why not?"

"The fence was blown down."

"I see," Lissy commented. "Vinny has five children, Dan has four, another on the way . . ."

"Margaret has none," I joked, "but she never tried to climb the fence, so it doesn't count." I stood looking out the window at the blank brick wall of the facing building, but what I really saw were the rough wooden fences, the tangled clotheslines and backyards of Warbisher Street.

346

I turned from the window. "Well, if I'm to start writing to-day . . ." I started away from the window; then, as I went past the drop-leaf table I noticed the color snapshots that were spread out on it, along with a jar of library paste . . . and a dark-green leather album. "What's this?" I asked.

Lissy groaned. "You weren't supposed to see that. A surprise for Christmas—and now I've ruined it." She came over to the table and opened the large and handsome album to the first two pages, which were already neatly pasted with snapshots. "You'd be sur-prised how many we've collected in six months," she said. "I thought I'd put them together, then we'd know where they are. Snapshots get lost or misplaced so easily."

"I suppose," I said.

"We'll want albums for our children to look at, won't we? To laugh at how strange and funny we looked. In any case, Robert—" She held out the green Morocco album. "Merry Christ-mas, three weeks early."

"Thanks. It's beautiful," I said.

Her arms went around me, the shining blond head tipped back. "Don't worry about fences, darling. I have a notion we'll have plenty of babies." She rested her head against my shoulder. "I don't doubt that we'll soon be wheeling a buggy in the park—by next summer, maybe."

We stayed in the furnished apartment on Ninety-third Street for another year. And there was no need to go shopping for a baby carriage. In one sense this was fortunate: the building was a stumbling block as far as babies were concerned. No carriage rooms, flights of stairs to climb, and halls so narrow they would have provided scant passage for a carriage. Besides, it wasn't a problem I could afford to give much thought to in the months that followed; there was money to be saved, the novel to finish, in the hope that it would provide extra income. I worked on the novel evenings and on weekends, except for the Sunday afternoons we spent at Warbisher Street.

The Sundays, that is, when my parents were at home in the brown-shingled house. The Greyhound bus had already whisked

them to Florida for a holiday, and to California for a visit with
Vinny and Peggy. There were shorter trips as well—to Williamsburg, with a stopover at Dan and Marijane's lavish new glass-and-
fieldstone house in Chevy Chase. Cape May and Atlantic City;
then to Buffalo to visit Margaret and Howard. If Bogotá, Colombia, were reachable by bus, it would have been next on the itinerary. Indeed, Dad was already looking into plane schedules and
the cost of fares. But when my parents were in Brooklyn, Lissy
and I took dinner with them every Sunday, the four of us spaci-
ously seated at the oak table, and Catherine busy at the task she
loved best, the serving of an ample meal.

The Sunday visits were pleasant and congenial, but I remember
one visit that lingered in my mind for days afterward. It wasn't
that anything untold occurred; the afternoon passed without incident, and then it was dusk and time to leave. I went looking for
Catherine, and located her, as I might have expected, in the
kitchen. But I didn't find her rinsing dishes or returning plates to
the cupboard. Instead she had pulled over a chair to the kitchen
window. Seated there quietly, lost in thought, she didn't even hear
the door swing shut behind me.

"What's going on in the backyard that you're so fascinated by
it?" I asked.

She laughed and returned the chair to the table. The pepper
and salt was gone from her hair. It was pure white, and she would
hear no talk about dyeing it. Old ladies should look like old ladies,
was Catherine's attitude.

I asked, "What were you looking at in the yard?"

"Absolutely nothing." Some glasses were set drying on the
drainboard; she picked one up and began polishing it with a dish
towel. "If you want to know, I was wondering about my sparrows,"
she said. "Didn't I tell you about the sparrows last fall?"

"No, Mom."

"Well, it was quite remarkable," she said, polishing the glass,
then starting on another. "Well, one morning last fall—must have
been late in November—I came down here to fix breakfast," she
related. "Dad was still asleep, and the house was utterly quiet.
That's why I heard the noise so clearly, I guess. A funny noise, a

sort of tapping or pecking at the window. And when I went over to investigate, Robbie, guess what I found?"

"What?" I asked.

"A sparrow was at the window," she said, "and he wanted to let me know he was darned hungry. I fed him bread crumbs, of course, but what do you think? The next day he was back—this time with a whole family in tow. One by one, they flew from the tree in the yard and lined up on the windowsill. For weeks I fed them—they depended on me—and every morning they came back."

"Then what?"

Catherine turned from the sink, holding the dishcloth, and looked over at the window where the sparrows had been. "One morning they didn't show up," she said. "I couldn't imagine what had happened . . . until I realized."

"Realized what?"

She went back to the drainboard to polish another glass. "Sooner or later, sparrows always fly away," she said. "It's their nature, isn't it? Good heavens, Robbie." She put down the glass and turned to me. "Listen to me prattle, while here you are ready to leave. Let me say good night to Lissy."

On the subway ride back to New York, and for days afterward at odd moments—at work in the office, eating lunch at a counter —I kept thinking of Catherine and her sparrows, and a question seemed to hover in my mind, which I could not adequately answer.

The question I asked myself was whether all of Catherine's sparrows had really flown away. *All six of them?* I asked myself. Or had one sparrow made the effort, only to falter beyond the fence?

Lissy and I stayed on in the furnished apartment. The money was maddeningly slow in accumulating, the novel stubbornly resisted completion. With each month the one cramped room appeared to grow smaller and more grating on the nerves, and in June the lease would be up for renewal. We couldn't, with any sense, afford a much larger rent, but as June approached we went apartment-hunting nevertheless.

We pored over the Sunday classified section, answered ads, trooped through the modern new apartments that were sprouting up by the blockful on the East Side. We gazed at picturesque apartments in Greenwich Village and Gramercy Park, whose rents we couldn't in any manner afford. We applied for an apartment in Stuyvesant Town, the behemoth housing development that extended along the East River at Fourteenth Street, featuring tree-shaded walks, playgrounds, and pleasant apartments at moderate rentals. A year's wait was the minimum, the rental agent advised us. Of course, if a baby was on the way and we were truly desperate . . .

I told the agent that only the part about being desperate applied to us.

Like so many fortuitous happenings, when we finally found an apartment, it was unconnected with any of our efforts.

It was June and the lease-signing was a week away. I'd finally completed the novel, Lissy had typed the manuscript, and to celebrate I'd bought theater tickets—orchestra seats—and had taken her recklessly to dinner at Sardi's beforehand.

Afterward we walked home leisurely from Times Square. We strolled up Broadway, cut into Columbus Avenue, and then instead of continuing to Ninety-third, we turned off at Seventy-fifth and headed toward Central Park West. The night was soft and balmy, and the vision of trees in the park ahead drew us along with their lush foliage.

"Sure I'm not tiring you out?" Lissy asked solicitously once more. The walk had been her wild country-girl suggestion.

"Nonsense, my legs are merely buckling. I'll wait till they fall off, then I'll be fine."

We had nearly reached the corner when she paused and pointed across the street. "Robert, look at that magnificent town-house," she said. "Look at the beautiful grillwork on the door. And you can tell from the windows that the ceilings must be enormous."

It was a five-story townhouse, built in the French chateau style of the turn of the century. The polished gray-stone façade was somewhat blackened with soot, but wrought-iron center doors were quite regal, and the roof pediment was elaborately carved. "Yeah, it's gorgeous," I said, starting away.

"Robert, *look.*"

I turned back in time to observe the regal door open and two young men come out, carrying a sofa.

"Oh, Robert, somebody's moving," Lissy said. Then both of us noticed something else: that glorious signal to apartment seekers, a U-Haul truck, was parked at the curb. Lissy glanced at me. I glanced at Lissy, and we ambled casually across the street.

"Help you with that?" I offered the two young men.

"Thanks, we can manage. Larry, you'll scrape the legs."

"Ha, ha, looks as if someone's moving."

"We are," said one of the young men. "Four rooms, wood paneling, stained glass, a Stanford White building, and Eric here has to move to the coast."

I took hold of the sofa as they lifted it onto the U-Haul truck. "Listen, I insist on helping. . . . I, uh, suppose the apartment's already rented."

"Not actually," Larry said. "We only gave notice yesterday. Eric, now it's you who's scraping the legs."

"That's a beautiful velvet sofa. What shade is it?" Lissy inquired.

"Persimmon," Eric said.

"I suppose the rent on the apartment is enormous."

"One fifty. Rent-controlled, really," Larry said, tugging at the sofa. "If we don't get someone to take over the lease we'll be stuck with it until October first."

"Rolfe says he definitely wants it," spoke up Eric.

"That'll be the day, when Rolfe makes up that dizzy mind of his," Larry said.

"Listen," I said. "If you've got other stuff to load, I'd be glad to lend a hand."

"And while Robert's helping you, we could have a look at the apartment," Lissy said.

We visited the management of the building the next day and arranged to take over the lease. The rent was half again as much as we had planned to pay, but idiocy had gripped us. We moved into the apartment in July, and we furthermore took oath that nothing could prevail upon us to move out of it, ever.

It was an apartment such as we had not dreamed of owning, and the rent, we decided, was the bargain of all time. The apartment was on the second floor of the townhouse and was reached by an elevator (large enough for a baby carriage), and by a marble staircase that curved up from the small faded lobby. The living room was paneled and measured thirty feet by twenty, with a fireplace and a carved ceiling thirteen feet high. The kitchen was fitted with ceiling-high cupboards, and there were two bedrooms. One was quite large, with a wide casement window that looked out on a green garden; the smaller bedroom was to be my study for the present.

"It's large enough for twin beds," Lissy said, measuring contentedly with a yardstick. "Or bunk beds—and we could put a bassinet in the corner . . ."

"Hey," I said, "what bassinet?"

"None yet, darling, but maybe you were right. The other apartment *was* jinxed or something." She put her arms around me. "We're bound to have babies here. So much room for them."

"We're certainly starting out with a lot of furniture," I said. "Mattress and innerspring, a kitchen table and two paint-it-yourself chairs in the living room."

"Robert. This apartment wouldn't have fallen into our lap so easily if we weren't meant to have it. Stop worrying."

Lissy sounded exactly like my mother talking, and, like Catherine, she proved that she wasn't far from right. A month after we moved into the apartment my novel was sold and I was paid a two-thousand-dollar royalty advance by the publisher. At my own firm I was promoted to associate editor, with a corresponding raise in salary.

Lissy viewed this windfall with quiet deliberation. "It means we can really put together a home," she said. "Now, I don't want you to argue, Robert. I want you to give me a thousand dollars. I'll furnish the whole apartment with it, I promise."

"Four rooms for a thousand bucks? Nobody could do that. Why, when we went looking at Sloane's for bedding—"

"I won't go to Sloane's," Lissy said. "Or Altman's or Bloomingdale's. Just watch me."

Nor did she go to Sloane's or Altman's or Bloomingdale's. For the rest of the summer, and after school hours beginning in September, my wife made forays into every secondhand furniture, junk, and thrift shop in New York. On weekends in the fall, while I worked at revisions on my novel, she prevailed upon her friend, Lynn Thomas, to drive the two of them around the Connecticut and Hudson Valley countryside on the trail of bargain antiques. Their trips resulted in an accumulation of barrels, cartons, and stacks of broken furniture, which appeared to have been reclaimed from some curb.

"Naturally, it has to be refinished and repaired," was Lissy's standard explanation for every piece of wreckage she lugged in. "Starting next week I'm taking a course in furniture restoration at the Y."

The furniture-restoration course claimed two nights of her week; the other nights, as well as weekends, were given over to practical application of her classroom instruction. For months the apartment reeked of pungent oils, shellacs, and varnishes. She slowly acquired a collection of tools and implements my father might have envied. In fact, he lost no time in becoming Lissy's collaborator in the refurbishing that was going on and showed up regularly at the apartment with his own tool kit.

Old copper pots, dented andirons, broken tables, chests and stands, a brass bed frame black with age, a cracked mirror that Lissy declared was authentic Queen Anne, highboys, lowboys, Quaker benches, footstools, torn hooked rugs, old clocks, apothecary chests, chipped china lamp bases, a marble-topped commode, dilapidated chairs, dusty carved eagles and roosters—when, by June, most of the labor was finished, the assemblage of junk had been converted into beguiling furnishings that made of the apartment a cheery, attractive, inviting home that I could not believe was our own.

The high-posted brass bed gleamed warmly in the bedroom, flanked by a Hepplewhite wing chair and a Federal-blue rug. The paneled living room glowed with pewter and brass, mixed with the brighter sheen of Lissy's wedding silver. A corner of the room, the dining area, boasted a cherrywood table and cane-bottom chairs, the polished floor was gay with hooked rugs of every shade. Facing the fireplace was a Victorian sofa reupholstered in crimson brocade, and draperies of matching crimson were hung at the windows. In all, the four rooms had cost twice a thousand dollars and more to furnish, but then I'd sold another story, and the paperback rights to my novel, which was to be published in the fall, had brought additional income.

Nearly a year since we had moved to Seventy-fifth Street, and very soon now—first week in October, the doctor estimated—I would be moving my desk and typewriter out of the study. The second bedroom had been painted yellow, and the white curtains Lissy had sewn on Ninety-third Street were in use on the window. Already a bassinet waited in the room, and a baby carriage was on order at Best's. And I was sleeping poorly at night, haunted by an event that I could not extricate from the joyful pending arrival of our first child.

I remember a sweltering, humid night in July. Sleep would have been difficult in any circumstances, and I sat down near dawn in the tufted black-leather club chair opposite the sofa in the living room.

How long I'd been sitting there I didn't know; except for the sheen of a street lamp, the windows were still dark, though traces of light were beginning to touch them. From the tree outside came a faint twitter of birds, which caused me to think once again of Catherine's sparrows.

"Robert?" A light switched on in the bedroom.

I went over to the brass tray, which, mounted on a luggage rack, served as a coffee table. I lit another cigarette, and as I went back to the chair I heard Lissy's steps in the hall.

She stood in her nightgown in the doorway, framed by the light behind her, her figure heavy and rounded. She pushed back the rumpled blond hair. "No sleep?" she asked.

"So muggy and close, not even the air conditioner helps," I said. "Tougher on you, I bet. How you feeling?"

"Bigger than a circus tent." She padded in bare feet across the floor, exhibiting awkward cumbersomeness, the rolling, off-balance gait of a woman in the final months of pregnancy. "If I could only find a comfortable sleeping position." She took the ashtray from my chair and emptied it into a silent butler. "So many cigarettes, Robert."

"I know," I said, taking another deep pull of smoke. "Listen, I'm sorry I got you up."

"You didn't really." She pulled over a footstool, lowered herself, arranged the folds of the nightgown over her distended, globular stomach. "It was the kicking that woke me." She laughed. "There he goes again."

"You seem certain it's a *he*."

"A quarterback, he feels like." She took my hand and placed it over her stomach. I waited, and under the taut, stretched skin I felt a thrust, a sudden movement. I started to withdraw my hand, but Lissy held it there.

"Oh, Robert, *talk* about it," she said. "This ghastly expression comes over your face and I know what you're thinking about."

"I can't talk about it."

"Wouldn't it be better than sitting up all hours of the night?"

"Felicity, my darling, darling—"

"Say her name, at least."

"Roseanne. There—and it means nothing." I withdrew my hand, ran it through my hair.

Roseanne was dead. Back in December, the week before Christmas. Up in the mountains outside Bogotá, the Santa Clara mission. Back in December. A Christmas party for the children, games and prizes and singing. Outside in the courtyard a car drives up. Men with revolvers pile out. La Violencia. Fists pound the door. The singing breaks off, and the thirty or so children huddle around the two nuns. In back of the mission is a thick grove of trees. One of the nuns gives instructions. The other nun is to take the children—instantly, without a second's delay—out the back door and into the shelter of the woods. Hurrying steps, as the pounding on the front door grows fiercer. Quick, quickly, the back door closes at last. Turning, the nun remaining behind goes and unbolts the front door. Opens it. She is not raped or sexually molested, but her face is shot away. Roseanne, my sister . . . *I'll offer it to God and He'll look after all of you . . .*

"She died bravely, Robert. That's what to think of," Lissy said.

"She was always brave."

"She died for a cause."

"For thirty children?"

"People have died for less. To no purpose or reason."

I stubbed out the cigarette. "I'll tell you what I'm grateful for. She wanted to be buried at the mission. I'm thankful for it. If we'd had to take her to Calvary . . ." I sat thinking for a moment, lit another cigarette. "Here's a contradiction for you," I said. "Children are supposed to be frightened of cemeteries and then grow out of it. I used to romp around Calvary as though it were Central Park, and now that my childish fears should have vanished . . ."

Lissy looked up at me. "You're mistaken about yourself, you know."

I brushed back her hair. "Oh, my darling Lissy."

"You see only one side of yourself. You're quite strong, Robert, only you haven't found out yet. Whatever happens, you always endure. Sometimes I think I'm waiting for you to find out."

I tilted back her face. "Aye, there's the rub," I quoted. "Whatever you believe to be true, *is* true . . . till something changes it, I guess. The other part of me that causes all the mayhem—I can't get hold of it."

"You will," she said. She nodded at the pale light that was suffusing the windows. "Like some breakfast? There's sausage, or I could fix a jelly omelette. Why are you smiling?"

I cupped her face in my hands. "Whenever we had a crisis on Warbisher Street, Catherine's first thought was about food. Talk about enduring, it's you ladies who specialize in that."

"Yes, sirree." She rose clumsily and started for the kitchen. "A jelly omelette would taste light and cool. Won't tell you what I'm having as a side dish. It's too disgusting."

"What?"

"Peach ice cream. Dr. Kelly says it's okay to indulge my appetite. Took him at his word." She turned in the kitchen doorway and hesitated. "Robert? One day you'll be able to talk about Roseanne—about all of it. You'll probably even write about it. Then you'll know the other part is over with."

I got up from the club chair and looked at her swelling breasts and burgeoning stomach, outlined under the nightgown. "When our baby is born . . . do you think he'll know?"

"Yes, Robert?"

"Nothing."

She stepped from the kitchen doorway. "No, tell me. Will he know what?"

I rubbed my hands, tried to make a joke of it. "Well, when he gets older, I just damn well hope he knows . . ."

"Know *what*?"

"How much we wanted him?" I said.

The nights through August stayed hot and humid. My sleeping didn't improve, and Lissy's rolling gait acquired an almost drunken lurch. Her stomach grew larger, though that didn't seem possible, and in September she stopped using the stairs to reach the apartment. Her ankles swelled if she climbed even a few steps. The elevator was old, clanking and exceedingly slow, but Lissy acquired splendid patience in waiting for it. Patience wrapped itself softly around her like a shawl, while the opposite held true for me. Originally Dr. Kelly, the obstetrician, had estimated the third week in October for the baby's birth, but by mid-September he moved the date up a week. The days dragged along, then it was suddenly October.

The first week in October . . . and unexpectedly one day I went to Warbisher Street, and upstairs in the brown-shingled house where I had been born, in a few blinding moments the pieces of my childhood were fitted together.

18

The Valentine Box

A Tuesday morning, the first week in October. The tree outside the living room window was still green and thick with leaves and shrill with the twitter of birds, and when I woke up I had no other plan for the day than to spend it at the office and perhaps meet Lissy for lunch.

"Darling, I can't," she said at breakfast, scraping eggs from the pan. "The appointment with Dr. Kelly's at eleven thirty—be lucky if he gets to me by one."

I watched her plod, stomach first, to the table. "My God, if he doesn't watch out, you'll start labor in the waiting room."

"He says it won't be till the tenth at the earliest." She placed the plate of eggs in front of me, lumbered to the coffee-maker that was plugged in at the counter. "He said the baby hasn't fully dropped yet, and there's still a wait."

"Well, Liss, if you can't make lunch, why don't I meet you at Kelly's office? I'll come sit with you."

"Surrounded by all those other ballooned-out ladies?" Lissy laughed and poured me a cup of coffee. "Robert, you're nervous enough as it is. Ten minutes in that waiting room and you'll need a tranquilizer."

I jabbed nervously at my eggs. "Expecting a baby is like living with a time bomb in the final weeks. Waiting for the bomb to explode. Long as I keep busy, I'm okay. But give me an idle hour, with nothing to do . . ."

She placed the coffee in front of me, moved the sugar and creamer closer. "You're so funny, Robert. Secretly you think it should all be accomplished in a month. Two at the most. Anyway, I'm meeting Sandra Earl after Dr. Kelly's. She's from maternity class, and we both need to go to Best's. Did I tell you about the carriage?"

I swallowed the coffee in one large gulp. "I'll hang around the office and chew my nails and get in everybody's hair."

"Imagine this," Lissy went on. "Best's sent a letter yesterday that the model carriage we ordered isn't available from England anymore. I thought I'd take a look at the floor sample, and if they'll give me a break on the price—"

"Ah, bargain hunting to the end."

At the door she handed me my briefcase and a kiss. "Take it easy, darling. Go to the office and concentrate on your work. I'll call before I leave Dr. Kelly's, just so you'll know labor hasn't started yet."

I looked down at her bulging stomach. "Can it seriously drop lower than that?"

"To my knees, practically," Lissy laughed.

"Oh, God," I moaned, and bolted in alarm down the stairs.

The morning passed crazily at the office. For one thing, there wasn't much work at hand. As with most publishers, the big push to get the Christmas gift books printed early and ready for the stores was over, and the galleys for the spring list were only starting to come in. There were some manuscripts to read, but I regarded myself as a poor judge of manuscripts at the moment. No, mostly I hung around the art department, interrupting other people's work. Then Lissy phoned at eleven. "Darling, I think you should go to a movie," she said. At noon Mac Forster, the editor in chief, recommended the same therapy.

"For God's sake, Connerty," he said, "take the afternoon off, go to a movie. One more look at that hound-dog face and we'll all go nuts."

"But, Mac, something urgent might come up."

"Like what, trouble with Aunt Fanny's cookbook? Get out of here."

A movie sounded like a good idea. Going down in the office elevator, I scanned the movie pages in the *Times*. Grab a sandwich, take in a flick—excellent idea. I flipped the pages to the art section. If the Matisse exhibit was still at Wildenstein's . . .

Five minutes after finishing lunch at Hamburg Heaven I was walking past a BMT subway entrance. I stopped at the corner and went back. It had been a month since I'd been to Warbisher Street. The subway stairs were out for Lissy, and the jolting train ride wasn't good for her either. I changed a bill at the coin booth, then I was on a train, rocketing underground and up over the Williamsburg Bridge. I hadn't phoned the house—I'd make a surprise visit.

Marcy Avenue . . . Lorimer, Hewes . . . Myrtle, Gates—the familiar litany of El stations. Then the train rattled into the Halsey Street station, the doors sprang open, I went down the platform, down the grubby, littered El stairs. Broadway, the clutter of neighborhood shops—Schmierman's bakery, Sciavelli's beauty parlor, Hymie's candy store, Jay's Outlet—they were gone.

I walked along Broadway toward Warbisher Street, and gone from my mind was the vision of the old shops, which on previous visits I had always seen. I walked among the scattered afternoon shoppers, the black citizens, and they were no longer strange foreigners to me. The avenue belonged to them now and I was the stranger. I turned into Warbisher Street, and the rows of porch-fronted houses opened to view. The houses looked old and venerable, like monuments from the past that bore no relationship to me. I exulted in this reaction. I had lived away from Warbisher Street long enough; it could no longer possess me.

Then, from the jumble of porches and gabled roofs, I picked out the brown-shingled house—and it was no different from the others on the street. I could approach it with untroubled steps. I had become a visitor at last. Was Catherine at one of the windows? Had she spied my approach and was already hurrying to open the door?

I turned in at the walk, mounted the porch steps, but the door didn't open, or a voice call a welcome—and in the hall a shock was awaiting me. I rang the bell—evidently Catherine had not been at the window. I raised my hand to the bell again, then the door was slowly opened by a white-haired man, stooped a bit, yet still erect, the eyes faded but still bright and kindly in the seamed, creased face.

My father gaped at me, his mouth fell open. "Why, Rob—of all the darned surprises. What're you—?"

"Had the afternoon off thought I'd surprise you. How are you, Dad?"

Why hadn't Catherine opened the door?

"I'm fine, Rob. Well, say, c'mon in. Afternoon off? Well, say, this is a swell surprise."

My father pulled back the door. I stepped into the front hall and—over near the stairs, standing there—what was it I saw?

Dad smiled in amusement. "Can't believe your eyes, eh, Rob? Yes, sir, that's what it is." And he went over and gave the curving paint-flecked handle an affectionate pat. "Hauled it up from the cellar this morning."

"The wicker buggy," I said, and the past rushed up and claimed me again, so that I couldn't speak.

My father gave the handle an experimental push; the wheels creaked and wobbled forward a few inches. "Not in such bad shape as you'd think," Dad said. "Needs new wheels, of course, oil the springs, and a paint job. It's all on account of you, young fellow. How's Lissy?"

"On account of me?"

"The baby comin'—and Lissy's fondness for antiques and the like. Your mother was convinced this old buggy'd be right up Lissy's alley. Been down in the cellar for thirty years. Old sheet covering it . . ."

"I remember," I said. *An old white sheet . . . and the wheels peeping out from the bottom had been eyes to me. And one day after Catherine had been taken away, I need a place to hide something where no one would find it . . .*

Dad released the buggy handle and turned to me. "Anyway, it's yours if you want it."

My head nodded dully, eyes fastened on the buggy. *An old white sheet and I need a place to hide something where no one would find it . . . and I'd gone down to the cellar . . .*

361

"It's great to see you, son. Let's go into the living room and sit down, why don't we?" The television set was playing, but only then was I aware of the sound. A quiz show, studio laughter . . . it shut off abruptly. "Rob? You keep standing in the arch. Have a seat," Dad said as he switched off the set.

I shook my head, as though to clear it, and went into the living room. Blue carpet, sofa reupholstered in rose brocade—but no other recent innovations. Since last December there had been no Greyhound bus jaunts for my parents either. Roseanne had died in December, and on the day they were told the news my mother and father, who for years had been growing old, *became* old. All in a day.

Where was Catherine? Why hadn't she answered the bell?

"Make yourself comfortable," Dad went on. He lighted his pipe and gestured at a chair. "Tell me what you've been up to lately."

I pushed the ghosts away and sat down. *The coal bin in the cellar, the pile of broken furniture across from it, the buggy covered by a sheet . . . and I need a place to hide something . . .*

"Lissy getting anxious about the baby?"

"What?"

"The final weeks are always the worst," Dad said. "Don't matter a bit how often you been through it."

"Guess not," I agreed. "Actually, Lissy's holding up better than I am. It's partly why I was given the afternoon off—I drive everybody at the office nuts."

"Well," Dad said, gesturing with his pipe, "when your mother went down to dust off that buggy after breakfast—'Never mind a fancy new carriage,' she said to me, 'Lissy will cherish this one.' "

"Yes, she will. Everything's ready for the big event. We painted the nursery yellow last week and put up the bassinet." *A hiding place, so I went down in the cellar and lifted the old sheet from the buggy . . . and there was my hiding place. Under the sheet, hidden in the buggy seat, where no one would think to look. Catherine was sick, ambulance drove her away. She was sick, maybe dying . . . and whose fault was it? Who had helped to make her sick?*

I looked across at my father and struggled to get hold of myself and continue the conversation. Words came from my mouth—I could hear myself speak, made no sense of it. Time had stopped; had never passed. The decades were years and the years were hours that whirled around me. I looked at my father and his hair was black, his shoulders big and strong, and he'd just come back from taking Catherine to the hospital. *Pneumonia. Who had helped to make her ill?*

"Letter from Vinny yesterday," Dad went on. "What a swell vacation he mapped out for the family. They rented this place at Toluca Lake—that's up in the mountains outside of Los Angeles. Swimming and fishing and boating—"

Dad, could I talk to you a minute? Listen, Mom will be all right in the hospital, won't she? People can recover from pneumonia. They'll know how to cure her at the hospital. "Dad?" I said, in nearly a shout. "Dad?"

My father was standing in the dining room arch. His hair was white again, and he lowered his pipe, his face slightly puzzled. "What is it, Rob? I thought you'd like to read Vin's letter. I was getting it from the sideboard."

"Mom didn't answer the door. I was wondering if she's all right."

He came back into the living room. "You were always the one to worry about her the most. I remember when she went to Greenvale—"

"*Isn't* she all right?" There was a hesitation— I could sense that he wanted to phrase his answer carefully. *Mom won't stay in the hospital long. She'll be home in a week or so, won't she?* "Dad, if anything's wrong, I'd rather you told me," I said.

"No, she's okay, Robbie, honest." He sucked at his pipe reflectively. "Of course I don't have to tell you, when we lost Rosie last year, it hit your mother hard. Nobody can try to deny that." He gripped the pipe, let out a thin stream of smoke. "It's slowed her down a lot—you notice we haven't been taking any trips lately. I keep after her to see a doctor, but you know how stubborn she is."

I got up from the chair. "A doctor?" I said, and it was April, the Saturday after the thundershower, and Catherine was upstairs in bed with a wracking cough and her breathing terrible. "I'll just run upstairs and see her," I said.

"Robbie, she's sleeping soundly enough up there not to have heard us. Believe me, there's no cause for alarm."

"I know, but I'll go up anyway, okay?"

"Sure, if it'll reassure you."

I went into the hall and past the wicker buggy. Time had stopped, had never passed, and the years were hours that whirled around me. I went up the stairs, and it was the Saturday that Dr. Drennan had come with his black bag and gold pen. He'd just left, and Dad had instructed Roseanne to go fetch Margaret home from work and had rushed out to the drugstore. Slowly I climbed the stairs to Catherine's room.

I turned at the landing, went past Roseanne and Margaret's room, and down the hall, the long, long hall, to the front bedroom where I had been born. Unlike that April Saturday, the door was closed, but as I raised my hand to knock, it swung open a crack, and glancing into the dim-shrouded room, I glimpsed a figure on the bed. *Mom,* a voice from long ago called within me. *Mom!* I pushed open the door wider. "Mother?"

The figure stirred under the coverlet, a head raised up from the pillow.

"Mother, it's Robbie. Are you all right?"

Catherine sat up in the dimness. "Is that you, Robbie?"

Guess what, Mom? I have suddenly figured out what I want to be when I grow up. An artist . . .

An artist, imagine that. Listen, Robbie, listen to me. Don't worry, do you hear? Promise you won't . . .

"Robbie," my mother said, throwing off the coverlet. "What brings you here? Good heavens, I didn't even hear the doorbell." She searched for her slippers at the side of the bed, brushed at her hair and dress. "Seemed to me at one point there was talking downstairs."

"Mom, are you all right? Dad says you need to see a doctor."

She waved her hand. "I'm an old lady who can't run up and down the stairs without my heart thumping a bit. What doctor's going to fix that, I tell your father." She smoothed out the bed coverlet, plumped the pillow. "Let's raise the shades and make it more cheerful in here." She started through the dimness, then stopped and asked, "Nothing wrong with Lissy, is there?"

An artist, Mama. It was the water-color set from Aunt Tilly that made me decide. I wanted to tell you about it first . . .

"Lissy's fine," I said. "I'm the one with the jitters. Took the afternoon off, thought I'd pop in on you and Dad."

She went to the window at the sewing table and raised the shade. The afternoon light streamed in, dissolving the dimness. "It's the nicest surprise since I don't know when," she declared. The sunlight fell on her white hair. It had lost its wiriness and was more the texture of cornsilk; her figure, too, seemed more fragile, the arms thinner, the neck gauntish. But Catherine's eyes, like Dad's, were still lively and warm. "Did Dad tell you about the wicker buggy?" she asked. "I bet you saw it when you came into the hall."

"Yes, I did."

My mother beamed. "It's old and needs repair, but don't you think Lissy will be pleased to have it? I said to your father when I went down to dust it off—"

"She'll cherish it. It's exactly what she'd want."

"That's what I told him—her fondness for antiques." She went to the other window and raised the shade, then over to the bureau. "Did Dad mention what else there was?"

"Else?"

"He didn't tell you what we found on the buggy seat?"

"The Valentine box," I answered without thinking, and my mother turned from the bureau, the pink heart-shaped candy box in her hands. She was holding it and staring at me.

"How did you know?" she asked.

I stammered out a reply. "I—I saw you take it from the bureau and . . ." There was a hammering in my ears and I couldn't keep the words straight. "It was lost, I remembered . . . we never could find it . . ."

"Yes." She carried the pink cardboard box to the sewing table at the front window. Carefully she brushed the remaining dust from it, smoothed the tattered gold ribbon that was still pasted across the lid. "Well, that's where it was," she said. "Under that old sheet, right on the buggy seat."

"Mom?" I started toward the door. "Why don't we go downstairs?"

She gaped in surprise. "This box was always your treasure, Robbie. Keeping the snapshots together—and now you've lost interest?"

The hammering in my ears was louder and I couldn't seem to catch my breath. "I guess . . . so many years have passed . . ."

"Come," my mother said. She sat in the rocker and lifted the lid from the heart-shaped box. I wanted to stop her, to shout a warning and to close the box, but I watched, dazed and silent, as she reached in and drew out the cracked, yellowed snaps.

"It did me good to find these again," she said. "All the pictures of when you were young—I'd given up hope of ever seeing them again." She sat in the rocker, the sunlight striking the white hair, and spread the photos across her lap. "Look, here's Vinny a week after he was born," she advised. "How precious Margaret looks— that was the knitted cap and sweater Tilly brought from Paris. Margaret was a solemn baby. And look at lusty Daniel, if you please . . ."

"And mine," I asked tightly, the hammering louder. "Are my baby pictures there?" She looked up at me, puzzled, and I drove on, despite myself. "How many baby pictures of me?"

Catherine returned her attention to the photos. "It's odd that you should inquire," she said. "So did I when I looked this morning. Dozens of baby pictures and only two or three of you."

Time had stopped, had never passed, and the years swirled around me. "Only two," I said. "Two baby pictures."

Catherine's head bent over the snapshots, her hands sifted through them. "Yes, only two, I couldn't understand it. Surely we took more pictures of Robbie than that, I thought."

"I remember," I said, the breath clotted in my throat. "I couldn't understand it either."

My mother selected two of the photos and raised them to her spectacles. "Here they are. I had to study them very closely. Even then I didn't come right up with the answer."

"Answer?" Something resounded in my skull, like metal striking. "What answer?"

"Come over here and I'll show you."

I shook my head, rooted helplessly to the carpet. "What did you find it was?" My voice sounded hollow and far away, and I knew that my mother was staring at me again. "Please tell me," I said.

"Robbie, whatever's upsetting you?"

"I'm all right. Tell me what you found."

"Well, it took some digging back, but I solved it." She held the two snapshots to the window light and peered at them closely. "First I noticed that these two snaps weren't taken with Dad's Brownie. They're a different size print, with straight edges. Some other camera took them. Well, I puzzled over it a while, and then I realized."

"Realized what?"

She turned in the rocker. "It was Mr. Jarecki's camera. Sure, it was.

"Jarecki?"

She gestured with the snapshots. "The Jareckis lived next door before the Fritzles moved in. You can't have been more than three, so I guess you forget. Mr. Jarecki worked for a wholesale meat supplier. Very pleasant man, big and friendly."

"What about the camera?"

A pause. "Robbie, you sound as if it's very important to you."

The metal clashed again in my head. "Please, it is important."

"Well, it all came back to me," Catherine said. "I remembered exactly. A day or so after you were born your father had the Brownie and had put it down on the porch steps. Forgot it was there, or something, and—"

"Broke it?" I said, and the conversation between Dad and Charlie Cronin roared back to me through the tunnel of years. The living room, Labor Day weekend, the party, Vinny passing around snapshots of Peggy McNulty . . . "Dad broke the camera when I was born?" I supplied.

"Yes," Catherine answered, "and didn't have the money to replace it. It took a year of saving nickels before I could buy him another for his birthday. It's hard to believe money could've been so scarce, but it was. Five babies in a row, doctor's bills and the mortgage to pay . . ."

A tiredness washed over me, the end of an ironic journey. I went past the bureau, over to the window that looked down on the alley. I leaned against the frame. "The camera was broken . . . that was why," I said slowly.

"If it hadn't been for Gus Jarecki, we might have had no pictures of you," Catherine said. "But a few weeks after you were born he saw me wheeling you in the buggy . . ." Her voice was suffused with memory. "Gus was standing on his front porch," she went on. "He had his camera, and he came down the steps and said, 'Mrs. Connerty, a fine baby like yours deserves to have his picture taken.'"

I leaned against the window, the curtain fuzzy against my cheek. "The Valentine box. I hid it," I said.

"He snapped you right there on the sidewalk."

"I hid the Valentine box," I repeated. "Down in the cellar, in the buggy under the sheet."

Catherine's narration broke off and there was a silence. "I know you did, Robbie," she said quietly. "At least, I always suspected."

"You knew?" I swung around from the window.

"When I came back from Greenvale and it was nowhere to be found, I knew you'd done something with it. It was your treasure, you'd always guarded it so."

"Oh, Mom," I said. "You never asked me about it. Why didn't you ask?"

"Would you have told me?" She got up from the rocker. "I knew that something had caused you pain or you would never have wanted to be rid of your Valentine box. I tried asking you a hundred times, but you wouldn't speak of it and I didn't want to accuse you."

"Accuse me?" I shouted. "I wanted to forget. Hiding the box, that's how I forgot.

Catherine's eyes were wide with fright. "Forget what? Oh, Robbie, what was so horrible that you had to forget it? Robbie?" I didn't answer, and she came over and grasped my arm. "What-

368

ever it was, all these years later you still remember. Something *wrong*—I knew it the day I came back from Greenvale—you were all gathered on the porch, then you ran into the house, Robbie, something was wrong, and it's been wrong ever since."

"No," I said, not wanting to grieve her. "It was nothing."

"The baby pictures—the way you asked about them now—"

"*No*," I said. "*No.*"

Her face implored me, her hands beseeched my arms. "Tell me, Robbie, I beg you. Those years you had such a hard time—here's the answer to it, isn't it?"

"Mama, it doesn't matter anymore."

"Yes, it does, it's still in your mind." She stared at me. "Only two baby pictures, you said. *Why?* Tell me why you asked, Robbie."

I turned away from her. "I'm crying and don't want you to see me cry. I don't want to hurt you," I said. "Children can think outlandish things for no good reason."

"And you, Robbie," Catherine asked, from behind me. "What did you think?"

I went over to the window, wiped my face, drew in a shuddering breath. "I thought . . . well, we were poor . . . four babies in a row . . . and maybe when I came along . . ."

"Yes?"

"Maybe you didn't want me so much."

The room was filled with a ticking silence, and my voice stumbled on. "Before you left for Greenvale, while you were still in the hospital, Uncle Al dropped by one night, and I heard Dad talking about it. The four babies, and how it might have damaged your health, and I remembered the baby pictures in the Valentine box. So many of the others, but only two of me."

The silence ticked on, then Catherine said, "Was that what you thought—that we didn't want you? Oh, my poor Robbie."

I kept my face pressed against the window. "I hid the box in the buggy so I wouldn't have to think about it. I'd helped to make you sick, and I promised God that if you lived and came back to us I'd make it up."

"You thought that God would want such promises?"

I shook my head. "I didn't know. But I knew how good you'd

been to me, and I loved you. I didn't care if you'd wanted me or not."

"All this you kept to yourself and never spoke of it?" Catherine asked. "All the years hiding it, like you did the snapshots? It means you never understood, Robbie. Spent most of your life in this house, living with us, and never understood any of it."

I turned to her, my face wet and streaked. "I never thought you didn't love me."

My mother shook her head in amazement. "Such a one for books and studying and couldn't make sense out of your simple parents," she said. "I'd award you no scholarship prize for it. I'd have to give you a failing grade. I fear I'll get angry if I'm not careful."

She walked over to the Valentine box. "I guess these pictures tell nothing, for what have they shown of the truth?"

I sat in the chair next to the bureau. "Mom, you don't have to explain. You never did. It's only—"

She turned to me quite sternly, and there was strength mixed with her frailty. "Never mind, you've done enough talking for the present," she said, and walked a step or two across the carpet and pondered. "I'm so poor at words—how will I tell you what you need to know?"

"Tell me what?" I asked.

She pondered over it a moment more. "Where do I start?" she asked herself. "With Papa dying," she answered. "That was the beginning. . . ."

And then, by turn pacing the carpet, standing at the window, or reaching to touch some keepsake in the room, my mother told me the story of her marriage and the meaning of it. There were pauses where she groped for words, silences when words failed her altogether and she would have to pace out a length of the carpet, afraid that the story was beyond her telling. But Catherine was not one to give up, and she kept on until she had finished and made me understand what her life, and that of my father, had been about.

"Papa's death, and Mama's a year later—I'll start there, because it was the first time I learned about myself," she said. "You see, he left debts, we had to liquidate his business, and when Mama died we had to sell the house . . . and Tilly and I were on our own." She paused, summoning back how it had been. "Well, Tilly went out and taught school and I got a job with the phone company. It wasn't the fancy life Papa had envisioned for us—young ladies pouring tea in the parlor and so forth . . . but, see, after I'd worked for a while I discovered I didn't mind it a bit," Catherine said. "I enjoyed it, in fact. It taught me the kind of person I was— somebody who didn't mind hardship or struggle. Hardly gave it a thought—a simpleton, maybe I was. Tilly and I rented a little apartment. We took little vacations in Asbury Park and went to Keith's vaudeville on Saturday nights. . . . Listen, I could have been working in a coal mine," said my mother, "and I believe I still would have been happy."

She laughed at the thought of her lightheadedness. "Anyway, it seemed to me I was happy," she amended. "It was only after Jim Connerty strolled on the scene . . ."

She stood at the sewing table, the light falling on her, hand cupped to her chin. "He lived in the neighboring parish, you know, and Charlie Cronin brought him over one Sunday to St. Gabriel's for Mass," she went on. "I wish you could have seen your father in those days, Robbie," she said. "I don't doubt he was the handsomest man in Brooklyn. Tall, and shoulders bursting out, black hair and fair-skinned . . . and a smile that could light the sky, it's the truth." She turned to me, radiant as a girl. "It was his eyes, Robbie. Those blue eyes that laughed and reached right in and warmed your soul. Listen to me go on," she broke off.

"No. Go ahead," I urged.

She walked the carpet again. "After Mass that Sunday we went to Schlack's for a soda—Jim, Charlie and me—then Jim walked me home. He stood fumbling at the door and asked if I'd go out with him. Well, I acted very iffy about it, and hemmed and hawed—but, God help me, I'd have run off with him there and then. Yes, I would have! Off anywhere he wanted, the ends of the earth. . . ."

She paused again, her hands trying to grasp the words. Then, turning, she leveled a glance at me. "I'm not sure how to tell this next part, so I might as well tell it straight," she declared. "I only had to know your father a few months," she said, "and I knew he was never going to be a Wall Street hotshot or set the business world on fire. It wasn't the kind of man he was, or even the kind I wanted. I'd seen with Papa what could happen with riches. The house and furnishings sold to settle debts, all of it gone . . . Jim was a clerk, he'd probably go on being a clerk, but I loved him, Robbie, and all I wanted was to give him my love and make him happy. He needed looking after, you know. For all his manly strength, there was something in him"—her hands fought to describe it—"something a little like you," she said. "A violin under all the brass . . . and there was nothing I wanted except to be his wife. In those days, you know, people believed in long engagements—hasty marriages were regarded with suspicion. As it was, we waited a year and a half, and that only so Jim could save the money for the down payment on this house."

She glanced slowly around the bedroom, remembering when she had first come to it as a bride. "This little house—I think he knew it was the best we'd ever manage," she said. "Your father was never fooled by himself. The night before the wedding he showed up like a wild man to warn me I'd never have pearls for my neck, or fur coats, or mansions. We'd have to spend our lives struggling, he warned, and if I had any sense—" She waved her hand. "Well, I told him I didn't, and please to kiss me. Besides, we both knew what our riches would be. We always knew, somehow . . ."

"Yes?" I prompted, though I already had surmised it—known it always, perhaps.

"Our riches," Catherine said, and her eyes brimmed, her words wavered. "I can't believe you never understood, Robbie. Our riches were our children. Did you never know?"

"Yes, I knew," I said. "Always."

Her hands reached out. "When Vinny was born you'd have thought it was the first miracle on earth. Margaret a year later, and Daniel after that. But riches aren't easily won, I guess."

She went to the foot of the bed where her children had been

born; her hand clasped the post. "Some women give birth without trouble, but not me," she said. "I was small and narrow-hipped, you see, and it was hard to carry my babies and get them born. After Daniel arrived, Jim got afraid for me. I wasn't in good shape, and he told me we'd stop if I wanted. 'Do you want us to stop?' I asked him. 'Am I in such poor shape that I need to stop? Do I cook meals, run the house? Do I drag around? If you want us to stop, then tell me, Jim,' I said. And he couldn't."

She gazed at the big double bed and her hand twisted on the post. "After Roseanne was born . . . I began losing my babies," she said, mentioning it for the first time. "Two of them in a year. None of them was far along, only a few months, but I still think of them, Robbie, and wonder what they'd have been like, if they'd lived. I still think of them," she said slowly. "Just as I think of my infant brother, Johnny, who I never got to meet." Her hand tightened around the bed post. "After I'd lost three Dr. Drennan said I'd best forget about having any more. I wasn't able to anymore, he said. Oh, Robbie, it's the saddest thing when you think there'll be no more babies. You see, Dad and I enjoyed having children around. I don't pretend it's all a picnic, but we took such happiness in it, and now we grieved that there'd be no more. But then . . . a year later . . . after we'd given up hope . . ."

She turned to me, her hand falling from the bed post, and I gazed across the small room at her and asked, "Yes? Yes? Then what?"

"You came to us, Robbie." She came over to my chair and stood behind me. "How could you have thought it?" she asked. "What sad thoughts did you hide away in that buggy?" She put her arms around my shoulders. "We welcomed you with joy. It's been joy we've had from you, how couldn't you have known?" she asked.

I sat very straight, with my head raised. "I did know," I said. "It seems to me with Lissy—I know about love. If you hadn't taught me love, from where did I learn it?"

Neither of us spoke, and silence ticked in the room again, then from downstairs came Dad's voice, muffled by the closed door.

"Cath? Cath, you okay up there? What's going on?"

She crossed busily to the door, went into the hall, and called down the stairs. "Rob and I got talking, Jimbo. We'll be right down."

"What were you talking about for so long?"

"Life," she called down in reply. "Rest your patience and I'll put on some coffee and fix a snack for us." She came back into the bedroom, stopped impulsively in the doorway, and found the words she had wanted in the beginning. "I'll tell you this," she suddenly said, "I'd do it all again."

She stepped toward me. "All of it, including the hard parts," she said. "Including the births and when I had to go to Greenvale. Including when I said goodbye to each of you and watched you walk out the door. Including these years of being old." She wrung her hands together and bit her lips to keep them from trembling. "Including even Roseanne dying . . . I'd do it all again, Robbie, because it's been worth it."

Roseanne's name—in the instant it was spoken, shadows rose up again after having been vanquished. "Roseanne dying . . . ," I said. "I can't think about it. I can't accept it."

My mother went over to the sewing table and ran her hand over the gold-threaded ribbon of the Valentine box. The sunlight fell on her, and she said, "Well, if you can't, then you don't accept life either, Robbie, for the two walk hand in hand."

We went downstairs to the kitchen. She put on coffee and fixed a plate of tomato sandwiches for Dad and me, and it was the last time that I saw her.

Three days after the visit to Warbisher Street Lissy phoned me at the office and said that her labor pains had begun. I rushed home, and the taxi waited at the curb while I helped her downstairs. I took her to the hospital, up to the maternity floor. A stretcher wheeled her into the labor rooms at the end of the corridor, and I sat waiting and praying and smoking cigarettes in the visitors' lounge. After three hours the doctors told me the wait would be longer and to go out to dinner. I returned in half an hour and began the vigil again. It was evening, and the babies in the nursery across from the lounge awakened, hungry to be fed.

Their lusty, bawling cries resounded down the corridor . . . and then, from the end of the corridor, beyond the doors that led to the labor and delivery rooms, I heard a different cry—faint and high, the cry of our daughter being born.

A daughter, seven pounds and three ounces, pink and fat, with a curl of darkish hair that later turned blond.

A daughter, and we named her Roseanne.

Catherine never saw my daughter. Five days later, in the front bedroom of the brown-shingled house on Warbisher Street, sometime during the night, without telling anybody about it, my mother died.

Her heart stopped while she slept, and she went away somewhere to find Roseanne, Aunt Tillybird, and her infant brother, Johnny, whom she had never seen.

Epilogue

It was getting dark, but I didn't notice until, looking up from the snapshots, I saw the long shadow that was spreading across the carpet. The afternoon light was drawing away fast—the front bedroom faced east and was the first of the rooms to give up the day. I stirred in the rocker and heard from downstairs the soft thud of the door closing. More funeral guests departing . . .

The Valentine box stood open on the sewing table and strewn around it were the cracked, yellowed photos. I reached over to switch on the lamp and my hand scattered a pile of them to the floor. I bent down and scooped them up: a baby photo of Margaret in the knitted cap and sweater; a snapshot of Roseanne in her graduation dress, her hair cropped short, questioning, uncertain face squinting in the sun. And here was a photo of me posed on the front steps in my knickers, left arm encased in a plaster cast.

Where is Robbie, where can he be? Rooobbbiiee. . .?

Once more I heard in my memory that cry that had sounded from every part of the house, upstairs and down, from porch and kitchen and backyard. *Where is Robbie, where can he be?* Seated now in the rocker in the swift-fading light, the lost snapshots clasped in my hand, I heard the familiar cry . . . but with a difference. It seemed to me, as I thought about it, that maybe for the first time in my life I could supply the answer to it.

Where was Robbie? *Here* I was, here in this bedroom. Robert Francis Connerty, age twenty-nine, married, employed, father of one child, author of one book. Earlier this day I had followed a hearse—not black, but gray—to Calvary. There I had climbed a hillside and laid Catherine to rest and had not run away.

I had not run away at last . . . and in any event what was there to run from?

These snapshots—what story did they tell? Of a family that had held fast and survived the hard thrustings of life with good will and laughter and closeness. Closeness, yet each of the family had been alone, in the way that everyone must be alone. Catherine had been alone at Greenvale, Roseanne had opened alone the mission door, and I had lived alone with my hidden fears.

Alone, all of us, and yet not alone, for when had there not been someone to help me? Catherine, when I'd broken my arm; Aunt Tillybird, when Catherine had been taken away; Roseanne, to dispel the ghost child who'd taken up a dwelling place in me . . . and at the end, Catherine again, with the Valentine box. Something always given for something taken away—at home, Felicity and my week-old daughter were waiting for me.

Hills to climb, so many of them, and now it was time for still another.

I gathered up the yellowed snapshots and asked myself this question: What if, when I was born, I had not been wanted? Who, I wondered, was ever wholly unwanted? And I thought of the children in the Santa Clara mission and the men with revolvers pounding on the door. Who among those homeless foundlings had been wanted at birth? Yet . . . and yet . . . someone had wanted them. My sister had loved them enough to die for them. Roseanne had wanted them, and since her death at least two of those same children had found parents. In June Margaret and Howard had flown to Bogotá after months of negotiations and unraveling of red tape. They had flown back with two-year-old Nina for their daughter and three-year-old Juan for their son. The unwanted, in any event, are wanted by God.

And how much had I been wanted? The answer, I knew, had been there always.

I got up from the rocker, my legs stiff and cramped, and heard the door closing again downstairs. The sound of voices saying goodbye drifted up. I turned with the photos to the pink cardboard box and, for a moment, ran my finger over the tattered gold-threaded ribbon on the lid.

If you can't accept death, then you don't accept life either, for the two walk hand in hand.

380

Slowly I put the snapshots in the heart-shaped box, then brought the lid down over them. I carried the box to the closet and returned it to the shelf, where it belonged. Only the envelope with *Robbie* written on it did I keep. *It's the saddest thing when you think there'll be no more babies,* I heard Catherine say. *But then . . . a year later . . . after we'd given up hope . . . you came to us, Robbie.*

I put the envelope in my wallet, crossed to the door and opened it. I didn't look back, but went straight out into the hall. Halls could be perilous to walk, and looking back made the steps more painful.

I passed the silent bedrooms, turned at the landing, and started down the stairs. My father was at the front door, calling goodbye to some departing guests on the porch. I reached the bottom step and faltered there. Each part of this house, each shape and stick of furniture was engraved on my heart. . . .

"Ah, there he is," called a voice in rescue from the living room. "Say, now, if it wouldn't be any trouble . . ."

"Yes, Charlie?" I went through the arch and over to the lone seated figure in the living room. "Can I get something for you?" I asked.

The solitary figure in the morris chair wagged his head mournfully. "Everybody's going home except poor Charlie. A sad day for us all . . ." He extended his empty glass and inquired thickly, "A bit more ice and Jameson's would help, if it wouldn't trouble you . . ."

I took the glass from him. "No trouble at all, Charlie." I went into the dining room, from which the quilting-bee ladies were all gone. The extra leaves had been removed from the oak table and Margaret stood folding the white damask cloth.

"Howard's getting the car," she said. "As it is, we won't reach Buffalo before midnight, and I dislike leaving the children a minute more than necessary. Juan's very manly about it, but Nina gets upset." She folded the cloth and smiled with red-rimmed eyes. "Listen to me fret, when really it's that I can't wait to get back to them."

"I haven't met Juan and Nina, except for those few moments at the airport," I said. "Maybe Lissy and I could bring Roseanne up at Christmas for a visit."

"Oh, that would be lovely. We mustn't let the miles separate us." Margaret nodded at the glass in my hand. "Charlie wants more ice, I'll bet. Here, let me get it for him."

"It's all right, Marg," I said, and went past the oak table to the swinging door, but then my legs halted, as they had done before. "Any ice left, do you know?" I asked.

"A whole tray in the refrigerator. Robbie, if you'd prefer—"

"No, I'll get it." I pushed open the swinging door and stepped into the kitchen. Across the blue-and-white tiles to the sink, where I rinsed out Charlie's glass. The drainboard was stacked with drying dishes, towels were hung on the rack . . . and up on the windowsill Catherine's coffee tin was empty of flowers. The clock ticked over the stove, filling the silence, and I carried Charlie's glass to the refrigerator, reached into the tray for cubes. On the top shelf of the cupboard the Waterford pitcher sparkled among the glasses and bowls.

Then I started out of the kitchen, but as I passed the white table I stopped for a moment and gripped hard the edge of the blue-sprigged oilcloth. I stood there and listened to the ticking clock, and then to the empty kitchen I said, "Goodbye."

The bottle of Jameson's was on the dining room sideboard, Margaret was putting the cloth in the drawer, and I said as I splashed some whiskey over the ice, "Don't forget—we'll come up at Christmas."

"I'll write Lissy and make definite plans."

"Have a good trip home, Marg. See you soon."

She reached over and kissed me. "Yes, Robbie."

Turning, I went through the dining room arch and over to the morris chair. *Engraved on my heart, each room, each shape and stick of furniture.* "Here you are, Charlie," I said, holding out the glass of Jameson's. "I guess I'll be saying goodbye. It's getting dark."

He nodded and brought the glass to his mouth. "Home to the loved ones, eh? That's the fellow."

"Well, take care of yourself. If you ever care to travel to Seventy-fifth Street and have a drink with us . . ."

"Kind of you, Robbie. Might take you up on it," Charlie said.

In the hall I got my coat from the closet as my father closed the door, finished with the guests. "Tell me, did you find the letter upstairs?" he asked.

I pulled on my coat. "It wasn't a letter. Just an envelope with my name on it."

He scratched his head and said, "Envelope, huh? Could've sworn a letter was in it,"—and I wondered if he would have sworn to the truth of it.

"But I'm glad I went up there." I buttoned my coat and went over to him. "Looking at those old snaps again— It was a good life we had in this house, wasn't it?" Unexpectedly my voice broke, sudden tears stung my eyes, and I put my arms around my father.

The frail hand patted my shoulder. "Me too, Rob. A good life it was."

"Will you be all right, Pop? I'll worry about you."

He pulled back from me, waved his hand. "Don't go worrying, I'll do fine. Leaving now, are you?" He pushed at his glasses.

"Something you want me to do?"

"Well, since you mention it . . ." He scratched his head, shuffled over to the phone table. "Wouldn't believe it," he said, "but this is the same item we took down from the porch when we bought this place," and picked up a cardboard sign to show me. The edges were curled and bore rusty nail marks, and across the front black letters spelled out FOR SALE.

My father dusted the sign on his sleeve. "Cath had it packed away in the cellar with all the other stuff," he said, searching the table for a box of thumbtacks. "Found it last night, when I went down there to do some sorting. Only trouble is . . . I can't seem to get myself to tack it up on the porch." The hand that held the sign quivered slightly. "Meant to ask Vinny to help," he explained, "but he's busy driving Mrs. Fritzle home."

My own hand was trembling. I took the sign from my father,

383

along with the box of thumbtacks. I opened the door, went out onto the porch, and tacked the sign on the pillar at the porch steps. For Sale . . .

"There," I said. "Ought to be able to see it fine from the sidewalk."

"Thanks, Rob," Dad said, and I put my arms around him again, and the wind blew across the narrow porch. "Listen, I can stay if you want."

"No, son. Hurry on home to Lissy."

"I'll call you tomorrow."

He walked over to the steps with me. "I'll want to see the baby before I leave for California."

"Come for dinner. We'll arrange it."

"Okay, son." He stood back as I went down the steps, the wind blowing at his thinning hair. "Well, goodbye. Safe home—and get some rest."

"Goodbye," I said, and waved at him once from the sidewalk, after which I started down Warbisher Street, past the row of houses. The wind blew at the tree branches, but I was thinking instead of rain. Of a thundershower in April, and someone hurrying up the street in a lavender print dress, laughing as the rain fell on her.

At the corner I hailed a taxi and went home.